REVOLUTIONARY PRAISE FOR
LAST REFUGE OF SCOUNDRELS

"A delightful new slant on the American Revolution...a wonderful tale told with passion, humor, and insight."
—Winston Groom, author of *Forrest Gump*

"Imaginative...irreverent....Lussier blends *Tom Jones* with *Candide* in an unflinching look at what really happened."
—*Seattle Times*

"Roars in as a brisk gale of reality, removing the musty and ridiculous notions we were taught about our American Revolution."
—*Denver Post*

"A chortling good time...a style that swings between Henry Fielding and Mel Brooks." —*TIME*

"Lussier so movingly grasps the promise of the American-grown democracy that his version stands for its own truth...marvelous."
—*New York Daily News*

"In Lussier's rollicking romp through the American Revolution, the Founding Fathers are a scream." —*Boston Sunday Herald*

"A big, bold story of the American Revolution...a gripping historical novel that includes the most famous historical figures in that epic event, as well as a cast of fictitious characters whose experiences convey a sense of what the Revolution really was like. You will not want to stop reading until you have completed the last page."
—John Ferling, author of *Setting the World Ablaze: Washington, Adams, Jefferson and the American Revolution* and *The First of Men: A Life of George Washington*

more...

LAST REFUGE
OF SCOUNDRELS

A Revolutionary Novel

BY

PAUL LUSSIER

WARNER BOOKS

An AOL Time Warner Company

This book is a work of historical fiction. In order to give a sense of the times, the names of real people and places have been included. Many of the events depicted in this book, however, are imaginary, and the names of nonhistorical persons or events are the product of the author's imagination or are used fictitiously. Any resemblance of such nonhistorical persons or events to actual ones is purely coincidental.

Copyright © 2000 by Paul Lussier Co., Ltd.
All rights reserved.

Warner Books, Inc., 1271 Avenue of the Americas, New York, NY 10020

Visit our Web site at www.twbookmark.com.

 An AOL Time Warner Company

Printed in the United States of America

Originally published in hardcover by Warner Books, Inc.

First Trade Printing: March 2002

10 9 8 7 6 5 4 3 2 1

The Library of Congress has cataloged the hardcover edition as follows:

Lussier, Paul.
    The last refuge of scoundrels / Paul Lussier.
        p. cm.
    ISBN 0-446-52342-9
    1. United States—History—Revolution, 1775-1783—Fiction.   I. Title.

PS3562.U7518 L37 2000
813'.6—dc21   99-086028

Book design by C. Sutherland
Cover design by Flag
Cover illustration by Victor Juhasz
ISBN 0-446-67813-9 (pbk.)

For David,
who knows.

———— ∞ ————

Patriotism is the last refuge of a scoundrel.

—Samuel Johnson

There is nothing more common than to confound the terms of American Revolution with those of the late American War. The American war is over, but this is far from being the case with the American revolution. On the contrary, nothing but the first act of the great drama is closed.

—Benjamin Rush (1787)

Historians relate, not so much what is done, as what they would have believed.

—Benjamin Franklin

Let me tell you . . . . : the true story of the American Revolution can never be written. . . . You must be content to know that the fact is as I have said, and that a great many people in those days were not at all what they seemed, nor what they are generally believed to have been.

—attributed to John Jay
by Edward Floyd Delancey (1821)

Oh, how I wish I had never seen the Continental Army! I would have done better to retire to the back country and live in a wigwam.

—George Washington

The history of our Revolution will be one continued lie from one end to the other.

—John Adams

Prologue

I came to be who I was, a man named George, no more and
no less, during my final three breaths as I lay upon my bed
at Mount Vernon trying to die. It is for this reason, and
this reason only, that it can be said my end was peaceful and joy-
ous and, more to the point, my life had been worthwhile. For despite the many public exploits and achievements for which I am
endlessly praised, I consider the privilege of knowing myself, if
only for six seconds—the time it took to inhale and exhale
thrice—my most remarkable feat; certainly the one of which I am
most proud and, of all my accomplishments, by far the most difficult—and rewarding—of my interminable and dreary career.

For a figure such as "George Washington," you see, laden with
accolade after accolade, beaten down as I was (like gold to gold
leaf: rather less value, but oh, what a shine!), a shot at becoming
a man is rare.

Thank God, on December 14, 1799, luck was on my side. The

dawn of a new century it was, and redemption, finally, would be mine.

Redemption: It came through . . . well, I imagine you'd have to call him an angel. A war aide of mine, long dead, who reached out to me on my deathbed and offered me one last chance to come home to the secret self I'd tucked away inside, about whom so few knew and even I had long since forgotten. He offered me an "opening." I'm sure that's what he called it.

Lieutenant Colonel John Lawrence demanded that I revisit the American Revolution—unflinchingly, in a way that hewed to the truth and not History's sacred pack of lies. All I needed to do was see the event through his eyes, let him and not the almighty General be the center of the show.

To my credit, I accepted.

You already know the History of the War for Independence, and no doubt you've come to accept it—as indeed had I—as the history of the American Revolution. But they were not the same struggles. And knowing that this is confusing is what compels me to come forward, now, to share with you my remarkable journey back, and by so doing give America a chance to come home to herself as a country, a promised land.

Rest assured this is not another History. It's a story not of bloodless heroes, but of people; really it's the tale of Deborah and Alice and George and John. A fable of sorts, you might aver, but as such, truer than any "facts" about the war you've heretofore been told.

Let's to the beginning, then. To my end.

CHAPTER 1

To Die

It wasn't until I was facing my final days that I realized I hadn't lived.

It wasn't until an uncontrollable terror of being buried alive emerged, of being stowed away in a sealed vault with the world deaf to my hoarse and frenetic screams, that I did all I could to feel my frailty, my humanity—just to convince myself that even I, General Washington, could die.

With pneumonia ravaging my lungs, I walked out into a hailstorm with my greatcoat unfastened, lingering outside from ten o'clock to three in the afternoon. And when the weather settled upon cold rain I bothered not with a hat or a scarf, wanting my neck moist and my hair drenched.

I went to dinner in my wet clothes.

I admitted to a sore throat but took no measures to relieve it, and at that point flatly refused to take any medicine for the "cold."

Nor would I allow Martha to send for a doctor until the following morning. Even then, it was only because I was confident that the many exertions on my behalf would fail that I consented to the mixture of molasses, vinegar, and butter for my throat; wheat bran poultices for my swollen legs; purges of calomel; gargles of sage tea and vinegar; and tiny fires put to my feet.

Past these remedies, however, I drew the line, begging the three doctors arrayed at my bedside (Craik, Dick, and Brown), "Please, do not interfere. You had better not take any more trouble about me."

They smiled, then ignored me.

Oh, didn't they poke and prod, urging me to cough, to sit up, to lie back, to stay warm one minute and to cool myself the next, shifting and raising and lifting and turning and tossing my frame as though I were an old rag doll and they the family dogs.

"Do not let my body be put into the vault less than three days after I'm 'dead'! Please!"

Martha, unable to hold back her tears, thinking me mad: "Quiet now, General, you need your strength."

At least my secretary, Tobias Lear, indulged my dark fantasy, assuring me he'd take personal responsibility for determining "the President's" death before burial.

Nice enough of him, but I knew, three days or no, I would never be entirely dead. Lear could no more curtail the ubiquity of my hallowed figure than I could. And images on engravings, portraits, busts, ceramics—even a line of handkerchiefs, pillboxes, and soap—while they may persist through time immemorial, being bloodless, never die.

Do I have any blood left? I wondered.

"More blood!" I bellowed. "The orifice isn't big enough!" I wanted evidence.

Enough of this trickling, anemic, brownish sludge the doctors were leaching from my arm, drops at a time. I wanted to see fluid,

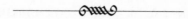

red and gushing, great gobs of it exploding from my veins. I wanted it now.

"More blood!" I again demanded, too weak to stomp my foot.

And when the doctors, in conference over my condition (quinsy, diphtheria, pneumonia, what?), did not jump to, I grabbed the fleam myself to slice at my wrist when Martha stopped me: "Please, General, no!"

"Call me George!" I found myself commanding her.

"You relieved him years ago, dear," Martha responded, thinking I was referring to a stable boy I'd long since retired.

And that's when I realized what needed to be done.

I'd not asked Martha to call me George . . . well, *ever*, really, now that I thought about it. Nor had she ever asked to so address me. Why, even my own children (Martha's really, from a previous marriage: a daughter and a son, Patsy and Jackie) could not be coaxed into calling me "Papa," let alone "George"!

And why should they have? It would be like calling Martha "Abigail" or a donkey a cat. Just plain wrong. For George was no more and hadn't been—since when, where and for how long?

I hadn't a clue.

I moaned, heaved, sighed, bellowed in unendurable pain. "Please, God, let me be!"

And then it came, a word that I'd only uttered (and to miraculous effect) twice before. It felt strange coming out, like a glass marble passing between my lips, round, slippery, and hard.

"Help."

And just like that, I found myself in a dream, nay a nightmare, all the more frightening because it was true.

In this dream, I was a man who despised being President.

The levees, the public speaking, the thick waistcoats, the unending dinners with dignitaries from countries whose names I couldn't pronounce. All of it I found tedious—a ceaseless, unremitting bore.

Since policy-making in particular left me cold, I'd pass my time in "cabinet" meetings jotting down gardening ideas I wanted the caretakers to try back at Mount Vernon, where I longed to return. I'd riffle through personal mail, with a particular interest in dispatches updating me on the ongoing mating saga of my beloved jackass, who, fussy about intercourse, rejected every suitor, no matter how well researched his lineage or well endowed his organ ("He's a bit more eager than the last, Your Excellency, but still, the jenny seems bored").

Never one to be caught off guard, I particularly loathed speaking in public extemporaneously. Even at my own levees, crowds milling past, I'd cling tenaciously to the fireplace and behave like a wax statue, so most would ooh and aah, but stay away.

When public speaking was altogether unavoidable, however, I'd spend countless hours preparing. I'd write voluminous notes to myself, recording particularly clever turns of phrase, bon mots, jokes, pleasantries, even bawdy puns—in sufficient variety and quantity to cover the wide range of situations experience had taught me I might confront.

Even so, I'd tremble in public and sweat like a horse.

Yet, despite all this, I didn't know I was unhappy, that I'd rather I didn't belong to the archives of History.

Advocates had me convinced the vague ennui that circled endlessly about me (like a summer horsefly buzzing unceasingly around one's head) was a sign of great humility and grace. That my mind-boggling array of ailments (recurring malaria, ague, fever, even a malignant carbuncle—you name it, I thought I'd caught it, rarely repeating myself, always something exotic) were signs of royalty, great compassion, blue blood.

And what of those ugly thoughts I'd had from time to time, like wishing I'd fled my inauguration?

What of the admission I'd made, while progressing from Philadelphia to New York (the capital then) for the ceremonies celebrating our First President, that I felt more like a culprit going to my place of execution than a man about to be made leader of his country?

What for the man consumed with all those gloomy thoughts when the ridiculous festivities took hold? The towns festooning themselves with flags, emblems, slogans, and mounted escorts to receive me? The massive applause on my approach and pandemonium on my arrival? And yes, who could forget passing under a victory arch as a concealed mechanism lowered a laurel wreath upon my head and a choir of white-robed maidens strewed blossoms in my path, singing "Hallelujah" at full tilt?

I could forget, that's who. Indeed, I had. All my unhappiness buried, along with George.

Why, I'd even begun to believe I was attractive. Who wouldn't prefer the portraits by Trumbull and Gilbert Stuart? No pock-marked face. No springs visible at the corners of my mouth, coils to fasten my wretched teeth to my jaw or, for that matter, Madeira-stained incisors or cuspids perpetually flecked with unremovable bits of food.

Who could blame the General for being so tyrannized by his own image he'd carry a self-help guide on his person as reminder of just how General George Washington should be expected to act? "Run not in the streets, neither go too slowly nor with mouth open," was particularly important to remember when dignity was required.

Poor embalmed President, Commander-in-Chief, His Excellency, General Washington, who didn't even know he'd lost George somewhere between those phony cherry trees a certain "historian" dreamed up and the real victory at Yorktown: the triumphant battle that won us independence and the end of the war.

And then one day, facing the end, all that changed.

I woke up.

———————— ᔕᔕᔕ ————————

Waking from the dream, I felt a new kind of pain. Not a physical sensation, neither the press of inflammation for the burning of blood (red!) seeping through my eyes. Rather, I was gripped by a certain sadness (Had I loved Martha as much as she deserved?); by fear (Did Martha love *me*?); a degree of fragility (Was I a good man? Am I as gawky and as potbellied as I feel?); and even paranoia (What if America finds out that it wasn't I who won us the war?).

I squeezed Martha's hand and she squeezed back. I felt deep and abiding love for the woman.

And love for my country.

And love for the likes of Deborah and John, whom I'd not thought about in years.

And that was all it took. . . .

Suddenly I felt as though I were being lifted from my bed and transported through the heavens to another time and place: to Boston Harbor, 1765, where I noticed a small boy beckoning me from the deck of a most splendid mercantile ship.

I recognized him as John Lawrence, my longtime aide-de-camp, whose death by suicide just *after* America's victory had for years mystified dignitaries and officers and, most importantly, me, the General himself.

One look at John and I knew instantly what I was about to experience. He didn't have to say:

"Not the events of the War, but the story of the Revolution, is your way back to George."

He flew to me—what a lark was this astral plane! We neither embraced nor shook hands; there wasn't time.

"Two breaths left, before you die or are permanently embalmed. Which is it?" he asked.

"The story!"

"Well, then, come with me and utter not a word! Just watch,

listen, and be proud of the legacy of Deborah and Alice and George and John. For this is the way back to George, to the Washington America didn't even know she had."

And now I could see into my bedchamber at Mount Vernon. I could see my body, my chest heaving for air. The doctors were scurrying all about the bed, panicked looks on their faces, thinking the end was near. But I was just getting started, preparing to come back to life.

And then, to die.

CHAPTER 2

Apollo in Boston

oston: 1765.

Jutting rocks, stinging winds, and whipsawing currents were threatening, quite suddenly, to take down our ship. Correction: *Daddy's* ship, for Papa insisted that I regard nothing of his as mine until I displayed greater interest in the shipping business that one day, were I deemed worthy of it, would be passed to me, John, his only child.

The purpose of this latest excursion, insofar as my father, Henry Lawrence, was concerned, was to instruct me once and for all in the mercantile way. I was fourteen now: It was time, by way of Father's glowing example, to persuade me to accept the destiny he had planned for me, the same one I'd been resisting since age four when I would piss in his tea barrels and blame it on the dog (until Papa shot her as a result).

God knows Papa had tried everything else to induce me to take an interest: paying me to organize his files (I took the money and made one of our slaves do it for me); including me in grown-up dinner parties (I'd crawl under the table and insist on being fed there, between the ladies' legs); buying me my own little ship (which I gave to a Negro escaping north); whipping me into submission at least once a month.

Nothing had worked.

But my Lord, had I known in advance how glorious Boston was, I would never have resisted Father so. He never would have had to drag me out from under my bed and strap me to a trunk to get me to come along.

I didn't know life could be so exciting, so free-feeling, so good. Of course Father didn't agree. He'd never been to Boston before either, and unlike me, he was frightened out of his mind.

We could only take the word of the captain that we were in the midst of Boston Bay, as we could see no trace of the city in the deep, dense fog.

But we could feel her.

By the time we reached the portal to this, the world's most bustling harbor, we had scraped against brass cannon perched on an isthmus, gouged our hull on a rock, and the Union Jack at our prow had snapped off and sunk to the bottom of the sea.

Oh, wasn't Papa taken by hysteria when that English flag was falling. Why, he nearly jumped into the roiling waves to retrieve it (it took six of us to hold him back!). As for my part, I was suddenly and strangely delighted to see it gone.

And only too mystified by Boston from the start. More hodge-podge than harbor, Boston Bay was a circus of merchant seacraft—sloops, schooners, whalers, heel tappers, ferries, lighters, and fishing ketches—a variety greater and more diverse than I had ever seen before. There were large ships back from overseas voyages unloading tea and turpentine; skiffs attached to swimming cows being herded from one harbor isle to the next by small boys with poles; schooners loaded with lobsters bigger than I. A rowboat piled high with sea coal, eel pots, mussels, and clams. A whir of piers, shipyards, distilleries, warehouses, and racks of salt-dried cod.

She was nothing like Charleston, South Carolina, my home. There wasn't a single curved pilaster or high-walled garden or gate of fretted iron in sight. And unlike every other colonial city I'd visited (always reluctantly) with my papa, Boston's appearance paid no homage to the Mother City of London either. For starters, there were virtually no brick houses (bricks were made in London); and her color scheme—shades of gray, sienna, and green—seemed uncultivated, unarchitectural, unmediated by man: like miles and miles of swamp grass that had run wild before growing preternatural heft, solidity, and height. There were no hurricane-proof tile roofs to protect her from the elements, as in Charleston. In fact, Boston's windows and doors reached right out to the wrathful waterfront, the long tentacles of her wharves straining to embrace the briny green sea.

And even more than that, in her outline I detected the shape of a creature, my tortoise Apollo, hunched and twirling, in fact. My beloved pet tortoise, who was forever at my side and whom Father had forced me to leave behind.

"Leave the goddamned tortoise to its tub!" he had demanded. But as far as I was concerned she had come along anyway—here she was, rising through the mist of Boston Bay to greet me.

Unable to suppress my delight, I hollered out, "Apollo! Papa, can you not see her in the city's shape?"

My father, already in a snit, was further annoyed.

"I see nothing but dim sunshine upon a chaotic shore."

"But Father, can't you see?" I asked eagerly, pointing out to him the ways in which the shape of my treasured tortoise could be detected in Boston's north-south line, her shell in the nearest hill and her feral eyes in the vermilion coats of the two British sentries standing guard on the approaching dock.

Over the course of the years I'd developed a habit of flinching whenever my father spoke French. Embarrassed by his lowly

Huguenot origins, my father rarely spoke in his native tongue un-less he was drunk and thus dangerous.

So of course I was trembling after my discourse on Apollo, when Papa called me belowdecks: "*Jean, viens ici.*"

Unfurling a map that flattened Boston's incantatory landscape to a dirty, sallow green stain, "*Pas assez grand que tu crois, n'est-ce pas?*" he declared, slapping his palm down upon the map. "It's not even as big as my hand."

Yet no matter which way Papa angled his hand, Boston seemed to protrude out from under it, its wharves like little fin-gers wiggling their way out of his attempt to quash them.

So Papa switched tack. Jabbing at various Boston locations with his thick, broad thumb ("This is Cambridge, where we'll find Harvard. And over here—take note, boy—the name of this river is the Charles"), he attempted to reduce Boston to simple geo-graphics which "a little later," he warned, he'd be testing me on.

But it was no use: The more Father poked and prodded the map, the more Boston, even in single dimension, radiated life that seemed to deaden Papa's gout-stiff fingers; to age him in some irrevocable way. Enough to make me wonder, for a fleeting mo-ment, his mere forty-four years notwithstanding, just how it was that I'd come to be so afraid of such a puny, wrinkled man.

"So . . ." he said, sighing deeply, his impatience mounting, "is she a peninsula, an island, or an isthmus? You tell me!"

She's Apollo, is what I wanted to say, *with her neck outstretched and feet splayed in the sun*. But I didn't, of course. I played dumb: "I haven't a clue, Father, *you* tell *me*!"

"It's really an isthmus connected to the land by means of a fragile, tiny neck that, right here, you see"—jab, jab—"when it descends into the water each day at high tide, Boston is entirely at sea, cut off and away. My feeling is that this is the source of her legendary mad, independent streak. From time immemorial Boston has had to . . ."

He droned on and on, ending on a high note, with the likelihood that Boston would one day be submerged and would wind up rotting at the bottom of the sea (along with all those damned independent-minded and unruly Yankees that the king, God bless him, found so hard to please).

At which point Papa released me to the upper deck, without hitting me. "*Vas-y* . . ."

He was speaking French, hadn't touched ale, and hadn't hit me. It was Boston—I knew it. Papa didn't *dare* raise his hand or insult me for fear that somehow Boston would protect me.

The only other place I'd ever felt protected was in my swamp back home, where I'd not only be free of Papa but, just as much to the point, the noise and bustle of downtown Charleston—the fishmongers' cries; the slave auctioneer's call; the carriages; the dustups; even the music of my father's lavish balls—all of it, once I was nestled in the reeds, was left behind. Just one mile and a half from our house, Mepkin Plantation, but another world away.

As we prepared to disembark the ship, I was feeling plain fine about everything. But as I went bounding along the gangplank, leaving Father to teeter and totter his way down on his own, I had the thought that perhaps Mother's death somehow had been nec-essary: a sacrifice of sorts, without which I might never have made it to Boston at all. Perhaps her death, more than a loss, was her final gift to me, her way of putting me in the world where I be-longed—even if the journey here had been roundabout and tinged with hatred for my dad.

The hatred started the night of Mama's death, specifically dur-ing the moment that Papa—after witnessing Mother's flailings for air—clutched me to his chest, held me in his arms, and sobbed. He was so close, so tight, so near, his hot breath had me sweating and his tears were dampening my hair. Holding fast to each other, together we helplessly watched my mother die: gasping, spitting, screaming, kicking, tearing her hair out, clump by clump. This went on for hours and hours and hours.

Even then, however, the true source of my misery was not my

mother's ugly demise. It was the way Father disentangled himself from me seconds after Mum expired; the way his face went to stone; the way he turned to me and begged my forgiveness for having "behaved abominably," referring not to a lifetime of the mania to which my mother and I had been constantly subjected, but to that "regrettable, unmanly moment" of his: "that hideous embrace" he and I had shared. Further, warning me that if I ever dared speak of it he'd lay a switch to me but good.

I, of course, had no intention of talking about what had transpired, but hardly because I was ashamed. Quite the opposite. I wished to remain quiet simply because speaking of just how good it felt to bury my tears in Papa's chest wasn't possible without trivializing what had been, to date, the finest moment of my life. "Not a way a man can be seen behaving," my father thought. Very well then, Papa, be not a man: Be my dad.

And it was in that moment that the journey to Boston, that is to say, my journey to Rebelhood—began.

For with Father's embrace I'd felt something new. Sweet. Something I'd never felt before: love.

My world opened. Now I had actual evidence that what in the quiet of night I'd barely dared dream of truly existed. Love was out there for the giving, and taking, and the only reason I hadn't felt it before was because to me, heretofore, it had been denied. Well, no more. Suddenly I realized that it wasn't that fathers didn't hug their sons or heave with sorrow while they held them fast. It was that this *particular* father, Henry Lawrence, didn't care to. And that the one time he did, he'd tried to turn it into a lie.

From this realization there was no turning back. Yes, that sensation of tingling from the back of my neck to my toes was love, and I wanted it, was unwilling to live without it ever again. Even if it took my whole life, I decided I would get it. I would demand, extract, manipulate, extort, fight for it if I must. But someone, somewhere would give me my due.

And so, not the soldier but the Revolutionary in me was born.

I began defying my father almost immediately. After my mother's funeral, I abandoned my studies, took to caning slaves, and started beating my horse. I set my tutor's wig on fire. I shat in our rice fields in plain view of my father's overseer, and for every stroke my father gave me, I pinched my governess.

Papa, at his wits' end, tried to straighten me out. Even a whorehouse to "move your adolescence along." Gentlemen with great big whiskers and big black leather bags showed up at our door, poking and prodding and asking plenty of questions: "Tell me, little man, what's wrong?" With luck, I'd have stored up a fart for a reply.

What *was* wrong?

Everything: the silk fineries that itched, the fine hose that fell, the fussy table manners (little finger up, tongue in, back straight . . . how about just chomping down?), the dumb quadrille, the grotesque fox hunt . . . on and on and on.

I couldn't have cared less that Austin and Lawrence, Ltd., Papa's famed firm (hugely lucrative, with profit from tobacco, slaves, Madeira, cotton, and, normally, rice) could one day all be mine. Bah! All I wanted was an embrace from my dad.

It was during this time that I developed my fondness for the swamp. Its stillness was all I craved. To doze in the moss, cradled by cattail and swamp grass; to listen, without moving, to the sweet warbles of bullfinch and the hushed footpads of lizard snake; to stare for hours at the fog while waiting for the landing of a loon or the leer of an alligator; to roll in the mud and think myself brine; to laugh with the sun and stretch myself into the shape of a cypress tree—this was what I craved.

Father went berserk, particularly when I came home with Apollo; or rather, when Apollo followed me home. Mucky and blinky-eyed, she showed up at my doorstep one sunny afternoon and stayed.

Standing there on the dock, I swear I could detect her presence in the howling of the ship's crew at the capstan; in the roar of the captain's voice; in the shriek of the bo'sun's pipe; in the familiar chirps, croaks, and caws of mallards and kingrushes and gulls.

Boston enfolded me.

Porters in leather aprons shouting; clerks with ledgers bustling; fat merchants in gold lace and great wigs counting; dogs barking; slatternly girls whistling; wary Redcoats firing warning shots at a particularly unruly crowd. The egret grabbing the catfish and the catfish the worm, the bear the egret and the alligator the bear.

Life in Boston: life in the swamp. I had found home.

Mother's death had been for good.

CHAPTER 3

The Girl with the Smile

rom now on, Papa, to better acquaint myself with how business is done, I wish to be your escort everywhere this business of selling rice in Boston should take you," I said to my father, offering peace, an inner shift of some one hundred and eighty degrees. (All the way from Charleston on deck when I wasn't cursing I had been silent or singing the hymns of the slaves.) "There'll be no more trouble from me."

The truth was, I had developed a plan.

My father looked at me as he did the day he forced me against my will to go fox hunting, then streaked my face with the fox's warm blood.

"As for our business here," Papa asserted, jumping to the agenda at hand with great enthusiasm, "remember, we are only here to help."

He explained that since the Seven Years' War with the French, Boston had fallen on terrible times. Merchants were foreclosing on their debtors, currency was scarce, and as I could see, people were starving in the streets. "Lying in the gutters, even too weak to be begging for food. . . . Smallpox is rife, although largely confined, and Boston's citizens are restive—very. So caution must be exercised," Papa said.

As we trundled down Ship Street in our coach (a clunky, inelegant box with rusted iron wheels which gave off sparks), my father eagerly detailed his plan to help.

Help, as he saw it, would be his offer to "select" merchants (that is, ones who owed his firm huge debts in bills of lading) a reduced wholesale price on "fine rice" which we couldn't unload elsewhere and from which, because of the reduced cost, they could turn out big profits. For his "generous assistance," he would receive repayment of debts owed him. And whatever precious little was left over would, of course, be theirs— "not to take advantage of all the suffering, rest assured, but to relieve it."

We were there to sell rice. Period. We had had a terrible season at the plantation. Too little rain, and my father's fancy irrigation innovations had been, he believed, sabotaged by some renegade slaves. The end result was rice that was dried out, musty, and worm-infested, and needed to be unloaded quickly.

I listened to my father and was amazed. Even by his standards, this was a crooked business, and the rationalizations that were sprouting from his mouth spoke volubly of his unuttered shame. Rice, he claimed, was the "new grain for the masses," the "key to renewed prosperity," the "only cure for dyspepsia," and, better still, would surely cure the "agitated spirit" for which New Englanders were well known. And if I didn't know it already, I would soon.

The Green Dragon, the oldest brick tavern in Boston, was where we lodged. We were to keep to a rigid schedule. Each morning, I was to accompany him on foot to his business meetings, then lunch, followed by my studies during his nap, then back together for tea at four o' clock, followed by touring about at six.

As soon as lunch was done (slabs of bacon with beans and corn, served with drams of ale—all brown, even the vegetables, and always the same, no matter the eating house) and my father had retired to his nap, I would take to the streets.

They were crooked, narrow, full of filth, at once both merry and grave, magical and mundane: rife with distractions and opposites. Rivulets of raw sewage coursed on each side of the lanes, smelling mostly of spoiled fish, but also blueberry and thatch. A clown found a rabbit in my waistcoat, and a gypsy woman read my palm—short lifeline, she advised. A crackpot exhibited his revolving model of the universe made of pins and steel next to where victims of smallpox, heaped in a cart, emitted muffled cries for help. A wax figure was made to walk as Redcoats uneasily stood guard. Lovers held hands—two even kissed!—while the poor stepped barefoot into the mire of the street, deferring to the privileged, who would pass unsullied on the sidewalk.

In this setting, then, it was without any real surprise that one day on my rambles I beheld gold coins raining down from the sky.

Actually, they were just pence (one hit me in the eye!) and they were coming from a glorious red- and gold-trimmed coach fitted with glass and beribboned horses that would with great impunity have run me down had I not leapt out of their way. Face first, I fell into the gutter, and for the rest of the day smelled of shit.

Trailing the chariot was a parade, hundreds of folk screaming, "Hurrah for King Hancock!" and laughing and catching coins in their fists, while tucked away in the carriage there sat a man in emerald velvet, waving absently to the human effluvia swarming his coach.

It was when lifting myself up out of the muck that I laid eyes upon a young girl nearly sixteen fastened to the stocks in the center of the square. To her, this clearly was no king passing by. To her, this Hancock fellow was a demon.

And it was at the top of her lungs that she was expressing that view, pointing out to the ladies in the crowd the size of his cock, "a mere pin," and that he deserved to "rot in hell and be set to ruin."

For she, as I was about to find out, was a whore, and Hancock a reg-ular, who one day had up and decided to turn her in.

A milk pail was hurled into her face. "Payment," it was, "for disrespect of Sir John," from an offended admirer clutching her scavenged copper.

"Naughty slut!" shouted a small boy, climbing the platform to which the girl's feet were chained, dropping a fistful of nails on her head.

Pilloried wide, arms stretched to the limit, feet bound, the girl could do nothing to defend herself. But nor did she seem to want to. She smacked her lips and lapped what milk she could from her face and caught one of the nails in her teeth, grinning.

I wanted to help but was unsure of how, or even if, she needed it. I approached anyway and, instead of speaking, just stared, offer-ing a soft, weak-at-the-knees "Hello."

I found her to be beautiful.

"Sod off!" she spat.

Beneath a sticky mask of rotting vegetables, milk, and nails were two indomitably green eyes, like algae in the bay. Her lips plump and pink, the shade of a shell. And her hair, waist-length, multishaded brown, reflected the late afternoon light, this despite a scum coat of debris.

I found myself reaching out to touch her.

She bit me.

I didn't say "*Ow!*" Instead: "I won't hurt you," uttered gently, soothingly, at which point a chicken carcass was slammed right into my back, the force of it pitching me to the platform floor.

"Damned cur!" a farmer yelled at me from across the way. "You'll soon be seeing a pecker full of disease for bein' sweet on that ugly whore!"

And with absolute mirth, her dimples deep and irrepressible, the girl shot back: "No chance of us fucking in this contraption! You can be sure of that, damn ye!"

By her face and saucy manner I was absolutely transfixed. I

picked myself off the platform and floated a few paces toward the well. "I'm going to get water to clean you up," I offered bravely.

Once I was at the public well, the crowd roared with disapproval and drew near. "Get that bastard!" I heard someone say; and next I knew, I was drowning.

Thrashing, gasping for air, I was oddly lucid. I thought through the forming of a fist (thumb outside the clamp) and before I even knew what had happened, the butcher boy was the one facedown in the freezing water. Had it not been for the pleas of the angel in the stocks—"Leave off!"—I would have kept him there, submerged under my boot, and killed him.

And so I stumbled back across the square to the stocks, water pail in tow, and began cleaning up the whore.

"You punch like a girl," was all she said as I was wiping her face.

I took no insult, for the observation was true. "Lowlifes . . ." I muttered as I dabbed at her face with my linen handkerchief.

She bridled. "Lowlifes, hardly! Good men with heads whipped about the wrong way, is all. But we'll be changing all that with the Revolution, we will!"

I was perplexed and knew not what to say. "'Revolution'?" I asked, wanting clarification, for this was the first I'd heard the word used outside my academics—outside science, mathematics, or my study of the stars.

"There's one starting tonight. You want in?"

"Why the devil not?" I answered, having no idea what I was agreeing to . . . perhaps some odd Yankee tradition I was too embarrassed to admit I didn't comprehend.

"Tonight at ten o'clock, then?" she asked, further committing me. I nodded.

"And the devil take you if you come back here again and be acting all sorry for me. I'll be fine. Now git. Meet me at the dock for Charlestown and I'll take you across."

And in the absence of sufficient mental wherewithal to ask

Across what or to where? I assented, knowing nothing about this woman, this river, this Charlestown, or whatever she had planned.

"You want in?" she'd asked.

"Why the devil not?" I'd answered.

And that, for me, was how it began. A naive exchange that, little did I know, amounted to a declaration of war . . . an exchange that in its innocence was more to the point of the Revolution than anything I have since seen, heard, or read.

And so it was on a lark and a crush, knowing little and feeling much, that I was soon to be initiated into The Cause.

CHAPTER 4

Taking Flight

T hat night, I waited and waited for Papa to fall asleep. It was almost half-past nine before I could pull out the map and determine the best way to the Charlestown ferry.

It had been a tough few days for Papa. He hadn't yet hit me, but with his frustration increasing over his failure to convince the Yankees to purchase his rice, I knew that it was only a matter of time.

For my part, Boston continued to distance me from my dad. I know I was supposed to be studying and learning from his entrepreneurial example, but this was difficult, as I began to view him in a different light. I saw few results from his rice-sampling seminars for prospective clients (I did the boiling), even combined with his latest spurious declaration that mildewed rice was an effective fertility enhancement.

What was it? Was Boston altering my perspective of my father, or Papa's touch? Or had he always been this inept?

"An aftertaste of mold!" the Yankees complained.

"Exactly!" my father buoyantly and triumphantly responded.

All I knew for certain was that the Yankees had Papa's number and hated him, his rice, and his king.

His king. Was it possible that His Eminence George III wasn't their king as well? Or was *their* king that Hancock fellow, the foppish charioteer?

This was one of the many questions I was storing up for the girl. Dammit, Papa! Go to sleep! Strike me, count sheep, do numbers on your stubby fingers and yellowing toes! Close your goddamned eyes!

"*Go to bed,*" I heard myself command—it just came out, before I'd even had a chance to work up my nerve.

Silence.

Papa appeared to fade, his figure flatten; his crooked nose, high brows, hazel, tired eyes, and bulbous upper lip retreating to single dimension, to a fading portrait of himself, hanging askew. Where had he gone? I wondered.

"Apollo, my eye!" he finally burst out. "How the devil could you possibly deduce a tortoise from a landscape?"

So he had wandered back on board our ship, replaying my recognition of Apollo in Boston's profile.

"*Answer me!*" he boomed. And there it was: the telltale fist, preparing to strike.

"Father—"

"*Answer me, sissy boy!*"

In my father's world, boys were men and tortoises were simply reptiles. Anything and everything he didn't understand was the enemy. Whether it be a tortoise of indeterminate sex or a tender son who could parry his blows and knock him out in the process: which was exactly what happened this August night of 1765.

After making sure he was still breathing, I left, racing like mad to the ferry like a boy who suddenly had sprouted wings.

CHAPTER 5

The Green Dragon

One thing for sure: The combination of Boston and this girl was working wonders. I was changing. Suddenly I was trusting my own impressions to be true.

Yes, I had been hearing voices in the middle of the night coming from below our room—I hadn't just imagined it. Furthermore, that was an actual fire-breathing dragon lurking about the hallway.

The Green Dragon was, of course, the mascot of our inn. Anyone would tell you she was just an image, hung on the iron branch above the door, hammered out of copper already green with verdigris and time.

Yet as I was flying out of my father's room and down the stairs, there she was, roaming the hallways, eyeballing me as suddenly I was stopped in my tracks. I realized that the entryway wall was not perfectly seamless, that within the pattern of cracks running from floor to ceiling was . . . the outline of a door.

I'd imagined it as the threshold to another world, one replete with secret codes and furtive men conducting nefarious business, dangerous as all. And I was right.

Through one crack leaking traces of orange light, I took a peek. I caught bits and pieces: shadows; specks of maroon, chestnut, and deep green; billows of harsh yellow smoke; and an aroma, too, of stale ale.

Then voices: harsh, throaty, male. I recognized in them the violence with which I'd grown up. And I wanted to run.

But the Green Dragon had another idea.

I found my hand rising to push open the door, despite myself, as if guided to do so by something other. Of course, no History book would ever include me in an account of what was taking place in that room, despite the fact that my presence there would change its course. And certainly no one would include the green dragon. But in fact, it was her breath of fire that got me into the room, and without it the Revolution may never have been won. So for those who say History and Imagination don't mix . . .

Inside was a devil's den.

Hearth ablaze despite the summer heat, the chamber was filled with men in midtoast cheering "Three huzzahs for the Stamp Tax!" and snickering that the king, with his latest salvo, had given them a gift from the gods. "What a blessing is the Stamp Tax!" cried a palsied man who stood near the hearth. I knew nothing of this tax, of course, except what I was given to believe: It was a curse. So why on earth were these men celebrating it?

The palsied man, tattered and filthy, suddenly noticed me.

"Who sent you?" he barked, grabbing me by the throat, his other hand poised to tear off my ear.

If it weren't for another man—tougher, plumper, stronger—who emerged from the darkness to stop him, I would certainly have received my second thrashing of the day. "Adams!" my advocate barked. "He's only a boy."

I hastened to add, in my most proper and obliging I'm-not-scared-to-death-despite-the-hand-clutching-my-windpipe fashion, "Forgive my discourtesy, gentlemen, it was an accident, I assure you. I'm afraid I lost my way."

Adams held me fast.

"I said, who sent you?"

"I—I couldn't sleep and—"

Then another man came forth, one who had been blocking my view of the table until now. He was the man in the red coach: "King Hancock." Tall, languid, graceful, with pearl-white hands graced with a gold signet ring and silken ruffles cascading from his wrist, a walking waterfall.

"You say you are a guest of the inn, sir?"

I gulped and nodded. "As a matter of fact, good sir, I was on my way out—"

"A little late, is it not? What business takes you? And you're here with a guardian, I assume. Where is he?"

"Upstairs, sleeping. I'm—I'm supposed to meet a girl—"

Another man—swarthy, portly—spoke sharply, but with a trace of amusement.

"A little rendezvous?"

Hancock smiled sweetly and turned to my feral captor, the dark man, and an aproned man.

"Adams, Revere, Dr. Church—all we have here is a little Romeo. Clumsy, perhaps, but hardly dangerous. I say let him go to his doxy!"

I stole a glance at the table, a slab of gnarled white pine, upon which lay a huge map stuck with pins. Their little gray bobs littered its surface. And drafts upon drafts of letters and articles and broadsides took up what room remained. The seats not occupied around the table were filled with newspapers.

Adams protested, "We can't take that chance. What if—"

Hancock shot back, "Tell me then, Samuel, where will we be when this is over if we cannot exercise a little trust?"

"Well . . . just . . . not quite yet," Adams insisted, relaxing his grip on me only slightly.

Revere stepped forward. "If not now, when? Damn if you're not mad, Adams."

And a melee ensued. Adams shoved Revere to the wall, but Revere quickly caught him in a hold. Adams could only slap out blindly, while Church struggled to pull the men apart.

This, then, was my introduction to the Founding Fathers. As John Jay would later write: "Dear me, I think History must needs be rewritten, some circumspect revision is in store, for we were not heroes as much as we were men, and History, nay posterity, might not be braced for that, not at all." From the disturbed faces of the frenzied men wrestling in the chamber before me, to the grave expressions of their polished alabaster busts lining the corridors of History . . . what a journey, what a fraud!

Hancock, having had enough, rapped on the floor with his ivory-tipped walking stick and, when that didn't work, applied it to the backs of his colleagues. "Stop it, stop it, you hear? Like children!"

In the confusion I skedaddled off, with Adams, stopping to catch his breath, calling after me, "Swear by God Almighty that you were never here tonight!"

"I swear it," I declared. And then I ran.

Through the narrow, jagged alleys of the night I lunged, making fast tracks toward the dock I'd learned was at the mouth of the Charles, where muddy effluent met the torpid, brackish sea.

It was two minutes to ten and I was in a panic. "Oh, Lord, please don't let me miss this chance! Please don't take her away!"

Winding around Back Street, dodging and weaving through flocks of crazed chickens and the random cow, I was struck by the drum of my heels echoing in the streets.

Suddenly my shoes felt too damned light, thin, delicate, effete for whatever it was I sensed in that moment I was meant to do. I stopped to remove them and my stockings.

And in those few seconds I suddenly heard it: a palpable silence. Similar to what I'd experienced in the swamp, reminiscent of the quiet which had followed my confrontation with my father, but more of it and thicker, denser somehow, carrying with it the blank sensation of something very big about to turn.

Barefoot now, I pushed on, as a whole new world unfolded to my zigzag path.

People were hiding everywhere, crouching behind bushes, ducking inside smokehouses, stooped behind barrels of dried cod. Tiny groups in haphazard formations were racing from tavern to hitching post and back again, speaking never above a whisper and only among themselves.

Otherwise, unbroken silence—not even the night watchman to wish Boston "good night" or a reassuring "all's well." Perhaps he was sleeping or was wiser than we knew, for although evening was well on, actually it was morning, and the Dragon of Revolution was awake, breathing fire, preparing to pounce.

CHAPTER 6

Ah, Ezekiel!

She was waiting for me. She knew I'd come. Ah, yes!

And when she reached for my palm without so much as a hello, we ran hand in hand toward the dock without needing or wanting to exchange a word, as though we'd been friends all our lives. Suddenly all the questions I had stored, all the talking I had planned, seemed beside the point. I didn't even think to ask her name. Even twenty minutes later, with the city of Boston behind us, swallowed by riverbank fog, and the choppy black hills of Charlestown fully in view, still we'd shared nothing but . . . yes, silence, like that which I'd discerned on Back Street, carrying the hope that I would never, ever have to let go of her hand, intertwined in mine.

I finally tried to break the silence, but she stopped me by tapping gently at my lips. Her finger felt moist against my mouth, and substantial, like being kissed by humid night air. She shook her head no, forbidding me to speak, and I obliged, squeezing her hand. It was bigger than mine and scarred, the nails dirty and chewed.

Charlestown, Massachusetts, was marsh also, but unlike any I'd ever seen before, of the most forbidding kind—moors, clay pits, and thorny scrub that drew blood. It was dark as coal with not so much as a moon to guide us on our path, and I had only the sounds of her footfalls to follow—squish, squish—through the bog, as well as the rhythm of her breathing and the reassuring pulse I could feel in her palm.

We ended up at a lone gibbet, a gallows abandoned but standing tall on a dirt mound that somehow seemed to attract light from stars which could only be viewed from that very spot. They hung in the sky expressly to illuminate what was hanging from the gibbet's arm: an assemblage of sticks and chain. No—it was the remains of a man, a ghostly skeleton, its bones clacking in the breezeless night.

I tried to run, but she refused to let go of my hand.

"Nothing here to hurt you. He's one of our own. In fact, he looks out for us. That's what I feel. I come to see him when I have a question. I need to know if tonight's the night. If it is, he'll let me know," she explained.

"But he's dead—an abominable horror." True, the skeleton bore no resemblance whatsoever to the man I had to take her at her word he once was. Birds had picked at his eye sockets, and the space between the two remaining shards of rib bone was the site of an abandoned nest, the eggs discolored, shattered, and dry.

"He's been hanging here for six years, thereabouts," she explained.

"Looks to be more like a century to me." I shuddered.

"Touch him," she advised, "then you'll see."

That, of course, was the last thing on earth I wanted to do, but she really wasn't giving me the choice. She dragged my hand toward the vestige of his heel and directed me to stroke it.

"*Do it,*" she ordered.

I obeyed.

On contact, the heel turned to dust and tiny bone particles drifting into the air turned luminous, iridescent, twirling in the moonlight, their ballroom the sky. "Ahhhhh."

It was a taste of the magic behind the Revolution, a hint of the dreams it would encourage, allow—require. No, this was not to be the last revelation she would share with me.

But for her, the girl whose name I still didn't know, this dust of angels was the stuff of life and death and serious business indeed. I could tell that by the way she concentrated to read the pattern the bone dust was writing on the soil.

"A bit like reading tea leaves, only I find it easier, you see." She pointed out the design the white dust made on the dark earth, seeing in the squiggly lines a circle that wouldn't close, the tail of a minnow struggling upstream, refusing to alter its course.

And that was all she needed.

"Okay," she said. "I guess then it's time—let's go."

Of course I had absolutely no idea what was happening, and still I didn't know the girl's name, but at that moment I didn't much care. I was caught up in her spell, in her wonderland: a world of omens, cadavers, and stars.

So back to the ferry we ran, the sea breeze encouraging our return while the *clackety-clack, clackety-clack* of the skeleton's bones played friendly accompaniment to our flight. It felt so much like living a song that I wasn't surprised when she stopped at the quay and urged me to "Listen up! For those are the bells! Let the Revolution begin!"

In the heat of the moment I asked for her name, but she demurred: "You don't need to know nothin', 'cept I'm a whore who knows what's up, what's right and what's wrong. You wanna call me something, just call me 'friend.'"

"Well then—friend—what's this stuff of Revolution?"

She plopped herself down on the riverside, tossed her hair off her face, and, cross-legged, back straight and tall, told me a story.

She explained that the skeleton at the gibbet was a Negro named Ezekiel who had poisoned his master. Everyone who knew Ezekiel—white, black, rich, or poor—wanted his master, Captain Simpson, dead too. The captain was so fierce and bloodthirsty and venomous that it took three tries to kill him, so the story went, because his body thrived on the poison. But when it finally worked and Simpson croaked, white people rallied around, suddenly afraid of a black man who knew how to do what was right. So they hanged him. The end.

Captain Simpson was her father, she told me. And she'd rather fuck men for money than her daddy for a beating any day of the week. At least until this Revolution of hers was won, when all this, of course, would change. Then there'd be fairness and good sense and no hypocrisy and people they'd be sweet and kind as all . . .

Sounded good to me. Did this have anything to do with all this fuss about a Stamp Tax and the Yankee hostility toward our English king?

She laughed. "Not really, but for now, it'll do."

"I'm afraid I don't—"

Again she stopped me. "Never mind now. You will." And she offered me her hand to shake.

"I'm Deborah."

"I'm John."

CHAPTER 7

Firedance

Back in Boston: more bells, but by now the churches were involved, Old North and New North and Cockerel. And as they tolled, farmers, smiths, coopers, apprentices, and even slaves spirited forth in the night, confident that they had received their call. It was time to come out.

Deborah was among those in the lead, at the head of a parade of hundreds on the march, down Beacon Hill, across the Common and on to the Liberty Tree. There, still more Bostonians were waiting anxiously for a party that was to begin with a beheading.

When we joined them, it was one of the queerest sights I'd ever seen. Thousands of people had gathered about a raging bonfire, the flames almost two stories high. Beyond the fire stood what they all called a cathedral: the Liberty Tree. It was of solid elm, without doors or pews, and boasted a magnificent clerestory of long limbs that rose above Washington and Essex Streets, high above the rooftops and framing the sky. She was one of the oldest trees in America and, rumor had it, unfellable.

People howled "Liberty!" and plied themselves with free-flowing ale that sprang from kegs, which I knew instantly were too expensive a brew for this particular crowd to legitimately afford in such abundance. The wine too was good enough for fancy soirees, the Charleston kind my father hosted.

Some folks chanted like Indians and sounded drums, circling the giant bonfire. Other people were part of a performance with actors. Farmers and shopkeepers, drunk as pipers, were lining up to bring goods to be stamped by a mock stamp master. Objects of all kinds: ears of corn and baskets of fruit, porringers, chamber pots, and urns, naked buttocks, bare breasts, and plump thighs. It didn't matter what—the stamp master, with his official mark (a nasty skull and bones) was only too happy to do his job, laughing all the while.

There was an effigy, too, marked A.O. STAMP MASTER. Stuffed with straw, strewn with tar, he hung from the Liberty Tree, and a small girl with her one-eyed cat swung from his feet, shouting "Liberty!" The tree branches bowed with her call.

"A goodlier sight who e'er did see? A stamp man hanging on a tree!" chanted the people as they circled the writhing fire. There, amid the rising sparks and roaring flames, the Green Dragon roosted, its head thrown back, its ivory teeth bared.

Deborah wanted to dance. But I was in no mood. Maybe it was because I had seen parties like this before, thrown by my father for his slaves. "Good times to assuage the bad," he used to say, but really to stave off the rash of rebellions that had become commonplace in the land.

Maybe it was those kegs of beer and casks of wine conspicuously initialed with the letters "J.H.," just as I'd seen on the door of John Hancock's glorious carriage and his ring. Or maybe it was the luxurious coffin out under the great tree, lined with silk and there to carry "A.O." away to the funeral pyre in high style.

Whatever it may have been, I sensed deception. And was certain of it, in fact, when a smattering of elegant gentlemen—faces dirtied, velvet waistcoats stashed in the shrubs, silken hose removed—wove their way through the drunken carousers.

These were the men I had seen before in the stifling room at the inn—Samuel Adams, Hancock, Church, Revere, and some others. Their air was patrician, save that of Adams, who was base. And when they commenced to speak, their rhetoric felt just like my father's when he explained that he had come to Boston on a mission to help: hollow and a little too loud.

I tried to listen, but Deborah grabbed me for a dance. "Never mind the likes of them," she whispered, tugging me toward the fire. I was shocked again, for she appeared to know exactly what I had been thinking. She warned me, "Boston is a dangerous place. You gotta be more careful." Then, hand in hand, we started circling the fire, forked tongues of flame flicking at our ankles.

But even with the clamor and the drums, I caught bits:

"Before long it'll be your tables, chairs, platters and dishes and knives and forks and everything else that will be taxed . . . just as you see up there on the stage!" shouted one man, his shirt too white and fine for his part. Deborah told me that one was a Dr. Warren.

And another: "Nay, I don't know that they wouldn't find means to tax you for every child you got, and for every kiss your daughters receive from their sweethearts. God knows, they would just as soon ruin you, the English would." This from a wild-eyed man Deborah said was an attorney named Otis.

And from Revere, my shield: "The people will starve, for imports will be too costly. As it is, there is not enough bread to feed our children!"

Hancock: "By the sweat of our brow, we earn the little we possess, and we shall not see it taken away. We will fight to protect what we know to be ours!"

From Sam Adams, by far the most frightening prognostication: "First will be the fever, then the characteristic pustules with their revolting disfigurements. After, the odor, at which point the fever will rise sharply and then, oh shame!, there will be no medicines! For they will not have been unloaded because of that bloody tax!" This struck a chord in the seething, fearful mob.

Not unlike my father's sales patter. Only in this case, the message seemed to be working. Women screamed. Children cried. And men shook their fists and offered to take up guns.

I didn't know of this "tax," or know these men. And I certainly didn't know these Yankees. I knew only enough to be sure that things were not quite right. But still, as Deborah pointed out, again reading my mind, things were exactly as they needed to be, adding an optimistic, "You'll see."

But though I'd only spent a few days in Boston, I had learned this much: The Yankees were not stupid. These were people who got what they wanted. For now, they were content to drink and wait . . .

. . . Until after the effigy was cut down and carried by procession to the home of Andrew Oliver, the new stamp master appointed to levy the tax: namesake of A.O. . . .

. . . Until after A.O.'s head was sawn off, crushed, and turned to ash by fire (just for the real Oliver to witness from his balcony) . . .

. . . Until after Oliver, barricaded in his home, finally fled . . .

. . . Until after the lieutenant governor, Thomas Hutchinson, arrived with soldiers, to be assaulted by a volley of stones . . .

. . . And until well after the bevy of disguised gentlemen, scared as shit, would run from the soldiers, hide, and later claim they had nothing to do with the ruckus. . . .

Then the Yankees would attack. In plain view they would rip the railings off Oliver's fence, the windows from casements, the cabriole legs from Queen Anne sofas, and the Copley portraits from their frames. All this they would destroy, along with A.O.'s English gardens and his croquet field—not just because it was En-

glish, or even because Oliver had elected to sell stamps, but because he was rich. And I would take part for the very same reason.
Because, though I too was a mansioned fellow, I knew the harm
that had been done me in our unhappy way of wealth.

And with the havoc in full tilt and the fire burning high, licking at whatever drew too close, I picked up a broken cobble and
pelted the lieutenant governor, who was chased away again, this
time by me. And as I did this, I also knew why: I had had it with
being my father's son.

And that's when I kissed Deborah. And with the stamp man's
Madeira still on her tongue, she kissed back, fierce and for a long
while, saying one more time, "Just trust me" and "You'll see."

I did. And I saw.

The next day, in the *Gazette*, these events became the "Stamp
Act Riots," plain and simple. And they would not stop until the
dreaded tax was repealed. The people had spoken, it was pro-
nounced, and "in a manner without design."

And while Samuel Adams disavowed all connection, he
would secretly see to it that none would be arrested and that justice would ensue . . . and (hush-hush) that the lieutenant governor's abode would be hit next. Hutchinson was the man to ruin to
get rid of that tax.

"Trust me," she said. For even back then, Deborah alone knew
who was really using whom. Different goals had they, the rich and
the poor, but for the first time they needed each other. And in
this need a new country could be born. Of this she was sure.

"Does this have anything to do with all this fuss about a
Stamp Tax?" I asked.

"Not really—but it'll do."

CHAPTER 8

The Governor Besieged

The next morning, Papa woke me in a state of nervous excitement. But it was not to discuss with me what had transpired between us the night before.

The pleasure of your company is requested for dinner this day at six o'clock sharp. Father was beside himself. "This is it. All our troubles are over! Boston is mine. It's a rice city now!"

Judging from his reaction to the delivery of this invitation (upon his awakening earlier that morning), it might as well have been from the king himself.

We spent the entire day shopping in preparation for the event.

Funny, I never asked the identity of our host. I more or less didn't care. And since Papa didn't seem to care that I didn't care, the combined lack of interest made for a very fine day. Father traded his traveling wig for a more formal bag replete with ribbon of indigo silk, and for me he insisted upon a new "cauliflower" wig, which on my head looked exactly like it sounds. He bought us new lace-cuffed shirts of the finest Holland linen and four-threaded Strawbridge knit hose. High-tongued shoes with sterling buckles and new silk waistcoats with buttons of agate, carnelian, and bloodstone completed the picture Papa wanted so much to compose: rich and full of class.

Unfortunately, he had, in his mindlessness, forgotten the August heat, and while we looked handsome indeed in our layers of satin and silk, we sweltered. Our armpits dripped, our powder ran, Father's cadogan wig slipped freely and frenetically about his sweating head.

As we approached the house (a "palace," my father called it, although it looked to me like a putty-colored cage), I was reminded at all costs to "remain impressive, look alive, and be smart"—on my life.

But when we arrived, he was the one whose ankles were collapsing from his new, too-high-heeled shoes as we tiptoed ("Old money is light-footed," Papa claimed) down a massive corridor filled with royal busts leading to our host's dining room.

I had never seen so many kings in one place. All the Georges, Queen Anne, "and over there, the Stuarts," my father pointed out, before crashing to the floor. "Damn it to hell!" he cursed as his wig slid across the parquet, to come to rest a few inches from the diamond-buckled toes of our host.

Dramatically posed, Lieutenant Governor Thomas Hutchinson stood reflected in the tabletop of highly polished black oak. He was still sporting the gash I had inflicted on his forehead from my volley of stone.

While a servant retrieved and replaced my father's wig, Hutchinson tendered me his hand. "How kind of you to come."

It was clear he didn't remember me as the stone thrower. Not because he hadn't seen me and not because his memory was weak, but because he hadn't ever really taken me in. Hutchinson just wasn't in the habit of looking upon the mob. To him, the lower orders were a malodorous mass of fuss and bother, comprising far too many unattractive earth tones, and he wanted as little to do with them as possible. Richer than my father he may have been, but dumber, definitely, than the Yankees he disdained.

Hutchinson, you see, had heard my father's pitch on rice as an "antidote for restlessness," was interested, and hence issued the invitation to dine. In the spirit of noblesse oblige, he hoped to bring rice to Boston to "help the body politic with their unhappiness" of late. He wished to strike a deal with Austin and Lawrence, Ltd., at a price commensurate with an act of charity, if my father was sincere in his wish to help the beleaguered of Boston. This much was clear: These two deserved each other.

As they prattled on interminably in the rice-as-medicine vein (Hutchinson's mute, cross-eyed daughter taking notes for posterity all the while), my state of agitation grew to terror. For suddenly I remembered we were doomed.

This was indeed the eve of the twenty-sixth of August, and I recalled that the mob was planning to chop down Hutchinson's door tonight. Any second now we'd be running for our lives. . . .

"Any second" had arrived . . . or so I thought. I heard a knock and screamed. "They're coming!" I shouted, leaping up and knocking over my chair.

Father's face went red with embarrassment and rage. Hutchinson's went white with consternation. His goggle-eyed daughter stifled a shriek. A servant, who had tapped politely before entering with the roast and inadvertently prompted my exclamation, hesitated at the open door, gulped, then deposited the meal on the table and scurried away.

Servants rushed to pick up my chair and I shakily deposited myself back into it. Papa, a fine scarlet by now, wouldn't even look at me and began stabbing at his proffered slice of beef. Hutchinson made a comment about the vintage of the wine as if nothing had happened. Silence descended.

It was short-lived.

A hacking sound ripped through the room. Cries of "Come out!" and "Hang the bastard!" rent the air and the sound of smashing glass reached us in our seats.

Hutchinson, daintily dabbing his lips, vowed to stay. But the door crashed open, torn from its hinges, and dozens of men, dressed mostly as Indians, stampeded into the front hall. Hutchinson's hysterical daughter clung to his legs, swearing she would die with him. But, dying not being exactly what the lieutenant governor had in mind, he rose and ran, managing as best he could with a braying, cross-eyed girl attached to his waist.

"We'll have him, we will!" the crew captain cried, giving chase with the rage of the devil, but without his wit. For he lost the couple at the first turn, in plain view, where the kitchen spilled into the garden.

Father and I crouched hidden under the table as another contingent ran upstairs to do damage to the bedrooms. Some were content to stay downstairs and tear the wainscoting off the walls, but four other men, especially enthusiastic, could be heard scaling the mansion roof, razing the cupola, and yanking off the slates, hurling them down to shatter on the walkway below.

As terrifying as all this chaos was, I was having a ball. Even while my father and I were hightailing it to the wine cellar, I couldn't resist tossing a sconce through a broken bay window.

But the fun didn't last long.

In the cellar, though it was solid black, I could make out some shadowy figures in the corner: ruffians who had preceded us with the help of a torch and had found their way to the wine. Their eyes glowed red in the flame and they resembled bears, except with breeches, which were down around their ankles. Between them on the ground was a tiny woman, her legs spread wide.

Judging from the homespun dress shoved high above her head and the absence of shoes, it was clear she was one of their own. But the bear-men had bashed her with a wine bottle and were taking turns with her. She was covered in blood and every available orifice was in use.

I lunged. And was instantly cast back, a shard of glass in my forehead, my eyes sealed shut with gushing blood.

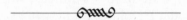

I must have blacked out for a good while, because when I came to, in the morning's wee hours, the rioting upstairs had dwindled to a growl. But the men in the cellar were still having their fun.

Although I was in terrible pain, I didn't dare move. I did, however, in the lightening gloom, finally get a bit of a look at the girl's face, and she at mine. It was Deborah.

She was smiling at me. Exhausted, and too frightened to speak, she could only mouth, *Trust anyway* and *Go!* before falling faint again.

Smiling.

But I did as she bade me and made a run for it. When I got upstairs (the house but a shell of what it had been, everything gone or laid flat), I realized I had lost my father. Or rather, he had lost me, for he had run and left me behind.

Outside, scavengers were fighting over useless bits of debris— a shelf from a china cabinet, the broken handle of a vase. An old couple was bent in prayer, on their knees.

Wary Redcoats stood guard—a little late.

"What a blessing is the Stamp Tax." The words of the palsied man from the secret chamber ran through my head. So for whom was it a blessing and for whom was it a curse? And what was this business of Revolution that felt so exciting one moment, so sickening the next? That had a father running for his life, forgetting altogether that he had a son? That had raped one of its own?

An article in the next day's *Gazette* made things even more confusing. It stated that while this attack on the lieutenant governor's house was obviously a "high-handed enormity perpetrated

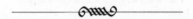

by vagabond strangers," it also implied that letters were found in Hutchinson's house which proved he was indeed responsible for the Stamp Tax.

It suggested that these letters were the target of the riot, the motivation behind the sorry unleashing of fury. But these letters, it was explained, would never be produced because they had been destroyed (conveniently enough) in the course of the night.

I knew enough by now to see that these were lies.

"The resistance of that day, however," the article went on to say, "has roused the Spirit of America. Britain best beware its Tax, for the People will fight!" Signed, Samuel Adams.

The journey back to Charleston passed in silence and I resolved never to mention to Papa his running away. Instead, I secretly decided to return to Boston as soon as I could, with Harvard my excuse. Bound and determined was I to rescue that girl.

CHAPTER 9

Rebelhood

*I*n 1769, the Rebel in me was born, inadvertently, as is always the case with a true Rebel. For as it is a Revolutionary's heart and not his mind which needs be engaged, usually his purpose hits him unawares. When he's not looking, so to speak, as when, too late on August 15, I realized my father, in heading down the hall, intended to crack my beloved Apollo's body to bits by slamming her against my bedroom wall.

Actually, in retrospect, I'm surprised it didn't happen sooner, because from the moment Father and I returned to Charleston from what he came to refer to as his "little stint in Massachusetts," four interminable years of uneasy truce between us began.

Father never again conducted business in Boston ("God will sink it, leaving my invoices unpaid"). He had all correspondence and addresses belonging to merchants from "that godforsaken place" struck from his files. And he absolutely forbade me ever to consider enrolling in Harvard.

I never mentioned Deborah to him, which was difficult, since I thought about her morning, noon, and night. Sitting on the edge of the swamp, I took up sketching and must have made five hundred portraits of her hand alone, both sides, driven as I was to have a permanent record of what, with every passing day, felt increasingly like a dream. I found hope in the lifeline on her palm, which I remembered being long (and I drew it longer, extending it down to the wrist) in the belief that the longer she lived, the better our chances of finding each other once again.

I tried running away, but only got so far as the swamp before realizing that without money or clothing I'd wind up sleeping in haystacks or sold into servitude. This is one area in which I differed markedly with the storybooks: I knew that love alone was not enough to keep me alive.

So I was trapped. And I acted like it. My only solace was thoughts of Deborah (I'd talk to her via Apollo, into her blinky red eyes) and the literature I read coming out of Boston, which made taxes, taxes, taxes synonymous with tyranny (I was learning). It was always the same old thing, but it had a quality that captured my attention. Evidently other people's too, for by 1769, the anti-tax furor had spread to Charleston and seemed to be taking over the town.

It was fun. We set up liberty poles and marched "offenders" (those who paid their taxes, I guess) around it. We said all sorts of nasty things about Parliament. And a boycott was set up to cripple merchants who sold taxable, British goods. I knew my father, for one, would persist in doing so and, hence, give me a chance to fix him but good.

He hadn't been that horrible, actually, during these years. Sure, he made me clean out the horse stables once a week and empty my own chamber pot, but mostly, thanks to times getting harder economically, he was preoccupied with what he loved most in life—making money—which kept him more or less easy to please.

Here in Charleston, you see, he perceived no threat in this anti-tax furor. That's not to say that Papa was flamboyant about selling British goods—he just didn't exactly advertise his oscillating clocks, pygmy dolls, and scented thatch in the streets. He was definitely more covert than that, secretly stowing goods in every available nook and cranny in the house. He conducted the majority of his business deals and deliveries and the unloading of ships from the docks in the wee hours of the night. Still, he was confident enough to let me attend anti-Parliament rallies, as long as I assured him harsh words were never spoken about the king (they weren't).

It was a bit odd, in fact, how King George was generally spared at these gatherings—never the target, per se, except as the butt of rumor and bad jokes. Certainly he was taken perfunctorily to task for being weak, with a Parliament beholden to mercantile interests. But mostly it was his eccentricities (was it true he dreamed of sex with piebald mares?) and obsessions (is every clock in the palace linked in absolute, to-the-second synchronicity?) that were the subjects of debate and ridicule.

Looking around me, I got the idea that very few people knew what the hell they were talking about, especially as regards taxes. The Stamp Tax, having long been rescinded, had been replaced by a less onerous usage tax on glass, lead, tea, and china, to mention a few items on the list. With the possible exception of tea, these were all luxury items, which few people in attendance at the tavern rallies could afford anyway. Really, now, all bias aside, what business did gypsies, jack-tars, tenant farmers, and yeomen have complaining about surcharges on china? And at the opposite end, for merchants affluent enough to afford such items, what was a few extra pence?

All very confusing, especially when in the same meetings I'd also hear rumblings hailing King George for "knocking down a peg or two the merchant seamen, the plantation owners, the bastard well-to-do"—people like Papa, who took more than they gave.

I understood nothing, nor did I care to. As far as I was concerned, I was on the right side and my father the wrong; he was a tyrant for amorally selling British goods. Heeding Deborah's words, which I'd etched in my mind—"No, but it'll do for now"— I simply took it on faith that this hue and cry about taxes would take me where I belonged.

It did.

So it was that in the feverish climate of one of these rallies, I took it upon myself to report my father. "Duty compels me, comrades, to report to you the heinous violation of the current boycott by Henry Lawrence, otherwise known as my papa."

Oh, didn't the crowd cheer.

When they raided our home, even though I was watching through the keyhole of an armoire where Papa had stowed me ("for your protection") and even though their faces were painted black and bodies swathed in Indian garb, I recognized every last one of them. (I think, momentarily forgetting myself, I even said "Hi!")

First they ordered Papa to dance to "Yankee Doodle" while singing it backward, then demanded he cease and desist from importing "taxable goods" from Britain.

Papa handled the feat surprisingly well under the circumstances ("Macaroni it called and cap his in feather . . .") and made a litany of promises to do just as these men bade. Not only did he put up virtually no resistance, he seemed relaxed, utterly unruffled by the whole ordeal.

I can't quite recall exactly how it was that Papa turned the situation around to his advantage. It all happened so fast. I just know it had something to do with quantities of bootlegged British rum and some little Chinese porcelain figurines he retrieved from a trunk in his bedroom and passed out in droves. "One of these could feed the entire city of Charleston bounties of bread," he bragged.

Not only did not a single comrade object to such decadence, they encouraged Papa to hand over more of the statues because, as one of them remarked, "They make nice gifts."

Then, after signing a petition of support for my father's campaign as a delegate to the South Carolina assembly, they left.

Needless to say, I was disgusted beyond words. Where was all that Revolutionary zeal I'd been hoping for? All that commitment? The Cause?

Father hadn't locked me in the armoire for my safety after all (I knew that was too kind to be true). He'd done so simply to be free of my interference while he took matters in hand as only Henry Lawrence, unimpeded, could.

Which of course meant two things: (1) From the moment he spotted "Indians" in black face (go figure) coming up the walk, he suspected me of colluding with them; and (2) afterward, should he prove triumphant, I'd have hell to pay.

"Papa! Let me out! I can't breathe! I've had quite enough!" I hollered. Then, playing innocent: "Are they really gone?" and "Are you all right?"

He released me. And for as long as I lived, for the balance of my thirty-two years, I never, ever forgot the look on my father's face at that moment and all that next ensued. The face and temperament of a wild, rabid dog, a snarling, hissing, snorting, sweating, bloodshot, vicious beast.

He struck me, his ring-bearing fist landing in my right eye.

"Get the point, son! And get it now!" He grabbed me by the scruff of the neck. "You are done!"

I still don't know exactly what came over me, but all I could think to do was laugh.

Henry Lawrence did not take it well. He kicked me to the floor and smashed a saucer on my head. Which I thought was even funnier.

"When will you learn, sissy boy, that these ideals you espouse aren't worth the paper they're printed on, that in the end, I will win out—and things will remain just as they are!" he roared, kicking my shin for emphasis.

I don't know why I bothered to reason with him, but there you go. "Papa, I cannot help but differ. Look, for example, at Apollo and her kind: The oldest living creatures on earth are those who adapt, not those who hold on to antiquated values. Apollo has endured precisely because—"

My next inhalation brought a vision of exactly what was to come.

Father running down the hall to my room.

His only son, now with a bruised leg, giving chase on all fours, screaming, "Please, Papa, no!"

Father at the bath, Apollo in his hands.

"Papa, please!"

He was gripping Apollo's neck. "Tell me you're dead wrong. That you're sorry. That you respect your papa."

I couldn't do that. How I wished I could.

So he snapped her neck in two.

He hurled her against the wall, full force, shattering her to bits.

"There!" he cried triumphantly. "So much for its talent for survival—now it's gone!" And he crushed bits of her shell under his velvet shoe. "Such is a tortoise's fate!"

My head, heart, and soul were silenced. Nothing mattered anymore.

That night I made a necklace of Apollo's shell shards, and I kept it with me to my dying day. I took nothing else from Mepkin Plantation when, later that week, I left for Harvard.

I didn't discuss my decision with my father. Somehow he just knew.

He agreed to pay all expenses provided I never speak, write, or seek to meet him again.

I accepted the terms.

In the course of a single week, my father filled in my swamp with topsoil.

But for the sound of my necklace rattling as I stepped up into the carriage Father had hired, nothing but silence accompanied my departure. Papa and I never even said good-bye.

Silence, but for the rattle of Apollo's scales, my own personal alarum.

CHAPTER 10

Harvard Days

When I wasn't escaping the tortures of my beastly Harvard classmates, I spent every moment looking for Deborah, and I made a promise to myself to stay alive until I did.

Things were that dangerous. Keeping one step ahead of the various mobbish factions roaming within and without Harvard's ivied walls was really and truly a full-time job.

I don't know what I'd come to Boston hoping for, except to find Deborah and, I guess, fight for something. To be where she and The Cause dwelt; to become a priest or a lawyer; to settle down and be free. This was, I suppose, how the scenario in my mind played out.

I had it all wrong. Deborah was nowhere to be found. And just attending a lecture in the wrong attire amounted to taking one's life in one's hands. One day I'd wear an English waistcoat to look very much the gentleman and keep Tory upperclassmen from making me their slave (no exaggeration here: I mean whips and chains!).

Another day, unassuming colonial homespun (ostensibly to protest dutied British cloth) to placate those sympathetic to the "Rebel Cause" (although I hadn't quite figured, outside of the tax argument, which was getting tired, exactly what that was). Never mind that I looked like a sack in homespun flax; if it kept my untimely eradication at bay, I could cope—although I dreaded that I might run into Deborah on one of my dumpy, unfashionable "colonial days."

I just couldn't seem to keep the infractions belonging to whichever side straight. One day my crime would be sneaking a sip of Bohea tea in the latrine, another day failing to refuse butter. That, as it turned out, had more to do with protesting the lousy— and I mean that literally—food than with manifesting either a Loyalist or Rebel sympathy.

For the apparently capital crime of sipping tea, would-be Rebel sympathizers (i.e., children of Rebel parents) were forced to renounce all loyalty to George III. In and of itself this wasn't a big deal. I'd learned quickly enough at Harvard that in order to survive a single day I'd need to tell anybody anything they wanted to hear, and by this point, three months into my first term, I'd already become situationally ambidextrous. Besides, I hated George III . . . I thought. But climbing that lightning rod, blindfolded, at night in a rainstorm—that was tough.

This was punishment for helping a boy, one Tom Troy. Tom had been tarred and feathered by Rebels for writing to his Loyalist father. The Rebel faction on campus was convinced he was a spy. And all I did was give him water after he was dumped, burned and sniffling in pain, on the dean's doorstep.

"Water is not the issue," Rebel bully Buck Sweet graciously clarified for me. "It's for being an accomplice to conspiracy that we're forcing you to do this," he explained, prodding me up the rod with a pitchfork. "Up you go now—show us you regret your action!"

I admit that, given the alternatives of jumping from a high window or being hung by the feet for six hours from a flagpole, the option of climbing a lightning rod in a storm was tame, but even so, I deserved better than an "up you go."

Had my father not forbade contact, I would have written him about the thoughts that crystallized as I was clinging to the rod:

I regret to inform you, Father, that I've made a terrible mistake. Please, let me come home.

Where in the name of God were all those high-minded ideas historians afterward touted as having inspired The Cause? Where was the evidence of British policy strapping American commerce?

Who knew? Who understood? Who cared?

And to make matters worse, Harvard looked like play school compared to the ruckus going on off-campus, in Cambridge and beyond.

Big, rusty cauldrons of tar were kept at a boil at the top of Copp's Hill and Beacon Hill, available and ready to spread on the next victims of the Sons of Liberty—perhaps an unsuspecting Tory shopkeeper, newspaper editor, or defecting partner in organized crime.

Small men were strung up, with scalding imported tea forced down their throats.

A bookseller was stripped naked and tied to a pole with a sign strung about his neck: *No friend of Liberty.*

And who was it that was behind all this rabble-rousing? Who was it that was ordering shops selling British goods closed, besmearing their shop windows with human excrement and cow piss?

Our esteemed and dignified Founding Fathers, that's who.

By 1769, the Green Dragon Tavern, having been bought outright by Samuel Adams's well-heeled friends, was no longer a secret den. These days, the Sons of Liberty met there and plotted openly. College students such as myself would gather there too, to enter competitions for free beers, the most "clever" curse against British soldiers awarded the three-mug prize ("Your Mother isn't England, she's your King George!" . . .).

His black Labrador specially trained to bite at the sight of the color red (as in Redcoats) at his side, Samuel Adams would rail on and on about The Cause of liberty, attacking the Townshend tariffs, which he claimed existed for the "sole and express purpose of raising revenue"—a statement of the obvious, to me, not the nefarious. But didn't the crowd go berserk anyway, hissing and booing and swearing revenge even as they had to be reminded who Lord Townshend actually was: the obese prime minister who chewed with his mouth open, hated America with a passion, and had much too much influence with the king.

"No Englishman is bound by laws made by a legislature in which he is not represented!"

That one always elicited a toast.

"No taxation without representation!" of course, was a very big seller, normally preceded by a refill of bumpers, which would always produce a cheer—at which point the rowdies and students who purchased no glass and had no business with lead (I think those were the items currently being taxed; it was hard to keep the list straight) would fall into the street, hooting and hollering and carrying on, taunting soldiers, who in turn would raise their muskets in protest, which in turn incited the ladies to turn out and command their husbands and sons to "shut in the name of God up" and get their useless arses home. And they would oblige, until the next night, which always promised another adventure.

Oh, the men from the Green Dragon, they ruled. There was Hancock and Otis and Warren and Church and, of course, the Adamses: Samuel and John. They were merchant and lawyer and doctor and poet and clerk and lawyer again.

All American gods. All American heroes. The furthest thing from lily-white. Each his own brand of mad.

Dr. Joseph Warren didn't speak much. Mostly he came and went under his pen name, "Paskalos," and hurled some of the best invective at England in Samuel Adams's rag, the *Gazette*. He was said to be a good man, who had earned his popularity doling out free smallpox inoculations to the poor and choosing to live amid

the ghostly, diseased, leprous forgotten on Castle Island. He said
all the right things: argued for compassion for the poor, fairness
under the law, even the need to raise our own army, which he secretly lusted to command. For the time being he was settling for
secretly leading the Sons of Liberty, those roving shock troops that
roamed the city and countryside clear to Medford giving innocent
citizens and others an impossible time.

Obsessed with death and glory, he'd routinely recruit needy
Harvard students (including me, one time) to dig up shallow graves
for him so he could dissect the corpses and wanted nothing more
out of life than to die with his knees steeped in blood. He did just
that, at Bunker Hill, after having predicted his death to the day.

James Otis, code named "Hampden," was the best-loved lawyer
in Boston—constantly threatening to hang himself, shoot himself,
or bash someone with a brick. Hailed across the globe for his sear-
ing speech denouncing the hated "Writs of Assistance" (general
search warrants issued by the crown to ferret out illegal goods), he
took up the issue of the right to privacy and, for the first time in
history, made it a viable cause (I read him religiously down in
Charleston). When he wasn't skewering Massachusetts's Governor
Bernard and his lieutenant, Hutchinson, in the press, he was bang-
ing his head against posts and racing through the statehouse during
business hours screaming "Fire!" He'd howl at the moon, fire his
musket without provocation, and, from his window, toss whatever
he could lay his hands on at pedestrians, shouting "A man's right to
his life is his liberty, no created being could rightfully contest!"
while alternately spewing "trash, obsceneness, profaneness, non-
sense, and distraction" (according to John Adams) into the air. He
was finally tied up, strapped down, and carried off to a farm, where
he spent the latter part of his life. He too predicted the manner of
his death correctly—by lightning.

Samuel Adams, "Vindex." The trouble with Adams was that although he said and wrote all the right things about liberty and was
far and away the most aggressive advocate of independence and,

later, war, he meant little of it and everyone knew it. Certainly, if one were to take his writings alone and were pressed in one's search for heroes (as History always is), one could ferret out in his scathing attacks against monarchy and Parliament powerful, forward-thinking notions about a new and different democratic state. One could also find shining proof of his respect for the masses in his insistence on having a balcony built in the statehouse where the people were let in to watch the proceedings.

But these records don't reveal the true story. The wisdom and attitude on the street held Samuel Adams to be a religious fanatic, with antiquated and dangerous puritanical ideas of, yes, an independent, deeply religious republic, stoic to the core, with himself the arbiter of morals, and with intolerance for Quakers, Jews, Catholics, even Huguenots (all together, a good twenty percent of Boston's population).

As for his celebrated lack of interest in money—demonstrated by his tattered vest and dirty hair—even his cousin John Adams attributed this and his hatred of the British not to Lockean ideas of freedom but to his family being bankrupted after Parliament clamped down on the illegal land schemes his father was counting on to make them rich. John Adams: "Oh, he affects to despise riches, and not to dread Poverty, but in fact, no man is more ambitious for an elegant life style than he." The greatest libertarian the world had ever seen? Maybe, maybe not. What we saw at the time was a not-so-well-meaning man, Boston's ex-tax collector, who was doing his damnedest to avoid a jail sentence hanging over his head (for embezzling seven thousand pounds from the state of Massachusetts) by gathering support to overthrow the British crown.

Hancock was another character who, in the intervening years, had emerged as an apparently bright and shining Patriot. Patriot, maybe. Bright? Decidedly not. Delicate, frail, whiny, tall, with eyes much too far apart, he was a sucker for flattery and had been complimented and cajoled into a friendship with Samuel Adams, who wanted access to Hancock's cash in case the Puritan state never took hold and he was in need of bail (in fact, Hancock did wind up paying his embezzlement fines). Not being a very swift fellow (complete sentences a problem), he was popular with the ladies, and although he gave the rhetoric of Revolution his best "I-never-quite-made-it-through-Harvard-College" try, he was much less convincing than the others. Maybe it was the fact that ten years later he was still miffed over not being invited to the coronation of George III. (Or perhaps it was those fantasies he had of being crowned king himself.)

Plagued by unreasonable fears, Hancock saw ghosts and lurking disease everywhere. Had it not been for the stress-relieving ritual executed by his loyal staff at his bidding of regularly smashing bone china because he claimed the sound cleared his mind, Hancock would probably never have lived to implant his gargantuan signature onto that famous parchment of the Declaration of Independence, written up in Carpenter's Hall on one sweltering July afternoon.

Then there was the "so very fat" John Adams who just wanted to be liked—another one History regards as a lover of the people. Which is particularly unsettling given Adams's phobia of crowds and any activity that involved small talk, flattery, kind remarks, or discussing under any circumstances horses, women, weather, or dogs. Instead of relating, he preferred simply to judge, and did so, harshly. Even his own wife, his beloved Abigail, he excoriated publicly for singing like a canary, and looking like a pigeon when she walked. It was widely believed, in fact, that his commitment to laying the foundation for our independent country was mostly an excuse to get away from his wife, from whom at one point he stayed away for well on four years.

Adams wanted to be seen as manly and also as tall—the latter, believe it or not, easier for him to pull off than the former (thanks to robes with vertical pleats and his insistence that he wasn't short so much as fat). He had a volcanic temper and conspicuous breasts, and in his barrister's robe of scarlet looked rather like an overripe, bewigged tomato.

Despite a history of "fidgets, piddlings, irritabilities, insomnia, rashes, failing eyesight and an array of nervous ticks," John Adams somehow found the stamina to manage long hours for The Cause. Good for business, he declared openly, all those political gatherings. "Good for 'my little reputation,'" he declared, while passing out his card: "John Adams, Esq." To "increase his connections with the people" (that is, to increase his roster of clients) was his motive; for, things being the way they were, "everyone was in trouble and in need of a lawyer, no matter the side." A slave owner who needed defending against uppity servants; a man accused of rape; or a man charged with fathering a bastard ("I fucked once, but I minded my pullbacks, I did"). They all got off with Adams's advocacy. So too did John Hancock once walk scot-free with Adams's help, despite the fact that he'd shoved a customs officer into a ship's cabin and then had him dragged through the street by his hair.

So Adams gladly talked the talk of Revolution, mostly because it paid. Even though privately he was rigidly conservative, fearing rebellion would dangerously "embolden the little people," that Britain was at worst misguided, never despotic, and that society required perfect submission to government: "Even in four-year-olds, for goodness' sake, there are constitutional inequalities. Pray let nature alone."

And finally, there was Dr. Benjamin Church: the last of the coven making himself known at the Green Dragon Tavern. Here was the one deemed the standard bearer of The Cause. His very existence had come to define Patriotism. The first time I went to watch him, to listen to his poetry, such an aura preceded him that I was trembling.

He turned out to be a British spy.

So these were the famous advocates of liberty I'd wanted to come to Boston to observe firsthand, whose reputations had awed me for four years, and whose oratory I'd read and been inspired by—all compromised, every last one of them. How shocked I was to find that few in their own environs took them seriously.

So how then did they come to hold such position, such esteem? The truth is: They didn't. When, soon after 1769, things started accelerating toward war, everyone understood that Venus was their inspiration, not Hancock, Warren, Church, or Adams—Samuel or John.

It is true that the road to war began with a rare event, but not trade restrictions or rhetoric of a new and unusual kind. The American War for Independence began with Venus' attempt to eclipse the sun. And those who choose to disagree with that are those who deny the truth: that human imagination, not documented facts or events, moves History, blow by blow.

In 1769, the same year I returned to Boston, Venus went retrograde in her orbit, passing directly and defiantly in front of the sun instead of, as was usual, politely around.

When news broke of the impending cosmic spectacle, the populace went mad. Although astronomers insisted that the event was insignificant beyond the scientific domain (a chance to better measure the distance of the earth from the sun), it was no use—the people would not be swayed.

All over Boston, telescopes were set up in strategic locations, and as far north as Newfoundland crowds of thousands wrestled each other for tickets to sit in attendance as the astronomers watched the sky, announcing their observations to the breathless assembly.

Prognosticators, soothsayers, and charlatans alike spoke from caves, mountaintops, and almanacs, predicting more rain, the world's end, even the assassination of George III, not to mention the discovery of an exotic new spice isle. "Venus, Venus be brave!" you heard until blue in the face. Tell me that the events that transpired about this time—particularly in Boston, where Venus fervor was especially keen—were unconnected to this cosmological phenomenon, and I'll tell you: Not so.

Tell me, then, why virtually overnight, customs commissioners sent by England "to ensure the peace" were silenced, mocked, and locked into cabins on ships, when nothing in their approach to policy had changed from what it had been before.

Explain to me why soldiers sent from England "to enforce the peace" and quartered all over town—fifteen hundred, all told, and more set to come—were only now barred from homes and lured into abandoned warehouses to be jailed, just for kicks, with a few vagrants, the diseased, and old whores.

Explain to me too why just then Governor Bernard ordered cannon positioned directly outside the statehouse door, why the long-held and cherished right of assembly in America suddenly was on the wane.

And explain to me why I chose to do what I did when I did: creep into the college library and cut a heart-shaped scrap out of the portrait of Governor Bernard. Not only that, but I fed it to some gulls, as if it were a real heart.

I did it because, like everyone else, whether rational or not, I was emboldened by Venus' example, by the possibility of the triumph of the tiny planet, and by love. I did it because Venus' challenge spoke to what was deep in my heart: a desire to break with tradition and win the day.

A burning desire, all too human, to cut the heart out of Governor Bernard's likeness, because to me the portrait lacked totally in human dimension anyway and looked more real this way. I had no political comment whatsoever in mind; I was simply a lonely, drunk young man, sick with lovelessness and disillusion, tired of the gap between representation and reality. Governor Bernard, I was certain, was no more brightly hued and beatific than my father was kind, or than John Adams was a Rebel with a legitimate Cause.

"So fine, let the records, the documents, the writings, and this oil before me be false! And let's not make any bones about it. Let's cut out the heart and let it be known that this portrait, ladies and gentlemen, just isn't so!"

It happened that this antic of mine was considered treasonous, and my claims to truth-seeking and not Tory-bashing fell on deaf ears. It didn't help, of course, that Bernard had fled Boston for his life a week before—so fast that he had forgotten his wife at the dock—and Tories were on the hunt for revenge. Little did I know that the who-cut-the-heart-out-of-the-canvas-painting puzzle would consume most of Boston and start me on the road to Revolution.

Within two days of my misdeed I was apprehended by a fellow student, a snot-nosed Tory named James Billingsley, who, as it turns out, had suspected me all along. Had I been thinking, of course, I never would have attended the Rebel fireworks display celebrating Bernard's flight (poor hapless governor; even the ship consigned to whisk him away had fallen into the wind and, a week later, being still barely offshore, he had the best view of the show). Of course the celebration was riddled with Tory spies, including the aforementioned Billingsley, the nasty Tory with mucus perpetually oozing out of his face, who apparently had been suspecting me all along.

For my sin, the rebellious defacement of the governor's portrait, I was dragged to an abandoned blacksmith's shop, cast to the ground, and roundly kicked in the head, throat, teeth, and stomach until I bled and pleaded for mercy. I quickly agreed, in exchange for my life, to do what I could to help my tormentors ruin John Hancock, who the Tories guessed (wrongly) was the ringleader of the Rebels and (rightly) the one financing the presses and the parties enjoining people to resist England, rise, and revolt.

"Sam Adams writes the letter, yes, but Hancock pays the postage," they used to say. "So break him, Lawrence. Or die."

They had just the plan . . .

CHAPTER 11

Father and Son

The Tories' campaign to break John Hancock was a sign of how out of touch they were. A series of essays running in their *Chronicle* was designed to sway public opinion. It attacked Hancock for being stupid and vain, but since nobody read the Tory rag but Tories (a case of preaching to the choir if ever there was one), the insults nonetheless added fuel to the fire about to rage insanely out of control, culminating with the Boston Massacre.

They called Hancock a "Milch Cow," a "weasel-brain," an "aristocrat with a skull of uncommon thickness and a brain so small that its contents would not fill a teacup." Excerpts were posted on tavern walls as entertainment. About the only individuals who didn't find them funny were the "Gang of Six," as they'd come to be called (Adams, Adams, Hancock, Warren, Otis, Church). It was joked that they failed to detect any humor in the exercise because they were the only ones who knew Hancock well enough to know the accusations, base language notwithstanding, to be decidedly true.

Sam Adams's belief that "the key [to successful propaganda] was the emotions, not the mind" was resplendently evident in his *Journal of Occurrences*, a "true" chronicle of the blazing-hot atrocities allegedly committed by the soldiers in Boston ostensibly sent to promote order and stabilize peace.

Unapologetic, uninterested in standards of decency or integrity, History's acclaimed *Journal of Occurrences* was so flagrantly spurious that it was first published outside of Boston, where the readership, a large percentage of which had never been to the city, was believed more gullible.

In the premier issue, British regulars were depicted as beating small boys screaming for their mothers and deflowering Boston's sweetest young virgins. There were accounts of babies being ripped squalling from their mothers' wombs, of soldiers shooting innocent, elderly citizens on sight. Oh, the savageries went on and on.

The British didn't know what had hit them. And, more importantly, what on earth to do about it. What if people started believing what they read? Indeed, there was so much chatter about the accounts, they wound up taking on a certain validity, a life of their own.

But now, with the help of the fuss over nonimportation of British goods, gentlemen like Tory fanatic John Mein, editor-in-chief of the *Chronicle*, saw their chance at last.

Nonimportation had not been enforced with any more success in Boston than it had in Charleston, which is why the Sons of Liberty had had to resort to disciplining resistant merchants with whatever it took: singeing transgressors with tar, clubbing them with fence posts, sodomizing their daughters—just the kind of heinous acts that the *Journal of Occurrences* was accusing the British of perpetrating. One couldn't help but wonder, who was inspiring whom?

It was the snot-nosed Billingsley's idea to expose the patriotic maxim "Buy Yankee" as a hoax and a fraud. But how?

Certainly I'd heard the rumors that Hancock routinely landed goods as far south as Jersey to avoid Boston's more vigilant customs commissioners and then, under cover of night, lugged them to Boston by carriage. I'd also heard he packed British tea as anonymous freight and stored it offshore in schooners, selling it to select customers on the side.

So for a start, my job was to dig up the ships' manifests that editor Mein needed as proof of King Hancock's betrayal to The Cause. Such exposure, it was hoped, would cause Hancock's followers to disband, for suddenly the boycott would no longer be a badge of liberty, its enforcement no longer proof of dedication to the common good. It would be seen for what it was: a wild and cruel manipulation of unwitting fellow Patriots, a ploy to keep competition down, a means to reduce Hancock's personal liability for English taxes. At which point, it was hoped, Hancock's cabal would collapse like a house of cards.

In truth, however, I must tell you that even the little Harvard Tory boys who sent me out on this mission didn't care a whit what Hancock or his kind were up to. Not really. They themselves were in it for the money, a crown apiece, to be paid by Mein, upon receipt of "the facts"—none of which, of course, I expected to be able to retrieve.

How on earth was I going to lay my hands on Hancock's dockets? What was I supposed to do, sneak into his office, his home, the offices of the *Gazette*? And, my Lord, what if I were caught red-handed rifling through his files? I'd be in a lovely mess then, wouldn't I?

These were the thoughts running through my head as I approached Hancock's home, comparing the consequences of failing Billingsley to being caught by Hancock. Since in both cases I assumed I'd be killed, the decision mostly involved selecting the way I preferred to go—whether torture would be involved, how quickly I'd be allowed to expire . . .

I ultimately decided to throw my lot in with Hancock, to tell him of the heinous Tory plot against him. I figured death-by-Hancock would involve too many questions and, especially if Sam Adams were present, be too brutal.

My decision wasn't entirely self-serving, however. I remember thinking, as I threaded my way to Beacon Hill through the Common, how sad it would be if this plan of Mein's ever worked. How discomfiting it would be to all those innocent, flax-clad, non-tea drinking, only-locally-grown-vegetable-and-fruit-eating families who had suffered loss of employment from the closed shops and the empty wharves, who had found themselves drawn into battle with once-beloved neighbors based on boycott participation—or not—to discover that these sacrifices had never been necessary or effective at all.

September 5, 1769, ten P.M. By now I was on Hancock's property, eyeing his front door (huge and forbidding) and reviewing my plan one last time from my hiding place behind a convenient boxwood.

I decided I would knock twice only, counting to sixty in between. I would introduce myself as a student of Harvard, Hancock's alma mater, and presumably be invited inside. For the first few minutes I would speak only of nostalgic college stories (a prospect every bit as challenging as stealing files, as I had none to tell). A few minutes more and he'd offer me a nice glass of fine (presumably smuggled) sherry. Once settled cozily before the fire (I know it was September, but the image of the fire gave me some nerve), I would silently apologize to God one more time for having cursed him four years ago and then go all out: spill my guts, tell Hancock everything I knew about Mein and his terrible plan, and be prepared to bolt if need be.

I would give no credence, of course, to Mein's suspicions, just explain that I felt bound to inform Hancock of the plot. Only if required, for purposes of verification, would I reveal my part in it. Then, if things went well, as I hoped they would, he would offer me more of the sherry and confide in me his counterplan to ruin Mein and his stooge, Billingsley, once and for all. Good. Very good.

I walked up to the door.

I grasped the enormous knocker and banged it once. Then once again.

". . . fifty-seven, fifty-eight, fifty-nine . . ."

Nothing.

I paced. I wrung my hands. I pissed behind a fruit tree. In the back of the house a cow eyed me stupidly and I stuck my tongue out at her.

I broke my rule, hoisted the knocker one last time . . . and suddenly felt myself swinging through space.

I watched my warped reflection in polished brass clinging to the door knocker for dear life just as Hancock's gold-knobbed cane came smashing down on my head.

"Begone, beggar, begone!" (I knew I never should have sported the damned homespun.)

Dazed for a second, I lay on the ground, blood streaming down my face, and opened my eyes. A comet of pinkish blue streaked across the night sky.

And there she was. Deborah. She stepped from the back of the house, cloaked in black from head to toe, and slipped through an alley, a black speck come and gone in the blink of an eye. Had I really seen her?

Hancock, satisfied that if I'd come for money I'd never do so again, whisked himself away and into a carriage.

I shouted after Deborah, but she didn't break her stride.

And so I heaved myself up and, dripping blood, bent over and, reeling, gave chase.

She picked up her pace, dashing left, right, left again. Yes, she was running away . . . for now, but to a place that ultimately would bring us together again, guiding me, inevitably, into that Philadelphia cave where, together, we'd plot the changing of the world.

Down Tremont, onto King, zigzagging to Cornhill, and past the statehouse, where she disappeared. 'Round and 'round the streets I twisted, bellowing "Deboraaaaah!" to no avail. No sign of her, just darkness all around, her cloak become one with the dark of night—no light posts, no fires, no comet, barely a moon.

I was lost, utterly without bearing, not so much as a recognizable wall to guide me. I felt empty, hollowed out, yet curiously alive. I clutched my side and gasped for air.

And then, a few odd sounds.

Tap-tap. Tap-tap. Tap-tap. Followed by just a few words, mumbled, that I couldn't make out.

"Hello?" I called out. My greeting sank into the darkness.

There it was again: Tap-tap. Tap-tap. Then three words: "Who goes there?" followed by: Rattattattattattatat . . .

A stick, that's what it was. No, a cane; a cane that was being rapped with panic against the walk.

"Pray, speak now. Or I shall start swinging!" the voice rasped. Whoosh-whoosh-whoosh!

But I had had quite enough of walking sticks that night. I tried jumping out of the way and shouted, "I'm lost and without malice. . . . Please—"

The swinging stopped instantly.

"Step toward me then, and state your business."

I did as bidden. Oh, what a strange world this Boston was.

"John Lawrence, sir." (I'd at least determined the speaker was a man.) "I was—uh . . ." I hadn't the slightest idea how to explain what I was doing or why. Where would I begin? As it turned out, this didn't much matter because it was quite clear that the gentleman of the dark wasn't talking to me anyway. He was now addressing a wall.

"I demand satisfaction!" he yelled at it. And again, "State your business!"

I could just make him out by the flicker of a tar-barrel.

He was James Otis himself—the mad barrister, sweating, scowling, and flushed with rage. He shook his stick at what wasn't a wall after all but a door, the front entrance to the Royal Coffee House—a Tory hangout if ever there was one.

As he stepped nearer the lantern at the entrance, a flicker of flame illumined his eyes. Red, beady, bulging, they were the eyes of a madman. My Lord, the eyes of Apollo too—that ancient gaze of hers. And his breath, reeking of spirits, was the dragon's fire. My heart pounded. I followed Otis inside.

"Satisfaction!" he cried as he crashed with a flourish into the tavern.

The place went still.

From the corner, a few titters. Then, "What satisfaction would you have, Mr. Otis?" from the far corner.

"A gentleman's satisfaction!" Otis barked back.

"Well, I am ready to give it!" was the answer.

From across the room, Customs Officer James Robinson, a notorious Loyalist lackey, mockingly waved Otis to his table and poured him a drink. But Otis, already well fortified, righteously explained that he wanted his due for Robinson's recent public declaration that Otis was a traitor to his country and an enemy of the king.

"Pray, be my guest, sir," Robinson said with a smile as he leaned back in his chair, his feet on the table.

But Otis wasn't interested in defending himself or attacking Robinson. He wanted simply to be understood.

"I am and ever have been a Tory," he stated simply and soberly. So far, so good. Robinson looked mollified.

"On the other hand, if to stand for the rights of men is to be characteristic of a Whig, I hope I am, and ever shall be, a Whig."

I felt as though a breeze were coming through an open door.

"I profess, however, to be not devoted to any party, but that of Truth and Reason, which I think I am ready to embrace wherever I find them."

Robinson swung his legs down and sat up.

Otis went on: "You may ruin yourselves, but you cannot in the end ruin the colonies. We have been a free people, and if you will not let us remain so any longer—"

For a while the white-knuckled Tory merchants simply looked on from their tufted chairs by the fire, their servants crouched on the filthy floor, while Otis went on to explain with his own inimitable logic that the privileges of the people were more dear than the most valuable prerogatives of the crown.

"Let the consequences be what they will," he cried. "In this vein I am determined to proceed! I will be neither Tory nor Whig!"

The breeze I was feeling came from Otis's words alone. It was hearing the truth spoken, as enlivening to me as it was unnerving to the crowd.

If Otis had gone into that bar to defend his honor and had declared his allegiance to one side or the other, he probably would have walked out unscathed.

But Robinson slowly rose and, in a low voice, said, "To be a friend of this country, sir, and a friend of the king, these are *not* one and the same."

A tankard fell to the floor. Someone screamed. And suddenly the crowd fell upon Otis—much as my father, back home, had fallen upon me—beating him with their sticks, fists, boots, and canes. And as I watched, I knew they didn't want to kill Otis any more than my father had been intent on killing me. They wanted what Henry Lawrence wanted: for this glimpse of the future—a world neither Loyalist nor Patriot, just fair—to be made to go away.

Three well-dressed gentlemen carried Otis to the back of the bar and, pinning him to the wall, beat him until he was hatless, wigless, and blinded by his own blood. They left him in a heap on the floor. I knelt down to him.

"Son," was all he said, quietly.

I'd never been addressed with such affection in my life. I grabbed hold of Otis's arms and, slicing my way through the crowd, dragged him across the floor and out to the street, fending off a trail of assailants and flying objects as best I could.

"Son," he said again, once outside.

I struggled to sit him up against the hitching post where the light through the tavern doorway would enable me to assess his wounds. There was a hole in his head big enough to fit my two fingers. I tried to plug the outrush of blood.

He clasped my hand tight and refused to let go, just as my father had done once so many years ago. Except Otis, I knew, would never, ever ask me to lie about this moment.

"*Help! Help! Help!*" I screamed, splitting the night wide open as Robinson advanced.

And suddenly . . . a miracle.

Up from the dark came a supernatural slew of arms and hands whisking Otis up onto their shoulders and away. Arms thick, muscled, scaled, and scarred. Arms of jack-tars and seamen, barmaids and whores who had been watching Otis from the dark, waiting and ready to protect him and, failing that, to carry him home.

Too afraid to declare for themselves, perhaps, to fight Otis's enemies hand to hand (just now). But nonetheless willing, able, and eager to hold out their arms for him.

It was love.

Seeing the ragged reinforcements advance, Robinson and his cadre withdrew.

I knew then I would never return to Harvard. Here, finally, was everything I'd come to Boston for.

Here was reason.

Here was respect.

Here was truth.

Here, somewhere, was Deborah, at long last.

All night long, back at his home, Otis still would not let me go, continuing over and over again to call me "son." I decided I didn't care a whit that he wasn't my flesh and blood. So the next morning, when Samuel Adams and the rest visited (Hancock displaying no recognition of me whatsoever) and Otis introduced me as his long-lost son, I went along, presenting myself as "Papa's secretary," which nobody, for fear of inflaming Otis, bothered to contradict.

For when Otis called me "son," he meant it, and that was good enough for me.

CHAPTER 12

Boston Massacre

A nybody who thinks that the Boston Massacre, the event which more than any other put us on the path to war, was a spontaneous, unprompted assault upon the people is wrong. And those few brave, irreverent souls who have insisted it was all part of Sam Adams's plan (goad the troops into firing upon innocent Americans to prompt a furor that would get these soldiers gone) are wrong, too. Although at least this last interpretation carries with it a degree of truth: Sam Adams did plan the Massacre in advance—every shot, every rock, every curse. I know. I was there.

But along the way, like the men, women, and children who came out of the shadows that night to save Otis, like Deborah, who had instantaneously emerged and just as swiftly disappeared (five months ago now), something else happened that no one could have predicted, its meaning elusive but profound. In February 1770 I watched as up from the darkness what began as an insidious project to dislodge soldiers from Boston wound up ex-posing an intractable class divide here in America, which after the incident would never be forgotten.

And while History stubbornly heralds the 1770 Massacre in which "British soldiers fired upon innocent Americans" for pre-saging the fight for freedom and delivering the message to En-gland to "Get lost!" that position, while inspiring, bears no relationship whatsoever to what the Massacre actually was: proof positive that Americans would have to come together first in order to fight England, and that, at present, we were indeed a "sorry, contentious lot."

It wasn't long before I was convinced that had I not fallen into Otis's life, he probably would have been bound and gagged, de-clared non compos mentis, and run out of town even sooner than he was—probably by his fellow libertarians, no less.

Oh, sure. These men called each other names and behind the scenes bickered like old dames. But none of the insults—like "cheesehead," "loathsome fuck," "no-brains," "tiny prick" filling the air like gnats and just as irritating, just as routine—could hold a candle to the wrath Samuel Adams harbored for Otis.

Although there was ample distrust between the two men based on principle and sound argument alone (whether or not the boycott should be abandoned, whether to malign the king himself or Parliament—things like that), Sam Adams seemed to reserve the better part of his dislike for Otis as an entirely personal vendetta. It was simple: This business of Otis being carried to safety on the shoulders of seamen and the poor was more than Adams could bear. Begrudging Otis the popularity such a rescue implied—popularity he'd been gauging for months—Sam Adams gave him no quarter whatsoever, denouncing him as a constitu-tionalist and, worse, monarchical, not to mention insane. And while Otis was down for the count, Adams plotted ways to turn that situation around, to steer favorable opinion his way.

What to do? . . . Well, the issue of putting all those pesky

British soldiers on a boat and sending them home—that might work, if the success of the *Journal of Occurrences* could be taken as any indication of the way to peoples' hearts. But here Adams had to be very careful, for should he go out on a limb publicly advocating for the position that the soldiers must, at once, return home and then find that the issue, for whatever reason, didn't resonate with the people, he'd be worse off than he was now. Not just fading, failed. Fine, then, he'd make it his personal responsibility to make sure the issue took, that more than anything the people would want the goddamned soldiers run out of town.

Easier said than done. . . .

While there had been a definite hostility generated down at the wharf when off-duty Redcoats were hired over Yanks due to their willingness to work for mere pennies, the truth of the matter was that for this dangerous trend the shopkeepers and ropemakers should have been held every bit as accountable as the Redcoats. For the crime of working for wages no one else would accept, a few soldiers on guard had been jostled off bridges and pushed off wharves. Some had been followed and taunted by small boys goading them with forks and chanting "Lobsters for sale!" but none of that had amounted to much. And as for the furor over the quartering of soldiers that, for all practical purposes, had by 1770 settled down to a low boil. Even the soldiers, under strict orders not to avenge their civilian tormentors, mostly deserted in droves rather than retaliate (punishment for which was being shot unblindfolded in broad daylight in the center of the Common).

Of course, the citizenry didn't like the soldiers; but still, until Sam Adams published all those horrible stories about them in the *Journal* and the *Gazette*, they were mostly apathetic. Adams had to seize upon whatever emotional ore he could mine. There was, after all, a climate of fear about town—whether one held the Sons of Liberty or the Redcoats to blame. Why, just last month an eleven-year-old boy had been felled by gunfire, and since that time a curfew had been imposed. People *were* rumored to be sleeping with guns under their pillows and walking to market with knives . . . hmmm.

Adams calculated adroitly that a group of British soldiers caught between a carefully chosen rock and a well-timed hard place would provide the perfect foil for this fear. All he needed to do was set the stage properly for a well-managed disaster that, had England heeded Samuel Adams's warnings, *could have been prevented.*

In the most Machiavellian sense, it was a great idea. But when he went so far as to suggest a time and a date for this "inevitable massacre" and tipped his hand, I thought he'd also exposed his private ambition.

He actually had small boys out there posting broadsides, giving a location for people to gather and meet to stave off the siege he was "dead certain" the Redcoats had planned.

Of course, you'd think that if the British really were plotting an invasion of some sort, if six hundred soldiers were intending a campaign against sixteen thousand people and Samuel Adams was known to have discovered their schedule, at the first sign of Adams's posted broadsides they might, at the very least, alter their plans. So one had to wonder who was more stupid—Adams for giving the British advance notice of what he knew, or the people for falling for it. Or, for that matter, the British, for showing up smack on time for bloodshed as Adams had warned.

Otis was out of his mind—that was no surprise—but this time with worry. He warned Adams repeatedly that no good would come of this plot, but Adams, on a tear, threatened to have him committed if he didn't shut his trap.

And what was I doing in the middle of all this? To tell you the truth, I was happy to be out from under Billingsley (for returning to Harvard and facing him was out of the question) and, thanks to Otis's wages, out from under my dependency on my father's cash (I'd written Father a bit prematurely, I'll admit, and told him what to do with his blood money). I wasn't thinking about Adams and his campaign nearly as much as my narrative implies. Mostly I was concerned with saving every penny I earned from "keeping" Otis's "books" (which mostly amounted to playing marbles with him all day long, I'll be the first to confess) in order to keep the tiny room I'd let—the one with the view of Hancock's back stairs, where nightly I'd watch for Deborah. To no avail.

And while I recognize that my preoccupation with saving my own hide seems selfish, may I remind the reader that it is only in hindsight that I figured out Adams's plan—and his motives. I also wish to point out that no one, no matter how cynical, could ever have predicted the bloodshed that the Boston Massacre would involve. Gravely and deliberately plotted, all right, but there's no question that once on its feet, the event took on a life of its own. Even Adams, whom I'm certain above and beyond anything else wanted to give England a good scare, could never have anticipated the carnage caused by it (at most, he expected a few shots in the air, perhaps, but no casualties). And as much as I hated him, I'm convinced that had he foreseen the debacle, he was not so obsessed that he wouldn't have called it off then and there.

So it was my first lesson in Revolutionary ways, in fate asserting itself with a purpose only destiny would eventually lay plain.

The Massacre occurred on Monday, March 5, 1770, exactly as advertised.

"Spontaneous gunfire," Historians would later declare. Indeed!

Sam Adams knew the sentry schedule, the various work shifts of the soldiers he had targeted. And for those citizens who would show up at the appointed time without their own weapons, he had in reserve a cache of sticks and stones. Cloaked in a red cape (a little bright and obvious, I thought, but then again, Samuel liked being noticed), he flitted from group to group in the square adjacent to the riot, supplying them with stirring words about liberty and, when those ran low, expletives characterizing the soldiers sent by the godforsaken king—foreign soldiers who had no business here at home.

And unfortunately for England, the King's Twenty-ninth was the regiment that went on alert—far and away the worst of the lot, the only soldiers who'd involved themselves in civilian skirmishes to date.

It was cold, unusually so for March, and had, in fact, been snowing. Spring snow—wet, hard, and slippery.

I was there, crouched behind a wall, acting as Otis's eyes and ears in the event things got out of hand (which of course they would) and the record needed straightening.

First up was a soldier, whom I could only assume had been targeted for goading once he entered the street. Almost simultaneously the church bells began to peal, signaling *Fire!* Mobs of men and boys descended upon the area instantly, armed with fire buckets, yes, but also cutlasses, scabbards, and clubs.

But then fate or planning stepped in—I still don't know which—in the form of a small child named Garrick, a wigmaker's apprentice, who happened to have a terrible toothache and a nasty tongue, who began pestering Captain Goldfinch (the targeted soldier) for money allegedly owed Garrick's master for a trim to his peruke.

"There goes the fellow who won't pay my master for dressing his hair!" the child cried, bawling at the top of his lungs, stepping on the heels of the captain, who was having little success breaking free of the brat, his sudden turnabouts and figure eights notwithstanding. My, my, did that boy hold on, and when Goldfinch produced a receipt which, from what I could determine, seemed to prove Garrick's accusation false, the situation became even graver.

"No, no! I want *cash!*" said the greedy little sod.

The fire-bucket-toting, cutlass-wielding dozens who had gathered around by now were looking to one another for guidance, privately wondering if this was real or part of the play. One thing for sure: *Someone* had told the boy that whatever he got he could keep.

Suddenly Garrick bit Goldfinch and, lunging like a rattler at the soldier's waist (which was as high as he could reach), screamed, "Give me the money, you cur!"

One Private Hugh White, a sentry who had been watching the disturbance from his solitary post at the Custom House across the way, came to rescue Goldfinch. At first he just tried to swat away the little dreadful with the butt of his musket. A little tap. Nothing more. But the boy went mad, falling into a heap on the cobblestones, and, pounding his balled fists and ragged feet into the walk (a little much, I thought), he tellingly hollered, "Yaaaagh! Yaaaagh! I've been shot!" over and over again, caterwauling until Goldfinch (and the rest of us) could listen no more.

My Lord—the sound coming out of that boy. It was as if he were one hundred times his size. So disproportionate that, thinking back on it now, I'm convinced my fleeting premonition in the moment had it right: That boy's squeal, as much as it might have been premeditated, wasn't springing from the boy, from the situation, or from Adams's design. It was emanating from God: This was heaven's cry.

Not a smidgen of honesty to the child's claim, yet his cry was every bit as real and hard as bone. And as much as the crowd was prepared to assault Goldfinch, I'm absolutely certain their approach wasn't due to any preconceived animus toward the British officer. Rather, it was a primitive, instinctual, automatic response to the boy's cry, a raw, bloodcurdling, mature-beyond-its-years manifestation of their pent-up rage—and mine—at injustice, at unfairness, at struggle, at never having been treated compassionately or understood. Decades of disappointment with the American fantasy of freedom and prosperity gone wrong.

Goldfinch continued down the street.

White tussled with the urchin. Despite my orders to stay clear,

I joined the fray, rushing the assisting officer with a group of two dozen or so who instantaneously decided to join us.

In the distance, as if right on cue, I heard, "Town born, turn out!" being chanted in unison, riding our way on the drizzle and the fog, along with fowling pieces, knives, sticks, and stones.

A runt, quite without intending it, had called the country to arms.

And to complicate matters more (or simplify them, depending on your view), across town, at the same hour, at Murray's Barracks where the soldiers were housed, another boy—equally obstreperous—tossed snowballs and rocks at that garrison's sentinels ("Get back, lobster-backs! Get thee back home! You are not welcome here!"). He too, chafed by a soldier's musket but claiming he'd been killed—even as he raced through the streets fully ambulatory, remarkably spry for a corpse—was stirring a good stew. Hundreds heard him and rallied to help, spilling onto King Street to avenge a death that wasn't. But nobody knew—or cared.

No matter what Sam Adams had contrived, this wasn't about the Brits, not anymore. This was the egret's call, the tortoise's hiss, Deborah's irrepressible smile. This was deep human need, yearning.

Across town, White was cornered by now, bayonet fixed and musket held low: "Molest me and I will fire!" he warned the ranks.

The Yanks, with their rusted swords, blunt clubs, and chipped cutlasses, dared, begged White to do just that. "Why do you not fire? Damn you, you dare not fire! Fire and be damned!" they chanted in unison, in counterpoint to Garrick's "YAAAAAGH! [sniffle, sniffle] YAAAAGH!"

Then came the grenadiers (sent by kindly Captain Preston, secretly viewing the brewing riot from the Main Guard) to rescue White. These men were the hardest, fiercest, tallest (even taller with those bearskin hats), meanest shock troops of the British army. Together, all six—Carrol, Kilroy, Warren, Montgomery, Hartigan, McCauley—formed an imposing and forbidding wall.

But the people, by this point seething with fury, were not to be daunted. They set upon the grenadiers and, rattling their rusted, rustic weapons, egged them on still more: "Damn you sons of bitches, fire! You can't kill us all!"

Seconds later the king's muskets were loaded with powder . . . and before anyone knew it, Montgomery had sent two bullets straight through Crispus Attucks's heart. And the sound of the black man's head hitting the pavement with an unforgettable *thwack!* was mistaken for another shot, detonating the powder keg, unleashing a disaster . . .

. . . In which Private Kilroy would shoot ropemaker Samuel Gray in the head and his mate Caldwell too—both falling dead on the spot, Kilroy further stabbing Gray's lifeless body with his bayonet . . . just because . . .

. . . In which young Sam Maverick would die holding the hand of his master's twelve-year-old son, both boys present for the fun of it, after their supper of stew . . .

. . . In which Irish teague Patrick Carr's hip would be shot off, separated instantaneously from the spine, chips of bone scattering through the air like so many snowflakes . . .

. . . In which people would fall to their knees in grief and in wonder as to who in the name of hell had commanded "Fire!" and how exactly this situation had gotten so gravely and irreversibly out of hand. . . .

Every one of us present at the scene was paralyzed with confusion, mute with shock, so much so that long after the shots had been fired, we chose to believe that the dead bodies lying about were only heaps of greatcoats discarded by good men and women fleeing for their lives, and we left them behind.

No one dared believe that what had happened actually *had*, that fellow countrymen soldiers (we were still a colony of England, after all) had murdered citizens in cold blood.

"What about the lives?" I cried, in a voice as full as Garrick's wail, directed to everyone and no one in particular all at the same time.

"What about the lives?" I asked for days thereafter as the scrambling to lay blame, to find opportunity in this carnage, conspired to erase the pain.

Back at the office of the *Gazette*, the propaganda machine lurched to life, feeding upon the recent dead, cranking out broadsides entreating Bostonians to attend a town meeting to "come up with our response to the sad and tragic affair." Anticipating that the soldiers would be called to account for the night's "murderous doings," the press panted for eyewitnesses, producing wildly differing, dramatic accounts of the scene.

Boston was in utter turmoil.

I hid out with Otis, who had locked himself up in his house and was shooting his musket off at will from the upper story. As one of my last duties as his secretary, he ordered me, his mind unusually lucid and keen, to burn all his papers. Piece by piece, every record of every speech, every copy of every letter, and every article he had ever written on behalf of "the Revolution" was consigned to the flames.

Two days it took to complete this destruction, which Otis, his eyes wide open, sat and watched, crying, "I meant well but am now convinced that I was mistaken. Cursed be the day I was born."

One day later they carried Otis away from me forever, per order of the court, hands, feet, and legs trussed and bound. The man who had made Hutchinson et al. tremble with his orations and rapier logic, sent south, to "rest indefinitely" at his kin's quiet farm.

The night Otis was taken away, the particular brand of silence which once before led me to meeting Deborah and then Ezekiel swinging in the breeze returned. Only this time there were no bells, no clackety-clack of bones. Just death, flat and morbid, hanging in the air.

"Promise me you'll keep to the point of Revolution," were Otis's penultimate words to me.

"Pray, sir, tell me, what exactly do you mean?" I asked, desperate for clarification.

And he replied, "Son, you must never stop asking: 'What about the lives?'"

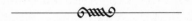

"The law is all and these men deserve a fair defense," was what John Adams had to say.

He was talking about the British soldiers, by the way.

Now, as if things weren't confusing enough, Adams was defending the soldiers who, just one month ago, his cousin had been scheming to oust from town. History has tried everything to justify this, to find reason and heroism in Adams's decision to take the Redcoats' defense, variously hailing him for his reasonableness (the argument being that the honorable Founding Father viewed all men, under the law, as deserving of a fair defense, no matter how heinous) and his innate goodness. Here, believe it or not, Adams's deep commitment to The Cause is cited as the excuse for his undertaking the soldiers' defense, the argument being that Adams, Patriot to the core, understood that the inevitable furor and cries of "Injustice!" surrounding any exoneration of them served the long-term goal of rebellion better than the soldiers' conviction. The latter might leave the people more or less satisfied, content with the status quo, the current English justice system actually reinforced by acting punitively in favor of the slaughtered victims. That would not do, and Adams's ingenious chicanery would see to it—what greater proof to the people could there be of the unfairness of British law than to watch an American attorney valiantly wield it to the letter, then have justice miscarry out of prejudice and concern for British interests over that of its subjects?

And what of the painfully evident risk to Adams's professional reputation in all this? Not a problem. The story goes that paramount in Adams's mind was his concern for his country. For liberty's sake he'd nobly take—and did—his lumps.

This is bunk. Adams took the post because it paid decently, like any lawyer would. And if he had any secret agenda, it was to teach the *people*, whom he believed had acted "mobbishly, scandalously and in vain," a lesson. To him, his cousin's plan notwithstanding, the Boston Massacre was indeed mostly a spontaneous outpouring instigated by a raffish mob. There was but one aggressor, according to John Adams: It was not any one of the soldiers, but the rascally "People," "the very Character of Boston's inhabitants," which precipitated the bloodshed.

But weren't the soldiers supposed to be taunted into firing?

Apparently.

Wasn't that the point?

Apparently.

Did they really expect people wouldn't get hurt?

Apparently.

What queered everything, you see, was the shocking two-fold discovery that: (1) the Redcoats' muskets *really were* loaded after all, and with shot (there had been some doubt about that); and (2) the people themselves were powder kegs of fiery, uncontrollable rage, a rage which had much less to do with quartered and billeted soldiers than anyone could fully admit or understand.

Of course, not grasping this last plain fact didn't stop either of the Adams cousins from attempting to manipulate it to his own advantage. While John was busy preparing his defense of Preston and his men, Samuel's acid pen scribbled a red streak denouncing those same soldiers his cousin was intending to vindicate. Which causes another dilemma for the History books, in that, for the duration of the trial, John and Samuel were as friendly as ever despite their apparently being on altogether opposing sides. Oh, there are theories, all of them struggling to adduce this seeming contradiction to some, as yet unknown, inscrutable overall grand plan of theirs.

Poppycock. John and Samuel continued to meet because there was no animosity between them. These weren't personal passions, these positions—they were issues, planks, differing opinions, which gentlemen who wished to be regarded as gentlemen *prided* themselves on taking in stride. This wasn't life. This was politics. Simply men jockeying for power and influence—understandable, perfectly respectable, and good. May the best man win!

So Samuel Adams would write that the soldiers were executioners, that "they were murderers of innocents, and this was plain fact. Curses from a crowd never gave soldiers license to kill," even going so far as to say that "soldiers [had been] seen greedily licking Human Blood in King Street" right after the Massacre.

And John Adams would say: "We have been entertained with a great variety of phrases to avoid calling this sort of people a mob. . . . Some call them shavers, some call them geniuses. The plain English is, gentlemen, most probably a motley rabble of saucy boys, Negroes, Irish teagues and outlandish jack-tars. And why should we scruple to call such a set of people a mob, I can't conceive, unless the name is too respectable for them. The sun is not about to stand still or go out, nor the rivers dry up, because there was a mob in Boston on the fifth of March that attacked a party of soldiers."

And the people would cry: "What about the lives?"

Shots had been fired, after all.

So while John Adams was, with great aplomb and equanimity, holding forth, and court stenographers, boredly bent over their quills, dutifully recorded his every word, people were lining up from miles around to view Crispus Attucks's embalmed carcass at Stone's Tavern, and men, women, and children were hurling themselves upon Samuel Gray's rigor-mortis-stiff corpse on display at the apothecary.

Every shop in Boston was closed, church bells tolled across the countryside, and a column, six men abreast, twelve thousand strong, proceeded from the Liberty Tree to the Old Granary Burying Ground, where the bodies of the five dead were lowered ceremoniously into a common grave.

The night of the mass burial I stopped by the Green Dragon, where the esteemed men were meeting. Actually I didn't stop so much as storm the place, crashing through the door (readily visible these days, by the way). I demanded to be heard.

It was like going back in time: the long, pine table, the roaring hearth, the dark, smoky den, and the image of the dragon breathing fire. Only now, five years later, I was disgusted, not afraid, and instead of apologizing for my presence I took the floor . . . before realizing I hadn't a clue what it was I had to say.

These days the gentlemen barely tolerated my presence. The only reason I wasn't thrown out on my arse or directly into the fire was due exclusively to the fact that no one wished to *appear* disrespectful of Otis's memory (as if he were already dead).

I pulled a tantrum: I beat my chest, I lolled my tongue, I leapt atop the pine table, and I shouted as loudly as I could: "What about the lives?"

They all thought I was crazy, that whatever Otis had been eating I'd been fed too.

They let my fit run its course and then politely asked me to leave. "Nothing personal, you understand."

Precisely the truth. Nothing personal. Sam's position was Sam's, and John's was John's. One made a career of inflaming the people and the other made his living in the law, and the others—Warren, Church, Hancock, even Revere—dwelt somewhere in between.

The soldiers got off, deemed "not guilty," and were set free.

Montgomery's and Kilroy's thumbs were fire-branded for having shot too furiously and fast, but that was all.

And the relative quiet that subsequently settled on Boston for the next three years was not due to England's ultimate repeal of the Townshend taxes or the post-Massacre truce in the war of words with Britain. It was like the three years of quiet my father settled into after our difficult Boston sojourn. It was cold war. Not between America and England, but among America's own.

The people had taken note—of Samuel Adams's manipulations, John Adams's triumph, and their heretofore silent, unconquerable rage.

The dragon was here to stay.

CHAPTER 13

Boston Tea Party

To look at the papers and, later, the History books, one would have thought that after the Massacre, Boston was steeped in more anti-British feeling than ever before, thus making the next step on the road to Revolution, the "Boston Tea Party," nothing but a further demonstration of patriotic verve. Which is only half the story.

Try as the Gang of Six might to resurrect anti-British sentiment anew and redirect the hate raging in the street back toward England where they felt it belonged, the people weren't taking the bait—not at all. Sure, there were speeches by Warren and Church in which they denounced "crimes acted by a King's soldiers against the people [as being] the highest treason against the highest law among men, the natural freedom of mankind," but they rang hollow.

Samuel Adams was ignored altogether. But for the occasional recipe, I stopped reading the *Gazette*. And things had become so unsafe for John that he had to leave town. *So, go—go your silly struggle with England alone!* is what the people seemed to be saying.

"It's farewell, politics," Warren wrote, adding, "Ah . . . The people, they are dead, and the dead can't be raised without a miracle."

Even Paul Revere, the silversmith and engraver always on the sidelines, succeeded financially but failed politically in his attempt to capitalize on the expected anti–British post–Massacre backlash with his engravings of the shootings—copied without the authorization of the original artist, Pelham. Offered at shops, street corners, wharves, and by post, for centuries they would come to represent to posterity the tragedy of the Boston Massacre. They sold in the thousands, but as entertainment, not as truth.

The engravings show the Redcoats opening fire at point-blank range while distressed innocents look helplessly on and gather up their dead. The Custom House, where the action had taken place, is renamed "Butcher's Hall," and Captain Preston, depicted as a fiend with sword raised, is urging his men to shoot. The sky is blue. The Yankee crowd appears defenseless. There's no Garrick. And Crispus Attucks, shown dead, is not black.

Nobody was fooled. Those days were gone.

The people knew the British soldiers had panicked, shot too fast, too soon, and that was that. Irresponsible, perhaps, but few thought them criminal.

Even young Patrick Carr, who was roused from his deathbed after the Massacre to give his account, wondered why the soldiers had not fired earlier, given the abuse they had endured. He refused to blame the man, whoever he was, who had fatally shot him. For his candor, the dying boy was denounced by Samuel Adams as clearly "Catholic"—as good as calling him a sinner or a fool.

And so it was that we came to the ludicrous view that the ensuing Tea Party was a nasty, whooping, and hollering patriotic riot that set us on a collision course with England.

For starters, the Tea Party was an event occurring in complete and utter silence. Rather than a riot, it was a moment of grace in our history—a collective prayer.

How in the world, you ask, was this missed? Not missed so much as ignored. You will find mention of this silence in most every detailed account of the Tea Party, but only in the margins, as side detail, as it is considered incidental to the story History chooses to tell of the people rising up to destroy taxed tea. The story History chooses to tell is not of Revolution but of war with England; they were not the same. In this story, the actual experience of the Tea Party as epiphanic—as a momentous occurrence in the history of America in which diverse strains of humanity cooperated and were joined in true democracy for a shining moment—simply doesn't register. All that counts are the details supporting the Tea Party's distinction as the single biggest event compelling us to war, from which there was no turning back.

In that story tea matters, taxes matter. Silence does not.

But the silence was all.

Then the miracle came.

In 1771, when the Townshend taxes were all repealed but for "a nasty little tax on tea," the problem wasn't the tax itself. For, if truth be told, the British, quite strategically, had so drastically lowered the price of tea by then (via the Dutch East India Company) that even with the tax included in the price, the tea was bought cheaper imported from England than from smugglers. The tax was designed to break smugglers' profits, not America's spirits, to quash the inroads the smugglers had made in Britain's market on tea.

Challenging America's independent streak had nothing to do with the gambit.

Yet, as a bonus, the British wouldn't be able to help but snicker and count it as a victory over the Rebels when Americans promptly checked their rage and chucked their principles to save a couple of pence and rushed out to buy the cheap, taxed tea.

But for the American spirit, it would have worked.

But for Sam Adams and Hancock yielding to that spirit, the American Revolution would have stopped right there.

Tea business was big. This situation, being desperate, called for desperate measures. It was time to appeal to the people, post–Massacre style.

To approach them respectfully, politely, and ask for their help.

We are in this together, they claimed. "Since we all love tea, how far apart could we be?" was the ditty of the day.

"Do you, the people, really want Britain telling you from whom you must purchase your morning cup of tea? Cheaper, perhaps; and yes, certainly the merchants have the most to lose, that we freely admit. But what about the jobs these merchants provide, what about our community—oh, forget all that, how could we persuade you to help?"

News of the plan had been circulating for weeks. Slowly and quietly word got around of the desire to dump overboard the first shipment of discounted tea, which was sitting on the *Dartmouth* in the harbor. There was alluring talk of all being equals, of dressing anonymously as Indians regardless of wealth or station, of swearing a vow of silence (there it was again), of the riot's ringleaders being selected not from the Assembly but exclusively from the street. There was talk too of three groups of fifty being formed, for which commanders would be expressly chosen for ordinary skills alone, from their whistle to their muscle to their sheer nerve. It was said that only hissing, clucking, or grunting would be allowed, class-distinguishing speech as countersign only, in pidgin Indian, no less: "Me know you" the only phrase allowed.

Lastly, word on the street was that lumberjacks and bricklayers and architects and blacksmiths and breeders and apprentices and masters would be coming together on December 16, 1773, in a way they never had before.

I was twenty-two now, working as a French tutor and doing some debt-collecting for Dr. Warren on the side. These days, my contact with the Rebel Gang was practically nonexistent, and what work I did was purely for cash and generally of the errand-boy kind ("Find me a pretty whore for fifty pence"—that sort of thing).

So it was purely as a rank-and-file participant, not as auxiliary organizer, that I came to what was dubbed the "event over tea."

There I was, approaching South Church, along with 5,999 others, the largest "mob action" in our history to date, fully intent upon having a ball . . . but silently, of course.

But the real reason I'd come was that as soon as I'd heard there'd be no talk allowed, in my bones I knew this was it: I'd find Deborah.

So with the de rigueur feather headdress on my head and a leather skirt with some rather colorful fringe; my shoes removed and too-thin legs painted red (much too bright: "colonial red," for the record, is altogether unsuitable for purposes of disguising oneself as an Indian); an attractive combination of turquoise and yellow war paint streaking my face; and a fierce tomahawk in my caking fist, I joined the fray.

Deborah, are you here?

There were candles everywhere. Bright white and tall, some as high as six feet, hundreds of them illuminating the damp baroque chamber inside Old South Church, which had been designated the meeting spot.

In search of Deborah, my heart racing, my breath short, I looked all about me: men of diverse fortunes and fashions and races come together as one—as Indians, no less, as beings indigenous to the land. Even comparative heights were erased; in some instances, to boost anonymity, shorter men had been advised to come up to the height of their taller brethren by nailing extra heels to their shoes.

So with the usual distinctions between men blurred, there we stood in South Church, a solid band of red faces aglow in the tapers' light.

'Round about six, talk began at the pulpit, something about these treasure troves of tea, about four hundred, stashed on a ship we wouldn't even permit the owners to unload, let alone pay the tax upon, and how it was our job to dump it overboard before it would be confiscated for nonpayment by the crown.

Sam Adams began with a few remarks about the nasty king and the abominable Governor Hutchinson, whom he described with what for him was uncharacteristic restraint as "a shadow of a man, with a withered carcass and hoary head." A doctor stood up and called the tea poison—that was a new twist. And according to another doctor, tea was now the root of apoplexy, palsy, or, worse, leprosy. Oh well. I spotted Revere in the crowd, and at the window, Dr. Warren (I was hoping he hadn't recognized me because this day's round of collecting debts owed him had proved fruitless).

Then Hancock appeared: "Let every man do what is right in his own eyes! And only that!" he hollered from the back of the vestibule, looming head and shoulders above the crowd.

So, as the drizzle which had been afflicting the day lifted, Sam Adams intoned, "This meeting can do nothing more to save the country!"—the prearranged signal to head for Griffin's Wharf.

The sound of bare feet (no fancy shoes for me now; how far I'd come!) gliding on cobblestone, feather-light and just as soft, replaced all talk as colonists proceeded side by side in specified groups. Shouldering tomahawks and axes, our faces streaked with color, smeared with soot, burnt cork, lampblack, and grime, we paraded as one toward the sea.

In the town, the British soldiers tried to stop us but, deterred by our threats, stepped back, allowing a "path wide enough for all" to pass on to the wharf unhindered.

"Me know you." . . . A message was sent to the cabin of the first mate of the *Dartmouth*, asking for his lights and his keys.

"Me know you." . . . Block and tackle were attached to chests in the hold, which were hoisted up onto the deck.

"Me know you." . . . Silence so total that the first blows of the hatchets on the chests could be heard all through Boston.

"Me know you." . . . The chests, broken open, were spilled over the ship's rail into the water, the staves tossed in after the tea.

"What a cup of tea we are making for the fishes," someone dared whisper, and together we all laughed.

The moonlight, combined with the lamps and the torches, made Griffin's Wharf as bright as high noon. Thousands of onlookers swarmed the surrounding area, remaining silent, in awe.

Convinced retaliation would come at any moment, we worked as quickly as we could.

But retaliation didn't come. The British naval commander, Montague, mesmerized by the sight, could only find it in his heart to stand on his balcony and admire the harmony and design of men from all different walks of life moving as one.

"Me know you." . . . Together with a fellow "savage" I voyaged deep into the black-as-pitch hold where the tea was stowed.

"Me know you." . . . Our routine down pat, we attached the block and tackle.

"Me know you." . . . We signaled above that it was okay to hoist the chest.

"Me know you." . . . The chest was pried open with so many axes, perched on the ship's rail, and on "One . . . two . . . three!" the contents were dumped overboard—WHOOSH! It was received by the sea.

But suddenly, as I was preparing to return to the hold, I caught sight of a fellow Indian boy in a ragged greatcoat filling his pockets and inner lining to the brim with stolen tea.

"Me know you," I intoned pointedly, but he ignored my warning. It was as if every fiber of his being were consumed with this task and he couldn't let it go. "*Me know you!*" I warned him a second time.

This offense of his was serious; it had been decided in advance that anyone caught stealing tea would be treated harshly by his peers, possibly maimed. Stepping closer, toe to toe now: all right, for the last time, "*Me know you!*"

Damn right I did: He was a she, and she was Deborah!

The contents of her greatcoat, pounds of tea, were spilling from her hem and pockets as she ran.

"East Indian!" someone cried, indicating the presence of a traitor in our midst. And another: "Get him!" But by that time she'd already leapt off the gangplank onto the wharf and was running for cover into the observing crowd. The spell of silence broken, the serenity undone, several men gave chase, I among them.

But I wanted only to hold her, to look her in the eye and tell her I was sorry for having run from Hutchinson's mansion. It was as if time had collapsed and we were back at Hutchinson's and this was my chance, the moment I'd lived for, to reverse that painful memory and rescue her at last. In that moment I cared not a whit about stolen, taxed, or drowning tea.

She wound her way—and I, mine—through alleys and into coves and along the quay, clear up to the Common and up past Mill Cove until (I knew exactly what she was doing, I could sense it in the air) we'd lost the other fellows. Oh, you should have seen us zigzagging through the streets, taking our cues from each other, anticipating each other's every leap, twist, and turn without exchanging so much as a glance or a word. Anyone observing would have said this was a chase, but like the dragon who had given me the courage to bust through that secret tavern door so many years ago, the event was not the experience.

The event was exhausting. The experience sublime.

It was as if we both understood that some of the energy between us needed to be depleted before we met, lest when we came together we'd explode. Finally, after having kept each other running in circles for well over an hour, at Old South Church's peal of ten o'clock, the pretty thief took cover behind a haystack. Not pausing to catch my breath, I did too.

I had no idea what to do with myself, what to say, think, or do once I was there at her side. Panting, trembling—not from my run—I reached for what I knew, what I'd never stopped sketching, not for a day: her hand. But she held it back.

It was exactly as I remembered it: hard, scaly, dirty on the top-side, pink and hot and tender on the palm. Oh, my God, I thought, Apollo . . . Deborah . . . all these years they really were one and the same. Creatures of nature, of revolution, embodying happy, purposeful opposites coming together to survive.

I was so nervous, I think I *called* her Apollo.

Seeming to understand, she smiled—*oh, to behold that smile again!*—and she whispered plainly, "Hello, John."

I took one step closer. "You know I haven't chased you down to do you harm. I would hide you, if you'd let me . . . for the rest of our lives."

Nothing on earth could explain this feeling that I couldn't live another moment if I didn't have her hand.

"Me know you," I softly whispered.

"John . . . I wasn't stealing tea," was her reply.

"Was that you that night—at Hancock's?"

She nodded stiffly. "I wasn't sure what side you were on."

I shrugged. "Yours, is all."

Again, we understood each other; we each knew exactly what the other meant.

She tried to stop her lip from quivering, biting down on it till it bled. I wanted that blood on my lips, inside my mouth, but instead I asked her for her hand.

She gave it to me.

That night, we burrowed into the haystack, our little tent, and she fell asleep sitting up Indian-style, her back against the hay.

I fought sleep, fearful that it would cause me to let go of her hand, which I refused to relinquish.

The first time she woke, it was to ask, "You were there, that night, at Hancock's, to report for Mein, weren't you? To bring him down?"

"I was simply trying to save my hide," I replied.

"You don't stay alive if you don't," she agreed matter-of-factly before nodding off.

The second time, it was I who awakened her. "I'm sorry I ran. For eight years I haven't stopped thinking about it."

She looked me in the eye. "I was okay. I've been raped worse than that." She squeezed my hand exactly twice and went back to sleep.

The third time, again, she woke on her own. "Can I trust you?"

I didn't bother answering.

"I was feeling it, and that was all. I really wasn't meaning to be stealing tea."

"Feeling what?" I asked.

She sighed. "Oh, you know, feeling what it's like to be together, like all one, kinda like it could have been if I'd had brothers and sisters and a father I didn't have to see killed. Never having had that, I dunno, and having it right then and there under the light of the moon, it kinda made me grateful . . . for tea, actually. So I wanted it, all of it, with me, on me, in me . . . the smell, the sensation, the feel of that memory of the night we spilled the tea—so I wouldn't forget. Nah . . ." She paused to reconsider her words. "So I'd be sure to remember, that's it."

She uncrossed her legs, no more sitting Indian-style for her. She'd had enough of that. And no more feather headdress either. She removed it. And no more war paint, to boot. She began rubbing her Mohawk marks away.

"That was it, John, you know. Tonight. That was it. What we both want. Do you know what I'm saying?"

I did know.

I must have fallen asleep because suddenly she was gone. Actually, that's not so, she was still there, outside the haystack, in what she'd left for me: a long, thin zigzag trail of tea. A path for Revolution.

CHAPTER 14

The British Get Serious

breadwoman, her basket full of hot baked goods cooling in the sea breeze, was sitting on the shore, weeping, not making her morning rounds. Watching the sailors trudging through the sea lanes clogged with tea, sweeping, sinking, dispersing, siphoning up the "damage" from the night before. Sad she was to lose that tea. Something about its eager removal had her mourning in advance about losing the love her husband had brought home to her last night, fondling and nibbling at her breasts as though they were still plump, pinkish, and firm.

She was afraid that the moment was just that, a moment. A fleeting dream that would be no more. That she'd have to forget it ever happened or, worse, that as with my father and his embrace of me the night my mother died, she'd be asked to lie. No, no, the tea affair had been a party, not a crime, and on her breast was a hickey proving her point.

That's what I imagined the weeping breadwoman was thinking

as she and I sat together in the sand (I'd been wending my way home from the haystack when I'd spotted her), watching sailors trudge through clogged sea lanes in what appeared to be a futile effort to rid the harbor of its tea.

And these weren't official British sailors at work, mind you: These were Yankee sailors, working for Yankee mercantilists, fortunate men who wanted to remain so and toward that end wanted this event forgotten and the evidence gone. So what had happened, I wondered, to warrant this shift in attitude? After all, most of these men—through to last night—had not only been supportive but had participated in the tea-dumping plan. My goodness, I'd even spotted Hancock done up as an Indian. So what of this clean sweep, then?

Well, not entirely clean. Weren't the breadwoman and I cheered now by the sight of huge, sodden floating dunes of tea (some looked more than five feet tall and as wide!), refusing to go away, using the currents to slip from their would-be captors' shovels, picks, rakes, and nets? Thousands and thousands of pounds of wet, black tea shining in the sun, enjoying an early morning chase.

"Guess the tea's meanin' to stay," the visibly cheered breadwoman explained.

"Seems so," I replied, tipping my headdress (I was still outfitted from the night before), bidding her good day, and resuming my journey home.

Crossing the Common, however, I came across, or rather was accosted by, a scared-to-death young man, not more than fifteen, with bits of last night's war paint still dotting his ears which he was only too desperate to remove, scrubbing, scratching, tugging at his ears like a dog fending off fleas.

"Go home, sir, and out of the street, don't be dressin' like an Indian, don't you know?" At which point, seeing a Son of Liberty coming, he shoved me out of his way and continued on, wanting nothing to do with me.

The Son of Liberty, one Cameron, didn't lose a moment to

order me off the street, threatening me with bodily injury if I so much as dared strut about in broad daylight in last night's garb.

"I don't understand where there's a problem."

"Just get out of my sight by the count of ten, and the feather headdress out of sight on three, and there won't be one." He began counting. "One, two, three . . ."

I fled.

Oh, weren't the Sons making themselves hated now, randomly stopping innocent men and boys on the street, checking faces and ears for remaining traces of Mohawk red paint, warning even women and children to talk to no one of last night's affair and ordering those who could not be trusted—such as young apprentices beholden to inquiring Tory masters—to flee from town. And underground Patriots who had partaken of the event—those who were publicly pro–Tory but in private defiantly Patriot—although vouchsafed clemency, were kept under close surveillance and tailed.

All of these security measures were allegedly for the "people's benefit," put in force to protect the identities of those who had participated in the "tea affair" from arrest and prosecution. And while I didn't have a better explanation, I didn't trust it—or like it—any more than I did the sight of tea being sucked out of the bay.

And in the ensuing days my sense that something was very, very wrong, that fears of British retaliation were exaggerated, only became more clear. While Governor Hutchinson wasn't exactly racing through the streets swearing revenge, he did, in fact, arrest a few men, so, to be fair, the Sons of Liberty weren't entirely wrong on this score. Actually, I reverse myself: They arrested *one* man—randomly, it seemed—an unassuming barber named Eckley, who, after a brief, perfunctory interrogation availing nothing, was released.

Now, everyone knew Eckley had said nothing, if for no other reason than he probably knew nothing. Indeed, Eckley had doubtless spent all of his life knowing nothing. Swift, old Eckley was not.

Did you see Adams, Warren, Hancock there? he might have been asked. To which he would have replied, *Who are they? . . . What riot? . . . What ship? . . . Did you make mention of tea brewing in the harbor? My, my, I must help myself to a cup!*

Yet after Eckley was released by the authorities, he was borne naked through the cold streets, strung up on a narrow pole with a placard that read INFORMER! and spat upon.

The fear was irrational. And when I realized that, I had an epiphany: that the Boston Tea Party itself—the vision, the model it represented—was what was feared most. The possibility—nay, plausibility—of a whole new world. More than anything else, more than a tax revolt, the *experience* of the Tea Party was what was historically significant, for silently and under the light of the moon, a way of being that to date had dared exist only in people's hearts came to life. A way of being in which differences among men and women, rich, poor, Jewish, black, Quaker, Baptist, retarded, fey didn't matter, except in the talents and skills they brought to the Party.

In the silence something eerie, something strangely intimate, had crept up and caught us unawares.

It was beyond language.

It was "Me know you."

It was finding Deborah.

It was love.

You could see it in shoemakers like Joseph Robert Twelvetrees Hewes (you read that right), who suddenly, the very next day, claiming to have worked side by side with Hancock while dumping tea, with a bounce in his step and a flower in his lapel, shared with anyone who would listen thoughts of revelation: that Hancock, all in all, Lord be, *was just a man!* So giddy was he that he knocked on Hancock's door.

But Hancock was not to be found.

Dressed like Indians, we'd touched America, which, before the Tea Party, was a concept not yet born.

Before the Tea Party, we were simply . . . not–British.

Well, not anymore.

Now, in the cold morning after, we were also not–American. Not-equal. Not-homespun. Not-indigenous. Definitely not–Indian, and not welcome at Hancock's door.

In light of this discovery of mine, the fads that developed in this post–Tea Party era made considerable sense to me. Trading the war cry of the Mohawk for the classical oratory of Rome, educators, priests, and pulpit hogs developed a way of public speaking that would have bored Caesar. Sons of Liberty took on nicknames like Herodotus and Demosthenes. Benjamin Church, in his Boston oration on the anniversary of the Massacre, came clad in a Ciceronian robe. John Adams spoke of the Boston Tea Party as "epochal," as one of the grandest events in the history of the world, its sublimity unsurpassed. Fine, then, spare us the high rhetoric of British tyranny, give us instead blunt proclamations of equality, of fairness, of love. And good old Sam Adams: His diatribes these days were addressed to his "fellow Romans," exhorting us to remain strong, to seek inspiration in these hard times from the "Virtue of our Ancestors" (by which he most certainly did not mean the Indians). Additionally, he spoke of America as the "imperial Mistress of the World." Imperial . . . us? You bet.

"So leave the Americans as they Anciently stood!" remonstrated one Whig in defense of America. And from the Tory side: "*Delenda est Carthago* [Carthage must be destroyed]!"

Plain English, please.

So it hardly came as a surprise to me that everyone in town with money suddenly wanted to be royal, not free; elegant, not frayed (hats were big!); and above all, to be fluent in Romance languages—and fast.

Actually, this last development wound up being wonderful for me, as my expertise in French made my living possible after I ran out of Otis's money.

So there I was, in March 1774, teaching French to the socially inept but aspiring—sometimes as many as thirty to a class! Wasn't

I on my way, though! Happily contributing to the demise of America and pocketing all that cash.

Lucky thing for America that the British finally retaliated in the way that they did—blockading all of Boston Harbor, thereby treating us equally, punishing *all*. As if to remind us that we could forget about playing aristocrat, that as far as the king was concerned we were his servants and, more importantly, that we were one and the same: a new species of man, albeit nasty little beasts, all in all. In addition, they replaced Hutchinson with a military leader. And laid down vindictive measures, the famed "Intolerable Acts," forbidding town meetings and the like.

The irony is that the British in their actions, not in their rhetoric, conveyed an understanding of the Tea Party that surpassed our own. For despite their declared intention to defend the principle of taxation once and for all (which, by the way, they were ready to concede if only they could get some cash back on that ruined tea), nothing they did in this period supported that position. They forbade town meetings and large gatherings of any kind and declared martial law. No new taxes were assessed and no additional arrests made for the "tea affair." Indeed, Hutchinson said it better than any so-called Patriot could: that to prosecute the tea affair would be "to issue a proclamation against the whole community."

Right. Tell that to the Founding Fathers.

Another irony of the British blockade was that it greatly contributed to our emerging sense of what "being American" actually meant, if for no other reason than Hutchinson was replaced by General Thomas Gage—a man entirely enraptured by everything American, from bean dinners to hunting getups. He held a mirror to the culture that suddenly we couldn't help but realize was distinct, rustic, and true to the land. From day one, Gage was in the "Yankee swing."

Gage had spent the recent past in New Jersey, had taken a gossipy, sluttish Jersey wife (thank God for that, as you'll soon see!), and campaigned for this new post as Boston's military commander primarily because he wanted desperately to stay in America. He just plain liked it here.

To get the job, the story went, he adopted the king's ministers' advice on how to ingratiate himself with his sovereign: bore George III unforgivably with conversation deadly dull, so as to keep the king from being interested in him, for George III would trust no one who stimulated him to think. Even Governor Hutchinson, after he was ensconced again in merry old England, in his one interview with the king, found it best not to discuss colonial unrest, but to stick to a tidy, monotonal brief on corn, the coarse bread it made, and the taste: "Well, rather odd, Your Majesty." But even that proved too much for the king, who replied, with a twinge of excitement the entire court had learned well to dread, "How very strange." Phew. That was all. This time Hutchinson would get to keep his head—consider yourself in luck this day, Governor.

In any event, Gage must have done something right, because it was about this time that George III declared, "The die is cast," and ordered Gage to "master them or leave them totally to themselves and treat them as aliens" (there's mention of that new species again). An order, of course, that because it required Gage to be something he was not—tough and ugly (John Adams might have been a better bet for the enforcement of martial law)—he was doomed to fail from the start.

Gage devoured baked beans, threw fabulous concerts featuring local artistes, and dined regularly with the men he was supposed to arrest.

He befriended Dr. Warren completely.

And to top it all, he sported a wig, custom-made in Boston, that left him looking *exactly like Samuel Adams.* A little older, perhaps, much cleaner, and more feminine, which was why we called him "Granny Adams"—a nickname the idiot not only didn't mind but encouraged.

Hardly a saber-rattler, one of Gage's first military efforts was an order to his men to be nice, denying them sidearms and dressing them up in farmers' outfits to cross the Charles for afternoons in the countryside. To be fair, these excursions were designed to be undercover reconnaissance missions to investigate stores of ammunition that were reportedly being secreted away by villagers.

It's just that his men would get a little distracted, and their outfits were, well, a bit over the top. Thinking they looked like Yankee day laborers, they wore gray greatcoats, leather breeches, blue mixed stockings, and silk "flag handkerchiefs" about their necks. Accessorize this ensemble with delicate walking sticks, with which they posed while asking for scones in taverns, completely forgetting not to speak in the best King's English, and you have men whom you couldn't pay enough not to give themselves away.

And when one of Gage's colonels, Leslie, proceeded to Salem to seize war stores and found that the bridge over the river had been drawn up by militiamen who were threatening violence if the Redcoats tried to cross, he backed right down and settled the matter amicably. Leslie swore that if they would only help him follow through with his order by letting the bridge down for an itty-bitty second, as soon as he reached the other side—just so he could say he had done his duty—he would turn back around and go home. Which is exactly what he did.

And Gage later praised him for his good sense!

Frankly, personally, I loved Gage. I loved having a father figure that I could imagine running circles around. Even though he possessed military might five thousand strong, soldiers quartered everywhere, and artillery and grenadiers all about, the "Americans" had Gage's number and we were relentless in our reminders to him of that sorry fact.

When the Provincial Congress gathered illegally in Salem to elect its representatives to the First Continental Congress (which it was decided would be convened in Philadelphia, in order to investigate the possibility of a "collective response" to the Boston blockade), Gage, of course, dutifully but halfheartedly sent emissaries to dissolve the assembly. To stop their interference, all

Samuel Adams had to do was lock the door. When the emissaries knocked, he called out from the other side of the door, deep inside the hall, swearing he couldn't find the key.

As Gage's men stood outside, politely waiting on our "search" for the key (as I was in attendance at this meeting, I witnessed this firsthand), we resumed our vote for the delegates to the Continental Congress and approved the illegal resolutions necessary to finance the expedition of our five "congressmen" (among them the Adams cousins, of course) to Philadelphia. Once that business was finished, Sam, presumably having "found" the key, and in "obeisance" to Gage's order, dissolved the session and unlocked the door, welcoming the emissaries in just as he was bidding his constituents good night.

And believe it or not, Gage was so pleased by Sam's accommodation of his orders, he proffered him an invitation to dinner, convinced this "change of heart" of Samuel's was a sign that finally the esteemed Mr. Adams might be open to a bribe. He offered one thousand pounds sterling annually for life to alter his course of action against the king, but Adams, valuing power and influence over money, declined.

So—even with the port closed, the Charlestown ferry disallowed, business at a complete standstill, and Boston more depressed, depraved, and impoverished than ever before (unemployment at 30 percent and disease and filth taking its toll)—we were, some of us, having a great deal of fun. Six out of ten of Gage's men were deserting, and not because they tired of being soldiers, but because they too got a kick out of life in America and wished to quit the military, settle down, and start a farm.

Maybe being an American wasn't all that bad.

CHAPTER 15

The First Continental Congress Convenes

$\mathcal{E}$xactly what Deborah did at Hancock's each night I was yet to know for certain, but long before she confirmed it for me, I had the right idea. Deborah wouldn't be fucking for money a man whom she wasn't, in turn, betraying.

She was, of course, a spy.

And how this squared with what I saw in her eyes, in Ezekiel's ashes, in the trail of tea, in her smile, remained for me to know. I only knew that it had to be all right. That a woman who was quite willing to risk her life to openly pilfer tea just so she could feel it on her body had to be (like Otis, who was neither Patriot nor Tory), too loving, too American, to be a simple thief, traitor, or whore.

I was right. About as much as I was in my feeling that we would meet next at the Continental Congress of September 1774, which, based on this intuition, I'd resolved to find a way to attend.

The First Continental Congress was a convention organized by the Gang and other "Patriots" of the colonies stretching as far south as Carolina, who wanted to meet to formulate an official but, of course, entirely illegal response to Britain's recent blockade and the installation of all those troops. Little did I know—or did *they* know—that the Continental Congress would actually launch the Revolution—from a cave in Philadelphia, thanks to Deborah and me.

My shot at getting to Philadelphia came quite easily, due to Hancock's obsession with the French language. I knew full well when he tried to attend group classes ("to swing with the multitude," as he put it) that this would not last. And it didn't. At the end of his first half hour, during what used to be called a tea break, he professed to be unhappy sitting next to people who were "more than a little smelly," and so offered me a post on the spot as a personal secretary to tutor him privately in French. I took the job then and there, leaving my other French students to their unfinished lessons, never to return.

My job, theoretically, was to teach Hancock French and record or fabricate only his best words, seasoned with French, whether he had actually uttered French or not, but before long I was dusting his cuffs like a valet, advising his cook on daily menus like a butler, and toting his gigantic damned trunk about town like a slave.

Mounted on his fine carriage, it was one hundred pounds of pine and hide and brass that followed him everywhere, a box into which I was forbidden, for some reason, to look.

"So heavy, sir! May I ask . . ."

"Just shut up and lug it, please," on a bad day.

And on a good: *"Emporte-le et tais-toi, s'il vous plait."*

"Papiers secretes" was what I was told it contained. Felt more like dead bodies. That trunk . . . that trunk. How I loathed it. Sometimes I think I signed on to fight in battle just to be rid of it. Even during the skirmish on Lexington Green, surrounded by showering bullets—oh, never mind, more on that score later.

Hancock agreed to furnish an elaborate cortege to accompany the Massachusetts congressional delegates and I was to be one of the amenities. Pleading illness, Hancock would not be among them but wanted me to be his eyes and ears in the proceedings—and on his fellow delegates. No one really knows why Hancock did not attend himself, but I believe the others thought him too stupid and preening to represent serious Boston, the infamous hotbed of sedition, and diplomatically suggested that he "take charge of the town" in their absence, which his vanity acceded to immediately.

Top priority after Samuel Adams was elected to the First Continental Congress was to get him properly attired. Adams, with raiment filthy and poor, was much too low-class-looking, much too scrappy to attend as he was, the rest of the delegates agreed. So I remade him as a gentleman with Hancock's money.

Hancock decreed that this makeover was to be a grand event, meaning it was to be total and complete. Toward this end, I spent whole days on Samuel trying to teach him how to ride a horse (he hated it, and arrived in Philadelphia with his backside chafed raw). I purchased everything necessary to make him look presentable. It wasn't easy. Oh, the strange lumps on that man (nothing fit)— shaped like a trapezoid, I swear to you. Eventually, though, I cobbled together an acceptable outfit: fine silver-buckled shoes, blue satin breeches with gold knee buckles, a brocaded blue waistcoat with a fine gold fob, a green velvet coat with gold sleeve buttons, and a much-too-small-for-his-dirty-fat-head tricorne hat, monogrammed with the insignia of the Sons of Liberty. The finale: a gold-headed cane.

By the time I was through he looked like, well, not much better than a discarded Christmas tree, draped with bright baubles but wilted and derelict, hanging around on the street to greet the delegates when they arrived in September.

Although another delegate also stayed home due to ill health (James Bowdoin, who probably didn't trust Hancock either), finally Robert Treat Paine, John Adams, Samuel Adams, and myself

crammed into a coach-and-four. Preceded by two white servants armed and on horseback and with four liveried blacks at the
rear (two of these were forced to keep up on foot!), we were off,
looking more like a parade float than a diplomatic carriage train.

As we passed through Connecticut over the next few days, every
town rang its bells and shot off its cannon. Cheering men, women,
and children crowded the doorways, and John Adams, with an ear-
to-ear grin, mentioned in passing that no governor, no general
of any army, had ever been treated to such ceremony. What a
delight!

En route, we discussed not Boston or the people and their
plight, but the watermelons in New Haven ("So red they look un-
true!"), the stunning statue of King George III in New York ("What
a sight to behold!"), and the seasonal flowers, with a few jokes
about birds and bees thrown in.

We feasted upon more sumptuous breakfasts than even I had
ever seen, served on rich delftware, in massive Revere coffee urns
and teapots, with luxurious lace napkins that were lovely but useless for the perfect toast and butter, followed by luscious peaches
and pears and plums.

John Adams's ecstatic state, however, varied on a meal-to-meal
basis, and then only if he hadn't come into contact with a lot of
people.

"Ah, the lack of good breeding in America," he bemoaned.
"Would that there was more evidence of real gentlemen about. . . . "
New York fellows, in particular, got his goat: "No interest in another's opinion, [they] talk overly loud and very fast and all at the
same time."

By the time we trundled into Philadelphia, we were dusty and
weary and in need of a drink. We couldn't resist heading for City
Tavern, where we mingled with a host of Philadelphians and met
Christopher Gadsden of South Carolina, my father's friend who
knew me in youth, yet was goggle-eyed at my appearance there in
Philadelphia. I asked him about Papa, and he started to stammer,

then shook his head: "Not well." Papa's gout was plaguing him, he said, and then finally explained his amazement at seeing me; he had been told that I had died after falling ill on a junket at sea. I nodded slowly, then dropped the subject.

The delegates at the tavern had their eyes upon the "three men from Boston" and from the start were wary and quick to judge: "Bostonians for Liberty—I see, but don't they hang Quakers?" Between the jellies, continual toasts in claret (the Adams cousins practicing their elegance, not raising their drinks "too low or too tall, but to that nice point which is above disguise or suspicion"), bits of Parmesan cheese (John came to be known as "Baconface"), almonds and raisins washed down with strong punch and rich red wine, trifles, curds, creams, and whipped syllabubs, there was enormous suspicion and paralyzing fear. More than that: deep, deep hatred.

"Those New Englanders—ranting, canting idiots. I will not be duped into fighting their battles against the government!"

As far as I could tell, most of the men who had come seemed to have a single surprising agenda: to free the colonies not from England but from the "Bostonization of the Republic." I had had no idea that Boston was so widely hated by those other than my father, and its misconstrued influence so widespread.

I had just settled into that little world unto itself and forgotten, I think, that the rest of the colonies were even there. And I certainly had no sense of any dangerous nationalistic agenda afoot, which clearly these men did, for to quell it was their aim.

"There is too great a nationality among the Bay men for the good of America as a whole."

What were they talking about?

She would explain.

It was in Watertown, en route to Philadelphia, where a gentleman on horseback had treated us to an elegant entertainment, that I noticed she was following. First as a lady in a carriage and riding dress. The next day as a courier, and the third as a milkmaid, pushing her cart into town—never once wavering from her path, trail-ing ours.

It was in the City Tavern, while the delegates, wary all, were hissing under their breaths, "This Washington—are those peas in his head or brains?" As they slurped flip and sucked their wine, I ap-proached her, dressed now as a housewife with a beribboned mob-cap, a spotted bodice with striped kerchief, and even a pail for fetching water.

"Nice touch," were my first words, pointing to the pail.

She chastised me with a "Shush," then: " 'Tisn't polite to com-ment on a lady's attire." It was as if we knew each other so well that we could bicker like husband and wife. In fact, taking advantage of this impression, she dragged me outside, careful not to take my hand, as this was not generally what old intimates would do.

"Am I to know who it is you're following and why?" I dared ask, once I was confident that the garden fountain was covering my sounds.

She rolled her eyes. "Shut up now."

"May I call you Deborah," I whispered, "or do you go by an-other name?"

She scowled.

I took the liberty of getting closer. "Deborah, I've thought of nothing but you since the Tea Party. I want to know everything."

"That's a tall order," she insisted. "I'm not sure you're ready."

"Yes, you are, otherwise you'd never let me spot you. Believe me, 'Me know you.' "

She giggled. "It's true."

"Then tell me," I pleaded.

"Then meet me," she countered, reaching for her pail, "at Hell's Caves."

I couldn't say no, not to something that sounded so good. Though I had no idea whatsoever what she meant.

CHAPTER 16

Hell's Caves

*I*t was to be my initiation into the other story.

Hell's Caves were essentially a series of holes in rock serving as taverns on the banks of the Delaware. They were like nothing I had ever seen before. Crevices splayed wide, black openings into which drunks and whores and those who wished to meet in secret would slip, checking their daylight identities at the entrance to the hole that served as a door. Inside, beer, wine, gin, rum, and meat pies were served to company of "lesser sorts" as bats swirled about heads and snakes slithered across the floor wet with water oozing up through fissures from a source that predated man. By "lesser sorts" I mean a collection of farriers, peddlers, Indians (real ones), cobblers, street sweepers, stableboys, and indentured servants who somehow, having managed the night off, were assembling for what looked to be more than a routine, casual affair.

"Welcome," she said.

At some level I must have understood hers was more than a

simple greeting, for the impact of her salutation was almost more than I could bear. Something about the cave, a wet, dark hole in the earth; the particular caste of people (whom I hadn't seen collected since the night Otis was carried away); the quality of candlelight, amber and flickering gold; even the shadows, tall, black, and jagged silhouettes of ladies and gentlemen whispering, caressing, conspiring, flirting, cracking jokes, and plotting Revolution all at the same time.

There was only one place left to sit, a bench, which seemed to be reserved for Deborah. It was carved out of rock and belonged to Benjamin Franklin, who, when not on ambassadorial missions to England, was a regular here, welcome not for his political work or his almanac, I would eventually learn, but because he was the man who had harnessed lightning.

Here upon Franklin's bench, no less, I was to encounter my own brand of lightning: the momentous power of Deborah's secret world, not particular to Boston, Philadelphia, or any one location or place, but pervasive and ubiquitous throughout America, up and down the seaboard line. Not an organized network as much as a common bond, all the more recognizable for going unspoken and undocumented. More or less a state of mind.

This power, by the way, was immediately palpable; the moment I set foot inside the cave it had me in its grip. Imagine a shining, vibrating ray with a sharp tip (was it the Green Dragon's fire, the tip his tongue?), attracting like a magnet all the bits and pieces of heightened awareness I'd accumulated over time (in the swamp, in beholding Apollo, in listening to Otis, during the Tea Party, and in the presence of Deborah's smile, to review a few) and reorganizing them, connecting them in a whole new way. In this new configuration, these moments were no longer merely separate manifestations of transcendence, representations of beauty that one could only dream of, but were nothing less than goads to action. Not about yearning but about doing. Principles not simply to contemplate, but to live by.

I can't say I felt *Ah, at long last—I'm home! Among my people!* Frankly, I found everyone there, even Deborah at the moment, somewhat fearsome, if only because I sensed—even if Deborah hadn't said a word to me—that the simple fact of having discovered this cave and its denizens was about to make my life more dangerous than I ever could have dreamed.

Revolution would have it no other way.

But alas, Deborah did talk, and a lot.

"If you think you're ready, I could use your help," she began.

"Why the hell not?" I said, causing us both to smile.

She started in: "You said to me you was no Tory or Patriot, that your side was my side." She paused. "That still true?"

I shrugged my assent.

"I'm a spy," she went on, "but I belong to neither side."

I waited for clarification.

She ordered an ale and settled in to tell a story, which I would learn was her wont when things got serious. She talked in stories, because that's how she saw life: as a tale with a beginning, middle, and end.

Tonight's story, an account of what would eventually come to be thought of by me as "The Missing Years, Part One" (sadly, there would be a "Part Two"), covered our time apart from the Stamp Act Riot of '65 to the night we spotted each other outside Hancock's home.

The morning after the destruction of Hutchinson's mansion, Deborah, still wet with blood from her attackers, walked right into the Massachusetts Statehouse while it was in session. She smashed her way through the heavy doors to a chamber where women were not allowed and, storming up the aisle, demanded that justice be done.

She insisted upon attention, exhorting the legislators to see to laws that would deter men from such savage acts upon women as she had experienced last night in Hutchinson's cellar. And of Sheriff Greenleaf, there in the balcony, she demanded that the men who had done this to her be tried and, when found guilty, hung. "Every last one of them, Sons of Liberty or no!"

She was tossed out for being a bunter and a crazed whore who stunk of menstruation and deserved what she got. The sheriff made nothing whatsoever of her claim. Furthermore, because she got caught during the attack and would not expunge the child growing inside her, she was cut from Madam Dorcas Griffiths's roster of "gentlemen's companions" available for hire through her agency. Consigned to the stable at the rear of the millinery shop-cum-whorehouse, she was given one week to move on.

Deborah hid in stores and silos and pens. She ate gruel and hay. She kept moving, stealing clothing appropriate for her to pass for a lady. And since fine ladies were usually given credit, she would often eat and sleep for free. Then, after purloining whatever she could to survive, she would flee.

By the time she was wanted for thievery in Boston, Deborah had moved on to Milton, Massachusetts, and there, after being hunted by dogs, it was on to Plymouth. Then back up to Salem, across to Concord and Lexington and Menotomy, zigzagging her way across the Bay Colony.

Moving, always moving, and in an unpredictable way so as to be difficult to pursue, Deborah stopped to rest for more than a day only once, at the gallows in the marshes of Charlestown. It was there, beneath Ezekiel's clacking bones, that she gave birth to the child misbegotten by one of her attackers in Hutchinson's cellar. Now, as the unwed mother of a daughter with a clubbed hand, her life situation was made worse.

Moving some more. Swallowing stolen gold so if she was apprehended she would not be found out. Tucking sugar inside a band wrapped around her waist. Raw meat inside her daughter's drawers. Carrots and corn in her bosom. Whatever survival required, until, luck having run its course in one location, she'd be spotted and sometimes arrested. But somehow, she'd flee again, moving to the next village, carrying a child for whom breathing, walking, simply existing was a chore.

"Please, daughter, just one foot before the other. That's all you need to do. Let God take care of the rest."

"Mummy, I don't think I can," burbled the tot. Then she would fall. And Mama would clean her face with a kerchief sticky with sugar, which would make Alice, the little tyke with the little legs, smack her lips, call out "Sweet!" and smile.

So when Mein came to town with his Tory rag the *Chronicle*, he made it plain on the streets that he needed prostitutes and stableboys. Because of their low profile and obvious access, they were in a fine position to do the state's bidding, to dig up defamation on the famous Patriots. Deborah was only too happy to volunteer. For the money, yes, but also to discredit The Cause, as it smugly styled itself. For she was every bit as angry with the Founding Fathers as she ever was with the Brits for all their finery and arrogance. Indeed, she saw little distinction between them, if any at all.

And besides, working for Mein, she thrived for the first time in her life. No pay up front, of course, but she was not about to refuse the chance to trade her considerable survival skills and wile for steady shelter, food, clothing, and, most importantly, a way of finally keeping Alice from harm.

First Mein liked her. Then Admiral Montague. Hutchinson liked her once, for a night. Gage twice. And Church, Benjamin Church, yes, the married Patriot most fiery of all, liked her enough to keep her as his own mistress, and then his personal British spy. Before she knew it, she was in deep, reporting on events she learned about in Hancock et al.'s beds. It was decided: It was on spying and whoring, then, that she would rely to keep herself and Alice alive. Why, in that mansion Church was building for himself with all those British pounds (didn't any of his esteemed colleagues wonder where a *poet* might be getting this kind of cash?), she and Alice were even given their own bedroom, if only to make it easier for Church to fuck Deborah on demand. There she lay, thinking of England, thanking it, for keeping little Alice alive. Every part of herself she would give them, from cunt to brain—every part but her heart and soul. These she would keep for herself, for the Revolution, for the day her country would call. In the meantime . . . call her traitor, call her Patriot—spying, no matter the side, was just a job.

So was she an enemy of her country, then? Or a friend? This was the question roiling in my mind even as I knew that the answer depended on which story, in the end, proved true: the story about the war with England or the story about the war for truth.

Finishing her tale, she proclaimed: "So now to the business at hand, to making war." Because, she decided, war would be the road, the vehicle, for Revolution.

"Without independence from England, the Revolution won't be worth a damn," she asserted in her own inimitable way. "And since war is the only way we're gonna make that necessary first step of announcing our independence, I'm aiming to have you help me start a war."

I guzzled my entire ale, which I hadn't touched while listening to her story, in one swallow. My head thought for sure she was a crazy woman, but my uncooperating heart had me uttering out loud, "Okay."

She went on to explain that although thoughts of Revolution had been voiced since the turn of the century by men and women like Ezekiel in every one of the thirteen colonies, they had never been acted upon in their own right. Rather, they'd popped up erratically, like the Stamp Act Riots and even the Boston Massacre.

But, she insisted, it was the blockade of Boston that had brought her to the sad but inevitable conclusion that war would be required. As she saw it, the blockade wasn't simply punishment or retaliation causing America suffering. It was more than that, a heaven-sent gift. For it was the blockade that had given her the idea to start a war.

"Have you seen . . . did you go out to the Neck to actually watch the caravan?" she asked. Her eyes opened wide at the thought of the endless parade of supplies that the closing of the harbor had prompted our fellow colonists to send to Boston—the first ever unified action of its kind. Normally colonies took competitive advantage in the extreme of each other's weaknesses or misfortunes. While others recorded the details of the Intolerable Acts of this period, what Deborah chronicled (in her head only—she could hardly read or write) was everything that she'd seen sent into Boston via the Neck, courtesy of the other colonies. She had it all down, to the last apple.

"Quintals of codfish from Baltimore, rye from Maryland, meal and flour from Philadelphia, money from Connecticut. Last week alone, three miles of sheep from Massachusetts, and from New Hampshire, so many cattle I lost count. More blueberries and cider and potatoes and molasses and wine than I knew existed if only 'cause I can't count any higher than a thousand fifteen, at which point my tongue gets all tangled and I lose track."

She took a deep breath, for she was nearly too excited to speak, then continued. "Our poorest of Boston citizens ain't wanting for bread, John. That's a first. That's the beginning . . . and all because Britain retaliated. All because we got ourselves that much closer to war.

"Wharves of Boston deserted, not a topsail vessel to be seen nowhere, nohow in the harbor, save ships of war. No work, no money, no medicine, and yet—food enough for everyone, like never before."

"God has sent speedy relief," I added enthusiastically, eager to convey to her that I was catching her point. But I wasn't.

"God, indeed! No, the colonies have. That's my point. With the trouble dealt us by Mother England, seems we pull together and recognize that we have to look out for our own. We're not separate colonies in hard times—we're all Americans."

She continued. "For you, it was all poetry, all verse—the tea riot and all. I know. All up here." She laid a finger on my head. "But it doesn't have to be like that," she added, clucking her tongue, furrowing her brow. "It can be more—it can be real. Those sheep coming over that Neck can be the way, every day, if only—"

I could put the rest together myself. For I knew full well from the days of trade with my father that generally New Yorkers were out for New Yorkers, Carolinians for Carolinians, Georgians for Georgians, and so on. In such an atmosphere, an interest in another colony that wasn't simply mercantile, competitive, was inconceivable. The notion of sharing, caring for one another didn't even exist.

"But you and I, we're gonna change all that!" she insisted.

Finally she reached for my hand.

Pure lightning. The real kind.

I was sold.

CHAPTER 17

The Hoax

er plan was as unlikely as everything about her, and just as ingenious.

It sounded simple, if you believed, as future generations would, that the Continental Congress, set to convene soon in Philadelphia in September 1774 was composed of sweet visionaries, enlightened men all, united in common rebellion against British tyranny and in making a case for freedom.

But because even I knew better than that, I was sure that Deborah's plan—to bring Congress together on a joint declaration of war against England—would require nothing less than a miracle. Which, as it turns out, she was prepared to provide.

As Deborah put it, "Without some kind of enemy to close ranks together and oppose, there ain't a pope's chance in Boston of us all getting along. Hunger and bullets have a way of making you feel like you're all together whether you really are or not."

"But if you're not *really* together, then what's the point?" I asked, fully aware that I was splitting hairs in an attempt to get out of what she'd planned.

"Well, sometimes you gotta put people side by side first, on a common footing. Sorta give it a kick and a start."

And with that, she sent me on her way.

My instructions were to tell her everything that went on, divided into two categories: to report juicy treasonous bits to keep Church and Gage "happy enough" (a challenge, as this was hardly an inflammatory crowd) and to note "possible openings" that might be exploited as the catalyst for war.

"Openings" . . . hmmmm. Of course, I hadn't a fucking clue how to provoke such a situation—short of pretending I was from a renegade British faction and storming the hall.

When I asked Deborah to share with me what she imagined an "opening" to be, she said, "Can't say. You'll know it when you feel it, though." Not much help, on the face of it. But ultimately, she was right—and I did.

So there I was, smack in the middle of the First Continental Congress, a lint brush at the ready in one hand (Hancock's marching orders were to keep Samuel Adams presentable at all times) and a pen in the other, for recording for posterity Adams's and the other Massachusetts delegates' every righteous word. In the main, my brush was kept very busy and my pen was conspicuously unoccupied. All the while, I strained to apprehend any openings to war that I might "feel."

My, my, I thought, what a strange process this business of Revolution is.

So why'd I agree to do it?

Simple. I couldn't say no.

Period.

Openings?

I must say, the prospect of seeing the Continental Congressmen declare war on each other was more likely to occur than spontaneous unity. These men seemed disinclined to agree on anything, down to and including where the illustrious body of fifty-six delegates should formally convene (rather poor advance planning, wouldn't you say?).

Some lobbied for a nearby church, others for the Philadelphia House Chamber, a tavern, a ballroom, even a farm. Oh, the debate went on and on and on, contentious from the start. New Englanders feared a religious setting, moderates were wary about the Pennsylvania House Chamber's "empire" feel. A ballroom, while lovely, just wasn't "right," unless someone wanted to spring for a little chamber music entertainment—that might be nice.

Carpenter's Hall was eventually decided upon because it had a pretty courtyard for pacing and gossip, should things get too boring. An understandable concern, for once this raging debate over where-to-have-the-party was over, I couldn't imagine these men would have a helluva lot left to say or do.

Things commenced at a place exactly opposite where Deborah wanted to take them. Patrick Henry spoke for nearly all when he declared, "There is not a man amongst us who would not be happy to see accommodation with Britain." So first we'd make a motion regarding formal unity with England, contingent upon the polite nonbinding suggestion that the king authorize a tiny branch of Parliament to sit here in America. Then we'd vote on it and go home.

To my surprise, the motion lost . . . but by a single vote.

"No possibility of a declaration of war against England yet here, friend," I would tell Deborah each night over grog in the cave.

"You'll know," is all she'd say, adding, "We'll wait." Which was the first she'd ever indicated to me what I'd intuited that first night in Hell's Caves: that whatever Deborah had planned, she was not acting alone.

"An opening always comes. You just need to be looking, and to trust yourself here when it does." She tapped my heart.

It came. And she was quite right: When it did, I knew. It was that swamp/Apollo/Deborah's smile/Green Dragon/Ezekiel/shattered tortoise shell/Otis's words/little Garrick's cry/Boston Tea Party/night in the hay kind of feeling, coming from the same Patrick Henry, the delegate from Virginia who had made the motion for our reconciliation and reaffirmation as England's dependent.

From out of the blue, the opening we had waited for sprang from Henry's sudden and instantaneous turnabout: "The distinctions between Virginians, Pennsylvanians, New Yorkers, and New Englanders are no more. I am not a Virginian—I declare as an American."

The entire hall flushed with vitality. Even the walls, pink in the setting sun, seemed enlivened, abashed, in a state of nervous excitation. Henry had touched a nerve.

I reported back to Deborah.

The next day word arrived from Boston from a "mysterious source" that Gage had laid siege to the town, that Boston was burning, and that people had been killed.

Reverend Duché, an Episcopalian, led ten minutes of prayer on behalf of Boston, "that once happy town." There was no controversy over his denomination. Samuel Adams himself had settled the debate by offering to hear any prayer from any gentleman so long as he was "a friend to his country." Quakers cried, Congregationalists sighed, and Anabaptists trembled with feeling.

While Duché read the thirty-fifth psalm to Congress—"Plead my cause, O Lord, with them that strive with me"—I prayed, gripping Apollo's shell necklace like rosary beads.

And then came that telltale silence, enveloping us all.

Rancor ceased.

We were colonists no more.

We were Americans.

Virginia's George Washington wrote home that he quite liked the New Englanders after all.

In the courtyard, more than one delegate found himself characterizing Patrick Henry's speech as "music."

And by the time it was determined that the news of the siege of Boston was entirely a hoax, it was too late. The state of unity that had emerged in the silence could not—as much as the delegates might have wanted to later—be called back quite so fast. Certainly not quickly enough to stop Congress from approving what came to be known as the Suffolk Resolves, brought into Congress by courier more or less simultaneously with confirmation of the hoax.

I never asked Deborah about it.

I didn't have to.

I just knew.

The hoax was immediately forgotten in the wake of the Suffolk Resolves. This document from the Massachusetts Provincial Assembly (and penned adroitly by the bellicose Dr. Warren) amounted to a virtual declaration of war in recommending that the Boston Port Act (the blockade) be disregarded and resisted. Furthermore, that the people should prepare for combat against England whenever Boston sounded the alarm.

To my absolute bafflement and delight, the Resolves were approved unanimously amid gushing tears and applause.

Deborah was merely pleased: "It's a start."

That night, we met in Gloria Dei, Philadelphia's oldest church, dating back to Philadelphia's beginnings, and made our plans. The church was similar to Hell's Caves in that it too was carved from rock, unornamented except for a bell, a baptismal font, and a wood carving of two cherubs mounted on an open Bible that read: *The people who wander in darkness have seen a great light.*

CHAPTER 18

Grape

We were waved through the checkpoint on Boston Neck without incident because, as one surly sentinel explained, Gage had ordered it so. "Lucky thing," he reminded us. "Otherwise we'd quite happily have blown you to smithereens. Welcome home, gentlemen, to the fine mess you've made of things. Suffolk Resolves, my eye!" he spat at our carriage. Then to his fellow officers at the other side of the gate he shouted, "Let the bloody Rebels pass!"

Where once Boston's quaint gate had stood was a shaved pine stockade, some eight feet tall, blocking the road. Two fences, barbed and sharp, spanned the entire stretch of isthmus between the bay and the sea; and a countless number of His Majesty's sentinels marked time, permission granted to shoot to kill anyone who gave them cause.

"Treasonous bastards," another guard sneered.

And another: "Ah, you'll be seeing the noose soon enough, you can count on that!"

As if this display of hostility wasn't shocking enough (particularly to John Adams, who had expected to be met at the gate by adoring fans), imagine our shock at having our carriage commandeered by Yankee roadsiders with supplies in need of transport just as soon as we crossed into Boston on the other side.

"Get out!" ordered the motley band of gun-wielding Rebel highwaymen.

"Right, then. Plain enough," John Adams assented, first out, pushing the rest of us out of his way.

"This is a loan, I take it?" Sam Adams inquired of the gang.

"Yea, with nary a date, time, and place for its return!" one of the brigands, a dirty squib of a woman, replied. And they drove off.

When we arrived at Hancock's two and a half hours after we were expected for lunch, we were in no mood for one of his snits, which we knew would be impossible to avoid when through the door we heard the sound of his staff cracking plates for him to keep him calm. His butler being otherwise engaged in dropping teacups down the staircase, we let ourselves in.

"Helloooo! Helllooo!" we shouted through the house, hearing an altogether unfamiliar echo resonating throughout.

It had been only eight weeks since we'd seen Hancock, but in that time his house had undergone a remarkable transformation. It had been laid bare, with any sign of extravagance removed. The silver chandelier, the Venetian glass vases, the onyx chess set, lacquered tea trays, even the Italian silk draperies—all gone.

"Helloooo?" Echo, echo. Crash, crash, bang.

Even our soup, two hours cold and laid before us sloppily by a hatchet-faced maid with a runny nose, seemed stripped down, thin, bereft, lacking in meat, cream, wine, or flavor.

"What a terrible day this is turning out to be," John Adams flatly stated, breaking the well-on-three-hour silence among us since our approach to Boston gate. Not a peep from a one of us during the episode at the gate, the theft of our carriage, the long walk to Hancock's, or the unhappy surprise of a sniffling bitch serving a piss-poor lunch with our host in the throes of hypochondriacal mania upstairs—until now.

John Adams had had just about enough. Now, ensconced safely enough in Hancock's home, he was ready and eager to bitch and moan.

"Is it me or has this town changed?" he asked, in what undoubtedly remains one of the greatest understatements of the era, if not all time.

Changed? Our walk had been like a forced march at double time through alien territory. We had witnessed an "open-air town meeting," during which a cabal of three denounced "all legislatures of all kinds" and declared "an enemy of the people anyone honoring Parliaments of any sort," be they British, American, or, for that matter, Whig or Tory.

"John Hancock could do without yet another carriage," is all Sheriff Greenleaf had to say when Sam Adams approached him to complain he'd been robbed.

"Robbed or confiscated? Which is it?"

"Robbed!" Adams answered defiantly.

"We'll see," Greenleaf responded indifferently.

Where Deborah once had been pilloried on the Common, there were women, hundreds of them, installed at spinning wheels. Skirts hiked up between their legs, bonnets loose and askew, they turned flax into yarn, with prizes being awarded to the "most industrious Patriot"—i.e., she who had spun the most. The prize, a jar of blackberry preserves, went to a little black girl who had produced four hundred yards of cloth and three hundred skeins of yarn.

Walking down King Street, we noticed a string of once-prosperous jewelry and silversmith shops, all closed. In their place were open-air markets, with sections designated FOR AMERICANS

ONLY!—the first time I'd ever seen the actual word *American* written down. In these markets, soldiers, Tories, and any merchant seeking profit over ten percent were disallowed. There were no luxury items available and not a single British import. But there were baskets of flax, delicate herbal teas, local freshwater fish (remember, the harbor was closed to commerce), seasonal vegetables, local dairy, and fruit. Connecticut brick was here for the bricklayers, New Hampshire hardwood for the carpenters, hide for the leathermakers.

And in the streets where once there was violence, there was barter: yarn for milk; milk for lead; lead for bullets; bullets for cartridges; cartridges for pouches; pouches for guns; guns for food.

And the talk on the street wasn't inflammatory, wasn't about "tyranny" or "taxes" or railing against Parliament or the king. It was about "making a go of it on our own." Releasing ourselves from the onerous burden of British influence, policy, and law definitely was part and parcel of the plan, but not the be-all and end-all. Freedom was.

Where broadsides announcing a "massacre" or denunciation of yet another tax once were posted, there were signed agreements posted by and for ladies not to consume or purchase English tea. Not just because tea was British and taxed, but because our love for it "inveighed against the new ideal," which was self-sufficiency. Literature was given out celebrating the housewife as the model Patriot because in her duties she actively contributed to this overall goal.

To do a job, faithfully and well, was all that was required to be included in The Cause. Anyone who worked, belonged: women, children, slaves, Jews, Indians, half-breeds, mulattoes, farmers, sailors, fishermen, even whores—the differences seemed blurred.

The spirit of the Boston Tea Party, it seemed, had taken hold. Right under everyone's nose.

No wonder I hadn't seen Deborah for all that time after the harbor uprising. While I was giving French lessons; while the ladies and gentlemen with two left feet were learning—and failing at—the minuet ("Too many tiny steps"); while the Sons of Liberty were harassing small boys and men: Otis's jack-tars and whores—of which Deborah was only one—were silently making the Tea Party a reality, duplicating Venus' trajectory into the sun.

The Suffolk Resolves, I soon would learn, had been but one tiny manifestation of this shift. Shortly after the Tea Party (Deborah would later tell me all this), political power in Boston had shifted almost immediately to include those normally shut out. This happened for one reason only: They showed up at town meetings, the unpropertied did, and demanded to be heard.

At these meetings, Sam Adams was dwelling on his usual bugaboo: the enforcement of the boycott, blah, blah, blah.

The people got smart. "Fine—you want our help? You give this damned fool boycott some teeth, and you prohibit not only importing, but exporting and the distribution, consumption, and stowing of any British products *at all*. Put us all in the same boat, on the same footing as the rich, living on our native wits and agriculture alone, and we'll back this boycott and make it work."

A document called the "Solemn League and Covenant" grew from these demands and, needless to say, it went nowhere at all. Sam Adams supported it and promoted it, but only—of course— because he saw opportunity for himself in the proposal: The chance to be a "hero of the people" was too good to miss, irresistible, you understand.

The Suffolk Resolves were indeed testament to the rising influence and ability of "the lesser sorts" to organize and bring about change, but pulling off the hoax was its crowning achievement. Had it not been for the momentary camaraderie occasioned by the hoax, the significance of the Suffolk Resolves might never have been understood, and the American Revolution, let alone the war, might never have followed.

Small wonder none of us expected Boston to be turned on its ear by the adoption of the Resolves. None of us, including me, understood them to be the genesis, the foundation, of anything more than a hardening of our stance against England.

Yes and no.

I remember sitting at Hancock's dining room table that afternoon, staring down at my pallid, congealing, tepid soup. Still in a state of confusion as to exactly what was going on in Boston, I was thinking of Deborah, confident that she'd be able to explain.

I understood nothing at this point, except one thing: that these men before me, and the melodramatic one upstairs, looked pathetic, exhausted, worn out, silly, and old. Not unlike my father at the Green Dragon that night nine years ago.

Of course, their bickering did nothing to help this perception. Finally it took Samuel's soup-slurping noises to provoke John Adams's wrath.

"It's neither hot nor thick, Samuel—must you do that?" John whined.

"I rather think it's better this way!" Samuel retorted, wiping his mouth with a sleeve that for some reason had been giving off the smell of horseshit since Philadelphia.

John held his nose in disgust. "And that's another thing. I've been insisting that you learn to ride a horse, to straddle his back, not wipe yourself against his ass. Why on earth do you smell so sour?"

I stopped listening, for I was back on Samuel and his "rather think," a mannered expression which he had adopted for the Continental Congress; part of his campaign to enhance his overall image and quell fears he wasn't to be trusted because he didn't have "class."

"'Rather think'?" John Adams continued. "How teddibly, teddibly British of you, Samuel."

"Perish the thought!" he shouted with a scowl, brandishing

his spoon like a mace, soupy drool dribbling from the corner of his mouth.

I knew then that his era was over.

John Adams didn't stop there. "Such a scuttle rat you are! I pray, cousin, that you'd never gotten me involved in this mess. We've done a fine job stirring up the rabble now, haven't we? Suffolk Resolves, indeed. They imagine war, they do, because they imagine themselves kings! Such folderol! I don't doubt it shall be necessary to call in a military force to do that which our civil government was originally designed for. That would be, to quote that dastardly sentinel at the gate, a fine mess now, wouldn't it? An army *just* to control our own? My, my." He laughed bitterly, pushing away his untouched soup.

The plate-smashing routine, from which we'd received momentary respite, had resumed. The shattering noise too grating to bear, I climbed the stairs to see what I could do to stop it. And there he was, wigless and gaunt, coughing consumptively and rubbing his eyes.

"Mr. Hancock, are you all right?" I asked.

"Never."

Wrong question.

"Are you ill?"

"Worse than that. I'm afraid this might be farewell." (Cough, cough, hawk . . .)

"Should I run for the doctor?" I offered.

He flung a vase at me in response.

"They hate me now. The people hate me. I have to dress like a farmer to get any kind of love. What on earth did you louts do down there in Philadelphia to cause me such harm?"

"I don't think it's directed at you, sir, not in particular. I think it's those Suffolk Resolves—they seem to have aroused quite a stir."

"You wish to help, little demon? Fine, then you get your ass out onto the street and you spread the word that I'm fabulous.

Toss coins, send flowers, offer them French lessons at my expense. Make them love me again or I shall die. . . . And get those Adams cousins out of my house at once! I hate them, always have!"

I left—to spread the word, I guess, figuring at the very least there were probably a few pounds in it for me.

Just how dangerous this mission felt upon my stepping foot into the street was an indication of how much things had changed. To shout Hancock's praises would be to take my own life in my hands. This was especially surprising given the deep regard in which Hancock had been held by the masses for so many years.

So what was it, then, this new life in the street? It was the din of chatter I was so struck by when I first arrived in Boston back in '65, come of age. Yes, that's what it was. It was talk parlayed into action, chitchat into community. From "each man for himself" to pitching in with the tribe.

"It's a start," Deborah reiterated later that night at the Green Dragon.

It was half past eight that evening when a child knocked at my door. "Tonight at midnight. Knock twice on the window and whisper 'Grape,' " she advised me without so much as declaring herself, her affiliation, or her name.

But I knew instantly who she was. Not more than eight or nine, sweet face prematurely lined, front teeth chipped, riotous hair thick as puckerbrush with berries tucked inside: Clearly she was Deborah's daughter, begotten in Hutchinson's cellar in '65. I could tell from the smile. And who else but Deborah's flesh and blood would be inviting me to a "top-secret, dangerous meeting—beware!" in a party dress, a little cobalt frock to which she'd pinned what had to have been at least a hundred silk ribbons in various mismatching shades of red, white, ochre, lime, and blue. A rainbow in the flesh, come to light up the sky.

As instructed, I appeared at the Green Dragon at the appointed time and knocked on a window which had been entirely blacked out with coal dust, whispering, somewhat embarrassedly I'll admit, "Grape." (How on earth did they come up with that for a secret code?)

The first thing that struck me when I saw Deborah was not her glowing green eyes, but the fact that she was sitting where Samuel Adams once had sat, back in '65, when the Dragon had led me down the stairs and into this chamber. And at her side— not Hancock, of course—instead was Job, a black man, who I could tell from the scraping, suspicious way he met all eyes was obviously a fugitive slave.

To Job's left were what looked like three Mashpee Indians, nicknamed Max, Joe, and Tan. And then seven white men: a distiller, a smith, two farmers, a barber, two dockworkers. Several women were also in company: a black nursing a child, an indentured adolescent who stunk of the gutter, and a dotty old dame muttering to herself "Someday—no, now!"

At the opposite end of the table . . . yes, that was indeed a British soldier. A deserter he had to be, with his arm about a drunken punk I'd met before, a farmer named Dawes.

And at the hearth, children making bullets, among them Deborah's daughter, her pretty dress already black as pitch. "Hey, you there, glad you could come, I'm Alice!" she said (the only one so far to have acknowledged my entrance) with an excited air that promised soon there'd be gifts, cakes, and lemonade.

The smoky chamber, in stark contrast to the vulgar morbidity I'd witnessed there in '65, seemed absolutely buzzing with happy, hot-blooded signs of life.

Indeed, in the weeks ahead it would seem as though the pulse of Deborah's meetings increased in inverse proportion to the Provincial Congress' decreasing power, vitality, and nerve. As her secret plans for war advanced, the more it seemed that the Provincial Congress dithered.

Oh, there was some pale talk in sessions about raising an army: yes, but then no. Endless discussion of how Boston must at all costs avoid alienating the other colonies by keeping on her best behavior. Lots of rhetoric about minimizing hostile exchanges with England in the press and keeping threats of war exclusively defensive in nature so as to avoid censure by Parliament (don't want that, no, God forbid we be censured by a country on which for all practical purposes we'd just declared war).

War? Now, when *that* subject came up there was admittedly some activity generated or, rather, a congressional semblance of action: the setting up of task forces to investigate the possibilities, assess the ramifications of war. A seemingly limitless number of committees were devoted to exploring every possible angle on the subject, except one devoted to actually making it happen.

One committee was appointed to nominate delegates to the Second Continental Congress coming up in May, even though everyone knew full well who the delegates would be—the same four plus Hancock. Another committee was charged to devise means to pay the delegates, and still another was charged solely with coming up with ways to reimburse a certain delegate who had accidentally "lost" the equivalent of forty-six pounds from his pocket en route to Philadelphia for the last powwow.

Ironically enough, the *only* evidence of life on the congressional floor during this period was Dr. Church, the undercover British spy who, to put everyone off his scent, was consistently and enthusiastically urging war. And, of course, Dr. Warren wanted war too, but everyone knew what his dream really was: an army to call his own.

But by far the most pressing issue of concern to the Provincial Congress was that of its own absenteeism. Nobody who was anybody showed, and those who did spent a good chunk of their time catching up on their sleep—a disastrous situation that left Samuel Adams wondering aloud "why the epidemic of bowel disorders, agues, rheums that seem to have hit Congress are confined exclusively to those of the Gentlemen [congressional] class."

Of course, John Hancock, his excuse still being his proximity to death, never showed up at the Provincial assembly at all. Or, for that matter, his scheduled French lessons with me ("How dare you ask a dying man to conjugate?"). Instead, he paid me handsomely to attend the few congressional sessions in his stead, my task being to note, track, and report back on any activity perceived as potentially threatening to Hancock's leadership and fast-disappearing influence ("in the unlikely event" of Hancock's survival, of course).

These days, however, mostly what interested Hancock were my daily reports chronicling my vast and far-reaching search to procure him smoked salmon (a rare commodity those days), which he'd decided was "just the cure" for what was ailing him. "I'll pay anything, even for just one little taste. A mere crumb will suffice to put off the Reaper, of this I'm sure!"

There were no ague or rheum or do-nothing committees or napping attendees at the Green Dragon. That much was clear to me from the start, that very first night.

Again, as in '65, there was a map spanning the oaken table, only instead of Boston it was of Massachusetts entire, with a single pin inserted into the town of Concord (famous for its hybrid "grape"—hence the code word).

Deborah introduced me. "Patriots, allow me to introduce John." She stood to greet me, casting her shadow across the large map. "He will be helping supply us with guns."

What?

The group applauded and raised their mugs to me in a toast. "Here, here!"

Deborah continued: "John has just the access we need. And the influence. Anything you might be wanting in your towns—necessities like powder, brimstone, beans, molasses, tents, and the like—he can get it."

"I—I think you're mistaken. . . ."

Ignoring my hesitation, she cut right to the quick. "John, here's what you do. . . ."

She outlined a step-by-step scenario for all to hear. It was her plan to raise an army—or, rather, the guns for one—which she knew full well she couldn't procure without "congressional aid," which would come down, as all things would with Deborah, not to working with policy or tools of argument or idle threats, but to trafficking in what she, as a whore at the margins of life, understood best: a man's heart, cock, and ambition confused with need.

She was looking to me to throw a party for Congress. A rather fancy soiree to which she'd be invited. "Just get it all going, Johnny, and I'll take things from there."

Fine. Consider it done. Why the hell not?

CHAPTER 19

To Arms

Oh, it was glorious. A chilly February night, 1775. I'd pulled off the party Deborah wanted and was eagerly awaiting her arrival.

It had been touch-and-go there for a while, as Deborah had absolutely insisted that Dr. Joseph Warren be there. But Hancock, the one I'd gotten to finance the party, hated him to such a degree that he made me promise that Warren would be excluded from the guest list—a condition requiring proof of execution before a single disbursement was made. This after three grueling weeks of bringing him around to the idea of throwing a party for the Provincial Congress at all.

"I still don't understand what there is in it for me." I had to pitch it to him as an opportunity for Hancock to regain his "fast-fading prestige." I insisted that Warren, in his sponsorship of the Suffolk Resolves and his recent advocacy of war, was set to steal Hancock's thunder. Hancock could one-up Warren, I suggested, not only by coming out plainly in favor of the increasingly popular position of mounting an army (never mind that privately he detested the whole idea) but by intimating that he just might be open to financing it. Since the raising of an army was probably inevitable anyway, why not be its most aggressive advocate and thereby increase chances astronomically of one day being appointed commander-in-chief?

Me: "You'd look so nice in epaulets."

Hancock, blushing: "You think?"

So the cash flowed forth. Even as Hancock was in secret conversations with Gage regarding a lucrative contract to build barracks for British troops, he agreed to host the party to muster support in the Provincial Congress for an American army and the institution of a draft. As a member of the Committee of Safety (whose meetings he never attended), Hancock ostensibly had influence in such matters, so he didn't think it'd be hard to get Congress to play along—especially if he first got the delegates good and drunk on the imported black market distilleds they shouldn't be drinking. Damn the blockade . . . sign them up! Finally, it seemed we'd come full circle, with Hancock testing some of his Stamp Act techniques on his own.

And as to the stipulation of snubbing Warren . . . not to worry. The night of his own party, Hancock pleaded cramps (or was it a distended belly?) and never showed.

By the time Hancock realized that Warren had been in attendance (if ever), Deborah's plan would already be well under way.

It had been an unusually arduous day for the Provincial Congress, engaged as they'd been in vigorous debate over a particularly pressing sartorial concern that, due to a lucky eleventh-hour streak of bipartisanship, had been settled to everyone's content. Resolved, "that in consideration of the season, and that the Congress sit in a room without a fire, all members who wish to do so may henceforth sit with their hats on while Congress is in session." Needless to say, in the wake of such grueling legislative exercises, the delegates were more than ready for a stiff drink.

He was a very good man, Dr. Warren was, kind to the indigent and diseased and, generally speaking, understanding of those who couldn't pay. His interest in raising an army, however, didn't come from this generous place, nor did his messianic dream of heading a mighty nation capable of fighting "fire with fire!," bathing in blood if that's what Destiny required. A loose confederation of states, democratic and plain, was not exactly what the visionary Dr. Warren had in mind.

In Hancock's absence at the party, of course, Warren seized the moment for himself early in the evening, working the floor, aiming to convince these wary men of the need to raise an army which would enhance and exceed the capacity and skill of the local militias. And to drink more. To blood. To Destiny.

I had been instructed to wait out back with the servants until Deborah arrived. To pass the time, I took to teaching them how to pronounce "hors d'oeuvres."

An hour of "whoredoovers" later, she finally showed up, as she promised she would, on Benjamin Church's arm, with dried marigolds in her hair, a lavender silk dress, a chiffon fichu, and delicate pearls emphasizing a *poitrine plus belle*: much more than I could have imagined. My Lord, could all that cleavage possibly be real? (It wasn't.) She really didn't have the "gracious lady" act down quite as well as some other identities of hers I had seen: Her feet protruded awkwardly out to the side from under the dress; her fan, which she brandished like a loaded gun, should have been left home; and the marigolds flaked.

But those tits . . . in a roomful of men. What a way to start a war.

Things happened so fast that it wasn't until later that night at the Green Dragon, while watching a noticeably energized Deborah still bedecked in her ball gown rattle off assignments new in focus and intent, that I realized we must have succeeded in what she had set out to do.

There was even a post-party addition to the group tonight. My old protector back in '65 who'd stopped Samuel Adams from strangling me: the fair-skinned, plump silversmith-turned-courier—the saucy but dignified "mechanic," Paul Revere.

Deborah introduced him as "one of us," someone they "should grow to trust," who would serve as liaison between "us and them," "them" being Congress by way of Warren, she explained.

So yes, I was right—something definitive had occurred on the party floor.

"Now it's just a matter of keeping their feet to the fire," she explained, "and we'll have all the guns we need."

Thanking me for the party—"planned to perfection," she claimed—she assigned me to a committee of fourteen whose job it was to get Warren whatever he needed to begin building an army, specifically information regarding British intentions that would keep Congress good and scared enough to comply with Warren's wishes.

By the end of the party, she had managed to win over Warren utterly to her Cause. How? She claimed it was simple: because Warren knew . . . that Church knew . . . that Deborah knew . . . that even Gage knew . . . that raising an American army was for each in different ways a good thing and that it would be best for them to work together rather than apart.

But since this explanation clearly was wanting, I concentrated good and hard and reviewed in my head the party as it had unfolded, detail for detail . . . one more time.

First, Church shows up, toting Deborah on his arm, who looks stunning, albeit disproportionately buxom. Warren, who has taken over as host for the party in Hancock's opportune absence, is only too happy to see Church, as he regards him as a strategic ally in the effort to encourage congressional support for a war.

Never mind that Church is a spy—Warren doesn't know that, although he's about to find out.

Church congratulates Warren for organizing this event and asks where Hancock is. Both men simultaneously intone, "Ill!" then chuckle. They then speculate as to what might happen should Hancock ever truly develop as much as a cold: "He'd be convinced he had passed on, and that the image left standing belonged to a ghost!"

Church and Warren, chatting like fast friends, move across the floor. Although it is chilly outside, Deborah heads toward the door to the courtyard, en route "accidentally" brushing Warren with her spectacular bosom, and continues on without looking back. Warren, after a too-short-to-be-discreet pause, sneaks out in hot pursuit.

Deborah passes through the garden. Old fallen leaves, still loose about the icy earth, scatter as she walks deep into the woods, her tread forming a footpath easy for Warren, who is by now practically hyperventilating, to follow.

Once in the forest, Deborah weaves through boulder and pine, ostensibly in search of a place to hide. Finding cover in a generous, preselected bower of Norwegian evergreen, she pulls from her bosom a pen and pad and begins scribbling, dictating as she writes, talking much more loudly than a spy ever should or would, with an air of desperation, as if she were loath to forget a single word.

Warren slows his chase and listens, without yet revealing his presence. He hears her utter a full account of everything he and Church have said thus far at the party, as well as bits of conversations Deborah has picked up from miscellaneous delegates who, deep in their cups, were talking of war. She leaves no detail out or unremarked—even the trifle ("too sweet") is given mention and so too her fears "that the ruse Church and I are contriving might be too hard-pushed," to wit: too clear. That she might, in order to remain useful to the king, from this point on lay low.

Her idea of "fancy lady" talk is, like the choice of the marigolds, also a bit crude, but Warren is much too stimulated—first below the waist, then above his reddening ears—to notice or care, once he has caught the intended import of her speech.

Even as he jumps out from behind the tree where he has been hiding, I can see from where I'm watching behind a holly bush that he is much more in lust than enraged.

Still, even with his tight breeches nearly bursting, he does an admirable job of seizing the offending paper and giving it a quick read. "Explain yourself, woman!" he demands, with an iron grip on her arm. Whereupon Deborah promptly bursts into tears and begs Warren please to let her go.

Upon her life, she belongs to the Patriots' side and is doing what she must to survive, adding that she could be of greater use to The Cause not dead but alive—for Church could take her life long before the legislature could have laws sufficient to prosecute and punish her as a spy.

The bet she's making, of course, is twofold. She wagers that revealing herself as a spy to Warren will amount to nothing because there is absolutely no provision in the law yet for spies that are ostensibly working for the Mother Country, of which we are still very much a part. The idea of a spy for Britain who isn't also a spy for the colonies isn't even a tangible concept in most people's minds. In a court of law Deborah would be a friend of the state, not a foe—it is Warren who would be the traitor if he made a stir, thereby revealing his own sympathies to the authorities. Oh, boy.

So please, she entreats Warren (tugging at her fichu, and not unintentionally uncovering a bit more of that bosom), for the good of the new country, reveal her not, seek not to punish her but, instead, designate an arrangement by which she will be only too happy to oblige him.

Something like that. You get the gist. She's offering herself to him as a double agent and . . . ?

Deborah has Warren right where she wants him. So he is just

plain stuck with information about which he can do nothing—except, perhaps, seek out a Son of Liberty to do her in. She also confidently wagers that the mesmerizing sight of her bosom, emerging in the moonlight from the splayed fichu, is insurance enough to prevent such ungentlemanly action by Warren.

It works. If the Provincial Congress can't yet be counted on for an army, it certainly can't be counted on for new laws, much less a law that defines a spy for England as an enemy of the Massachusetts colony or the not-quite-extant American republic.

Oh, Deborah lays it on thick. "Please, sir, let me do for you better than I do for Church, better even than for Gage! Let me help you raise an army—by giving you access to all of Gage's planned retributions and military strategies intended to subdue The Cause! Let us, together then, scare Congress into raising an army and into rousing this dear fledgling nation to fight."

Warren is no fool. All that and a shot at what lies between her legs—she is unquestionably an expert at "raising" and "rousing" of all sorts. "Woman, say no more."

Warren marches himself right back into the pavilion and takes Church to one side. . . .

If he, Warren, were to "accidentally" come across "secret" information about Gage's stores, revealing British military preparations, threatening and vast, Congress would have no choice but to mount a defense . . . and wouldn't Church agree that Warren had this right?

Church, who should have been the enemy, was now the friend. Oh, this business of Revolution, would the twisting and turning of opposites never end? Not until the categories were viewed differently or were to change, no, they would not.

Although initially he was startled by Warren's blunt question, the plan was also perfect for Church. Which, incidentally, is what made it perfect for Deborah . . . and then, in its turn, also suited the Revolution.

Church himself needed a steady flow of information from the

Rebel side in order to keep his job—and to keep construction going on the palatial estate outside Boston that he (a poet, an execrable poet) was building with fees extorted from the king.

So the information would flow, via Deborah, from Church to Warren to Congress and to The Cause of Revolution . . . which is what Warren and Church and all the rest would never, ever know.

The plan was indeed remarkable in its breadth and scope. Even easy, or at least fun for all involved. All Warren had to do was fuck Deborah, keep that a secret from Church, keep Church's duplicity a secret from our side, help Church maintain credibility on their side by feeding him whatever it took to get what Warren needed from Church in turn for our side: secrets juicy enough to get Congress to scare up at least an army, if not a war.

And in the middle of it all: Deborah, a woman, secure in the shadow job of running, storing, and distributing all those guns for which Congress would almost instantaneously begin allocating funds.

From top to bottom, wholly her idea. Sure, the Founding Fathers were making it all happen, cluelessly—and with Deborah and her kind as their puppeteers.

CHAPTER 20

To War

ithin a week of Hancock's party Deborah had ordered Max, the Mashpee Indian, to raid British military stores in Boston via rarely trod footpaths and
convey the plunder out of town.

Two nights later, she commanded Dawes and me to haul field
pieces away, urging us to take the route through the Neck, insisting we'd not be stopped by Gage's guard.

We weren't; the next day six hundred pounds of cannon were
allowed to roll lazily out of town directly past the checkpoint, totally unmolested ("Let them pass!").

According to History, Gage was flabbergasted . . . outdone
once again by the too-clever Yanks. Bah! Gage was daft but not
dead; his men bumbling, not blind. Gage was *letting* us steal that
cannon (directly off the Common in broad daylight, to boot) and
that's all there is to say about that.

So how did History come to think Gage had been played for a

fool? By basing its analysis, as it always does, on so-called "facts." Hard, verifiable data, not stories, where the stuff of life resides.

Yes, I too read the raging letter Gage wrote to Parliament expressing his shock and dismay over the theft of the cannon (thanks to the Church-Deborah-Warren underground, the letter was intercepted), and thanks to my experience with Deborah, I had learned by now not to take documents like this at face value. Instead, as Deborah would advise, I probed to "find the story going on."

Gage *wanted* us to steal the cannon so he could hold out its theft as yet another "debacle" that might have been avoided if England only paid the colonial situation more mind. Send more of everything—arms, men, money—or face ruin, is the message he wished to send.

But even here, in his increasingly desperate demands for help, Gage was easily as disingenuous as his Founding Father counterparts. Since he knew that British attention would not be forthcoming anytime soon (and in any event could be counted on to be insufficient to his needs), he wanted his complaint on record in case he needed an excuse for not doing more than he had ("I was without capacity to fight"). And if and when he did act, he must be able to blame the British ministry for what he knew would most likely be defeat ("I was without capacity for victory").

All of which was simple cover for the fact that Gage had no desire whatsoever to engage "this pretty country" in a godforsaken war ("Can't King George just let bygones be bygones and send the troops home? Without their commander, of course, as I quite like it here!").

History views the cannon theft event as but one incidental, barely noteworthy step in the escalating war with England, or usually does not mention it at all. This is one of the best examples there are of History's flawed judgment at work, due entirely to the misguided belief that its characters behave not as people but as historical figures, allegiances to respective countries and causes always primary and intact. In fact, the cannon episode was a major turning point toward war, not for its practical, obvious results (it did indeed inflame England further), but for the human stories it set inexorably into motion. And for what it did for The Cause. Well, to perceive that, one must ignore History entirely and look directly to the men and women at hand.

I know Church had to have been delighted, because any gutsy moves on the part of the Rebels translated into more anxiety on the English side, which translated into higher fees for his services and greater job security—good for us, as we needed to keep him around.

As for Warren, anything that vexed Gage (or had Gage feigning vexation) was fine by him, for Gage's ire always translated into another military exercise or parade that History would regard as threatening to Americans, which would in turn have Warren jumping up and down in delight, since any aggressive action by Gage served his personal campaign to keep Congress "thinking army."

"Gage means to do something soon! Evident it is in his military moves! Order up more guns! Organize the militia into a fighting force! Replace the local militia leaders with those sympathetic to the emerging Cause! Be brave! Be prepared! England means to have a war!" etc.

From that point on, I have to admit, things became rather fun. Church would sit in Congress and take notes for Gage. To keep Church's identity a secret in the event of interception, I would translate these notes into French poorer than my own. And, of course, even I, being human, couldn't resist a little embellishment, a little poetic gratification now and again. It's just that everything sounded so harmless in French, I found myself pushing a bit more than perhaps I should in order to ensure the desired effect.

In a letter on March 30, 1775, I wrote (in French), "The Congress have been all this Week employed in adapting the Articles of War and the regulations of the Army to their Militia. Many of the articles they have adopted entire! Several grand debates have arisen in this Committee such as fixing a Criterion for assembling the militia together. . . ."

I left out that whatever resolve there was, was piddling, and that by the end of this session any hope Warren had of getting a full-scale army ready for action had been virtually destroyed. In truth, the "grand debates" that had occurred that day were precisely about the issue of what would constitute a threat from England, with the general opinion being "nothing short of an active and self-evident military exercise," defined by Congress as one "including baggage and artillery" and to which any countermoves on our part would still only remain "at all costs, purely defensive in nature." After which, Congress adjourned.

Church wrote it all down, but we both figured there'd be no purpose served in the British knowing all that.

Warren was miffed at the Provincial Congress that day, depressed about his progress. Unjustifiably, I thought, because in fact, in just a few months, the path to war had been well laid. An elaborate alarm system, consisting of express riders triggered by word of mouth, lanterns, and church bells had been designed by Warren, Revere, and Deborah to warn the entire colony/state and beyond, in the event of a military maneuver by Gage. Although it was stressed over and over again (even by Warren) that any action, once taken, must be carefully planned and might never be "the spontaneous efforts of unorganized farmers," Deborah was essentially doing what she wanted, salting away weapons. She knew full well that once the weapons were stored (and their whereabouts *made known* to the British via the communication underground, so as to direct Gage to Concord, where she knew he could be beat), Gage would have no choice, as much as she knew he hated to do it, but to launch an assault.

Guns, powder, brimstone, beans, molasses, tents, and the like, plus cannonballs and artillery, all had been raised and stowed by

the time the Provincial Congress disbanded—enough for supplying an army of fifteen thousand men, "just in case a defensive war
were to ignite."

It was not as though the Provincial Congress was altogether in
the dark, you see, regarding Revolutionary intentions like those
of Deborah's gang. This was one of the reasons congressional support always came with the caveat that Warren's committee was to
keep tight control of all weapons at all times. Supposedly this was
to keep them from the British, but those living history, not writing History, understood the situation to be a tad more complex.

It was further advised that the location of these stores should
be known only to a few. Militia Captain William Heath, Joseph
Warren, and, if you can believe it, even Benjamin Church were
specifically named (which, of course, meant Deborah, John
Lawrence, and the entire Massachusetts countryside too).

Oh, weren't we just going to town!

*A Concord, il y a pour le moins Sept Tonnes de poudre a feu. Il y
a aussi dans la même Village . . . une quantite de poudre, des Balles,
des Fusils et des bayonets*, I wrote from Church to Gage on April 3.

I admit to having no idea whatsoever how much "seven tons
of powder" was, that I was laying it on a little thick—by a factor
of seven, I later learned. But still, my gross exaggeration seemed
to yield results, for Gage, who certainly must have known better
but didn't dare do nothing, shortly thereafter stepped up military
exercises all the more. Encouraged, in the next installment I
pushed the estimations even higher, reporting a full fifteen tons
from Worcester, just for kicks.

And that was the last straw.

CHAPTER 21

Planting Guns

Clearly word had gotten around that there was to be war. Normally, all night long, this being planting time, the road to Concord would have been clogged with oxen bound for market, peddlers, farmers with produce and jam, and laborers searching for work to carry them through until the coming harvest. But tonight, midnight, April 17, 1775, the road was overrun with farmers toting not food, but pounds and pounds of musket balls and cartridges, cartridge paper, loads of tents, pickaxes, spades, hatchets, wheelbarrows—a trail of carts twenty to thirty long loaded with ordnance and covered with dung (to conceal the contents). The smell—shit and sulfur—was rank, yes, but enlivening. Many a farm field was seeded with oiled metal, black flint, and powder that come summer would yield not crops, but guns.

The branches of the trees on either side of the road—tall, white pine, maple, and elm—had entwined over time, forming a kind of roof, filtering the light of the moon and showering the faces, the carts, the weapons, and my cannon (yes, another one stolen from the Common) with shards of white light. From high above, I'm sure we looked like moving stars, a new, earthbound constellation: Minnows Swimming Upstream.

Concord was the perfect spot to launch the Revolution and I was certain Deborah had decided to stockpile arms there not only because it was situated at a crossroads between two protective ranges of hills with vantage points to spot invaders as far as two miles away. But also, it was beautiful: rich soil, glacial rock, brisk streams.

I had sensed beforehand that Concord—like Mesopotamia, Egypt, Greece, and Byzantium before it, fertile river valleys all—had it in her to foster civilization anew. For here, it was said, people and seasons and life were all one. The preponderance of Concord citizens were Sagittarians, conceived during planting time, born around Christmas, most likely to die in the dead of winter. Sagittarius: the sign of fire, of war, engaging every generation of Yankee here since 1630, from Indian ambushes to innumerable expeditions to Canada against the French. And now, the Revolution.

Spring it may have been elsewhere, but not so in Concord, where the only season now acknowledged, in the words of the Reverend William Emerson himself, was "the season for wartime preparations"—the season for planting guns. Warmer than usual.

The Charles never froze that year, and the temperature, for the first time in recorded history, never saw freezing, not once.

As we trudged into Lexington, en route to Concord (ten miles farther up the road), two hundred farmers, a six-pound cannon, and I were directed to the center of the town green by the same kindly Reverend Emerson. There townsfolk had gathered amid tootling fifes and rolling drums to applaud the arrival of this latest weapons cache.

The ladies as well as the men carried guns.

The supplies were immediately commandeered, taken to locations organized by Deborah and the committee of fourteen. Gunpowder was carted to silos, farmers with ox teams dragged the cannon to common land and hid it in a huge hole, sacks of saltpeter were concealed in gristmills, and guns were stuffed into hay or buried in furrowed fields between plantings of corn.

Under the protective cover of night Minutemen, the youngest and strongest of militia boys trained to be called out on a minute's notice, presented arms on the green under the command of Colonel Barrett, an old-time citizen whom everybody knew. Most of the militia, numbering some 265, knew each other well, coming as they did from not more than fifteen different local families. And indeed, there on the lawn, marching proudly in their homespun breeches and hunting jackets, they looked more like a family reunion than a drilling army.

Deborah winked at me from the line's left flank. On the field she was a man named Buttrick, presenting arms and marching to the drum. And to Buttrick's right and front was his "son," Robert, a.k.a. Alice, as a drummer boy.

"War's here," Buttrick/Deborah said. "Just a matter of hours."

"Not if Congress has anything to do with it," I retorted, because I was getting the picture.

She shot me a look. "They don't. You do."

Uh-oh.

"Just make sure Gage gets here. Enough of the letters. Enough of collecting guns. This is where it begins. Here and now. We're ready. We'll be here. And we'll wait. On you."

It was as if she'd just asked me to fetch her an apple or some other trifle.

"It'll have a life of its own," she continued. "We just need to make sure it happens, that Gage gets his men under way to Concord by the full moon, tomorrow night, April the eighteenth. Not before. Not after. Just then."

"Oh." I grunted. What else could I say?

A voice came from within the line: "Later, I'll tell you *how*—you'll be at Buckman Tavern, no?"

It was Alice—excuse me, Robert—who, in drummer-boy blues, a too-large liberty cap falling into her eyes and her face smeared with powder from a busted cartridge, looked like she should have been toting not a drum and a gun but string and a ball. Turning this little girl into a boy soldier, I thought . . . well, this was all just one step too far.

I shooed Robert/Alice away like a fly, and he/she didn't like that one bit. "Is it a date?" he/she commanded, stomping his/her tiny foot.

Well, didn't I find myself agreeing to meet this little girl less than half my age well past her bedtime—and mine—at two o'clock A.M. "Sorry I can't do it any earlier," she apologized. "Way too much to do. In fact, you'll forgive me in advance if I'm a little late."

She smiled, knowing full well I couldn't help but take pleasure in her precociousness, and I was as good as there.

To think that History regards Lexington and Concord as a spontaneous uprising of farmers in revolt against taxes. That's like saying a bird learns instantly how to fly for no compelling reason, rather than what actually occurs. An instinct for survival, generations old, pressing at and preparing the baby chick for this moment since birth, pushes her from her nest. Preordained. Just a matter of time.

At Reverend Clarke's invitation, Hancock and Samuel Adams had been "lodging" (hiding out) for some time at the Clarke parsonage in Lexington, just south of Concord, because Boston had become "too dangerous" for them—there was a royal warrant out for their arrests. This wound up being wonderful for The Cause because John Hancock, even as a fugitive, wanted what he wanted when he wanted it (usually *now!*). So I was given a perfect excuse to be in Concord to keep track of weapons depots for Gage via Deborah via Church (the goal being eventually to force Gage to action), while also collecting a paycheck from Hancock ("Here's the fine hose you requested, sir, and your sterling eyebrow tweezer, too"). Not to mention the clever hiding places it afforded me for the few messages it was decided could not be intercepted.

I had big news on this day. After six months of looking, I had finally found Hancock his precious smoked salmon (a little dirty, as I'd stowed it inside the stolen cannon's bore, knowing full well there was a greater chance of this delicacy being confiscated than the big gun itself), even though—for credibility's sake—he'd long since stopped claiming his life depended on the salty fish. Lately the perfect antidote to death were luscious, ripe, red, off-season strawberries.

I had also managed to sneak out of Boston his massive, god-forsaken wooden trunk which he held so dear, filled with mysterious items he swore the world would never see (heavy as cannonballs, but most likely the contents were personal effects such as books, letters, and jewels—I can't believe I never peeked).

"So where is the trunk?" he asked, clearly aroused.

"Safe with me in my room at the inn," I replied. It was thanks to Hancock's purse that I was "stored" (his word, not mine) at Buckman's Tavern whenever he "needed" me to be in town.

I tried to share with him how truly challenging it had been to lug the trunk up the inn stairs, but he didn't care to listen; he was cross-eyed with distracted pleasure over his smoked fish.

The country on the brink of war and there they were: the militia drilling just down the street, Hancock, Adams, and their entourage, gorging on cod and oyster pie, fresh hot biscuits, and buttered squash. And, for their amusement, a game: truth or dare. Will you run—the truth now!—if Gage or any of his troops come to Lexington? Answer: Faster than you can say "Tax!"

Hancock's ladies too had fled Boston: his fiancée, Dolly Quincy, and his hideous Aunt Lydia, both of whom he hated and was forced to pander to, the latter because he owed his fortune to her now-deceased husband, and the former because the latter loved Dolly and thought she was "plumb perfect" for John.

Tonight, drunk and clearly obsessed with the fact that Hancock was still not married, Aunt Lydia was practically shoving Dolly into her nephew's lap, insisting he "take a good, hard look and marry her now!" What cataract-plagued Lydia didn't realize—plain as the mole on her crooked nose—was that the last thing to inspire a proposal would be Dolly's looks.

It took till pudding, but finally Hancock did, in fact, touch Dolly, his velvet cuff brushing her lace sleeve. Aunt Lydia, breaking into an instant sweat, screamed "Thank God!" before reluctantly fleeing the scene, Bible in tow, to beg forgiveness from the Lord for having cursed.

In response to my soft query, "Uhm, well, does anyone think there might be war?" the remaining women looked at me as though I had just relieved myself on the table. Samuel Adams, from whom so far I'd heard little but those unimproved slurping sounds, wasn't much happier. Only Hancock, eager as he was to get Dolly the hell off his lap, responded enthusiastically, reaching for his rifle and swearing he'd start polishing it and *"toute suite"* (in captivity I guess he'd caught up on some French).

"Someday we'll have an army. Congress is just about there," Hancock cooed confidently, rubbing his gun, which was stashed taut between his legs. "And I will run it."

"Run *from* it, more likely," I said to myself, perhaps even audibly (I couldn't help it), but no one seemed to hear.

I figured out that, despite what the characters in this room thought, should Gage actually come to Lexington to arrest Hancock and Adams as rumored, he would be indulging in a pointless exercise. For Gage had no better understanding of "popular rebellion" than Hancock and Adams did. Otherwise, Gage would have realized that the removal of Hancock and Adams would have little or no effect on the real business of Revolution.

To Gage, as with the Founding Fathers, this conflict always would be, first and foremost, a gentlemen's pissing contest.

Which is where I would come in: by getting Gage to commit, not to a mere police action or to a raid to arrest Rebel ringleaders, but to a war.

"And how on earth do you expect me to do this?" I asked, seeking the counsel of the nine-year-old girl come traipsing into my room, bright-eyed and bushy-tailed, half an hour late at two-thirty A.M.

She was situated smack-dab on Hancock's trunk, which once and for all I would have opened had she not helped herself to it as a chair.

"Fancy pants," she called me, repeating the words over and over again only because the sound of it made her laugh. "Fancy pants, fancy pants," she sang to a little dance which mostly involved sticking her buttocks out and shaking them as vigorously as she could while also talking "business."

"Mum says we can't rely on Gage's stupidity or even his nerve to get him to Concord. She needs us to make sure he sticks to the plan."

So Gage needed our help in mounting a siege against us. Would the illogic of Revolution never cease?

No. Illogic being a way to the heart, it was precisely to the point.

This is why Alice could act as if what she was explaining to me were perfectly sane. "All you'll need to do is make certain he comes, by the night of the eighteenth."

"And once I've done that?" I asked incredulously.

"We win. *Ta-da!*" And with that she resumed her little fanny dance, this time punctuated by a practice drill. "Poise your firelocks! Cock your firelocks! Present! Fire!"

"Listen to me, little one. Whatever it is you've been told to ask me to do, forget about it. I can't do it." I was losing my nerve.

I meant it as a refusal, but she took it as a sign of my lack of self-confidence.

"Mum and I know you can," she said softly, as reassuringly as a nine-year-old could.

"I'll be needing air," I insisted, as I stormed out of the room, bounding down the stairs to get away . . . only to run into "Buttrick" downstairs, poring over a map with her fellow militiamen and discussing—what else?—preparations for Gage's arrival in Lexington the day after tomorrow. That exact. That precise.

And from the top of the stairs came Alice's confident response: "I'll wait here. I've got all night."

Deborah summoned me to the bar. "Revere and Warren have worked out a warning. He'll just need to be told whether it'll be by land or by sea that Gage will come. Got that?"

I said, "Uh-huh," recognizing that in so doing I was committing myself, if only because I couldn't say no. And if that sounds unheroic, then so be it: Remember, I'm not a historical figure, only a man.

As I was packing for my journey back to Boston, sweet "Robert," tiny nipples trussed, hair shorn, watched me like a hawk to make sure I didn't "go chicken" for as long as she could.

Even generals need their rest, I suppose. For as I prepared to leave I noticed she'd finally surrendered to sleep, curled and twitching atop the trunk, clutching her gun and her drum.

Still just a child, I thought. A child with a club fist. A child marked for squalor and rejection and early death, whose best hope had been and always would be her mother's legacy: the capacity to dream, which she would live on for as long as she could.

And in that twisted fist of hers, I saw a note clearly intended for me, albeit crumpled and smeared with blueberry jam and bits of chocolate. On it were written details of my mission, and directions which Alice, still being a child, had just plain forgotten to share.

Clearly written by Deborah, it read:

> My dear John,
>
> The address is Province House, King Street. Throw pebbles up to the window first. Afterward, talk to anyone—WORD WILL GET OUT and we'll take over from there.
>
> > Yours, Deborah
>
> P.S. This is it—the Big Bang!

She had written My dear John.

Kissing Alice on the cheek, I tiptoed out.

I checked the note yet again. Yes, there it was, in her scrawl: My dear John.

Once outside, I took a look through the window at Buttrick, still hard at work with her men, slugging ale and chomping on bread. I wondered if her comrades knew she was a woman, or if they even cared.

In this moment, her commitment seemed so staggering to me it brought water to my eyes.

"My dear Deborah, I shall carry on. . . ."

CHAPTER 22

The Big Bang

She had big tits and wanted me from the moment she laid
eyes on me.

On the night of the eighteenth I threw rocks at the window, as recommended, all the while terrified out of my mind because, yes, this was Province House, General Gage's mansion and headquarters, where he and his aides and his wife—the powder-white slut at the window—lived, slept, and worked.

Gage was out, presumably plotting Hancock's arrest. His wife had me brought in directly through the front door and mounted me almost instantly.

Having stripped off my breeches like an expert, she grabbed my cock and yanked it to her bosom, where it lay soft at first, between her breasts. She groaned with pleasure and asked me to suck the breast on my left (not her left). I did as told. It tasted of powder. Really not that bad.

She was almost instantly made jollier, and as she moved my

lips from her right breast to her navel and, ultimately, her pussy, she started to speak, blunt and to the point.

"Ooh! He'll be crossing the Charles, heading for Concord tonight—aaah . . ." And she seized my cock again.

"Not quite what I had in mind," she complained, having a look at my appendage, "but it'll do." And she stroked it like a fusil, priming it for insertion.

I came as it was going in, but, thank God, she did too. At which point she shoved me out of her self and tossed me to the side.

"That was lovely. Now go."

So there it was. I had lost my virginity to the honorable, venerated, and allegedly demure Margaret Gage. So was she a Patriot? Was she a spy? Was she one for the Rebels? Or just a horny dame who spilled state secrets for a good fuck (or in this case, a terrible one)?

I hadn't a clue, and didn't much care. But one thing for sure: Mrs. Gage's motivation didn't seem any more venal or selfish than anyone else's I'd run up against since this business of Revolution began and certainly it wasn't mean-spirited. Unless you consider betraying her husband and her king not a nice thing.

From entry to entry, exit to exit, a full five minutes had elapsed and I was back in the street. And that includes two of those minutes spent climbing the stairs up and then down, each way.

So all in all, I have to say my first experience with intercourse was rather dull, a thin sandwich compared to the feast I could conjure with my own hand. Certainly the earth never moved, the room didn't spin, and ejaculation, the reputed high point, was a most definite low. (The memory of her chortle—"Oh, to eat you with a spoon!"—upset me for years.)

Gratified nonetheless to have successfully(?) executed step one, I referred again to my note for guidance: *Talk to anyone . . . and we'll take over from there.*

Talk to ANYONE . . . The implication of this directive, on the face of it thoroughly preposterous, had me thinking for the first time that maybe Deborah was just out of her mind and I was nothing but a character suckered into a particularly captivating hallucination of hers. The moment of weakness was short-lived, however, for as soon as I did exactly as bidden, approaching the first stableboy I met with my top-secret news, all of Boston began to turn.

"To Concord. Tonight. It'll be tomorrow then," I said, just like that.

I thought sure the stableboy, clearly German, considered me a vagrant (*"Raus!"* he had threatened, pushing me aside) and either didn't understand English or was feigning ignorance of the language in order to deflect what he mistook as a request for cash.

So I approached a street urchin: "Gage is going to Concord. Tonight. Tomorrow then."

"Piss off, fuckface!" this one shrieked, shoving me to the ground.

Not to worry. My friend the German, as things turned out, had the situation entirely under control.

Ten-ten P.M. Suddenly the church bells, off-hour, began to toll.

Ten-fifteen. The German stableboy got to Revere, but Revere, having already been notified three times over (didn't word travel fast!) by various men and women on the street, was by this point well on his way to the Charles River to cross into the countryside and give alarm. His mission, as he understood it, was to rouse the militia to secure the safety of Hancock and Adams, whose arrest and hanging were still believed to be Gage's goal.

Gage, of course, had no such extreme plans. But the news of the Redcoats coming by sea was nonetheless key, for it enabled the people to prepare, to begin to set things into motion, according to plan.

The Minutemen in Lexington gathered in Buckman Tavern

within minutes of the signal indicating that the British regulars were on their way, well before they could possibly have received word via courier that two lanterns had in Christ Church steeple been hung ("One if by land, two if by sea . . ."). Was it coincidence, intuition, confidence? No, faith, like the chick who takes the leap because he knows it's time to fly.

Revere couldn't help but smile when out from the dark (on no more than tonight's advance word) popped two boatbuilders, Joshua Bentley and Thomas Richardson, offering to row Revere safely across the Charles, their journey in turn abetted by a young woman who appeared ready and willing to toss the renegades her warm flannel petticoat as a wrapper to muffle the boat's oars.

And we'll take over from there, Deborah had directed. *We*, I was about to discover, meaning not only human agency, but much, much more. . . .

We included Revere's dog, who showed up just as the rowboat was about to shove off, his master's forgotten spurs attached to his collar, without which Revere could never have made his famous ride.

We included the moon, only too eager to play a part. Near full in the clear night sky, normally the moon would have caught Revere's boat in its beam, making it highly visible to the H.M.S. *Somerset*, the British warship anchored smack in the middle of the Charles.

But not tonight, April 18, 1775. They called it a lunar anomaly, a freak event in the sky, described (but never explained) by astronomers as an abnormal positioning of the moon a few too many degrees to the south. Be all that as it may, to be standing on the corner of North and North Centre witnessing Revere's crossing was to behold a miracle. For Revere's little boat—amid a river ordinarily lit so well by the moon that its currents could be read from afar—passed under the hissing tiger on the *Somerset*'s prow hidden completely by *Boston's own shadow* thrown far across the bay and, thus, passed undetected.

I was in absolute awe.

"By the full moon, April the eighteenth," she'd told me. Was this what it was, then? A way of availing herself of the parallax moon? Dark for Revere's crossing, but bright on the road to Concord to the northwest—all the better to detect the scarlet of Redcoats coming our way?

I wouldn't put it past her. Things like this, you see . . . she and her farmers, they just knew. Not from Newton or Spinoza, but from the land, or perhaps, in a pinch, the almanac.

Small wonder that the moment those Redcoats disembarked on the Charlestown side of the Charles (bound for Concord) they were doomed to be picked off like flies.

To be sure, I could now see that these soldiers mustering reluctantly about Boston (apprehensive about all the activity and the tolling bells) would be no match for men who worked with the moon.

The story was all in the hats.

The Redcoats sported heavy hats made even more cumbersome by the canvas slipcovers required to prevent their cracking in the sun, snapping in the cold, and soaking up the rain. Additionally, they towered so high on the head they had to be cinched tight to the scalp with straps.

The American militiaman's tricorne, on the other hand, fit low, capably redirected rain, and was contoured to the head by the weather.

The Redcoats' hair was plaited and powdered and waxed; breeches kept bright white under penalty of court-martial; coarse red woolen fabric that chafed; horsehair neck collars bound tight and rising to the chin. All this as compared to the Rebels' natural locks, caught back with a ribbon or a thong; loose-fitting, homespun camouflage brown attire, or a grayish blue that echoed the night sky.

No match at all.

Just after midnight. The wee hours of April nineteenth.

Gage's soldiers, having been roused from their beds, were finally lined up at the riverbank and given orders to embark—without any direction as to where they were to go or why. Lucky for them the townspeople knew and amiably directed them to the dock, filled them in on the pertinent details.

"You're taking the cannon back from Concord," one towns-man advised, clueing in a half-asleep Redcoat.

Another Bostonian cracked, "And you're sure to miss your aim!" prompting laughter all around—even from the British sol-diers, who couldn't help but agree.

About this time, Lord Percy, in command of the Fifth Regi-ment, was taking an evening walk. Overhearing a group of Yankees casually discussing the evening's "top-secret" troop movements through town, he went berserk. Thinking he was the only one who had not been informed of Gage's plan to raid Concord, he raced to Province House and stormed into Gage's office to announce what he had just learned "from civilians in the street, good sir! How can this be?"

Gage, fearful for his job (rumor had it that three new gener-als—Howe, Burgoyne, and Clinton—were already on their way to replace him), felt it was now or never to regain favor with the king; a show of strength at this point in time was of the essence. If word were ever to get out that Gage had not persevered in his plans because the civilian population "found out," he'd be sent packing back to England faster than his wife could come. Better he fail in playing the hero than play the fool by backing down.

"Persevere," he instructed Percy, commanding him to ready his brigade. For many years afterward, whenever the dramatic story of the Battle of Lexington and Concord was acted out in the street by the citizenry, as often it was, here Gage was portrayed peeing his pants.

Percy was to help Colonel Francis Smith (God knows why—possibly because this was a battle that Gage was meant to lose; there's no other explanation), to whom Gage gave command of the action along with orders to take to Concord twenty-one companies of soldiers, Loyalist militia, and volunteers.

Of course, as much as Gage thought Americans canny, lovely, and smart, he couldn't bring himself to believe they were psychic (not yet). At least not until he excluded the possibility that his sluttish Jersey wife had opened her not-quite-wide-enough-for-him fat mouth and betrayed him. One look at her and, well . . . suffice it to say, she was history. Soon thereafter she was plopped onto a ship to England, never to return: "Madam, begone!"

Unfortunately, Colonel Smith, more than needing help, required full-scale rescue. The journey across the Charles, which Revere had executed in a matter of minutes, took Smith's men well over three hours. And once they did reach the opposite shore of Back Bay, they were already too tuckered to trot.

Actually, they never really made it to shore—not by boat, anyway—for the British longboat keels, always too deep for the Charles, ran aground, forcing the soldiers to jump into waist-deep water and drag themselves to shore with their hats, boots, wool uniforms, and 125-pound packs in tow.

Then there was the regrettable combination of fatty Colonel Francis Smith and fey Major Pitcairn sharing command (they had gotten out of town, oblivious to the fact that Percy and his just-mustered outfit were still in Boston, scrambling to get ready). Not all opposites are happy ones, I suppose.

At odds from the start, the ever-hungry Smith insisted they await food provisions before pushing on (two days' worth, he required, even though the expedition was designed to last at most several hours). At first a waiting period was fine for the ever-fastidious Pitcairn, who used the time to order and reorder his troops, insisting they stay in the water until a design he liked had been achieved (so as to make them attractive on shore). But then Pitcairn wanted to march. What would Smith say? "Not before my sandwich arrives!"

So it was that a full four hours after leaving barracks—Smith, miserable; Pitcairn, prissy—the Redcoat company finally shoved off through the Cambridge marsh, breeches full of soggy water, thick mud sucking at their shoes. One hour later I made that same trip in thirty minutes.

Fifty feet into the marsh, Smith halted his troops once more. Ostensibly concerned that the soldiers' wet, muddy footfalls would awaken the countryside, he sent his men, all nine hundred, down a slippery embankment into a stream, which he ordered them to ford. And with their backs turned, he caught a nibble of salt cod ("A tiny bite—nothing more!"), along with his breath (apparently he was hyperventilating so badly his men thought surely he'd die).

Meanwhile, back in Boston, Percy was still waiting on Smith (via Pitcairn) for his orders. He would have had a long wait: Gage's instructions conjoining them were sitting on Pitcairn's night table, delivered long after Pitcairn had departed.

Pitcairn would be trading bullets with Yankees on the Lexington Green by the time Percy had it all figured out and was finally leaving Boston. It was not until nine o'clock that morning, April 19, 1775, that a puzzled Lord Percy, with two cannon, a baggage train, and eight hundred men, finally trickled out of Boston to reinforce a battle that had already been lost before Percy had even shouted "Forward—march!"

And by the time Percy's parade dawdled into Lexington, the skirmish there was over and Smith's men had already taken it on the chin at Old North Bridge in Concord. News that one of their soldiers' heads had just been tomahawked off by a sixteen-year-old Rebel did little to spoil Smith's tidy breakfast and Pitcairn's brandy alexander, which during the battle they'd demanded be served them on the rather pretty Concord Green.

Where Percy's brigade became invaluable, however, was during the British retreat from Lexington. All that artillery power worked wonders in beating back the farmers stashed behind fences and in the woods chasing the Redcoats off, "assassinating" them "in cold blood" with clumsy fowling pieces, one by one by one. . . .

I had cantered back into Lexington much earlier, around four that morning, well ahead of Pitcairn and Smith, and far ahead of Percy—a full five hours before the skirmish at Concord's Old North Bridge. As soon as I crossed the river (with the help of Revere's oarsmen), I was met by a courier offering me a horse ("from Buttrick"), warning me to "ride like the devil" and warn the countryside through to Lexington, to act as backup for Revere.

I arrived just before that first shot: the one "heard 'round the world."

Upon my arrival, Lexington didn't, to me, seem at all prepared for battle. I thought for sure something had gone wrong. The Green looked like Harvard Yard did back in '70, except instead of soused students picking food fights and torturing underclassmen, there were Minutemen rolling around, playing at boule and beer-chugging competitions.

They'd been drinking since midnight, just after news of the "two lanterns" had been passed on, and they were drop-down dead drunk.

Not exactly the vigilant, austere Patriots of lore.

Women and children, as if preparing for a show, were competing for viewing space in upper windows, atop chimneys and roofs, urging the militiamen on in an exercise that bore no resemblance to any military drill I'd ever seen (soldiers tripping over their own two feet and each other's, another attempting a cartwheel).

I didn't have to look very far for Buttrick and Robert, standing there in the tavern's yard, Robert rolling *rub-a-dub-dub* on his drum, as if nothing about the scene before us were out of the ordinary or disturbing at all.

Half an hour later, at four-thirty A.M., a discouraged Revere shuffled into town, on foot. I approached him immediately. For while it had been evident during my ride that Revere had managed to alert the countryside as planned, I wondered, as I arrived in Lexington, why no one had seen hide nor hair of him. "Where have you been?" I asked, figuring there was no point in not getting right to it.

He explained that when he'd reached Lexington he'd gone immediately to the Clarke parsonage (around three hours ago, at one A.M.). After a chilly, annoyed reception from Hancock and Adams, who hated being roused in the dead of night, he left, urging them to break from town as soon as possible. From there he was traveling to Concord when he was arrested by a British advance man, taken prisoner, and soon thereafter released predicated on his bluff that there were thousands of Rebels awaiting the British in Concord. This caused the advance guard to panic, take Revere's horse, and run.

Revere further explained that having marched his way back to Lexington just moments ago after being unhorsed, he was astonished to find John Hancock and Samuel Adams still hanging about the Clarke place.

Subscribing to the school of thought that would have held Adams's and Hancock's arrests an unmitigated disaster for The Cause, he was resolved to induce them to go. Toward that end, he wished to procure Hancock his trunk, without which Hancock refused to make a move. Wondering how the hell I'd ever gotten it up those stairs all by myself, he asked for my help. "Would you mind terribly . . . ?"

Wouldn't you know that it was while dragging the goddamned trunk from my bedroom at the tavern that all hell began to break loose down below.

From around the bend, Pitcairn, the British officers, and six companies of Redcoats appeared: an orderly flood of scarlet and steel meeting swaying lines of brown and blue on Lexington Green. (Smith, of course, was well behind his vanguard of regulars.)

As to the millstone of a trunk: Now what? Drop it? Toss it?

Use this opportunity to take a forbidden look inside? Continue to drag it toward Hancock?

We carried on as before, figuring that if some action were to occur, it wouldn't be anytime soon.

We were wrong.

"Let the troops pass by and don't molest them without they begin first," were militiaman Colonel Barrett's orders, just as Revere and I were crossing the Green with the monstrous trunk.

"Disperse, ye Rebels, ye villains, disperse, lay down your arms!" cried Pitcairn. At which point I tripped and fell.

"This fucking lug! I'm gone. Let it drop!" I shouted to Revere.

Then, from someone on our side: "If they mean to have a war, let it begin here!" My, wasn't this escalating quickly . . .

The shot.

I ducked.

More shots.

Smoke, fire, splattered guts and blood, yelps and whimpers and screams of pain.

Minutes later, eight were dead.

Who shot first? Was it my shouting that had triggered it? Who fired at whom and from which side?

Nobody would ever know.

The question of who fired first would forever remain a mystery, which as far as I was concerned was proof enough that the Battle of Lexington was just what Deborah prophesied: the Big Bang, a paradox of new life, transcending opposites like a British or an American side.

Robert dropped his drum, Buttrick his gun. Both came running to me.

"John," Buttrick said.

"Colonel Buttrick," I countered, extending him my hand. "Robert." I reached for an embrace.

And so it was that we clung to each other out in the open in the middle of the square, a little drummer boy and his dad and the man who loved his dad holding on to each for dear life, rocking themselves in sorrow on the grass.

And nobody cared.

And all was silence. Even the tread of the British soldiers marching on, moving out, couldn't disturb us.

Pitcairn (and Smith) would get theirs on the march back to Boston.

And the trunk? Somehow it arrived at the parsonage safe and sound, Revere managing to affix it to Hancock's carriage.

"Oh what a glorious morning!" Sam Adams was heard to exclaim as the chaise carrying him and Hancock raced out of town, leaving behind their women, the dead on the Lexington Green, and all memory of truth or dare.

Not so glorious a morning for Hancock, as things turned out. Realizing too late he had forgotten his smoked salmon, and that with all this frenzy he certainly could use a bite right about now, he sent a servant back for it, a black man named Todd.

The salmon never came to him, because I had pilfered it and was at that time feeding it to my brethren on the Green. Wasn't it delicious, though.

In the end, all Hancock ate that day was potatoes, baked on dirt in the woods.

Yes, the Big Bang had come.

CHAPTER 23

Food and Guns

How on earth did I move from vowing, after the battle at Lexington, never to be parted from Deborah again, to being grateful to see her shipped off to the West Indies as a traitor to her country?

The answer is in the story of how I became a scoundrel.

Of course, Deborah's attempt on Washington's life had a lot to do with it. Indeed, had I not been well on my way to scoundrelhood at the time of Deborah's capture and arrest for her purported crime, I would have seen things differently. For in truth her transformation into an assassin turned out to be not nearly as reprehensible as mine into a dutiful soldier of war. If for no other reason than that her alteration was for the good of The Cause and mine was merely because of jealousy and fear.

Shocking as I know all this is, I must tell you that my journey was rather simple, plain, and ordinary, and, I would argue, reasonable, in light of the language I would need to adopt to get

Congress to support the battles at Lexington and Concord. It was a seductive and rewarding language which, from the moment I adopted it, began the change in me to a new man, fluent in the "gentleman's tongue." Soon I, along with the language, would also become a tool of the "gentlemen" of substance whom I sought to inveigle into supporting The Cause.

Cowardly? Certainly. But it's tricky to know that in advance, you see, because on the face of it, the language of the Second Continental Congress seemed not only natural, but heroic.

Funny how being scared to death distorts one's perspective: Hewing to the safe and familiar becomes honorable and lies become true.

I didn't know I was terrified, of course. Few scoundrels do. I didn't know that after the Battles of Lexington and Concord (as the "actions" would come to be known), literally tens of thousands of yeomen flocked to the hills just outside Boston to pin the retreated British into the city ("Starve them if need be!"). That was when I actually grew scared that we might be in over our heads and wouldn't stand a chance.

I didn't know I was jealous either. I'd convinced myself that Deborah's objections to my plans to travel to Philadelphia and appeal to the Continental Congress for food and guns were misguided and wrong. Of course, if I hadn't been made heartsick by the hundreds of men suddenly adulating her and by the distance wrought between us by the protracted and complex war-preparation period that followed Lexington and Concord, I might have thought differently. I might even have seen my way clear to the truth, as she saw it: that we couldn't trust Congress as far as we could throw them, and that as far as the majority of her "soldiers" were concerned, they were gathering to fight *all* tyrants—be they British, Tory, or arrogant "gentlemen" of any stripe or origin. The advent of a burgeoning American consciousness aside, it's important to remember: We were *all* British then.

I don't know exactly what I had been expecting the Big Bang

to bring, but certainly my fantasy did not involve losing Deborah, especially not to hordes of men primed for an all-out, full-scale, dig-in-your-heels, settle-in-for-the-long-haul kind of war.

And for sure I didn't expect her to act as if our embrace on the Green had never occurred. That's what put me over the edge.

Pity that my experience with my father's infamous denial of our single intimate moment had worked its way so deeply—and at such a tender age—into my heart. For in clouding my judgment, inducing me to see red where there was only pure, white light, I was myself set on the road to infamy. After all this time, I was still not so much a Revolutionary as my father's wounded son.

Indeed, for me to learn to live the thoughts I held so dear, I had a long way to go. The smashing of Apollo's shell had taken me this far, but now, to go the distance, I'd have to suffer the torturous shattering of my own. All a long way of saying that this business of Revolution was quite fraught and much, much harder than I ever thought possible.

Small wonder that few of our Founding Fathers wanted anything to do with real Revolution.

(And as if my campaign for food and guns among the wealthy elite weren't looked upon with suspicion enough by Deborah's side, wait until you see what happened when I delivered a general to her doorstep—a real, dyed-in-the-wool commander-in-chief . . . of a sort.)

Thank goodness, though, I had George Washington to save me from myself. Otherwise I may well have died a man lost, not a man found. Although in the story that is about to resume I recognize it is hard to imagine Washington ultimately being the savior of Deborah's Cause, imagine it anyway. Like the figment of the Green Dragon, it'll help you through.

For in this tale, the very qualities for which Washington is famous were abhorrent, inimical to The Cause. And other of his qualities since hidden or obscured would prove indispensable to it.

George Washington deserves to be famous, you see; not for the ridiculous, hollow personage he couldn't help himself from becoming (and the world saw fit to revere him for), but for the one, by war's end, he turned out to be: just a man named George, who in order to win freedom for America merely needed to exist.

I can remember with near-exactness the images and thoughts visiting me en route to Philadelphia. The hills of Charlestown looming behind in long, flickering good-byes, thousands of tiny fires dotting their slopes like so many stars in the fall of evening, marking the individual encampments of the soldiers and their families taking part in the siege of Boston. Memories of full-grown men, minutes after the battles, ringing their hair with daisies and on bended knee singing to plump, coy women standing in the river. Dancing, naked children, their torsos streaked with the dye of first-growth, fresh violet, jumping off the remnants of Old North Bridge and turning the river water an iridescent purple.

It would take three years for these memories to come back, scratched from my mind by personal ambition. Three years before Lexington and Concord would reemerge as more than just a "dangerous skirmish" and three years before Lieutenant Colonel John Lawrence, preeminent aide-de-camp to His Excellency, the commander-in-chief, would return to being John.

The tragedy starts out innocently enough.

I hadn't left Deborah on hostile terms, not at all. She fully understood my reasons for wanting to supply the underfed, poorly armed farmers with the basic tools of war. She just didn't believe that hounding the Founding Fathers was the way to do it. Be that as it may, she and Dr. Warren, who after Lexington and Concord claimed for himself what he'd always wanted, the role of de facto commander-in-chief, decided against resisting me, urging me instead simply to keep to the issue.

"Food and guns. Food and guns is all that we'll need! Under no circumstances should you let them distract you from this goal. You must absolutely ignore all the rest," Deborah and Dr. Warren

had, with great foresight, warned me. But even given my exten-
sive experience with Hancock and the rest, keeping to "food and
guns, food and guns" was hard, and ultimately impossible.

Hancock was the first to spot me in New Haven, Connecticut,
on the Boston Post Road.

"Sweet boy!" he hollered, leaping from his carriage, barreling
toward me like a man on fire, suspiciously happy to see me. Food
and guns, food and guns, I kept repeating to myself, somehow
sensing that just by laying eyes on Hancock I would be sunk in
trouble. I also remember being shocked and thinking: My Lord,
they left Lexington three weeks ago—and haven't gotten very far!

Whether it was drunkenness, hunger, gout-induced faulty eyesight, or just plain dumb luck, I'll never know, but Hancock ran
past me altogether (maybe once he'd gotten started, he simply
couldn't stop?) and plowed headlong into my hired steed's belly.
Sarah, after whinnying, bounced me off her back and, kicking and
rearing, ran as fast and as far away from us as she could.

I should have done the same.

That was it for the horse, who was gone forever. And that was
it for me, the moment I climbed into Hancock's carriage, tucked
between John and Samuel Adams, one unremittingly gabby and
the other indefatigably flatulent. Hard not to be distracted by this
pair of "gentlemen." Yet I continued to mouth silently, to myself,
Food and guns, food and guns . . .

"Sirs!" I said aloud, firmly, politely, steadily, and began to
speak to them of my intention to give report to the Second Continental Congress, due to commence session in three days (and we
were only in New Haven!) on the "urgent, desperate, and immediate need for food and guns to supply the farmers and tradesmen
who had fought so valiantly at Lexington and Concord."

They were unimpressed. Instead, they instantly began pump-
ing me anxiously for news of these battles—news they would have
had firsthand had they not run away.

It didn't take me long to learn why, even in running, they

hadn't gotten very far. As we rode south from New Haven to Fairfield and beyond, inching closer to New York, I noticed behind us what looked like a military escort, and on either side roaring, cheering crowds. In New York alone, why, the spectators of our passage turned out some seven thousand strong; nearly one-third of the entire city lined the streets to catch a glimpse of the men their own advance pamphlets promised were the emblems of the Revolution: the very men behind the triumphs of Lexington and Concord.

Oh, didn't the crowds push to our carriage, at one point unharnessing our horses and pulling us along with their own power to show approval, devotion, their infinite glee. And, of course, if the crowd got *too* close, there were always those militiamen at our rear who, at Hancock's behest, would "push them back where they belong."

Hancock was utterly convinced I had been sent by Warren in response to Hancock's many letters stating: *Please, I beg you, send me information as to the disposition of the troops. Urgent!* The "Hero of Lexington and Concord," as Hancock now wished to be addressed, could, without my briefing, pretend for only so long he knew everything about which he knew nothing. Eventually audiences would grow tired of his repetitive vagaries and want facts. My supply of credible news was his way to save his ass with the crowds.

I reported on the disposition of the troops, as requested, again emphasizing the need for food and guns. "If something is not done soon, sirs, Gage will rush back in and decimate—"

(Hancock interrupted me to wave at the crowd and shoo away a small, pug-nosed girl wanting his autograph: "Be gone, you ugly little rat!")

"—the citizenry. To stop this, we'll be needing food and guns, sir."

"Perfect!" Hancock replied, in what I would realize later was not at all a non sequitur.

On the tenth of May we trundled gracefully (read: slowly) into Philadelphia, part of a procession led by two hundred to three hundred mounted militiamen with swords drawn. Once more Hancock took the post of honor at the front and, with John Adams in the seat beside him, made a grand entrance into Philadelphia.

While we crossed the city limits, bells pealed and trumpets blared to commemorate the convening of the Second Continental Congress. It would soon become apparent to me that Congress had gathered not to celebrate or even debate what had occurred in Lexington and Concord, but to put an end to it—*to discourage the man on the street from perpetrating any such kind of action again.*

And if you're looking to understand what follows, I'm afraid you'll have to look past the accepted, Historical myth that Congress as a body now moved with great fervor and dispatch to appoint a commander-in-chief and create the American army and look instead to the strange brew of quirk and cupidity that coalesced (with my prodding) into this momentous decision.

"Food and guns, food and guns, gentlemen!" I made report on the true status of Boston's militia army whenever and wherever I could—inside committee meetings, courtyards, taverns, and whorehouse parlors. But clear it was from the start that the "opening" through which the Suffolk Resolves had passed had now slammed closed, was buried and forgotten by History. These delegates had been tricked once with the hoax and would not be tricked again.

"What? Supply the local militias with additional arms? Certainly not. What if these men were to turn against us?"

"If they've made it this far without arms, why supply them now? Isn't the skirmish over?"

Or, more flatly: "No. Now leave me, or I'll call the sergeant-at-arms."

As one delegate wrote to the Massachusetts Provincial Congress: "The people now feel rather too much their own importance, and it will require great skill in gradually checking them to such a subordination as is necessary to good government."

The events of April 19, 1775, were never once referred to as a "battle," let alone a "victory."

For the first few days, Congress didn't even speak of the British or how to remove them from Boston. Instead the body obsessed on how to "keep the growing military power in Massachusetts in check"—and by that they meant the *Rebels*, not the incoming British Generals Clinton, Burgoyne, and Howe. Reports of armories being robbed and weapons being distributed freely among the citizenry is what Congress worried about, as well as stories of women and children up and down the eastern seaboard being taught the "manual exercise": how to handle a gun, a knife, a bow and arrow, and even a rock.

No, to this group of "gentlemen," the shortage of arms for the twenty thousand unwashed men, women, and children gathering outside Boston to hold Gage in was good news, not bad.

And on top of everything else, there was that awful mess at Fort Ticonderoga giving the delegates a fright.

Ticonderoga was a British fort up the Hudson on Lake Champlain. It was the key to holding Canada, controlling New York, and, as far as England was concerned, the way to keep New England Rebels split off from the rest of the colonies by isolating and vanquishing them at once.

On May 10, the very day that Congress called itself to session, New England militiamen (led by Benedict Arnold), together with a paramilitary force from Vermont (Ethan Allen and the Green Mountain Boys) seized it without firing a single shot.

It was a magnificent defeat of the British, one which came with the particular humiliation of the commanding officer, Lieutenant Feltham.

It was early morning when the fort was taken. Feltham had been sleeping. When Ethan Allen woke him ("Come out, you bastard!"), Feltham was so frightened that he appeared at the door forgetting to cinch his breeches about his waist. As a result, raising his arms in surrender meant dropping his pants. And so the British exodus from the fort amounted for Feltham to a miserable hop to the Hudson with his exposed prick flouncing (what little there was to flounce!) from side to side as he went.

It was devastating: a royal fort attacked and captured; the king's cannon and munitions seized; a British officer's penis left dangling in defeat.

Yet at the time, this wasn't considered funny by either Britain or Congress. Congress immediately put plans into motion to guarantee that "one day soon" Britain would get all her weapons back without hesitation, demands, justifications presented, or questions asked or answered.

News of this disturbing event fueled debate as to whether or not Congress should move its quarters closer to the Boston army, so that Congress "could act more expeditiously in regulating operations in that quarter." But the fact was that "being so close to an area with so many questions referred would leave Congress without the leisure they ought to have to digest and perfect matters of *greater importance*."

"Perfect!" Hancock had said, which turned out to mean that at first he considered food and guns a windfall issue for his campaign for president of Congress, his feeling being that advocacy of arming the Rebels might be just the thing to put him back on the road to popularity. Needless to say, it didn't take long for him to change his tune, or at least to moderate it intensively, covering all his political bases by mixing enthusiasm for supplying the Rebels with food and guns with rank disapproval of "the actions at Lexington and Ticonderoga."

And the muddle worked! John Hancock became president— but only after Peyton Randolph (Delaware), who actually won the election, required a leave of absence for health reasons and the Carolinian who was subsequently offered the job declined it.

Even then it was stipulated that Hancock had to relinquish the post upon Randolph's return. Oh, well.

So when Randolph did return, Hancock was sent packing, back to fishing for another plum post. Lucky for him (or so he assumed), there was a juicy one coming right at him—one that would put him on a collision course with General George Washington, who, unfortunately for Hancock, looked much better in uniform. Which is how Congress preferred their military men—valiant but pliant.

Commander-in-chief of the American army. My, my—what a ring to it! The concept was just now beginning to emerge in the ranks of the Committee of the Whole, where somehow the discussion had moved from providing food and guns for the current siege forces (discussed for all of three minutes at best), to the subject of raising an army (hastily dropped as well), to the top-priority subject of electing a commander-in-chief. Now, *there* was a subject that proved capable of setting the collective congressional tongue wagging. For which they would have me to thank.

The Committee of the Whole, created earlier to study the Massachusetts Provincial Congress' request that Congress adopt the New England army for its own ("We are without a civil power to provide for and *control* them. *Please help*"), suddenly went wild. Up until the issue of a commander-in-chief came up, the recommendations of this committee had been modest, to say the least. Despite my bleak, dire predictions of the terrible fate that would befall the Rebel soldiers should England retaliate against them, the committee's best effort thus far was a proposal that New England alone supply the farmers drawn up before Boston with food and guns. This despite my explaining ad nauseum that if New England could afford to do that, I never would have come to Philadelphia in the first place.

But suddenly the mind-numbing indifference toward "New England's rotten little military escapade" gave way to talk of taking command of the prevailing situation—and all, as it happened, because I had accosted George Washington en route to the latrine.

It was about ten days into the Second Continental Congress session and I, having made absolutely no headway at all, decided that I must portray the Lexington Rebels differently than I had. Instead of stories about what disasters might befall undefended New England Rebels no one cared about, I decided on a different tack: cheap sentiment evoking pity for the damned and dreams of glory in their deliverance. Some poor sap might be induced to feel sorry for them and agree to lead their ragged asses to victory. And if there was a commander-in-chief, there would eventually be food and guns, of this I was sure. This new leader simply wouldn't be able to manage anything without them.

Friday, May 21: I was standing in the courtyard of Independence Hall rehearsing my narrative, waiting for the delegates to break—yet again—for lunch, when George Washington, the pear-shaped planter with what must have been a button for a bladder walked urgently past, as he had thrice before within the hour, bound for the privy. I knew very little about him (none of us did), but I decided that he was my man, since I could make him my captive audience by pinning him down in the line for use of the facilities.

To enhance my credibility, I spoke in even, dispassionate, inhuman tones. I'd learned that the trick with these gents was to act like you cared not a whit about that which you spoke. I informed Washington coolly, as if I were talking about the weather, of how the latest dispatch of stories from Lexington and Concord seemed to point "quite scientifically" (it sounded good) to a "profound change of heart" on the part of the Rebels. That of late the Rebels had been turning sweet, compliant, respectful, deferential—their wrath reserved exclusively for a bloated Parliament, not Mother England, not King George, and certainly not those born of the American gentleman class.

Instead of speaking of the Rebels' right to freedom (a subject which I mistakenly had broached on a previous occasion and very quickly left behind due to the alarm it engendered in the discussion's participants), I spoke as monotonally as I could of their sad and pathetic travails: housewives risking their lives tossing billeted British soldiers out on their ears; still-breathing Yankee soldiers being kicked into mass graves by angry Redcoats; wailing wives and children jumping in after their men's bodies and being buried as well; children losing their fathers, and fathers their sons and daughters and limbs. Mothers by the hearth at home on bended knee, praying for peace.

"Stop, stop!" George finally insisted, clacking his unruly teeth and clutching his heart. By which time several congressmen and, for some reason, a curly-haired poodle had gathered around to hear my story: There wasn't a dry eye in the line for the latrine.

Planter Washington's turn came up and he left me only long enough to relieve himself. After wiping his hand cursorily on his breeches, he shook mine and said, "The Rebels are lucky to have you in their court, young man. You speak their case well—very well."

"Their plight speaks for itself, sir, through my heart," I said, tapping my sternum for effect.

Washington continued, "And so we must attend to it."

"My heart, sir?"

"No, no—their plight, their plight. You expect me to care about your heart, son, when there are naked, starving children roaming the streets in search of a crumb of food and defenseless women holding vigil at graves while Redcoats just across the river mock and abuse them and plot their ruin?"

Eureka! I'd ignited an imagination even more fertile than my own (and a temper infinitely more volatile, for which his odd shape helped me forgive him . . . all those years of being compared to a fruit must have been tough).

Washington invited me to have a port with him that evening back at the Robbins house, where he was staying.

"I think I can be of help to your friends; indeed, I feel I know just the thing to do. But I'll need to know more first. . . ."

I was so excited now that it was my turn to run to the latrine. That afternoon I wrote Deborah and Warren:

The tide, I do believe, has turned. I seem to have inter-
ested a tall Virginia planter with a hot temper in The Cause.
Apparently he's not terribly bright—the story goes that he al-
most single-handedly started the French and Indian War when
he mistook a Frog for an Indian and shot him dead. But be
that as it may, I don't care! Home soon—with food and guns,
plenty for all! Keep Granny Gage guessing.

Your comrade, John

She never wrote back.

He was much too big a man for a parlor so red, so small. It seemed that there was no place to lay my eyes without his being in my view. A second before he sat down, I thought there had been a tiny chair in the corner. Maybe it wasn't such a tiny chair. Maybe he was just bigger than he had previously struck me at first meeting and the piece of furniture that had vanished under his body actually was sizable, perhaps even a winged Chippendale. In any event, the effect of the combination of Washington's bulk, this room, that chair, was that he appeared to be seated comfortably on thin air, a demigod from the start.

I knew this was my chance. Hour by hour, blow by blow, I chronicled it all: the current crisis in the Charlestown hills, Revere's ride, the skirmish on Lexington Green, and the assault on Old North Bridge. Hanging on my every word, not interrupting me except to fart ("Whoever heard of turtle soup?"), Washington listened intently. And drank, deeply.

Several ports later, he extricated himself from his chair (a Queen Anne with mahogany arms and legs, as it turned out), ducked behind a japanned screen, where . . . yes, he proceeded to disrobe, flinging his shoes and scarf out into the room like a man primed for a revel with a whore.

Oh, dear.

"Now, on to why I've brought you here." He veritably shook with excitement as he flipped his coat over the top of the partition, his breeches soon to follow.

Please, God, no—say not that the planter is a poof!

"... how you could be of great help to me ... and I to you," he quavered. I blanched; it was true!

"I—I must be running along," I blurted out, and tried unsuccessfully to rise from my minuscule seat.

Out from behind the screen came his left leg—not a bad calf, I have to say, especially in the white stocking—which he appeared to be modeling for me in a teasing, music-hall kind of way.

"Good-bye, dreary planter, and hello . . ." With maximum dramatic effect, he leapt out from behind the screen. I covered my eyes.

"I promise you, you'll like what you see," he wheedled, then commanded me: "Open your goddamned eyes!"

What I found before me was a very large man encased like a sausage in a moth-eaten military uniform, so tight it looked applied with adhesive.

Washington walked about, admiring himself. "I recognize it's a bit small. I was twenty-four at the time it was made, allergic to cream and seeking to make a beneficial match. This dates back to the French and Indian War."

No doubt.

He leaned in to me, taking one of my hands and guiding it to his open waistcoat. "Now, if you take one side, and I the other, and we pull nice and hard, I believe the stomach could be forced into compliance with the size. I'll exhale. Don't fart too, I pray!"

His prayer wasn't answered, but his vest buttons did manage to find their holes rather nicely. "As long as I remember to keep inhalations slight, I should be fine. I brought this old thing in the event a situation such as the one you've described presented itself. High time, as you say, for Congress to appoint a commander-in-chief!"

He broke off, gazing at himself in a cheval glass, and fixed me with a stare.

"Promise me you'll keep to your stories—the better ones, weeping widows and all that. In the meantime, I'll 'allow' myself to be seen in this. We'll regard ourselves as a team, for which I promise you'll soon receive ample reward. But, to disguise our mutual purposes, we will appear unallied, unacquainted. You story-tell while I parade, and— Oh dear, if I get too excited, I'll pop! Slight inhale, deeeeeep exhale, there we go! Well, just you wait and see! Before you know it, you'll be writing your friends, telling them help is on the way, faster than you can say 'His Excellency George Washington, sir'!" (Faster than all that, I certainly hoped.)

And so, like a vision, a premonition of what was to come, there George Washington stood, posing mute as a statue in his outfit of buff and blue with gold epaulettes, brandishing his sword, and dreaming of the glory days to be.

Food and guns, food and guns. Oh well. Where there was a commander-in-chief, food and guns would be certain to follow, I surmised. And I was in much too deep to back out now.

By morning of the next day, before I had even set up my soap-box in the courtyard, things were already starting to change. Nothing impresses Congress more than a man in uniform, I guess.

About the only two delegates who were unfazed by Washington's parade were Benjamin Franklin and Thomas Jefferson. Their objections could not be entirely trusted, however. For Franklin, even at seventy, was never really interested in anything that wasn't female, naked, and hot to play; and Thomas Jefferson was a resolute pacifist across the board, considered too queer ("He eats only vegetables, the silly squirrel!"), and his views therefore summarily dismissed. (Eventually, in fact, they handed him the onerous task of writing the Declaration of Independence, mostly to get him out of their powdered hair. Lucky for him he was landed gentry and owned slaves, otherwise he'd never have stood a chance with those gents.)

But as for the rest, now weren't they cowed? The glint of that regalia of Washington's must have gone to their heads, for this is the only possible explanation, as I see it, for what happened next.

Suddenly everyone wanted in. A few days more and the Committee of the Whole had indeed created the position of commander-in-chief.

No weapons, no army—just a commander-in-chief.

Overnight, Lexington and Concord suddenly became "assaults upon the people," a replay of the Boston Massacre, but "this time the colonists defended themselves." "Bloody Butchery by British Troops!" it was written, rivaled only by "Redcoat cruelty and barbarity such as this has never been perpetrated even by the savages of America."

A job title had finally brought the Founding Fathers willy-nilly to The Cause.

And oh, did Hancock, screwed out of his presidency by the duly elected Randolph, want that job! He was absolutely driven to distraction by the possibility, making a complete fool of himself—popping pills, swatting flies that weren't there—and I'm dead certain that was his tapered foot that tried to trip George Washington the day he walked down the aisle to accept Congress' nomination of him as commander-in-chief of the (nonexistent) American army.

John Adams, who had more or less been pushing for war with England—even for arming the natives for it—was the one to make the nomination because he correctly assumed that Congress would back a discreet (if conspicuous) Southerner over any fiery mid-Atlantic Scotsman or Yank. ("Discreet" isn't exactly the word I would use to describe Washington's approach, but never mind.)

". . . A gentleman who is among us here and very well known to all of us . . . a gentleman whose skill and experience as an officer, whose independent fortune, great talents, and excellent universal character will command the approbation of all America . . ."

Hancock half rose from his seat in anticipation of bounding to the fore. Adams paused to beam and gesture. ". . . General George Washington!"

Hancock sat down quickly and practically sprouted horns.

Washington, like a virgin bride, had to be begged to reenter the chamber out of which he'd begun strategically to tiptoe as John Adams put forward his name. What a show.

The General blushingly claimed he was not fit for the post and further insisted on serving without pay!

This last condition History has always loved, but his wife Martha didn't. She hit the ceiling, although she was ultimately reassured by the huge stipend Washington later privately demanded—and received—in lieu of salary. One in which he made a sizable dent immediately with the purchase of a new carriage and a team of horses to whisk him (and his aides, of which I was automatically made a member) off to Cambridge in true commander-in-chief style.

Next came the wrangling over the suitable number of generalships to be allotted under Washington and, even more troublesome, the assignment of them. Here all pretense was dropped: Not bothering to make a case for one nominee as better qualified than another, congressmen made no bones whatsoever about proposing their favorite sons. And why shouldn't they? Since Washington, the new commander-in-chief, had been refused promotion as an officer while serving in the British army time and again, and in fact had never won a single battle during his earlier military career, why exert oneself to justify one's own candidate in terms of his skill, talent, or experience in war?

The upshot of all this was, of course, that within hours there were dozens more names in Congress' hat than there were available generalships. So, in their infinite wisdom, to keep the peace,

Congress simply created more posts than would ever be required. The New England contingent uncorked champagne to celebrate their receiving half the major general posts and seven of the eight brigadier general slots. Artemas Ward of Massachusetts was named first, as compensation for his essentially being stripped of the commanding generalship he currently held, in favor of Washington.

Then too, Charles Lee, a former English officer, was named as a major general. I don't know who he got to swing his appointment, just that he was a vile, filthy man who toted Pomeranians about in a bag. Lastly commissioned were Philip Schuyler of New York and Israel Putnam of Connecticut, both sweet bores.

The appointments complete, teeth securely in place, Washington dashed off a letter to Martha, promising he'd be home by Christmas—not specifying for which year—and then we were off to realize America's . . . what?

Bid for war?

No.

Hankering for freedom?

No.

Fight for justice?

No.

Who knew anything, but that a fine new commander, in a newly lacquered phaeton with a brace of good horses, a covey of aides in tow, was on the road to Cambridge?

Beaming, seated at Washington's side, I believed that with this triumph, Deborah and Dr. Warren would come around.

Food and guns. Food and guns. No, better than that: a commander-in-chief!

And so my journey to scoundrelhood had begun.

CHAPTER 24

The Arrival of the Commander-in-Chief

It wasn't long before it became clear that we were headed to Cambridge to train, not to assist, the farmers gathered there. Then, on June 23, just as we were leaving Philadelphia, a courier arrived with news of a massacre of Americans on Bunker Hill. No other information was yet known.

I was shaken by the news. Where was Deborah in all this? Was she still alive?

The trip was agonizingly slow. To his credit, Washington was anxious to get to Cambridge, although several of his brave new officers were not quite so eager to join the fray.

En route, Washington spoke reassuringly of his commitment to preserving civilian rule, but also of the need for order and subordination in the army he would create: one to make his country proud. Later, as he was describing it to the thousands who would gather to listen, I realized that his vision resembled England's organization of forces down to the same drills, boots, and buckles.

He promised to enlist men who, along with his generalship, would provide, as Congress had insisted, "the kind of example youth can look up to as a pattern to form themselves by," their conduct in every respect "guided by the rules and the discipline of war."

So "to our lives, our fortunes, and our sacred honor! Hear! Hear!" the crowd would cry, followed by thunderous applause for His Excellency, General George Washington, for whom fireworks fetes were held up and down the eastern seaboard to honor "Him."

Britain could not and should not be expected to deal with terrorists, the "gentleman's" argument went. Under no circumstances should the farmers at Lexington be allowed to represent the colonial cause of freedom, which they were deemed to have adopted as an excuse for errant, bastard behavior, and little more.

Credibility was held to be the key here. The English needed to see their opponent as nobly forbidding, formidable, and worthy of attention, not barbaric and unshaven. This was a "gentleman's" spat, not guerrilla war, Congress reasoned, and filthy, undisciplined hunters shooting at Redcoats from behind wheelbarrows and trunks of apple trees was no way to a fine end—a fine end by definition being a country that looked, acted, ate, played, fought, entertained, and conducted its affairs like England, but a tad freer, maybe.

And if too much damage had been done already, not to worry—Commander-in-Chief George Washington could be counted on to set things straight.

It wasn't that Washington was mean, you see. It was just that he spoke a different language, as described—that of the "gentleman." In the "gentleman's story," which History would adopt, there is no mention of what the "gentlemen" refrained from doing (not sending food and guns, for example), just what they had sent (a general). Furthermore, there would be no account of how the post of commander-in-chief came to be, or of the squabbles that ensued. Or the flies. Or the drink. Or that Hancock wanted to kill George Washington for taking what Hancock regarded as his own job.

Instead the language would be noble and grand and self-congratulatory. And because, as they saw it, there was nothing noble, "gentlemanly" about dirty little rabble-rousers encamping half-naked, half-starved and poorly armed outside Boston, the talk would not be of the Rebels' victory (this is why the word "victory" was strictly forbidden to characterize the engagements at Lexington and Concord), but of the defeat which would prove imminent if organization and respect for order were not brought about soon.

If the Rebels were not taught their place.

And it was persuasive, very, if only because it was the only story being told—until we got to Cambridge.

On the morning of July 3, 1776, the event occurred that History says signaled our readiness as a country to stand up and fight against England. George Washington arrived in Cambridge. A spectacular event made all the more moving by the first documented display of the star-studded colonial flag.

Documented, perhaps. But do the documents reveal that the flag was flown at half-mast? That when we arrived at Cambridge, there was absolutely nobody there to greet us? No military band regaling us with a perky tune. No crowds to greet the five horses, three generals (Washington, Schuyler, and Lee), three aides, and the escort of soldiers that at one point in the journey had ballooned to some five hundred strong—this despite John Adams's assurances that all of Cambridge would greet us "with the pomp and circumstance of glorious war displayed."

Instead . . . nothing. Not one militia officer, soldier, or civilian in sight. Just a bored, lone sentry standing guard in a Sunday afternoon downpour who hurriedly rounded up a small escort to shepherd us to our residence, the home of the president of Harvard College, which, as it turned out, was conveniently situated in the line of fire of the British gunboats anchored on the Charles.

There were twenty thousand soldiers gathered about Boston at this time, hailing from colonies and provinces far and wide in answer to the express riders who had run themselves ragged north, south, east, and west spreading news of Lexington and Concord (and, more recently, Bunker Hill). They had left their plows, their fields of wheat, tobacco, corn, their harvesting of peaches, slaughtering of turkeys, firing of bread, preparing of conserves, hammering of silver, and sewing of shoes, to walk to Boston from as far away as Georgia with only muskets on their shoulders, haversacks of biscuits on their backs, and strands of field grass in their hair.

Twenty thousand! And not one of them led there by a commander-in-chief, or eager to greet us that Sunday as we trundled tardily into town.

But we had come to save them, didn't they know? Where was the gratefulness, the appreciation, the show of obedience and respect for a general, a "man of talent, skill, and great fortune" who had "risked the ruin" of his reputation in assuming the terrible burden of power of the commander-in-chief, without pay—all for the sake of his country?

There it was: evidence anew, as if there weren't enough of it already, of "what an exceedingly dirty and nasty people" had risen up against King George. And oh, was Washington shocked all the more by what he witnessed on the road to our housing: a *colonel* shaving a *private's* face; officers and enlisted men drinking together in the tents, women lolling about at their sides; dirty children leapfrogging over fires; grown men mucking about naked in the river, mooning women and wagging their penises at passersby; American sentries fraternizing with British pickets who had crossed enemy lines to play whist! Blacks lying with whites and Indians with slaves. Fair women holding hands at the roadside, chanting "New lords, new laws—no! New lords, new laws—no!"

Where were the weeping mothers? The wounded fathers? The heartsick children missing their parents who'd been tossed into mass graves?

"The situation is not what I was expecting," Washington said to me in a darkly threatening tone.

"I see that." At which point yet another argument might well have ensued were it not for the sight of Deborah and Job to pre-occupy him: ostensibly two male soldiers, one white and the other black, holding hands.

Washington noticed the couple first. Ordering the horses stopped and silencing those of us in the coach (I remember that at the time Joseph Reed, a secretary, was squawking at top volume about how he wished he'd never come), Washington pointed, I thought rather rudely, at the black man and the white. Then, chin on fist, he simply stared for some minutes. And some minutes more. More than incensed, he looked confused.

"Shall we go, sir?" I asked.

He was roused from his reverie, but before we could move, the white soldier spotted me in the carriage.

She called out, "John!" smiling.

Was she happy to see me or more surprised by my place at Washington's side? I didn't know. And in truth, I didn't care, my relief at knowing she was safe after the Bunker Hill debacle turned to nausea by the company she was keeping: another man's—a black man's, to boot.

Ah yes, when threatened: still my father's son.

Washington was transfixed. "I'll be. So she's a woman, then?"

I simply nodded, wishing to commit myself to as little knowledge of her as possible, then added with calculated nonchalance, "So it would appear."

"But she knows your name."

"So it would appear," I repeated.

"You do see that she's a woman, do you not?"

"I do, sir."

"So do you, or do you not, know her? Are these the types with whom you consort?"

At which point Deborah kissed Job, causing me to bristle all the more.

"And the black one—he *is* a fellow, then, no?"

"I believe he's male. Yes, sir, it would appear that—"

"That nevertheless she makes a very convincing man, indeed," he said, directing the coachman to move on. And to me: "Your first assignment is to find out who she is . . . and remove her. She disgusts me."

"John!" Deborah yelled.

I froze. "John!" she yelled again, running toward the coach, which passed her by.

I didn't look back.

One day later, Washington laid down the law. He immediately set to revising the Massachusetts military penal code, adding sixteen more clauses and a vast assortment of punishments, including a provision for treason: death by hanging.

Henceforth, soldiers would be expected to avoid profanity and drunkenness. There would be no more dances around the fire. Any cider found in camp would be confiscated. There would be no naked bathing by the river, although the General "does not mean to discourage the practice of bathing to wash."

Deserters would be shot, as would any soldier who refused to serve under an officer appointed by Washington, never mind if he was from the soldier's region or not. "Level" intercourse between officers and men would be disallowed until "every officer and private begins to know his place and duty." Physical differences between officers and enlisted men were encouraged: A system of rosettes and sashes in different colors was devised to distinguish rank, with higher officers ordered into richer fabrics, colors, and better tailoring for purposes of commanding respect.

Women were to cook and clean and live apart from their men and were not to be seen drilling or on parade.

Sodomites would be forced to "ride the rail"—that is, tied, sitting up, legs straddling the narrow edge of a two-by-six plank (firmly set against the balls), which was held in midair by men at either end and then bounced up and down.

Time to get serious about war, boys and girls. Time to get the job done right.

In a whole different language. The language of "gentlemen." Determined to do what the British could not: tame us, control us.

No event delineates more clearly the resonant effect of a story told in different languages than that of the recent Battle of Bunker Hill.

After receiving a full account, Washington sided with reports characterizing the "rout" as avoidable, nothing proper leadership couldn't have prevented. A subsequent report indicating the exact opposite—that Bunker Hill wasn't a triumph for the British after all, but rather a humiliating defeat—was resoundingly ignored and taken as false. How much of a defeat could it have been if in the end the new British Commander Howe (Gage's day was done) had seized—and was still holding—the battlefield?

To Washington, the Rebels had failed. They had stupidly fortified the wrong hill (Breed's instead of Bunker's) and as a result the distinguished Dr. Joseph Warren, among others less notable, had unnecessarily lost their lives. And on top of this foolishness, the Rebels had withdrawn—worse than that, turned tail and run—just as Howe's men, climbing the hill in an out-and-out frontal attack upon it, were reaching its peak.

"Blasted cowards, all!" Washington exclaimed.

But others pointed to the facts—as Deborah would—that we lost only twenty-six men to Howe's *two hundred and twenty-six*, with an additional full thousand wounded (half his force). That controlling a hill covered with thorny blackberry bushes was hardly a major strategic coup. Gage's own words about the battle were proof enough of our success at Bunker Hill: "The people are now spirited up by a rage and enthusiasm as great as ever people were possessed of—we must proceed in earnest or give the business up."

Washington's ignorance (or ignoring) of these details was to the American farmers who fought and were wounded there nothing less than a declaration of war—on them.

It was not that Washington was oblivious to their view. It was just that in the language he spoke, that of "facts" which fit with his own gentleman's ideology, it simply wasn't possible to lose a hill and win a battle. Never mind that the lone fear of another Bunker Hill would keep Howe distracted and unwilling to attempt a frontal attack again; these considerations didn't rate with "gentlemen" the same way losing the hill did.

A language of fact and not of feeling.

A language disallowing nuance, thus humanity.

A language of fear.

George Washington was inclined to agree with Loyalists that our "Just and Righteous Cause" had been betrayed because, once again, at Bunker Hill we had behaved like "murderers." Ours were not regimented soldiers acting upon the orders of captains—one forward line firing while the rear loaded in orderly, predictable fashion. No, this, as reported, had been steady, relentless fire erupting without interval, without proper display of military etiquette. The Tories would say (and Washington wouldn't disagree) it was the handiwork of "banditti, desperate wretches of whom not one has the least pretension to be called a 'gentleman.'" Simply because we hadn't waited for orders to fire.

This was just not how a "gentleman's" war was fought. Or won. There were rules to follow, hierarchies to hew to, customs to obey.

Fortunately for America, the Rebels didn't see it that way then and never did quite get the hang of it. For in their language, Bunker Hill had been the best kind of triumph, and in the end it was their language that would win the day once Washington adopted it too. Which he would finally do, albeit secretly, although I wouldn't apprehend this for several more years—only just in time to turn 'round the war at the point when we were right on the brink.

Remember that I told you this was a story about getting past appearances?

Pray, read on. . . .

CHAPTER 25

The Battle of Breed's Hill

*I*n Cambridge, I was repeatedly rebuffed in my attempts to speak to Deborah. She would have nothing to do with me after I had snubbed her in front of Washington. "Lieutenant Robert Shurtleffe" ("Psst! It's me, Alice!") went so far as to show up at my door, warning me to stay away, that "Colonel William Buttrick" would not only look unkindly upon my continuing to call but would forcibly deter me from doing so.

Now that Dr. Warren had died ("knees steeped in blood," as prophesied) and old Artemas Ward had been placated by the generalship Congress had granted and been corralled into Washington's camp, "Colonel William Buttrick" (commission granted by Ward and Warren) was the one remaining "hero to the people." He was praised for his commitment and fiery dedication to The Cause, particularly his brave, patriotic showing at Bunker Hill, and stories about his courageous, defiant—and triumphant—

stand at that battle were legion. The same stand he was about to be court-martialed for.

In a different language.

Neither Washington nor Congress could abide the fact that so-called lieutenants and colonels had, in the last moments of battle, directed their "soldiers" to run from Howe, off the hill. To avenge this sad turn of events, Washington wasted no time authorizing the issuance of eight court-martial writs for cowardice and corruption demonstrated during the battle of Bunker Hill, Buttrick's indictment chief among them.

Of course, I tried to change Washington's mind, even going so far as to admit Buttrick was a woman I once had loved, an admission which, had I not ducked, would have afforded me a lethal head wound by flying candlestick.

The truth is I was in such utter disbelief that I hadn't even let sink in the possibility that Deborah could, in fact, be hanged. The objections I voiced to Washington were mostly driven by my fear that pursuing this course of his would make it impossible for me to convince Deborah that Washington was a good man and that this, for now, was the best we could do for her Revolution (the case I'd been wanting to make to her personally when I tried to visit her tent and was turned away).

But this, now, was my wake-up call. How in the name of God had I convinced myself that dragging Washington to Cambridge was somehow part of the piecemeal progression toward my goal of obtaining food and guns?

The mercilessness of the language of the "gentlemen" had hit home.

Of those eight court-martial writs, I recollect three: Samuel Gerrish and Joseph Matthews for running from the engagement, and, of course, Deborah, a.k.a. Buttrick, for leading the retreat. Joseph Matthews was sentenced to ten lashes on his bare back in front of his company; I can't remember what happened to Samuel Gerrish; and Buttrick, to my stupendous relief, escaped.

Three days after the writ's execution, guards went to his/her tent to arrest him/her, only to find him/her gone. (I had snuck her a note via Alice: *Very dangerous! You must go!*)

My secret and very private joy over her escape, sadly, was short-lived. For Buttrick certainly resurfaced in a nefarious way that spelled her end. Amid dense fog, she was found rowing ashore off a British gunboat anchored on the Charles and was accused of plotting to shoot Washington while he was lazily sipping his morning tea (was it British?) under his portico. A sentry spotted Buttrick in his spyglass and wounded his left leg.

She was leaving me no out.

It was decided that Buttrick was to be hanged two days hence.

I went mad, begging, pleading, cajoling Washington not to follow through. Yes, I understood she was an assassin and all that, but still, the scenario as it was playing itself out felt so sad to me, so wrong. I wasn't quite the gentleman—yet.

Washington was not only unmoved, he further assigned me to Buttrick's watch, threatening me with dereliction of duty, punishment being death by firing squad, should the prisoner escape.

Still I tried to save Buttrick's life, with one final plan. I offered to have Deborah—and her daughter—sold into indentured servitude in the West Indies, never to be allowed to return.

"Hang her!" Washington insisted.

"You *can't*, sir!"

He just stared at me. "And why not? Perhaps I'll hang you with her too!"

"You're not a king, sir, not yet! You'd do well to remember that!" I glowered.

I thought sure this was the end of my life. That Washington would drag me out to the Charles and have me shot, dismembered, and my bits tossed to the sea. He didn't do that. Instead he kept drinking Madeira and one hour later inexplicably reversed his course. "Indenturement, eh? Your proposal has appeal," he slurred. "Do it."

I did it.

She told me that she would rather have died. Alice didn't know what to think, except that the West Indies couldn't be so bad because it was warm and there was a lot of sugar there.

Visiting her in the safe house that evening, I confided, "I will make sure you are comfortable, and when this is over I pledge to work tirelessly for your return." The truth was, I intended to send her to a particular plantation belonging to an old business partner of my father's, but I didn't share that with her because she wouldn't have cared and I was concerned that the guards outside the door might be listening.

"So—you've joined the enemy."

"I'm afraid you've got that wrong, Buttrick," I replied, hoping that calling her by her soldier's name would reduce my heart's affection for her. But it only made things worse. "Oh, why the devil did you plot to kill the General, after all? If only you'd have let me speak to you. If only you could have been made to see it wasn't so bad—"

"Stupid moron," she hissed, kicking her chained foot against the wall. "He's not my general!" She spat at me, covering my cheek with her warm saliva.

I couldn't bring myself to wipe it off, not straightaway, finding in the hot, viscous spit strewn across my face confirmation of what I'd been looking for and otherwise had been unable to find: rage, fury, shame, embarrassment that I'd ever had anything to do with her at all. The conviction that she, with her chains, shorn hair, filthy neck, face, and arms, and those venomous eyes, was mad—and had been so all along.

A silence fell between us. Only this time, no stardust, no lightning, no tea . . . if only because I wasn't listening.

I turned to leave. "Let me help you," she whispered.

She sifted dirt through her fingers and her chains clinked; she toppled the bowl of gruel that had been served to her on the dirt floor. "It's not as it looks," she whispered again.

"What's that?" I asked, breaking the spell. In consequence, the next opening that might have altered the course of History passed me by.

She even went so far as to beckon me closer with her finger, obliging me to descend before her on one knee. I wanted to feel nothing between us but the cold, dark crust of the oxidized chain.

She said nothing; she only smiled. It was the surest sign of her love I could imagine.

"You listen to me now, I'll opt for the Indies, I'll take Alice and I'll go."

I took her hand. I was crying. "Deborah, please—"

"Let me help you"—she repeated the entreaty that in light of the circumstances struck me as odd, coming even from Deborah—"by leaving you with a story," she continued, "of the Battle of Breed's Hill."

She rested the stretch of chain between her wrists on the floor and folded her hands comfortably atop the pile of links.

"They say such a slaughter the king's men never knew. They also say Gage has been going around telling the king and such, 'Those Rebels ain't the despicable rabble too many have supposed.' Now, I know Gage ain't probably saying 'ain't,' but you get the gist, and I imagine the rest is pretty near on."

She shifted to sitting Indian-style, just as she had the night of the Tea Party. "I say Gage better sit down with your General Georgie—have you noticed that he looks an awful lot like a pear, by the way?—and tell him what he knows . . . set George straight before it's too late."

She leaned forward, eyes wide. "By my calculation, every musket in American hands counted for one Brit gone or hurt bad. Those Redcoats, they went down. Major Pitcairn, remember him? I'm the guy who shot him, good for me! Bam! Bam! Bam!" She simulated firing her musket.

"And you know why they were beat? (And they *were* beat, makes no difference what nobody thinks.) They expected their pretty little soldiers to keep their pretty little lines while they were climbing a not-very-pretty, steep, prickly hill. Steep like this. . . ." With her thumb and forefingers she illustrated an angle of at least eighty degrees and chuckled. "Stupid fools.

"I'll be the first to admit it," she resumed. "Whatever good came of Breed's Hill, it was due a good amount to dumb luck. But I ain't afraid of luck. Luck don't take nothing from me. Don't make our winning any less likely the next time, and so on."

"But you didn't win at Bunker Hill," I protested defiantly.

"Not Bunker Hill, no, we didn't, quite right. But then again, there wa'nt a battle there."

Now I was confused.

"That's another thing. High time we start calling the battle after the damned fool hill it was fought on, don't you think? Breed's. It was fought on Breed's Hill. That's where people died."

"So Howe took Breed's Hill, then?"

"All Howe took from Breed's was a bloody wound and the scared-as-shit feeling that he was a sparrow staring at a cat. And the reason everyone keeps calling it the Battle of Bunker Hill is 'cause that's where the battle was *supposed* to be. It's only one hill over, so nobody's bothering with changing the name, especially since doing so, they think, would kinda be like rubbing salt in a wound. Bad enough, they say, the dumb Rebels ran. We can't be advertising to the world that on top of it all, the stupid Yankees met the British on the wrong hill. What kind of assurance is there in that?"

I was fascinated.

"Sure, Breed's Hill was a mess, as military things go. But that don't matter. What matters is that Howe—precisely because he thought we were stupid to fortify Breed's Hill—got cocky. But somehow, somewhere, we knew—this was the hill where we could beat the Redcoats.

"Because Breed's Hill was not defensible according to any book he'd ever read, Howe thought he'd spare himself the usual tactic of coming at us from behind the hill (which woulda locked us in without an escape, 'cause there wasn't nothing but a tiny neck he could have blocked at the bottom of the hill's backside). Thinking we were too stupid to waste time sneaking up on, he just crossed the Charles in his big boats, disembarked his troops in broad daylight, and headed right for us, straight on up."

She stuck her face in mine and continued in a whisper.

"Only to be completely undone. Up they came, big red and white lines, three deep, shooting at us, salvo after salvo, as we tucked ourselves behind rocks and prayed we had enough powder (we didn't) to ward them off (we did). With fifteen paces between us, two bayonet-lengths apart, finally we unleashed all we had left: a barrage of musket power so loud that people across the Charles watching from Boston thought there was an earthquake going on.

"Oh, you shoulda seen their bearskin caps flying in the air, big ol' hairy things in the sky, and all those soldiers who didn't know what hit them falling, somersaulting down the thorny hill, wondering how the hell our useless fowling pieces and itty bit of powder could have done 'em in." She couldn't stop herself from talking about it. It was like she was on fire.

"Just one big blast of firepower that came out," she continued, enthralled. "No command, no order, no design, still every shot perfectly timed. Seventy guns up against their two thousand, and they were the ones with prickers in their behinds. And according to Howe, according to Washington, according to all their military rulebooks, *it never should have happened.*"

She stood up, high up on her tiptoes, brandishing her chained hands like a torch, like Washington with his sword.

"And that's how a few stupid farmers on the wrong hill put the fear of God into fifty thousand king's soldiers. Bring 'em on!"

I noticed she had tears in her eyes. Oh, how I wanted to hold her, but didn't dare.

"So . . . why'd you run then? If everything was looking so fine?" I asked, chastened but bewildered.

"We ran out of powder. So we disappeared like raccoons in the light of day, leaving Howe the hill, but knowing that jackass would never in a million years underestimate the Rebels again."

She plopped herself back down into the dirt.

"And that's my point. Men won't be winning this Revolution with guns and smarts and big ol' plans, John. They'll be doing it like we did with the hoax, with 'openings' coming at them, openings they'll see only if they're open themselves. Just like your turtle coming to you up from the swamp—you gotta be ready."

I didn't know what to say. It wasn't that I wasn't moved; I was near to tears, in fact. Every fiber of my being wanted to think she was right. It's just that, right or wrong, I didn't think she, in her state of mind, could ever win.

Sadly, I thought for certain she was a lost cause. That she would go the way of Apollo and be smashed to bits. And that I, unable to survive that since I'd be smashed to bits too, had better run now.

"Your way isn't the way, Deborah. England will cut you up into little pieces and serve you for dinner. This is serious business now."

"My point exactly."

"What you want wouldn't have been made right by killing Washington."

She smiled. "Wouldn't you like to know?"

She clutched at the soil. Frustrated as all get-out, she clumped dirt in her palm and squeezed hard until traces of earth began to leach between the fingers of her hand.

"What happened to you down there in Philadelphia, Lieutenant?"

I had nothing to say.

"I'll go," she finally agreed. "Just tell me when and what ship."

"I think that's wise. And as I said, I'll work tirelessly—"

She stopped me, just as she did that first night on the ferry, by covering my mouth with her salty hand, then she spoke. "I was just hoping . . . you'd have come around."

It would be years before I'd realize that all along Deborah had been the one working tirelessly to rescue *me* deep in the safe house that day. Years before I'd realize that already she and Washington were a team, not *adversaries*, and that I was the one in the front lines making History, but not Revolution.

I was simply too scared then.

CHAPTER 26

Valley Forge

There I was, sitting in Washington's fieldstone headquarters, preparing for a council of war demanded by Congress to help explain the three-year-long string of pathetic failures that had landed us in this hellhole called Valley Forge. Since Washington'd taken command, the war, as Deborah had prophesied, had not gone well. And Congress was spittin' mad about it.

If hell were cold and snowy, its name would be Valley Forge. Just outside the window in Washington's headquarters (where I resided with General and Mrs. Washington, Alexander Hamilton, French import Lafayette, painter Trumbull, and several other aides—yes, we were a very cozy lot) was a picket, a lowly enlist, shoeless but for a piss-drenched hat he was standing on as protection against the snow.

He'd be dead by nightfall.

As Washington and the rest spoke, the subject was how to

handle the soon-to-arrive congressional committee who most assuredly would be giving us a hard time. I, having heard this conversation too many times, chose instead to look outside upon
the cart carrying those who had frozen to death in the night to the
mounting carcass pile just outside the hospital: more food for the
wolves.

I watched a soldier beating himself with a stick for warmth,
drawing ninety-eight-degree blood to heat his flesh. I spotted another boiling a rock for the broth. History would have it that this
action was merely an example of irrepressible Valley Forge gallows
humor. It wasn't funny. The poor, starving sod was entirely serious.

And here I was installed in Washington's headquarters: a
warm, reasonably well fed wretch whose most pressing assignments this day would be an unsuccessful quest on Mrs. Washington's behalf for quality table linens and, later tonight, the
whipping of a soldier whose only crime had been that he'd been
caught in the countryside foraging for food.

And I thought I was doing my duty for my country.

My time with Deborah, who had been shipped with Alice to
the West Indies on a slave ship, I considered a dark (but somehow
never forgotten) mistake of my past. And believe it or not, I'd
resumed uneasy relations with my father, who was president of
Congress these days.

I should have known then, with Father's election, that something was amiss with this war effort. For one thing was certain:
Henry Lawrence, who most assuredly had never suffered a change
of heart with regard to his dislike for The Cause, was no friend of
freedom. Now, on the advent of the congressional visit, I prayed
for snow.

I understood, of course, that snowfall might result in the loss
of yet more soldiers. I wasn't completely insensible to that (yet).
Still, given a choice between having the decaying remains of
soldiers, horses, and dogs visible to the visiting congressmen or
sacrificing another soldier, I would, regrettably, have chosen the

latter. That's how desperate we were to keep Congress on our side. Besides, if it didn't snow, the quartermaster general was threatening to have one of us burn the carnage, and nobody wanted that noisome job.

Particularly troublesome were the dead horses. Horses would die of starvation standing up; when their bones were too dry to hold their weight, they would collapse with an unnerving thud onto the ice. They were a problem about which no one knew quite what to do. The ground was too hard and the men too weak to dig a hole and bury them. And there was no way in this hell, no matter how hard it snowed, for there to be sufficient accumulation of it to cover them up before Papa and the rest arrived. Heaps and heaps of snow were required for that.

For it was decided that at all costs Congress must not be allowed to see just how destitute, hard-up, and dispirited we were. Otherwise they just might do as threatened and blow out the candle on this ridiculous, failing campaign for independence.

Congressional support had been scant even in the best of times, which were generally acknowledged to be confined to the evacuation of Boston by the British after the Siege of Boston and the encouraging Christmas engagement at Trenton. But now, with the abysmal and embarrassing losses of New York in '76 and Philadelphia in '77; Brandywine (again, we lost hundreds); Germantown (we ended up, in the fog, shooting at each other instead of the British); not to mention the wholesale massacre at Paoli (three hundred men were bayoneted to death by the Brits), their support was particularly unenthusiastic.

We knew full well, in fact, that if we were not able in today's meeting to persuade Congress to continue with their support, all would be lost and we'd be surrendering to King George within days.

Unfortunately, Trenton didn't count anymore because it happened over a year ago and wasn't much of a battle to begin with. A nice morale boost, perhaps, and certainly invigorating—navi-

gating ice floes and rousing drunk Germans and all—but strategically insignificant, Congress well knew. And to call Princeton a
victory was a stretch, as it was an altogether pointless escapade
from start to finish.

So we were not about to take any chances with Congress, not
now. If we were to be brought down, it must be by the enemy, not
our own governing body. Anything else was simply unthinkable.
Better that the body of the soldier who was thinking of eating
that rock for dinner be covered in snow.

The problem was that the only way to please Congress, at this
point, was to indulge them in this dangerous fantasy that we had
what it took to take Philadelphia back. For well over six months
now they'd been railing against Washington for having lost that
city, for his October '77 retreat to Whitemarsh after Germantown, then, in December, planting himself in Valley Forge for the
winter and not budging.

"What about Philadelphia?" Congress screamed. Didn't Washington have any idea the kind of trouble the colonies were in?
France, upon whom we had been depending for assistance provided that we first declare independence from Britain (which we
did primarily to please her), still was dragging her feet. Holland
and Spain didn't care and never did.

And meanwhile every black man, every Indian, and every
woman was storming the delegates' doors and demanding that the
Declaration of Independence be taken at its word and its doc-
trines applied to them! The very idea: "All men are created
equal." That cursed vegetarian Jefferson, we should have known
better than to turn to him. How presumptuous! How anarchic!
How delusional! How silly!

Congress wanted to know why Washington couldn't understand that a full-out victory, such as retrieving Philadelphia, was
our only hope of pulling ourselves back together again, uniting
the country behind a single effort and attracting international
support. Without that, in all honesty, there was simply no point

in continuing on with this exercise in futility, this so-called War for Independence. Without Philadelphia, it was all a sham.

But everyone knew that the real bug up Congress' collective ass was being denied Philadelphia's entertainments and the relative comfort of Independence Hall. York, in southeastern Pennsylvania, to which Congress had been displaced, was, after all, dark, dank, drab, and reportedly low on quality prostitutes. Why was Howe, the enemy, the one having all the fun? Why was he the one dancing quadrilles, living in a fine stone house in Philadelphia's most desirable neighborhood? Why was he the one fucking a woman whose husband considered it a royal privilege to hand her over to the commander of the British army in America? Tell us, General Washington, where is the justice, the freedom, the sovereignty of America in all that?

Needless to say, it came as no surprise when, within minutes of their arrival, Congressman and Pennsylvania Governor Joseph Reed (or was it Gouverneur Morris? Or was it my father?) brought up the subject of winning back Philadelphia.

"So one more time," he asked, wishing to settle this matter once and for all, "exactly why is it that Your Excellency has given up on Philadelphia altogether?" He was hoping that by referring to Washington as royally as possible he might be flattered into giving a different answer than he'd granted in the past.

Washington replied, with practiced politesse, "Because we are particularly without guns, powder, cannon, food, shoes, boots, horses, medical supplies, and even potable water—the bluffs above the Schuylkill River are covered in ice, by the way, making access to drinking water impossible short of melting snow. And to top it all, soldiers are deserting to the tune of six or so a day. So saving Philadelphia would be a challenging, if not impossible, task at present, sir."

An understatement if ever there was one.

"Congress is a body made of men, sir, not all-forgiving gods," was a congressman's retort. "With all due respect, the feeling among those of us who meet—not many of us, you'll understand, because raising a quorum has proved utterly impossible due to lack of interest in the war, which, because of your dull performance . . ."

At which point the speaker abandoned every pretense of interest and simply sighed with the utter tediousness of it all.

Nathaniel Folsom now jumped in and resorted to pleading. "Do you have any idea how ugly York, Pennsylvania, is, General? Truly it's a horrid place. Please, please, please, get us out of there." And then bribery: "Do that and I promise you'll have all the food, clothing, and gear money can buy."

At which point General Wayne, a pal of Washington's in attendance, braved an affront. "So in the meantime, sirs, let's never mind about the quorum. If Congress cannot legislate because they cannot convene, whether that is due to lack of interest in the war or not, I take as none of my affair. About that nothing can be done just now. But what about the uniforms for the soldiers I ordered from the quartermaster's office months ago with nine thousand dollars of my own money? What about that? Where the devil are they?"

Morris sighed. This was his attack to parry, as he was the money man. "No, the order has not been lost or stolen, just stalled. An order placed with private funds poses serious issues which Congress needs to consider before proceeding. An armed, standing army financed by government is one thing, is in itself problematic, but the specter of an army financed with personal monies is a precedent much too dangerous and fraught to ignore without thorough and open debate." And since without a quorum there could be no debate and without a Washington victory no quorum . . . well, this line of logic led Morris to the dirtiest tactic of all.

Morris knew full well that the mere mention of the name Horatio Gates might be enough to cause Washington a rash, but he didn't stop there, he reminded Washington—as if the General needed reminding—that there had been several in Congress wishing to remove the commander-in-chief and replace him with General Gates, leader of the northern army.

"Remember the little matter of the Conway Cabal?" Reed grinned like a cat. (Uppity Colonel Patrick Conway had engendered a plot to replace Washington with Gates.) "Talk of change is again in the air," Fulsom said.

My, my—this was getting nasty.

The distinguished gentleman went on. "None of the other generals in the army seem to have this problem of yours. This habit of getting nothing done. Gates has had to endure all manner of adversity. First, Benedict Arnold: brilliant, but nearly impossible to command. And then there were all those blackflies in the backwoods of the Hudson River Valley, where Gates was stuck beating back the British who wanted to isolate New England from the remaining Mid-Atlantic states. These challenges couldn't have been easy, yet neither Arnold nor the flies seem to have stopped Gates from managing the British defeat at Saratoga, New York, in October this year—the single greatest humiliation of the British since the war began. So really, General Washington, what gives?"

"It's cold up there in Saratoga, too, by the way," John Harvie piped up. "October in the north is much like February in Pennsylvania, yet somehow, Gates pulled it off. As we speak, the defeated General Burgoyne and his men are being marched through the countryside, vanquished prisoners in chains. And what do you offer by way of comparison, General Washington—dead horses and men stewing rocks?"

In case you hadn't realized it already, the snow I prayed for hadn't come.

At long last the men came around to the real reason for their visit: "We feel it is incumbent upon us to acquaint you with Friedrich Wilhelm August Heinrich Ferdinand, Baron von Steuben, who will be arriving shortly."

Congress was sending an inspector general all their own because they had lost faith in Washington. "Just to discipline, drill, and organize the troops in the European style. To teach them how it's done."

"I see," Washington muttered, shifting in his seat, visibly reining in his famous temper.

"Congress would be most grateful if you'd receive him well."

Nothing more was said. At least Washington would keep his job, and all assurances were given that Steuben would be working under, not equal to or above, Washington. At least we weren't being altogether sacked.

In any event, Steuben ended up being quite a charming and helpful fellow. The only real difficulty he ever presented to us was learning his full name. One of the congressmen suggested turning Steuben's name into a tune for easy memorization. Truly I think one of the most ridiculous memories of the war was the scene, that night, of ten men of the highest military and legislative echelons in America trying to fit the name Friedrich Wilhelm August Heinrich Ferdinand, Baron von Steuben, to the melody of "Come jolly Sons of Liberty, come all with hearts united . . ."

Soon thereafter, the meeting ended and the deputation from Congress headed back to York.

In their wake, in celebration, plans were laid for a party for the General's forty-sixth birthday, for which it was decided a military band would be paid fifteen shillings. The menu was chosen: veal, potatoes, and cabbage. And since there would not be quite enough silverware or pewter dishes to go around, my job was to see to it that one of the blacks, perhaps Washington's loyal slave Lee, would stick to the kitchen and wash over and over again the few pieces that we had.

We drank while Washington crushed hickory nuts in his fist. Clearly he was nervous, distracted—more so than I'd ever seen him since the inception of the war.

"Everything all right, General?" I asked.

"Quite, quite," he replied, seemingly unnerved.

But of course, Washington was a wreck. And not because he'd just had yet another run-in with Congress.

I was about to learn that such encounters were of little or no concern to Washington. What he worried about was winning the war, and toward that end, what was preoccupying him was not Congress or even Steuben, with his new drill techniques promising greater efficiency, discipline, and facility for battle.

What Washington was obsessing on was me. He hoped that in whipping tonight's soldier (who had stolen and killed a cow) I would finally, at long last, be of real help to him in his campaign to win this war.

"Patriotism . . . whosoever builds upon it as a sufficient basis for conducting this bloody war will find themselves deceived in the end. We must take the passions of men as Nature has given them. . . . I do not mean to exclude altogether the Idea of Patriotism. I know it exists. . . . But I venture to assert that a great and lasting war can never be supported on this principle."

Remember, reader, that George Washington said that around this time, and then join me, if you will, in the whipping shed at Valley Forge.

CHAPTER 27

Finding The Cause

February 7, 1778, was the date I moved from officer back to soldier, from lieutenant colonel back to John. The day I moved from chief aide with responsibility for tabulating the Historical details of war—the count of missing bodies and the wounded, powder supply and ordnance, things like that—to living the real story of the Revolution. And the irony was that George Washington himself was the one bringing me back where I belonged—with a little help from his friends.

I remember having been astonished, over the years, at the General's extraordinarily high threshold for Congress' infinite idiocy. Even during that night's "council of war," for example, his relative calm found me befuddled and, in all honesty, dismayed. How was it possible for him to sit there amid such deliberate insults, maintaining for the duration that soft, ridiculous smile portraitists liked so much?

Wait a minute. That smile . . .

Maybe the failing commander with the pockmarked face, the gawky body, and the soft heart, the one who'd suffered such illness all his life, wasn't so passive after all.

Maybe it was simply that he knew what Congress would and could never know: that like it or not, this was a war for *Revolution*, and everything they wanted from Washington—a bankrupt show of military excellence and prowess to grace the accounts of History—was wrong. And maybe he knew he could never breathe a word of any of this, that should Congress discover it, they'd sign a peace treaty tomorrow and shut us all down. Maybe he had faith, and thus the stamina and confidence, to take criticism in stride. To be more or a less a yes-man (except for his constant whining to Congress for more food and guns—sound familiar?) so as to keep Congress off his back and to buy himself time to deliver to the people what they dearly sought: freedom.

But maybe Congress, given that the war had been going so badly for so long, finally was at its wits' end. The arrival of Steuben aside, maybe the game was pretty near up indeed, and it was time for George Washington to step up his timetable, take bigger risks, and go full-tilt ahead for Revolution—and a more profound kind of civil war.

Maybe George Washington wasn't at all who we thought he was. Maybe he knew much more than he'd ever let on. After all, he said himself that he'd decided well in advance of that Second Continental Congress session to bring that ratty old military outfit along.

History likes to say Valley Forge was the turning point in the war. Actually this is true, in that it was only after Valley Forge that we won any battles to speak of at all. Like I said, prior to the winter of '77–'78 we could boast "victories" at Trenton and Princeton, but neither were battles, really. More like sneak attacks.

And if truth be told, even during the post–Valley Forge years the victories were very few and far between (Cowpens, King's Mountain, Guilford Courthouse).

In any event, for the war's more successful turn after 1778,

Steuben, the general with the long name, is most often given the credit. The argument being that he turned a loosely organized, undisciplined, ragtag group of men into a professional army once and for all. Ah, there we are, blaming the soldiers again, not Congress or our Founding Fathers for their lassitude, apathy, and unwilling frame of mind.

But the discipline Steuben inculcated in his men is, as usual, less than half the story. The fact is Steuben got his men to love him. He supervised his own drills, cursed a blue streak in several languages, and brought his huge, gentle Italian greyhound, Azor, with him wherever he went. Additionally, he threw dinner parties for his men for which the dress code—"*sans culottes, s'il vous plait*"—gave the half-naked Valley Forge soldier a hearty, good-natured laugh at his ragged plight. Additional traits redounding in his favor were his love of beer and loathing of church and the lies about his rank, which he claimed to have earned in service to his Prussian king, when it was quite clear that Franklin, who brokered Steuben's consultancy, was solely responsible for his sudden promotion from captain to general. Be all that as it may . . . yes, it is true that Steuben's involvement in the war was critical, not to mention colorful.

Frankly, Valley Forge was a turning point for another reason: because it was during this time that George Washington stepped up his commitment to the Revolution, figuring this as the best way to win.

I like to think that the turning point was Washington commandeering the likes of me for his top-secret, brilliant little underground Revolutionary War.

For sending me to the woodshed that night and insisting that I whip this derelict soldier myself, I will forever be in his debt, for it taught me what he perceived in his vision and wagered his career upon: the possibility that I still had a heart which could be broken (open). Thank God for that, otherwise there'd have been no hope. I'd just have continued on as an officer: bloodless, feckless, and cruelly clueless as to the real story of the Revolutionary War. Which was Deborah's story, redux.

Fifty lashes was the punishment, to be suffered in a pitch-dark room, the soldier attached to a whipping post strategically placed by the fire so that the whipper could get a good look at the target and only the target: the soldier's back, an abstract, headless, legless, armless rectangle of thin, bony flesh. All that the whipper could stand to see.

I detested the thought of whipping soldiers, as Washington well knew. He had always, until now, excused me from the terrible duty. Why *now* was he forcing me to undertake this hideous task and stare into the black hole that was my life?

As I stood in that shed, staring at the faceless soldier's naked back, I blenched at my task and trembled at what I'd become.

John Lawrence, you wretch, what are you doing whipping a starving soldier for stealing food from a local peasant? Who the hell cares that as far as the military is concerned, starvation is a crime?

I reached for the whip, felt the leather in my hand. . . .

Who was John Lawrence fighting in this war? Who exactly was the enemy? More to the point, what was I fighting for?

I wrapped the snakelike instrument around and around my fist. . . .

Was I fighting for or against the "gentleman Patriot" plantation farmer who, in refusing to supply the Continentals with hay so as to fetch a better price from Howe, was denying the naked American soldiers the simple cover of a thatched roof?

I unfurled the whip to its fullest length. . . .

Was I fighting for or against the "gentleman Patriot" wagon masters who, after demanding to be paid in advance for the delivery of provisions to camp, would dump barrels of goods over a cliff at the first sharp or rutted turn?

I raised my arm and cracked the whip to test its weight. . . .

For or against those fish merchants who, during the arduous journey to Valley Forge, would lighten their load by emptying their cod casks of brine, causing the fish to arrive rancid and poisonous?

I recoiled at the gunshot sound the whip made, while my victim-to-be held steady. . . .

And what of the merchants who would sell barrels of rum cut with water? Deliver cattle so emaciated they were translucent, so thin that one could watch the worms wriggling their way through the intestines and brain?

I fought the rising bile in the back of my throat, breathed deeply to keep the vomit down. . . .

And why the devil is this godforsaken place called Valley Forge when it's neither a valley nor a forge?

Nothing made sense anymore.

What on earth were we doing?

One more second. One more torturous thought.

What good would ever come of a Revolution that, to save on horses, treated their men like beasts and refused the hungry soldiers even the means to convey logs to build their rude, drafty huts, ordering them instead to harness their own skeletal bodies to the felled trees, some trunks as long as eighteen feet and fifteen inches wide, to drag them to the building site?

I raised the whip and let fly, my arm angry as a lightning bolt. And there was the blood, dripping from the deep slash across the pale back.

And then, something else: a vision of Apollo as the soldier twisted in his bonds to face me, his eyes red, squinting with fire. And from his mouth—lips and tongue chewed raw from holding back his scream—came five quiet words:

"Mother wants to see you."

Alice looked at me as from another place, another time. She collapsed, but because her hands were bound to the post, she couldn't fall to the floor. She dangled.

"Mother wants to see you," she said once more, barely audible. And then she fainted.

My body, in shock, became teeth-chatteringly cold. So cold I was absolutely convinced my arm would stay frozen in midair for a lifetime to come. I felt stiff, hard, fragile, lonely. An image of my own body splintering to bits flashed through my mind, nobody in sight to pick the pieces up, let alone to join them into a necklace to be worn close to the chest like Apollo's shell.

Heaving myself to sensibility, I untied the girl and brought her immediately to the hospital. At some point after Dr. Thacher left surgery to give me a report on her condition ("battered, exhausted, otherwise fine"), she somehow fled.

It was as though the earth had suddenly sprung a hole into which I'd been dropped. Everything was changing, and fast.

The soldiers' ritual chant—"No bread, no meat, no soldier"—which nightly would spread through the camp like fire, wasn't the same. Tonight I was hearing "First Congress, then the Brits, then the world." Had it changed? Or had I?

With extra interest compounded on the agony delayed, it all came back:

. . . The terrible fear and jealousy and fragility that had informed my misguided campaign for food and guns . . .

. . . My hatred of Deborah's lover, Job (which I'd never acknowledged, not even to her, for fear of being vulnerable, exposed) . . .

. . . My hatred of my father (which I'd forgotten, in the interest of pretending to be loved) . . .

. . . My love for Deborah . . .

Mother wants to see you.

Had she traveled by slave ship to the West Indies now to return? Had she escaped?

Had she never gone?

Of course she hadn't. Of course she hadn't. Oh, how could I have missed it? How could I not have seen that the Revolution was being fought all this time right under my nose? That Deborah had not only been alive and well all along, but . . . oh, my . . . could it be?

Yes, as sure as I'd remembered only one of the soldiers' chants

("No bread, no meat, no soldier") but not another ("First Congress, then the Brits, then the world"), I'd convinced myself that the Revolution never could happen and therefore, like John, my own former self, wasn't worth remembering at all.

All along I was the one who'd been shipped in chains to a faraway land, not Deborah.

"Mother wants to see you."

To the Revolution, Johnny . . . *come home.*

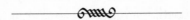

Suddenly, events of record that I'd lived through took, in my mind, an entirely different character.

The Evacuation of Boston: March 13, 1776 . . .

The Historical Account: Washington was hailed a hero and awarded an honorary degree from Harvard for sending Howe packing from Boston. Specifically he was praised for having induced his men to climb Dorchester Heights (looming above Boston) under cover of night with six hundred pounds of cannon and to entrench themselves there with guns and artillery pointed down to the city, directly at Howe. Guns that dared Howe to come up or to make good on his threat to burn the city. Guns that warned him to get the hell out of town.

The Revolutionary Record: Washington, taking a page—and specific suggestions—from the lowly Yankee book of tricks, fooled Howe into evacuation. The cannon were actually empty—we had no powder. And we knew that the British knew the cannon were powderless. That's why, in addition to the cannon, and on their own cognizance, our soldiers lugged thousands of pounds of garbage up the hill with them: vases, milk jugs, latrine scrapings, chandeliers, broken baby cribs, axes, muskets, hoes, even mildewed butter churns.

What they did with this kitchen refuse and household discards was stuff them into barrels placed at cliff's edge at the top of the

Heights, set and ready to roll. One look at the debris that would have been heaped upon him should he attempt the climb and Howe decided to run. Shooting at the barrels was pointless. Cannonading the hill simply wasn't possible: The Rebels were too far up, too high. And God forbid Howe attempt another Breed's Hill–style frontal attack. This time, even more humiliating than being routed by Yankees, he would be pushed back by waves of shit, junk, and debris that would only be made more putrid and horrifically runny by the surprise gush of rain that suddenly and instantaneously began drenching the hillside just as Howe was deciding what to do. *We slipped in shit, Your Majesty, and so were beat* was not exactly what Howe wished to report back to the king. Better: *Boston was no longer capable of being defended, so I took what I could and repaired to New York,* tossing into the sea cannon, baggage wagons, artillery carts, horses, and, rumor had it, even a few desperate Tories clinging to the prow of his gunships—anyone and anything that would slow him down.

The Battle for New York: July 1776 . . .

The Historical Account: New York was a sorry miscalculation on Washington's part. Howe took Manhattan and Brooklyn and White Plains and Forts Washington and Lee there, handily. Whole units of Continentals were killed or captured. Thousands upon thousands of men were left for dead, and just as many in retreat made a beeline for New Jersey and deserted. Hundreds of cannon, muskets, and vast stores of other ammunition and supplies were stolen away. The consensus was that Washington should have known better than to divide his troops or to set his men upon an exposed hill in Brooklyn, one that Howe could easily access from the nether side.

History later made excuses for Washington, insisting that in light of the circumstances (his untried, panicking soldiers were too quick to retreat) this was the best Washington could do. In fact, Congress was enraged at the commander-in-chief.

The Revolutionary Record: Ah, an entirely different story. Howe actually considered the successful battle for New York another miserable defeat for him, and it broke him. From this point on, he lost interest in the war, choosing instead, in his despondency, to spend days, nights, weekends—in fact, the remainder of his entire military campaign—obsessing not on his fortunes in war but in bed with his mistress, Elizabeth Loring, the Philadelphia bombshell he dragged around with him and was fucking wherever and whenever he could.

True, we were cornered in Brooklyn. And as if Howe's fleet of five hundred ships controlling the East River didn't make things grim enough, with darkness came surging northeastern winds and a wall of fog thick enough to dash plans for the crossing we might otherwise have chanced. On top of all this, when the wind died and the fog didn't, there came a silence so deep that the slightest sound, down to and including our tongues panting in fear, brought risk of capture and murderous defeat.

Silence again.

Another opening.

Another miracle, as command seemed to shift, without comment, from General Washington and his officers and aides to some cranky Yankee fishermen, the Marblehead sailors of Massachusetts, able to navigate the fog with ease. One by one, we formed what essentially amounted to a six-hundred-foot human chain to the water, guiding each other by feel (the fog was that dense!) to the rowboats that would, by dawn, ferry every last Continental soldier to yonder shore without so much as the sound of a dipping oar.

Not a military maneuver—no, it was a high-wire act, a ballet this night that had saved the next day. And to complete the show, the fog lifted just at dawn on Washington, sashed in blue, stepping confidently ashore onto Manhattan. Too late for Howe, across the sound on Long Island, to do anything but watch and swear: "God have mercy and I'll be damned!"

As for the subsequent chase through Manhattan, uptown and past Kip's Bay, the Continentals' mass retreat was considered by History to be the battle's worst hour. Yet even in this, there was triumph, signs of a thriving Revolution embedded within the defeat. I could see that now.

It may well have embarrassed Congress, the scene Washington made that day as the scared militia and Continentals streamed by him heading north to Harlem Heights in retreat, as he slammed his hat to the ground and cried aloud how on earth he was *ever* going to win this ridiculous war! But the sight of our commander-in-chief, hysterical and out of control, also moved whole hordes of men. When a lowly private helped the hatless, babbling General out of harm's way, put him back on his horse, and took Washington's reins into his own hands to guide him away from approaching danger, the Battle of New York was thereby transformed into victory of the most sensible kind. The letters written home by the soldiers featured moments like these, leaving the matter of success or defeat to those who cared about such things.

The commander-in-chief was tethered to a private, they would write, and that, to them, was as important as the status of our struggle with our king. As were stories of officers stripping themselves of their colorful insignias and taking cover behind privates whose native tunic of homespun provided better camouflage in the landscape dotted with limestone, cattail, and scrub.

After the Battle of New York, the war entered an even more precipitous downward slide. Enlistments were near to the end of their terms, and Washington was out of options: no money, no food, no arms, no congressional incentives to enhance recruitment and assist reenlistments to keep the army propped up. As far as Congress was concerned, Washington was a failure and his men renegade nuts. By Christmas of that year, 1776, the General was pronouncing the game "pretty near up" unless the troops could somehow be made to stay.

No word back from Congress. The implication: Make it work or go away.

Washington made it work.

To his soldiers he offered no bounty, no land, no fee—no empty promises he knew he couldn't keep. He simply asked them, please, to remain at his side. Stay past your enlistments, if you would, and we'll all help each other along.

Even at the time, the Historical accounts and the Revolutionary record were for once in synchrony about Washington's brilliant performance. We lauded him for his direct and candid approach to his troops. "Approach" and "performance" be damned: The tremble and quaver to the General's voice was coming from his core. And every soldier who stepped forward from the line that day to indicate his decision to stay on and fight did it because the man before them was real. Was a revelation.

Most of the soldiers stayed.

And so we come to the Battle of Trenton, at Christmas 1776. And the discovery, had I been open to it enough to perceive it, that Deborah was Washington's top-secret spy.

The Historical Account: Trenton was an ingenious strike, a strategic blow to Howe, Cornwallis, and that ruthless Prussian mercenary working for the British, Colonel Johann Rall. Washington crossed the Delaware River in the dead of night, standing tall in his longboat, and brought that nasty Hessian to his knees without a single life lost on our side. So Washington was "king" again, for a short time.

True enough in point of fact.

Now the Revolutionary version: First of all, if Washington had indeed been standing in that boat he would have tumbled into the icy water and been crushed to death by the jagged floes of ice. So let's put an end to that fiction right here and now.

Second, Washington was mostly attracted to the idea of besieging Rall at Trenton not because it was strategically so ingenious, but because lately he'd been learning that "enterprises which appear chimerical often prove successful," and there was no question that the intended attack on Trenton to this dubious category belonged.

To snare this "chimera," he again called upon the peculiar skills of John Glover's Marbleheaders, the same men who engineered

Washington's "dishonorable exodus" from Brooklyn to Kip's Bay. He wanted sixty Durham boats bent into the gale-driven sheets of snow and he wanted it done by midnight Christmas Eve. Could Glover do it? Word from a mysterious source was that Rall would be drunk and celebrating the holidays and never in a million years would he be prepared for an attack. Battles simply were not fought at Christmas.

Says who?

It was "a terrible night for the soldiers," Washington later would write, but he would not hear a single man complain.

Of course not. Because Washington was with them, kicking, pushing, tugging at the ice threatening to sink the little Durhams. Hunkered down, bent over in the cold, with ice forming in his lashes and across his brow and his breath icy wet, he was the best kind of leader, a comrade-in-arms who would let himself be taught how to twist an oar without tipping his craft, and how to jam through ice shards better than twice the boat's size without causing a whit of damage to the hull. He had learned how to recognize when it was time to put down the military textbooks and go along for the ride . . . that Deborah, as "Honeycutt," had engineered.

Oh, how could I have missed it?

Was I deaf, dumb, and blind?

How could I have believed that one "John Honeycutt, a Jersey farmer," captured three nights before Washington ordered up the boats, actually was a Tory "spying on our camp" from the opposite shore? What's worse, I was the one who interrogated double agent Honeycutt, keeping him under close arrest while Washington was allegedly deciding his fate.

I should have known: A Tory spy found by the pickets outside our camp—what was there to decide? Hang him, reel him in, and put him on the rack, stretch him to pieces!

But no, what I took to be Washington's "common decency," a collection of halting actions followed by a private one-on-one "trial" at which Washington solely presided, were actually ingenious maneuvers designed to give them both time to hatch this Trenton plan.

I could see it clear as day now.

Two days into Honeycutt's prison sentence, suddenly Washington had scads of information about Rall, his penchant for the bottle and for gambling, possibly even advance knowledge of the particular card game that Honeycutt no doubt promised would be keeping Rall occupied as Washington's forces stealthily approached on the night of Christmas Day.

After the battle, we found a note under Rall's card table warning him of Washington's Yuletide advance in Deborah's scrawl, warning the Prussian commander to stay in Honeycutt's trust, fully confident that her message would be blissfully ignored (it had the markings of Deborah).

A few days before the actual Delaware crossing, Honeycutt escaped. *I* was chastised for permitting his escape, even accused, for one brief moment, of possibly helping him along. How rich. I was asked how on earth Honeycutt set fire to the tent in which he was being held. Hadn't he been body-searched for flint, for the potential to create flame? Yes, he had been—but before Washington arrived, a flint secreted in his own pocket.

Top secret.

Not even I could know.

Dating back . . . oh, my Lord, all the way to Cambridge, just days after our arrival.

I was reminded of that first stare of his, chin in palm, when Washington, even with his terrible vision and at a distance of at least one hundred yards, had somehow determined that "Buttrick" was a woman.

I was reminded of Washington's decision later that night to have her dragged kicking and screaming to his headquarters, ostensibly to warn her against conducting herself like a man . . . a meeting she allegedly stormed out of, climbing onto his desk and out of his window . . . with the help of his own tall shoulders, I now had no doubt.

I was reminded of Washington's first expense in Cambridge. The next morning he had asked me to pen a note in the amount of $333.33 (a number handpicked by Deborah if ever there was one) for supplies that never materialized.

Of course they did. As Washington's first spy.

The assassination attempt, then?

Nothing but a ruse, which Deborah, in her story of Bunker Hill, was attempting to convey. Hoping beyond hope that her story of Breed's would replace mine of Bunker's and in so doing bring me to an "opening," to a new way of seeing things, enabling me to share in what really would be happening in the months and years ahead, above and beyond the expressed strategies and affairs of war.

Why didn't she just come out and tell me? Possibly she had orders not to, or it was simply too dangerous. But more than likely she did think she was telling me, in her own way.

In the way of the story.

Finally I understood her parting words: "Let me help you" . . . and "It doesn't have to be this way."

Not anymore.

Back at Valley Forge, I didn't even have to ask where Deborah would be that stinging cold night. I knew. I simply followed Washington on his "nightly walk" through the watershed, down the mountain, and into the nearby forest, there to be transfixed yet again by that radiant, incandescent, mysterious, irrepressible, inexplicable, send-joy-to-my-guts kind of smile.

I could breathe once more.

CHAPTER 28

Mission to Philadelphia

remember coming upon Washington and Deborah atop
Valley Forge's Mount Joy, she whispering in his ear, me
crying out, "Oh, heavenly woman!" and dashing to enfold
her in my arms; and Washington crying, "Arrest that man!"

Meaning me.

I remember running through the woods, Washington's sentries
giving chase.

I remember ducking, along with Deborah, beneath a dark
coniferous bough and then being knocked on the head with a log.

After that, nothing.

Oh, this business of Revolution never seemed to become less
confusing. Just when I thought I had it all figured out . . . oh, how
in the world did I get from there to here, and why? And where is
here?

I snuck a peek out the window of the office to which I'd been
brought: red brick, gas streetlamps, a wagon going to market with

snapping turtles, crab, and pie. I was in Philadelphia. Terribly attractive surroundings, I thought, for someone who must be a prisoner of war.

I could only assume that the tall, distinguished fat man was talking, since his lips were moving. But my vision was still too blurred and mind too dazed to make out his identity or to discern any of his words.

I was still thinking back on Washington wanting to arrest me (my memory was slowly coming back), and Deborah crying out: "*Run, John, Run!*" Then, out from the laurel, Washington's corps of bodyguards, each of whom I knew firsthand. "Sergeant Morris! Lieutenant Musgrave! It's Lawrence here!" I called out to two of the six men barreling toward me, bayonets fixed.

Since it was patently obvious that if I stayed still I'd be meeting the jailer or possibly the Reaper, I did as Deborah bade and fled for my life, with no idea why. And I remember, as I was turning to run, the sight of Washington tucking a parchment into Deborah's dress and sending her off in my direction.

Deborah must have taken a shortcut because within minutes she was sprinting ahead of me, jumping directly into my path and beckoning me to follow. With Washington's guard approaching fast, there was no time for explanations. I followed.

I distinctly recollect my fears for my life vanishing as I ran, along with thoughts of how on earth I could possibly have put myself in such mortal danger in simply responding to Alice's call.

I wanted only to watch Deborah. To observe her tough, muscled legs fording creeks, jumping moss-covered trunks of fallen pine, and her great brown mane riding high and wild behind her on the wind. I wanted only to run behind her until I died, whether that be for two seconds, two minutes, or eighty years.

It was in the grip of this reverie that I lost my footing on a rock and was sent careening down an icy incline, tumbling over boulders and branches and headfirst into a tree.

Here my memory dims. Was that Deborah dragging me into a

fir-shrouded cavern in time enough to save me from Washington's soldiers, whom I could hear passing just overhead?

Was that Deborah who said, "I'm so sorry to have to do this," before clubbing me from behind, felling me like a tired old tree?

My God . . . I think it was!

So who was this fat, tall man, not as distinguished as I'd thought moments ago?

He sat behind a heavy desk, clawfooted and of mahogany, and tipped back on his chair. He had an olive complexion, slack face, broad nose, and a thick but squeezed, pouty mouth that somehow, in my dazed state, invited comparison to a sphincter.

Additionally he had the most severe case of the hiccups I'd ever seen.

I'd laid eyes on him before, that much I knew.

Keeping my gaze away from his mouth, I fixed upon his forehead and asked the great balls of sweat beading his brow, "Do I know you?"

I tracked a drop. From forehead to nose bridge to nose tip, directly into his hiccuping mouth.

"Oops!" I heard myself say.

I guess I was coming to.

My muscles ached, my body was bruised, and my ankle probably broken or sprained. My waistcoat and breeches were torn, and I was filthy and caked with dried blood.

I stared upon the gaudy, red-jacketed aides at the gentleman's side scratching busily at their quills, recording his words, which here and there I was beginning to make out: "Mount Joy" . . . "impregnable" . . . (hiccup) . . . "there, you see" . . . "not altogether grim" . . . (hiccup) . . . "hmmm, nice!"

But it was Howe's pug who finally clued me in to who this gentleman was. Sticking to his corner, staring me down unblinkingly, the nasty little asthmatic canine with the menacing growl clearly remembered both that he hated me and probably even that he'd bit me once before.

My encounter with that vile little jaw of his dated back to last year, in the hills above Whitemarsh, north of Philadelphia, where we'd retreated in November after it was clear that we'd lost that city, but before we'd decided to winter in nearby Valley Forge.

We had just routed Howe, not enough to win back Philadelphia but certainly enough to send the British forces flying back to what was now the safe refuge of Philadelphia and to stay parked there for eight more months.

Maybe the mistake I made with the pug was naming him Lucifer. I spotted him on the battlefield, after the skirmish at Whitemarsh was done. He was trembling and whimpering near what had been the British line.

It was all an act to get what he wanted: some food. After that he went at me like Satan after God. "I saved your ridiculous little life, you porcine beast," I reminded him each time he drew blood. Oh, wasn't he a terror, running through the encampment nipping at ankles and whole casks of salt cod! And I, a lieutenant colonel, held hostage by an ungrateful little dog—a dog who belonged, we eventually determined, to none other than General Howe.

"Step on him!"

"Shoot him!"

But since neither of those oft-repeated suggestions seemed right, Washington settled the matter, ordering the pug returned, a polite note attached to his collar, to the British commander-in-chief. Out of spite, I thought. Although everyone but myself thought Lucifer had run away from Howe, I thought it more likely the reverse. If we'd only had that little demon on our side, we'd soon have routed the British.

So here he was again, mangy but loyal Lucifer, staring me down. My thanks for having risked life and limb in toting him all the way back to enemy-occupied Philadelphia's city limits.

And yes, before me was Howe himself, the "Duke of Dally," "Lord Snore of Neverup," who seemed nothing if not enamored of me and was now thanking me profusely for having "deftly delivered up the goods" to him.

Oh dear.

Stretched before Howe was the same parchment I was sure Washington had handed to Deborah, which now I could see was nothing less than a *map of Valley Forge*, with every embankment, redoubt, and powder house underscored; the configuration of troops arraying the field amply illustrated; the location of the hospital and the respective residences of officers Varnum, Pulaski, Wayne, and Washington outlined. The whole damned camp in plain view of the enemy!

And I was the man who'd delivered it? Thank God I was smart enough to keep to myself my ignorance of what I'd done! Howe clearly imagined me to be a spy for England.

How had this come about?

Dimly . . . yes, that *was* Deborah ordering the throng of Loyalist soldiers clad in green to carry my unconscious body to Philadelphia and directly to Howe.

Yes, the crinkling sound I remember coming from inside my shirt was the map Washington had passed to Deborah, which she had apparently passed to me, and which Howe had soon found on my person.

She and Washington wanted Howe to have this map. Why?

Was it possible that Washington was in the end nothing but a traitor? That this underground Revolution he was running with Deborah was a turncoat operation?

There it was, after all, the map of Valley Forge, in enemy hands.

No!

"Mother wants to see you." . . . "Arrest that man!" . . . "I'm sorry to have to do this, John." Even Howe's "Welcome to the fold, my man." All of it had to be—*had* to be—part of a plan.

I had to believe that sitting here in Howe's office, taken as a traitor to my country, I was executing a very important errand for my General and The Cause. I had to believe that Deborah and Washington were involved together on a mission important enough to get Alice whipped, me pummeled by Deborah and then praised by Howe.

But when the talk in the room turned to the subject of how the map I'd brought would make possible the wish of Generals Howe and Clinton to see George Washington kidnapped, I couldn't help but lose hope. Maybe Deborah *was* a traitor, after all. Maybe Washington had been duped somehow into handing her a map of Valley Forge, not knowing he was about to be betrayed.

No, that just didn't feel right.

I decided simply to listen for a while.

There was talk of inviting me as a guest of honor to the "farewell Mischianza" being held later this month for Howe. Apparently this Clinton fellow would soon be taking over for Howe, who would be "retiring" to England. ("Getting the hell out, to tell it right," Howe cracked.)

Also there was a rumor that a signed Franco-American treaty was making its way across the Atlantic as we spoke, in response to which George III, panicked to death, was ordering an evacuation of Philadelphia at an unspecified date so that troops could be marshaled to protect what was most important to England: the West Indies routes and New York.

Clinton, Howe's successor, was there, in the corner, near the damned dog. He never introduced himself and he squinted a lot.

I must say that despite my confusion and shock over everything that had happened to me in the past several hours, more than I felt frightened or threatened, I felt ill-prepared. Especially when, on my short but grand military-escorted tour of Philadelphia, I was asked to speak against the Rebel Cause (I begged off, pleading that I was a newish turncoat who needed, for the moment, to remain discreet).

I never forgot that tour. First of all, the city stank to high heaven of shit. I mean real fecal matter. Everywhere I looked there was evidence of turd. In the statehouse yard. Spilling out of genteel houses through open front doors.

Eighteen thousand soldiers were occupying Philadelphia, nearly doubling the population of the already overcrowded city and quintupling the number of horses. I could only guess that they'd run out of places to evacuate their bowels and that this, more than any fears of a Franco-American alliance, was why Howe wanted out of the city.

And, mind you, not a single British officer or aide in the carriage acted as though Philadelphia didn't smell anything but damned fine. God save them and their king.

The statehouse, where the Declaration of Independence had been debated and signed, had undergone a conversion into a hospital for prisoners of war (it stank, too, of human carcasses). And the Bunch of Grapes and City Taverns, once the sites of drunken political chitchat, without which there might never have been war, was surrounded by whores and scores of Redcoats playing dice, backgammon, and piquet. I could only imagine what had happened to Hell's Caves: probably became a diabolical love nest for this Elizabeth Loring and Howe. (By the way, where the hell was *she*? Oh, there, making out in the opposite seat with Howe. My, my, quite a tongue on that woman.)

The famous families' homes of Philadelphia—the Wisters', the Norrises', the Drinkers' and such—all had been taken over by the troops for use as barracks and stables. Evidently the Darraghs' home was where I was to be housed, because that's where the carriage dropped me off (Howe was deep into precopulation by now, so I decided not to disturb him with a good-bye).

"Ta-ta!" the jolly coachman cried, waving me off. "Until tomorrow then."

Oh, was that the plan?

So why wasn't I surprised when "Lydia Darragh" turned out to be Deborah, a housewife who milled flour when she wasn't "agenting" for Howe (and double-agenting for Washington)?

A sharp little home, brick front, two stories. Her husband "Charles"—who, naturally, didn't exist—was "a sailor, always away at sea"; and Lydia, as far as the British were concerned, was a Tory lass, a nonpacifist Quaker (nice touch, Deborah), who'd been a native of Philadelphia for years.

Striped linen dress, starched bonnet, wide apron, even a sprinkling of flour on her hands and stew simmering in the Dutch oven. Deborah had this particular act down cold.

Of course I wanted to fall to my knees, plead and cajole finally for some explanation to all this madness. But taking my cue from Lydia's sidewise glance to a handsome, tiny man at the table cutting pretty shapes out of silk cloth and presenting nosegays in various combinations for Deborah's survey, I got the message: Now was not the right time to speak. Not yet.

"John," she chirped matter-of-factly. "Lovely to see you. Stew?"

"You're too kind," I assented. What else could I do?

"Tea?"

Of course, tea. She was a Loyalist at the moment.

As for Captain Major John André, the elf whom Deborah introduced to me as a boarder, he was the man in charge of decorations for "the Mischianza" (that word again). He seemed thoroughly uninterested in my presence, except when Deborah offered me up as someone "particularly good at cuttin' and pastin'" (a Tory lady, maybe, but she still spoke like a Yankee trollop).

Believe it or not, I spent *three more hours* helping Deborah and André design floral bouquets and servants' costumes for this Mischianza, which turned out to be some sort of grand gala send-off for Howe.

It was midnight, the thirty-some-odd-year-old André put to bed with his rag doll, before Deborah and I were finally able to huddle before the fire.

"It ain't as crazy as it all looks," she said, taking the lead. She thought again. "Well, maybe it is."

I jumped in at last. "I'm still back at discovering Alice! Everything else is a blur! Tell me, tell me that the whipping—oh, I am sick, sick when I think of it now—is part of some . . . Oh, Deborah—and what about Washington? And the knock to my head? And the map? Oh, I'm so perplexed and vexed and confused I don't know where to begin. Are you a traitor? A friend? Am I on a mission to assist or undermine The Cause? Help!"

She was staring into the fire, already focused ahead on the business at hand. "Calm yourself, John. Everything's fine. Alice, too. It was a sacrifice she was only too willing to make. There was simply no other way of getting you to come without risk of detection."

"To come to you and Washington?"

She stopped me. "For the moment, John, please, I beg you, we must stick to the assignment."

I tried to hold my tongue. Then: "I must insist—"

She ignored me. "At Howe's, did they discuss kidnapping Washington?"

"Yes, they did!" I answered urgently. "So is all this madness of the past twenty-four hours in the service of thwarting such a plot?"

"No," she answered flatly. "In fact, you need to know that Washington wants you to help them with exactly that."

"I give up." I sighed.

She actually smiled. Then: "Not here," she warned, leading me to the back.

She took me out to the garden. After scaling the wall to make certain the alley was clear, even beating through the rosebushes to be sure no one was hiding in or behind them, she escorted me to a raggedy patch of sod, which, when she lifted it, revealed a hatch door.

I followed her down into a damp, rocky hole, entirely without light. I couldn't see her anymore. But I could feel her groping for my hand, which I surrendered.

The hand. The ferry ride. Ezekiel and the minnows swimming upstream. All of it came flooding back.

"Deborah . . ."

"It ain't so horrible as it looks, John. You ain't helping kidnap nobody, not really. You're just getting in there and winning their trust. Getting in on their team, so I can do what I gotta do."

"And that is . . . ?"

"Get this war moving. Finish it up, with your help."

"Still thinking small, I see."

She shrugged. "Just doing what it is I gotta do."

I couldn't help myself. I hugged her. "I want to say I'm sorry, about food and guns and Bunker and Breed's and shipping you off and all, and I *am*—"

"But you're mad 'cause all along you were taken for a fool, I know. I wanted, I *tried* to tell you the only way it was safe for me to do."

"When did he first approach you?"

"You know all this."

She's right, I did. From Cambridge to the whipping to Lydia Darragh, I now understood it all.

"The only part that worried me was whether you'd be alert enough to keep cool with Howe and the map and all. For that the General and I were counting on you spotting him handing me the map—"

"And the chase?"

"To give you credibility as a deserter first with the Loyalists and then with Howe," she explained.

"Why me?"

Silence.

"The Revolution needs you, John. George needs us to win this thing."

"You call him *'George'*?"

"Someday maybe even to his face. Ain't quite there yet, though. We made a deal."

"Three hundred thirty-three dollars and thirty-three cents?" I asked, remembering the odd amount.

"And Alice. He had to have Alice. As insurance of my loyalty and secrecy."

"You sold your own daughter?"

"No, I freed her, to a bet I knew Washington would never lose. That's why I couldn't say anything more at the safe house or Trenton or . . . oh, there were countless times I could have gotten to you, if only you knew."

"I get the idea," I mumbled.

So all along, Alice was an enlistee and also a spy.

Yes, I got the idea.

"And since that's what *she* wanted more than anything else in life, it all worked out."

"And all along she was fighting right under my nose . . ." I was shocked by my blindness. "So . . . why three hundred thirty-three dollars and thirty-three cents?" I found myself asking.

"Three, three, three, three, and three adds up to fifteen: the number of times my father raped me."

Suddenly there was a knock, vaguely rhythmic and absurdly long. Clearly the "tune," if it could be called that, disappointed Deborah.

"She can't get 'Yankee Doodle' right to save her butt. That's our code. I pray to God she don't ever come at me wantin' money to learn to sing and dance, 'cause I'd say 'Sure, sweetheart,' when truthfully I'd be dyin' inside 'cause it'd be like sending my pennies to the moon."

"Alice?" I asked, altogether stunned and unable to say more.

"Sure," she said matter-of-factly. "Alice with the club fist— but *that ain't no excuse!* She's gonna get that damn song right before she's welcome in here! So tonight since André's snoozing and there's no one around—she'll wait!"

This, from the mother of the girl I'd just whipped twenty-four hours before.

Was there nothing that this woman could not take in stride? Friend, soldier, master spy, doting mum, cranky mum, my love, all in one. A woman who treated the plotting of war as equal to teaching an obdurate daughter—handicap and stinging, bloodied back notwithstanding—how to knock out a melody.

Of course, she got what she wanted. Eventually Alice tapped out "Yankee Doodle" to Deborah's liking and was allowed to descend below.

One look at Alice and I understood how her scars had served her well. As with Washington's soldiers' pursuit of me, the whipping had given her all the credibility she needed to cross enemy lines. She was a "deserter" now too. And, after months and months apart, was reunited with her mother, at long last.

Alice hugged and kissed Deborah like the sun would never rise again. She kissed me too.

So Alice had been summoned to service as well. So she and I were to work together on whatever it was that was being planned.

I assumed faith and abandoned suspicion, because here, back with my family, I could.

"Welcome home," Deborah said.

CHAPTER 29

The Mischianza

So, things being as crazy as they were, when the British abandoned their plans to kidnap Washington I was inconsolable. Crazier still, my objection to their new, alternate plan to kidnap Congress—wholesale—was based upon my fear that I'd be left out.

Of course, none of us was thinking or behaving rationally. Howe dropped the plan to kidnap Washington because he lost the map. Per Deborah's orders, I was to commit myself to anything that would stick me close to Clinton or Howe (who, by the way, in the middle of all this, was mostly holed up with Elizabeth Loring, counting down the days until he'd get to go home).

The scheme to kidnap Congress was nothing but Clinton's attempt to keep me around as a conduit for the massive disinformation campaign he was about to mount. For Clinton, his vision unobscured by Loring's blond curls and big tits, had suspected me of treachery from the start.

Of course, as I was volunteering to help crazy Philadelphia Loyalist Joseph Galloway scout prospective prison sites for all sixty-five congressional delegates, I had no idea that Clinton was on to me. And certainly Galloway, an ex-congressman himself, a bona fide idiot, was too delighted at the attention he was getting to suspect for a second that the British command recognized full well that he was out of his mind.

I also have to say, the ridiculousness of the plan notwithstanding, I didn't mind passing in and out of York (where Congress was still convening), working up plans to lasso that esteemed body into the gargantuan pens Galloway had become convinced we'd have to build, since houses in the country tended to be too small.

It even took Deborah a while to see that we'd been found out, or at the very least been rendered suspect. Clinton recognized that in distracting me (and by extension, Washington) with go-nowhere, harebrained schemes, and by keeping Deborah reporting on military activity in and around Philadelphia (news of which he knew was surely bound for Valley Forge), he was weaving us into his web.

Didn't she make the job look entertaining, though! Combing the countryside as she and Alice would for bits and bobs of information, sewing Alice's notes inside the button covers of a coat, poking them into a jacket lining or the mouth of a freshly caught fish. Oh, there was invisible ink made of lemons and milk, and a coded system of communication based on various colors, sizes, and densities of different balls of yarn that Deborah, perched on a hill and knitting, would drop off rocks to be found by Valley Forge contacts.

She sent news of everything: the profusion of construction on the New Jersey side of the river and the redoubts being built at Cooper's Creek; the horses, some five thousand in number, being ferried back and forth over the Delaware; news of a shipyard destroyed in what turned out to be a purposely set conflagration;

and orders issued to the Redcoats to begin collecting supplies, up to twenty days' worth, to be loaded into wagons and carried across the river whenever the signal arrived.

Clinton was smart but Deborah, smarter. The construction, the ferries, the transporting of weapons, horses, and guns across the river—before long it all made sense to her. Clinton had overdone it and tipped his hand. Too much activity, too fast, not amounting to anything.

In the wake of the recently announced Franco-American alliance, it was common knowledge that Clinton would never be able to hold on to both Philadelphia and New York, and would likely decide in favor of holding the latter. So activities like these, clearly pointing to the evacuation of Philadelphia, weren't—and for Deborah indeed had never been—the big news. The news would be: *when* Clinton was going to do it.

"Wait a minute, this is all a ruse! He's got me coming and going, looking at ferries and horses and soldiers, can't you see, 'cause that's where he *wants* me lookin'! He's no fool! Clinton knows Washington needs lead time—what, two, three days?—to move out of Valley Forge and intercept him, and he ain't about to just give it to us! Forget the guns. Forget nabbing Congress. He's keeping us from what we need to know!"

Well, maybe Washington needed a few days, but Deborah's friends in the countryside didn't. So if push came to shove and she wound up with less time than was desirable, there were always the Jersey Rebels to blow bridges, fell trees, and block pathways to halt Clinton's wagon train northeast while Washington gathered his army, his supplies, and his nerve.

Still, "Absolutely, positively—we gotta know *when*."

Now I realized, that first night in the hole, what Deborah had meant in saying she intended to "finish off this war." From the beginning, as soon as rumor of the Franco-American alliance hit the street, she clearly had anticipated evacuation (as had Washington) and wanted someone on the inside of British army headquarters—in this case, me—to obtain the all-important news of the actual date of the British evacuation. Washington's kidnapping had been nothing but the "opening" to get me on the inside.

"And what if the kidnapping had been pulled off first?" I would later ask.

"Never," she answered confidently. "I woulda raced ahead to the Forge and foiled it: 'Georgie, hide!'"

Finally it all made sense. But unfortunately that did nothing to help us with our little problem. We decided that I must continue pretending to take the Galloway Plan seriously, even though it was just another Clinton ruse to keep me away from what I really needed to know. He wasn't to know that *we* knew. The point was to carry on our duties as spies *even more diligently*, to continue to support and not disabuse Clinton of his suspicions. To encourage him in his campaign of disinformation by making goddamned sure that he received all manner of confirmation that what was "leaked" to us was "spread around real good." That every lie of his was disseminated quickly, clearly, and exactly as he'd hoped.

Why? To make sure Clinton kept us close, closer, closest. Fine, then let's be spies he thinks he's duping! Give him a reason to keep us around!

So now Clinton, Howe, Deborah, and I needed each other. What a war . . .

Deborah worked up a counterplan to provide proof of delivery of whatever Clinton wanted Washington to know. If Clinton issued an order to remove a siege gun or burn a barn, we'd make sure he *knew* ordinary folk on the street knew it, that merchants and farmers knew it (here all we had to do was spread word on the street to create gossip Redcoats would overhear and report back on). Last but not least, he was under the impression that Washington knew it and believed it. For this, we resorted to the Lexington trick of making sure "intercepted" letters of Washington's fell into Clinton's hands.

Meanwhile, militia captains were under strict instruction, thanks to grocery lists interlaced with messages written in that invisible lemon ink, not to move on any gossip, any missive, unless it was sealed or verbally accompanied by a secret code of Deborah's devising.

Clinton was loving this, so much so that eventually he had me sitting in councils of war. In fact, things became so fluid, so routine, that once it only took forty-eight hours to present to him proof of Washington's belief that Clinton's men were estimated at twenty thousand (when in fact Washington knew they were only ten).

The problem was that none of this was putting us any closer to the news we needed in order to "finish off this war," which Clinton seemed to be protecting with his life. We did everything we could: break into his office, lace his tea with herbs thought to have truth-telling properties. At one point, with the help of a gypsy woman, Deborah even attempted to read his mind. All to no avail. His was a secret even telepathy couldn't crack.

Then finally, one day, after tailing Clinton's valet down State Street, Deborah figured out what to do.

"I got it," she said simply, careful not to reveal her meaning to André, who now, some weeks later, was putting the finishing touches on the designs for the flower centerpieces and candelabra installations for the great and glorious celebration to be held three days hence: the fabulous Mischianza, a.k.a. the Good Riddance to Howe party. Little did Howe know that what awaited him was a final hurrah before the onset of disgrace and infamy. He would be known for the rest of his life as the man who mucked up the British campaign to retain America.

Her idea, Deborah said, involved gunpowder, Clinton's personal belongings, and getting ourselves into that Mischianza. That's all she would allow. Claiming it would be "unlucky" to tell more because "pink and flush was the sky" when the notion came to her, and "that's always a sign to keep mum!" Oh, well. So far, scurrying minnows, bone dust, and mystic numbers in sums ($333.33) seemed to have taken her pretty far.

Actually, she did elaborate a bit on her resistance to revealing more than I think she intended: "I just don't want you knowing, is all—no point in you knowing something that could get you killed when only one of us needs to know to make it work."

She was scared. Of losing Alice. Or me. I knew it when, for a brief moment, her emerald eyes lost their glimmer and the corners of her mouth turned down.

"However you wish," I consented gently.

She bounced back. "Just get yourselves into the party and I'll take the rest from there." Her voice tightened. "And remember, do exactly as I say."

She kissed Alice.

"This is our one and only chance. We can't fail."

She shook my hand. Hers was trembling.

Getting into the Mischianza was a cinch, since Captain Major John André, in above his head, desperately needed help with the party setup.

Eager finally to make the splash he felt was his due and that had been denied him in battle, he'd gotten more than a little carried away. What was meant to be a pretty little theme celebration along the lines of *The Thousand and One Nights* mushroomed into a tournament, complete with knights mock-jousting on gray chargers for the hands of fair ladies costumed in polonaises of white silk; spangled pink sashes, shoes, and stockings; towering headdresses decked with pearls; and veils edged with silver lace. A boat parade would feature men-of-war rigged with gay flags, garlands of roses, and stocked with naked soldiers done up in blackface and dressed as Nubian slaves, with silver collars and bracelets, surrounding Howe. And a military procession would pass under two triumphal arches built just for the occasion. A fire-works display would follow at ten, followed in turn by a supper of twelve hundred different dishes carried in on the backs of the Nubians at midnight. Finally, after the feasting, dancing in the great hall would commence from four to nine the following morning.

André was already tired.

"Right now, I couldn't care if Washington himself offered a hand—I'd take it!" Alice overheard André saying to a co-worker at an all-night "work party" to weave garlands and cut menus in the shape of paper dolls.

I must admit that I felt demoted a tad, having gone from attending a council of war to designing table runners, place cards, and ladies' fans. By comparison, the scheme to kidnap Congress felt like serious business. Still, there was much to do: eight hundred mirrors to install, three thousand candles to ensconce, poems to write for the spangled ladies to recite.

And when André discovered he was short a lady, I thought we'd lose him for sure; he was hyperventilating so much I thought he'd rise into the air and fly away.

There were to be two separate pavilions at each end of a four-acre lawn. Each would hold a total of twelve bejeweled, begowned ladies for the favors of which twelve shining knights would mock-joust. Losing a lady threatened to ruin the symmetry of the entire design.

"Everyone will think me a failure and a fool!" André whined. (Which is nothing compared to what those of us watching you pound your feet and fists on the floor over this issue began to think of you, my lad.)

The missing lady was Peggy Shippen, Philadelphia's premiere beauty. Apparently her father, a Quaker, took one look at the low-cut gown André (and I) had designed and said he'd rather see his daughter tossed into the sea than attend.

Finally, after three rounds of smelling salts, pungent spice, and ice inserted directly up his nose, André was brought to his senses.

Hard to imagine that this nervous wreck of a man was the same whom Benedict Arnold would later entrust to deliver the plans of West Point to the British.

A handsome and charming youth who bought a commission in Britain's Seventh Foot Regiment, André, a "daddy's boy" par excellence, hated Rebel Americans' blood and guts with a passion exceeding anything I'd come across before. He put his disgust down to his having been captured during the Canadian campaign of 1775. Pelted with human shit, forced to sniff a hatchet his captors promised would split his skull the very next day, the dainty major was freed fourteen months later in a prisoner exchange. Yet I did not believe this to be the primary source of his ungodly wrath. This was a man born to be vexed—and born to be punished for it. Arnold would get away, but André would be hanged.

"A little loose about the waist, don't you think?" he asked me, jabbing yet another pin into our substitute lady's soft, pink flesh before I could respond. Deborah didn't even say *Ouch!* as he yanked the silk fabric about her person, while talking of his days as an aide to Major General Charles Grey at "Paoli '77," as he liked to call the scene of the most haunting massacre of American Rebels thus far in the war. For him, it was an all-time career high that also brought him to the brink.

"There I was, bayoneting the few Americans I had not already clubbed, stabbed, or sliced the faces and genitals off of, doing spectacular work, and where did it get me? Billeted in a tiny little Philadelphia home with this dowdy Quaker housewife—"

Deborah couldn't help but object: "I'm saving your ass, André!"

"Stop twitching, you flat baggage!" he seethed, his pin drawing fresh blood. He shoved Deborah off the dais. "Tomorrow at dawn—be there. Pavilion A! Wear your hair up high—no less than two feet to give your otherwise squat, plebeian face a nice, rich look. Eat light, drink less—and mind you, don't bloat!"

Deborah winked at me, as if to say, *Put up with the fool. He's our way to the happy end.*

André turned, sticking his face into mine. "So, fine—they want a party. I'll give them a party so spectacular, so grandiose, so memorable that finally I'll be in the pantheon of greats where I belong! This will be the night of all nights! Tomorrow, for Captain André, the world begins anew!"

Was he in for a shock. I'm surprised he lived long enough afterward to be hanged.

In the middle of all this festivity the next day, I was to sneak into the gunpowder supply house, where the fireworks André had planned were stored. Not a problem. And Alice's assignment to get hold of horses for the "escape" was made possible by her volunteering to take care of Howe's military carriage for the procession, putting her within reach of four fine beasts, of which she would commandeer two.

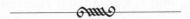

May 18, 1778. Four o'clock. Midafternoon. The plot to obtain the exact date of Clinton's evacuation is on.

Under the protection of the British warships on the Delaware River, the queens and their knights and all the notable guests, headed by Sir William Howe himself, board decorated barges while being serenaded by military music. They are then rowed from Knight's Wharf to the landing place at Old Fort.

As soon as the guardian ship leaves the dock, I steal to the supply house for the fireworks.

Five o'clock. From Old Fort, the procession moves along an avenue one hundred yards long, lined with soldiers in gay regimentals, then passes under two triumphal arches, one featuring a gilded figure of the goddess Fame blowing her trumpet, from which a banner wafts bearing the motto, YOUR LAURELS ARE IM-MORTAL.

The crowd joins a herald in proclaiming Howe's praises in horrible verse as scripted by André. Meanwhile Alice, scheduled to water the horses attached to the now-parked military carriage, secretly releases two of Howe's horses from their harnesses, whispering to them to remain in their positions. Deborah and Alice are to share one horse, and I will be spurring the second.

Five-thirty. The clash of arms. The knights mock-joust with lances, swords, and pistols as the fair ladies in the pavilions on either side of the four-acre field cheer, coo, and pray for their chosen knights. André must be so pleased, until . . .

Deborah, fair and bloat-free, installed in Pavilion A as ordered, suddenly faints. A mortified André tries to slap her awake. Being in a public place is the only thing deterring him from blacking her eyes in the process.

"Reviving" her (if you can call it that) fails, of course, but it preoccupies manic André sufficiently to prevent his close observation of the fireworks installation at the perimeter of the estate. Which is a good thing, because as Deborah is swooning, I'm stealing barrels of gunpowder, stowing them in the bushes, and preparing to blow them up at Deborah's word.

Six o'clock. A tiny flare emanating from a bedroom window in which Deborah has been placed by André to recover (or else!) appears in the sky. A hopeful sign to continue as planned and for Alice to ready the horses.

Alice jumps onto one of the horses and grips the reins, wrapping them tight about her club fist like leather around a ball. Guiding them about the perimeter of the mansion court, she reaches a labyrinthine garden replete with rushing fountains, arbors of morning glory, and twisting raspberry vines. She enters it, cautiously, quietly, making her way to a spot just beneath the window of Deborah's recovery room.

Six o'clock and two minutes past. The crowd retreats to the ballroom, made gorgeous by all those candles and garlands of roses we spent the night hanging, especially when reflected and magnified by the hundreds of mirrors we painstakingly fastened to the wall. Once the crowd is tucked inside and the pavilion strained to capacity, there is another discreet flare from another window.

That's my cue to blow.

I ignite the barrels of gunpowder. Serially detonating all twenty kegs, I cause massive explosions and much damage to the estate's outlying brick wall, gardens, fountains—even to the mansion itself.

Inside, terror ensues as the banquet hall turns into a rumbling, crumbling, crashing, hellish heap of horror. Candles set tablecloths, seat cushions, men's waistcoats, and ladies' wigs on fire.

The waiters, costumed as Egyptian slaves, slip and fall, sending 214 dinners into the air, splattering guests with bits of duck, currant sauce, and roasted boar.

Upstairs, Deborah keeps an eye peeled on the guards posted across the hall at the door of Clinton's changing room. In the melee and ruckus, the guards can't help running for cover, scraping and ducking their way down the hall.

Now is Deborah's chance.

Figuring that she has less than two minutes before the pickets discover that the gunpowder explosions are neither fireworks gone awry nor enemy fire after all, she moves like lightning.

Deborah searches purposefully through Clinton's changing room, knowing what she's looking for, but without a clue as to whether or not it's here. Is it on the desk? Hidden in a pile of papers? Her fingers slide across the bureau top, through a chest of drawers, in and around Clinton's armoire, beneath his bed, inside his trunk.

Too many minutes pass. She can hear the guards returning, close on the threshold of the changing-room door.

Damn! How in heaven's name did she come to leave the cursed door ajar?!

No place to hide. The steps draw near. But she won't leave yet. She looks for a disguise, the valet's work coat.

Aha! Tucked inside the pocket. Yes! The little green work diary that can turn the tide of the war.

And there it is—a homely entry, listed under the heading, JUNE 17:

"Retrieve general's new uniform."

She knew it! Days before, when she'd observed the valet entering the tailor's on State Street, she'd followed him inside. Eavesdropping, she'd learned of the order for Clinton's new battle uniform: the softest scarlet broadcloth, the finest gilt lace, the richest velvet stock. But she hadn't caught the date it would need to be ready. That was whispered. And why? Because it was a date earmarking an event requiring the most splendid attire. Victory attire. For surely Clinton, like any self-respecting officer, foresaw triumph in his evacuation from Philadelphia and his march on New York.

June 17 was when it would all begin. By June 18 he would be across the river and deep into New Jersey, just in time for a total solar eclipse.

How divinely helpful.

How miraculously timed.

How terrifying to be staring down the barrels of two muskets. . . .

Deborah kicks one of the guards squarely in the balls and rams her head into the other's teeth.

"Goddamn you, woman!" the first soldier gasps as he falls to the ground.

"*Now!*" Deborah screams, hurling herself out the second-floor window and into a ranunculus bed, where Alice and her steed are lying in wait.

"June eighteenth!" she whispers, spurring the horse. "Keep to me like I was your own backside!" she orders her daughter. "*Hold on!*"

She gallops off at breakneck speed, jumping hurdle after hurdle: shrubbery, statuary, and a man-made pond, clearing the estate out to open road, where there before her, atop the second of Howe's carriage horses, am I.

Off the road and onto a tiny trail we fly, deep into the woods.

Deborah and Alice are bound to the countryside to alert militia, Rebel boys, their children, and their wives. Well in advance, Deborah has prepared her countryside network to receive the date she is soon to bring them.

And I am headed for Valley Forge to let Washington know personally: that June 18 will be the date to intercept Clinton, to overwhelm his wagon train, to outflank him, both sides, and get him front and rear. To bring Clinton, begging, to his knees.

No.

Instead it will soon be Deborah, Alice, and me doing the begging—pleading with the Redcoats for our lives.

CHAPTER 30

Monmouth Woods

The thundering hooves followed us like a menacing storm cloud about to burst.

"Halt or we'll shoot!"

Clear enough. We obeyed.

With an extra bounty and possible decoration undoubtedly promised the Redcoat whose bullet took our lives, these three men could have been expected to shoot us dead on the spot, no questions asked.

They didn't.

Perhaps what deterred them was the sight of a beautiful, begowned woman still in her high heels wheeling off her horse, approaching the soldiers, reaching for the barrel of one of their guns, and bringing it directly to her heart.

"Go ahead—I dare you."

"Step back, woman!" the soldier warned, trying to wrest his gun from her grip.

She held on.

"You reckon killing us is your duty, I know. And that's true, if your duty's only that of a king's soldier, not a man, not a daddy, not a husband, not a granddaddy. If you're just some rat who's forgotten he was once a boy who at one time or another thought the world was piss-poor unfair—"

"For the last time, step back!" said another soldier, for the one whose gun Deborah was holding had gone quiet.

Deborah pressed on. "So shoot! And remember when you do that you're gonna regret it like you shot one you loved. . . ."

She blinked. Was it fear?

"And when your kids ask you, 'Papa, Grandpapa, why'd you slaughter that lady, her daughter, and her man?' Ah, hell! Let me give you our names—this way you can say, when we're famous all over the world, that you knew us when. I'm Deborah, there's Alice, and that handsome fellow, he's John!"

The Redcoat's gun was shaking. Deborah's foot was twitching. Other than that, her mien was cool.

"So where was I? Oh, yeah. . . . 'They just wanted a world made right, Daddy! How on earth could you have been so wrong?' And all you're gonna be able to say is ' 'Cause the king told me to!' Now, won't that be a sorry time?

"I know it looks like I'm the enemy, but I ain't, unless you're happy shoveling shit, getting whipped 'cause your breeches aren't white enough, being tossed into prison 'cause you're carrying debt, getting your finger chopped off for saying what amounts to 'boo' about the king—the same king that thinks you're a worthless turd he'd sooner jail, even kill, than meet."

The soldier: "Madam, give me back my gun!"

"So what is it, then?" she asked. "Is it shoot me dead or let it rest? Is it murder or 'Let them go!'?"

The Redcoat gave way. "Goddamn you, Jenkins!" one of the others cried, raising his musket and training it on Alice, her face in his sights. He cocked the hammer.

The girl looked to her mother. "Mummy, it's coming on. . . ." Suddenly, wracking convulsions shook her body. She fell to the earth, drooling, trembling, kicking in the dirt. The fit was on her.

The sickening sight of the girl with the crippled hand thrashing uncontrollably was enough to make all three Redcoats dismount their horses and take direction from Deborah as to how to help. Ordering one to place a stick in Alice's mouth, another to hold her gently, and me to stroke her head, Deborah knelt beside her, whispering "Hush, now, little darling. Mama's here. Everything's fine. Tap out 'Yankee Doodle,' sweetheart—can you do that?"

The concentration required of Alice was a lifeline, and she began tapping her way back from her fit of falling sickness, a condition which until this time I didn't know she had. Small wonder Deborah had been so insistent about Alice getting the tune right.

Slowly but surely, Alice came to, by which time the soldiers had lost a good deal of their resolve. Was it a state of heightened lucidity, or of mania, or of inspiration, which compelled Alice to make her next choice?

As the Redcoats were kneeling over her, debating among themselves exactly what to do with us ("Should we at least wound them to slow them up? Take them prisoner?"), Alice pulled a knife from her jacket and slit one soldier's throat. The other she managed to stab in the gut. And before the third could comprehend what had happened, she leapt up and ran, compelling him to follow.

"Run, Mother, run!" she screamed. Deborah, in shock, could no more run than I could. The remaining soldier felled the girl with a single shot, which echoed across the field.

Silence.

Deborah ran to her daughter's limp body. Ignoring her, the soldier lunged at me, stabbing me in the leg with his bayonet. Then he mopped the excess blood from my leg, wrapped a cloth tight below my knee, and tied me to the saddle of one of the dead men's horses, tethering that horse to his own.

Turning to Alice's mother: "Run along now, to your General. And pray—end this bloody war," he said quietly.

He left Deborah alone.

Tipping his hat, he rode away with me in tow. When I craned my neck, I could see that Deborah was in a tragically altered state. Her face was buried so deeply into her dying daughter's bosom I was certain she was trying to suffocate herself and die.

I called out, "Run, my love!"

She didn't call back. Not even to say good-bye.

Over and again in my mind I played back this scene that had left Alice dead, Deborah as good as slain, and me a prisoner of war. The queer thing is, I couldn't imagine it having gone any differently. It seemed meant to be, I suppose.

I gathered it was.

The series of events occurring thereafter I never witnessed; I only heard tell of them. Ultimately, in fact, they became legend, told and told again by plain folk hundreds, nay, thousands of times. Every teller adding his or her flourish, the end result being a tale that in every respect but one I trusted was true.

The ending was what was false. The ending which held that Deborah Simpson and John Lawrence ended their lives justly famous, given full credit for putting America on the path to freedom in winning the great war.

According to "The Legend of Deborah and John" as told at hearths and kitchen tables, after John was taken away, Deborah clung to Alice for several hours more. In a small clearing ten minutes' ride outside Philadelphia, off the road to Germantown, she held her daughter in her arms and watched her die. This was how the tale began.

Another ten minutes it took for little Alice to choke on her own blood. Although she died of a bullet to her body, such was her spirit that she did not die instantly, not before tapping out with her fist a particular tune. . . .

Deborah waited until afternoon the next day, until her daughter's body was cold to the touch. At which point, unable to leave her side, and unwilling to bury or burn her, she strapped Alice's dead body behind her on her saddle and together they rode away.

Some thought it ghoulish, the sight of a grieving woman with a dead girl tied to her saddle riding through the countryside, screaming out news of Clinton's oncoming exodus: "Turn out, citizens, turn out!" But mostly people viewed her as an angel from heaven, for the Rebel folk were so pleased finally to be executing their long-planned and long-awaited shot at vanquishing Britain on their own that had Deborah been a decayed skeleton in a tricorne hat they still would have cheered her, welcomed her as one of their own, and helped her on her way to Valley Forge.

"*Now! Now! Now!* Ambush his baggage train and send his vehicles careening into the mud! Fell trees onto Clinton's path! Farmers, kill your livestock so as not to have them stolen by the British! Fill your wells with sand to deprive them of water! Shoot the stragglers in Clinton's right flank and blow up so many bridges that his passage is slowed! Ready the way for General Washington!"

Notifying Washington of Clinton's withdrawal was more difficult. Having been a spy for the commander-in-chief for some time now, Deborah normally knew full well to take every precaution not to be seen or heard in the vicinity of the General except as someone other than herself.

Today she was much too distracted to care.

Today she rode right into camp, lathered in grime and demented with grief, and demanded to see the General, alone.

The General, of course, would not come.

"Fuck it!" she cried. "Tell him the eighteenth it will be! June the eighteenth Clinton will evacuate Philadelphia! He will have a ten-mile-long supply train of artillery, baggage, provisions, pontoon trains, fodder wagons, private carriages, rolling bakeries, traveling blacksmith shops, fifteen thousand soldiers, five thousand horses, and at least two thousand terrified Loyalist camp followers. In short, plenty and more!

"But also there will be on this day a solar eclipse. No shadows. We will hide in bushes, lie in wait, and make sure that Clinton is given the hardest of times. We will pick his men off like at Lexington and Concord—like flies! By Monmouth Courthouse, in New Jersey, Clinton will be slowed to a near halt.

"Tell the General this is where he must come, by way of the ravine, to do the final harm! Tell him he must prepare without delay!"

At which point, nearly falling from her horse in a faint, she regained her balance, wheeled her charger, and galloped away.

Upon hearing the news, the General raced to the top of Mount Joy to have a look through his field glasses at the woman the sentry described as "crazy as a loon." Satisfied that it was Deborah, though disturbed by the sight of Alice's body draped over Deborah's horse, he ordered immediate preparations to move out and away from Valley Forge.

The time had come to resume the war.

For well on a month (June 18 was by now just twenty-eight days away), Deborah aimlessly wandered the hills, taking a position overlooking Monmouth and camping out, living on rabbit, acorns, and herb brews. She was worried. Would Clinton be sufficiently harassed? Could Washington vanquish him?

Odd that Deborah found the mental wherewithal to ask herself such questions, for, in fact, her cognitive state by now had deteriorated to the point that had she been asked, she'd not have been able to recollect her own name. And she believed that Alice was still alive. So not only did she refuse to bury her daughter, Deborah kept her body propped up against a tree beneath a protective bough and each day would update Alice on the state of things in the coun-

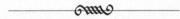

tryside, whether the match-to-end-all-matches between Clinton and Washington was—or was not—soon to transpire.

Just Deborah and Alice sitting there upon the hill amid the white wreaths of shadbush, yellow forsythia, and lilac, waiting on Clinton, on the people, on Washington, on the eclipse of the sun.

The date arrived.

One can't help but feel sad, not only for America but for Deborah, that the Battle of Monmouth Courthouse turned out to be a draw.

It all started well enough, Washington scaring the living daylights out of Clinton in dotting the hills along the British column with thousands of troops ready to come at both his flanks, pincer-style.

Deborah, viewing the parade from across the ravine (she was not willing to leave Alice behind to fight), was delighted with her and Alice's work (although not for a second had she forgotten about John).

"My Lord, finally, it seems we've done it, dear! It seems we've reached just about everyone we needed to in time! Clinton's baggage train looks less than half its size, the soldiers and stragglers look depleted, and I can see that bridge after bridge in his path has been destroyed! And, oh, my love, Washington has arrived!"

Yes, indeed, it seemed as though Deborah had done everything right. Except, that is, to set straight Washington's all-too-ridiculous gentlemen-in-command.

The players: Charles Lee, Alexander Hamilton, the Marquis de Lafayette, Anthony Wayne, Nathanael Greene, Lord Stirling. To Deborah, they were just names. But names can still do damage, and these certainly did.

They disagreed on everything from the start. Shortly after Washington spotted Deborah in his field glasses, he decided to dispatch fifteen hundred men to harass the British. His aides and generals met to discuss the proposal. Hamilton thought such a number not nearly enough. Charles Lee, who disapproved of the attack altogether, thought it too much.

Somehow the number of Continental regulars to be involved escalated to five thousand nonetheless, with a thousand New Jersey militia and six hundred sharpshooting riflemen planned as backup. And when that happened, General Lee changed his tune. Well, if this is going to be a grand battle, then, he thought, let me lead the charge. "I wish to request complete command!" On the other hand, we could lose: "Never mind." Then again, we just could win: "Well, then bring it on!"

Washington, fully appreciating the "anxieties of honor" that were occupying Lee's mind, caved, giving supreme command of the engagement to the man who couldn't decide whether the whole idea of attacking Clinton was a pitiful waste of money, men, momentum, and time, or whether it was worth a shot if it meant that he would obtain the glorious post he desired: major general, first in charge.

Of course, Lee's heart wasn't in it. But steeped in military protocol as these august men were, few argued against Lee, a ranking officer (a former *British* officer!), being assigned the command. His Pomeranians danced circles of delight.

There was a civilian doctor who snuck into Washington's tent that night and, after begging five minutes with His Excellency, shared his reservations about the good General's bad choice of Lee.

But the physician was politely shown the door.

Unfortunately, Lee, on top of being arrogant and delusional, was stupid. The next day at dawn, he quite literally had his men marching back and forth over the same bridge, yet remained convinced that it wasn't the same. He spat back at a lesser general who tried to alert him to "a better way" that he knew his business and to please shut up.

Lee's men were the ones Deborah spotted coming over the hill, sending Clinton into a panic. Unfortunately, once he was over the hill, Lee realized that he was without a battle plan (had he forgotten it? mislaid it?). So naturally, at the first sign of Clinton adding reinforcements to his rear guard to defend himself, Lee lost what little mind he had and began babbling orders and contradictory counterorders "with a rapidity and indecision calculated to ruin us," said one soldier. The only clear command from Lee being one—and, regrettably, it was an outright lie:

"I have orders from the Congress and the commander-in-chief not to engage."

You do?

Had it not been for a fat little fifer who waddled back to Washington and, begging his mighty pardon, told of the retreat that had been ordered by General Lee, rank, wanton disaster would have been ours. We would have lost the war then and there.

Washington, unable to believe his ears, galloped into action. He rode forward, with the chaos before and around him as proof of the fifer's claim (soldiers screaming, crying, ducking, running every which way but to the front). Then Washington blew his top, laying Lee out in lavender and ordering the attack anew.

The delay and vacillation, however, had taken its toll. As had the heat. By now soldiers and horses on both sides were parched, exhausted, and stark raving mad, for at some point the mercury had climbed to one hundred and five degrees!

From atop the hill, the sight of five thousand soldiers in total confusion proved just the jolt to heal Deborah's muddled brain.

"*Noooo!*" she cried, her voice caroming through the wood. This was not to be endured! What in the name of God had gone on?

Suddenly Alice looked stiff, and even in this ferocious heat felt cold to the touch—every bit as dead as she was. Flies surrounded her, and maggots; tiny bits had been removed from her stony gray flesh. This wasn't Deborah's daughter. Keeping her about was insane.

Quickly conveying Alice's body to a little gully and covering her with branches, Deborah, breathing dragon fire, leapt, jumped, lunged, even rolled down the hill—desperate to get to the battle-field fast.

She entered the scene on Englishtown Road, due west of Mon-mouth Courthouse, amid an orchard rimmed by shrubs. An hour or so had passed since Washington had ordered his men back to the fray, commanding them to re-form a defensive line on high ground.

British grenadiers were advancing in her direction in perfect formation. She was just inside the American line, behind the hedge where panicked soldiers, desperate and unable to remember their drill ("Poise firelock! Take aim! No, no—cock firelock . . . Oh wait, what's become of my blasted bayonet? Fix bayonet . . .") were crouched, some praying to the Lord for help, and others crying out for their mothers.

The heat, as if in apology, was sucking as much moisture as it could from the earth, resulting in long, wide vaporous swaths of steam refracting the fire and sparks of exploding muskets and ar-tillery, but doing little to cool. The field was an oven, hot enough, it seemed, to boil the blood that was drenching the area in ever-increasing streams.

Deborah had never seen such carnage: soldiers darting back and forth through the bushes, hacking and chopping and shooting at each other, retreating only long enough to reload . . . or, rather, fumble clumsily with powder and ball while crying out "God almighty, we're in hell!"

Screams, shots, curses, fire, the sickening *chunk* of sabers lop-ping off heads and limbs.

A flying ear.

A grenadier walks about with a sliced neck, his head lolling to his left shoulder.

A Continental loses his stinking bowels in a death agony, tug-ging without success at a bayonet lodged in his gut.

A militiaman, shot down and writhing in pain, is trampled by fellow Rebel soldiers running helter-skelter; surely they see him, but they just don't care. One soldier even gets his boot caught in the wounded man's mouth.

Thirst so intense that cheeks are purple, tongues are cracked, throats so closed that wrenching calls for "Water, water!" never make it into the thick air.

Yet Deborah fetches it anyway.

Carrying a sack made of her skirt in one hand and a scoop from a dead soldier's boot in the other, she totes gallons of water from the stream. Cupping it in her hands, she funnels it, dribbling the cool wet into dying soldiers' mouths, reviving far too few. The heat is simply too great. Soldiers not killed by whizzing bullets and cannonballs are suffocating to death anyway.

Suddenly calls of "Retreat! Retreat! Retreat!" emanate from outside the hedge, nobody quite sure—or caring a whit—from which side.

Deborah, seeing her plan dying before her eyes, wants things to be different. But how to go about it, what to do?

Her eyes fall upon an unmanned cannon, the artilleryman wounded or dead.

She reaches for a cartridge.

She grabs a rammer and fires ball after ball after ball after ball.

The British fire back.

A ball actually passes between Deborah's legs, but she's too far gone to feel fear. Instead, she's reminded of the pain of childbirth, of how much she loved Alice, of the memory of her beloved daughter.

She rams the cannon and she fires another ball.

And all at once she sees it. Alice is dead. John is gone. I loved John. I have failed. We can never win this war; Revolution thus will never be. A dream. A flight of fancy. A sham.

She tosses the rammer to the wind. No more balls. No more guns. This is not the way. *I will fight no more* is her last thought before she falls, exhausted, her body tumbling down into a thorny and parched ravine.

She never laid eyes on Washington that entire day. Although it is hard to believe that Washington had not spotted her in the last savage hour of the Battle of Monmouth Courthouse, still he made no attempt to speak with her. Neither did she attempt to find him. For his part, it was because he was ashamed. For her part, she was disgusted and forlorn.

Deborah knew that Washington knew better, and that mistakes like this, with the tremendous balancing act Washington had to perform, were bound to occur. And he was still a "gentleman," after all. Nonetheless, by the end of the day, Deborah was unwilling to allow him slack. I'm through with him, she said to herself. Leave him to his own devices then, I'll run this Revolution my way. I started it and I can finish it. Just you wait, my darling Alice, my lover John, just you see. . . .

And so she slithered out of the ravine back up to her hill. And after burying her daughter, she slept atop Alice's grave for three whole days, deeply, soundly, peacefully.

And Clinton retreated into the night, his baggage train battered but unhalted. Monmouth had amounted to nothing but a nasty draw. All because the "gentlemen's" respect for military custom—over instinct, wisdom, common sense—had ruled.

And Deborah left. Meandering her way to Long Island, she began life anew as a lone fisherwoman with only a small dory to call home.

But one day a week she wouldn't fish. Instead, she'd row herself to the *Jersey*, the British prison ship anchored off the Long Island coast, and feed prisoners fish and sundries in excess of what she needed to survive. She found herself living for this day, for the off chance it promised of a sighting of dear, beloved John whom at Monmouth she'd come to learn she desperately loved.

CHAPTER 31

The Legend of Deborah and John

lease, Lord, let me see him, let my palm at the least brush his cheek, she prayed every day as she handed food through a porthole in the decaying warship, searching the hundreds of faces crammed into the black, noisome hold for some sign of John. Oh, wouldn't they fight for space at the hole for a bit of apple, a chunk of bread, a pipe, some tobacco, a comb, and, failing all that, a breath of air!

The *Jersey* was the most notorious of the fleet of eleven miserable vessels anchored off Walkabout Bay. Retired warships pressed back into service as British hellholes, they were rotten sewage-maggot-smallpox-infested prisons.

After John's capture in 1778, it was here that he'd been carried, bound in irons, stripped down, and then ordered below, under the gun deck, into the pit of the undead: an unfed, unclothed, unwa-

tered mass of men packed so tightly together they would sleep—
and die—standing up.

It was early 1779 when Deborah first rowed to the *Jersey*,
having heard that this was where John was stowed. Disguised as
a "little biddy" or, as one British sailor put it, an "ugly hag," she
offered to supply the guards and officers in charge with items for
their pleasure, everything tidily wrapped in paper.

"I set my price, now and it don't change! So there'll be no quib-
bling, no bargaining, or—mind you—I shall not return!"

The prison guards, a woefully underfed and bored-senseless lot
themselves, didn't want that, no!

"Pray, woman, stay. Whatever it is you require, you will have!"

"Meeting the fee will do me just fine," she said. But deep down,
of course, Deborah had another idea. Once she had the guards
where she wanted them—unwilling to go without her goods—she
would exact a greater price.

"Open the porthole, then, and let me feed the prisoners
therein. Do it or else this day will be my last here!"

The porthole door was flung open wide.

Two more years, one hundred and fourteen visits, after never
missing a chance despite squalls, sleet, snow, and rain, Deborah finally laid eyes on John.

Careful not to tip off the sailor on guard, she was unable to
speak. Her eyes watered and her knees buckled a bit, yet somehow
she managed a smile.

Even in her costume—gray hooded cloak, big boots, fat belly,
salt-and-pepper fright wig—John recognized her smile. And knew
better than to breathe a word.

Although she could see but a piece of his face, one of his eyes,
a cheek, and an ear, it was his hand that brought her the joy, the
hope, the inspiration to give the Revolution another go.

Eight visits later, Deborah, as was now customary, ordered the
porthole opened. She stuck a note inside a piece of fruit: *Bring me
John.*

Although it took much more time than she would have liked to bring John to the hole, for by this point he was weak and could barely walk, he eventually appeared.

She risked speaking. "Don't move," she whispered under her breath, with one eye fastened to the guard, who, thank the heavens, was only too happily preoccupied with today's especially delicious goods. "I'll be coming inside," she whispered. "Keep still."

She waited a moment more for the guard, as he always did at this point, to move out of eyeshot to the quarterdeck where he could, in peace, munch on today's particularly spectacular feast: pears and salt cod and cold fish soup with bread.

Once inside, Deborah tossed John her cloak, instructing him, since the wig fit miserably, to at all costs remain covered by the hood.

"Row for your life, my friend! Your country calls!" she whispered. She turned to John's fellow prisoners. "Help me lift him through!"

Even with the additional time made possible by today's generous meal, Deborah knew well that any second now the guards would be lifting the ladder. "Until next week then, Dame Grant!" they would say, as such was the name she'd taken. And Dame Grant's impostor had better be in the dory by this time!

"I will be safe here, waiting for your return," she whispered to John. "Go to shore and you'll be told what to do: the one thing that hasn't been tried."

"I don't understand—" John croaked out the words as best he could.

"Nor should you. Just trust me, love—*my* love—and do it."

"I can't leave you."

"You'll be back. I know you will."

"How do you know?"

"Because this is it. Finally—*the way*. You can't fail to meet with success."

Abovedecks, the guards could be heard stomping their way to the rail. "That'll be all for today, missus!"

There was no more time. With strength Deborah didn't know she had, she nearly flung John through the hole into her boat.

John, passing undetected as a picture-perfect "Dame Grant," rowed without direction for hours. He had been without light for so long he was unable to see.

He was reminded of sailing into Boston Harbor with Papa, where this entire journey had begun, of how impossible passage seemed, yet in the end how effortless, how sublime. He recognized his dory experience as being exactly the same.

Without even so much as a single thought about how to get there, John somehow landed himself safely on shore. He was met immediately by a small farmer, who was hiding out in the reeds, waiting. Within seconds of John's arrival, "Mr. Smith" dragged him to a stone fence and issued instructions.

"Take cover, now, while I indicate to the others that you're here!"

Indicating involved arranging and rearranging stones according to an understood code visible from clear across the bay.

Finally, John's vision was beginning to return. And with it his mind became clearer than ever before.

He recognized this farmer, Smith; he knew he did. John had seen him at least twice before: in Boston, the night of Otis's rescue; and in Philadelphia, deep inside Hell's Caves.

"Who are you?" John asked.

"It doesn't matter who I am, there isn't time. The task before us is to get you to Boston, and from there to France!"

Oftentimes the story would end 'round about here, because mostly it was understood that the audience could guess the rest all too easily. "The Legend of Deborah and John," you see, wasn't meant to document the couple's role in turning around the Revolutionary War, for this was considered common knowledge: fact and not news. The point was to rivet the listener not with what they did but with how and why. Not everybody knew *that*.

And that's how and why Deborah and John came to be heroes of the Revolutionary War.

CHAPTER 32

One Thousand One Hundred and Forty Bottles

Why, after the war, were Massachusetts farmers like Daniel Shays up in arms all over again, just as they'd been at Lexington and Concord—but this time to make war on Congress?

Why were "patriotic" speculators driving up land fees, pushing generations of American tenants off their own property?

Why were Continental soldiers who stuck it out for years and years in large measure never paid by the republic they stoically served?

After the war, apparently, there was money enough for fireworks, for inaugural balls, to entertain dignitaries and commission alabaster busts—why not enough to pension real Patriots? To forgive war debt? To feed the widowed, orphaned, and poor whose land, families, and fortunes were devastated by the war?

Why were women and blacks and Quakers and Jews and Baptists and Catholics and gypsies and John Adams and Samuel Adams just as reviled as ever before?

As usually told, "The Legend of Deborah and John" claims that Deborah, after Monmouth, lost heart. This reveals more about the postwar malaise of those who told our story than it does of Deborah.

That said, "The Legend of Deborah and John" still comes closer—much closer—to the truth of the American Revolution than History does in its chronicle of the Revolutionary War's battles, its generals' lives, and its Founding Fathers' exploits.

However, while it's indeed true that by February 1781 I was on my way to France, the Legend errs in giving Deborah the job of sending me on my way. In fact, Washington sent me.

The Legend's generations-old insistence that Deborah was acting alone was testament of just how desperate the people were to have a hero of their own who made the difference between defeat and victory. As far as the people were concerned, George Washington was beside the point—victory was effected by France's navy and cash, and this in turn was due to the likes of Deborah and John.

But what people couldn't know was that Washington was the one who sent me to France, and that in so doing he was more of a hero of the people than History *or* the Legend has ever allowed.

History, for example, does not miss the fact that John Lawrence was sent to France by Washington, any more than it misses any other event for which there are official, "reliable" records for support. It even notes the title Washington and Congress decided upon for this suddenly elevated diplomat (me): Minister Plenipotentiary to the Court of Versailles.

What it doesn't bother to elucidate is the dire necessity of my mission, and the humility and genius required for Washington to realize the need to forgo traditional diplomatic channels and send *me* instead.

And one last detail, before sharing the tale of my sojourn in

France: I was indeed taken prisoner, but in Charleston, South Carolina, after the fall of that city to Cornwallis, and not aboard the
Jersey prison ship. Deborah was the one jailed aboard that floating
inferno, after being captured by the British as a spy. (Code number:
355. I never figured that one out. Thirteen stars and stripes, perhaps?) I was released almost immediately in a prisoner exchange.
And she was the one to be rescued by me, rather than the other way
'round, by war's end. Yet she never stopped working with Washington, right through to the finish.

So . . . to my story, subtitled: "Deborah and John and George,"
a tale depicting how Washington turned to the people—not the reverse—to win him the war. . . .

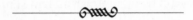

By the time I had boarded that ship to France, I had been brought
up to speed on the ever more disastrous state of affairs of the war.

After Monmouth, Washington basically sat out the war for the
duration, not budging from the Northeast (Morristown, New Jersey; New Windsor, New York), using his need to keep an eye on
Clinton in Manhattan as his excuse. Meanwhile, the British, turning their focus southward to Georgia, the Carolinas, and Virginia,
launched a savage reign of bloody terror, taking Savannah,
Charleston, and Richmond, in the correct belief that winning
these objectives would be easier than subduing the Northeast. Now
seemingly unstoppable, they began to make plans to take the
Chesapeake and Philadelphia (again) from below.

For our part, well, we had little to show but shame. During this
same period (1778–1780), General Horatio Gates, the "hero of
Saratoga," fled the brutality of battle at Camden, North Carolina,
galloping fast and furiously away from his own soldiers. His ignominy was to be rivaled only by General Benedict Arnold (the
real but unacknowledged hero of Saratoga, believe it or not) who

'round about the same time attempted to betray his country by offering up West Point to the British for large sums of cash.

The war was losing a sense of itself, what precious little it had, and the civil war that had always been threatening finally exploded at center stage. Roving Tory troops roamed the South, such as bloody British Major Banastre Tarleton's gang of Loyalists and Dragoons, engaging Rebels in swamps and on mountainsides, on bridges and at crossings. Sawing off heads, hands, and arms, and ripping fetuses from wombs even as soldiers and innocent women waved white flags of truce and begged for mercy. "Liberty be damned!": Tarleton would give no quarter.

Economically too, anarchy had taken hold. Speculators such as Robert Morris, signatory to the Declaration of Independence, cornered markets in flour, guns, and rye and drove prices up so steeply that by 1779 it would take forty Continental dollars to equal one gold coin—to wit, ten thousand dollars to purchase a single cow.

In an attempt to keep up, Congress printed so much paper currency it became worthless. Stories of farmers using greenbacks as livestock feed and toilet tissue were legion and not mere lore.

"Mock money and mock states shall melt away, and the mock troops disband for want of pay" was the 1781 war cry, coming first from the soldiers of the Pennsylvania Line and then New Jersey. Would Congress give them the food and supplies they needed and the money they were due to continue to fight the war or not? Otherwise they would quit.

The Pennsylvania Line received their due.

The New Jersey Line, however, lacking sufficient numbers, were shot, executed for their presumption.

At this point (with History's hindsighted apotheosis of the General still to come), Washington was basically regarded as a dullard, a dolt, and a poltroon—better off stashed in the Northeast doing essentially nothing.

But this is exactly where History is wrong. For this period offers Washington at his most fertile. Washington was plotting his last great gambit, which he was smart enough to realize mostly had to involve getting himself and Congress and all the ambassadors and diplomats out of the goddamned way. To let the American Revolution happen as it was meant to, just as it had at Lexington and Concord and Bunker Hill (still our two greatest victories of the war): as a great and God-fearing Coming Together.

Time to stop duping Congress, playing too many roles. Time to hide from the spotlight and just let go. To surrender to this vast, superior task force of coopers, miners, housewives, Indians, retarded boys, apprentices, butchers, whores, journalists, teachers, ministers, and slaves (including his own), some of whom he'd assembled with intent, but most of whom predated Washington's involvement in their devotion and commitment to Liberty by decades . . . even generations.

Washington wrote: "The knowledge of innumerable things, of a more delicate and secret nature, is confined to the perishable remembrance of some few of the present generation."

I was one of those few to whom George Washington, in these waning days of the war, had turned to ask for help. Just one. But my job was to secure tons of money and a naval fleet from the French king, Louis XVI, without whose help Washington quite clearly understood he hadn't a prayer of winning the war.

Another part of my job was to get Benjamin Franklin, dispatched as French ambassador since 1776, the hell out of my way as I tried to accomplish this. For all the treaties, the promises of aid, and the alleged enthusiasm for The Cause which he reported from France, Franklin's efforts, by 1781, had availed next to nothing.

All I had to do was spend one day at Franklin's villa in Passy, France, and it was easy to see why.

". . . In a word, we are at the end of our tether and now or never our deliverance must come. Yours, General Washington." So read the letter Washington had supplied me for those who might inquire of my instructions. And how was I to accomplish all this? I hadn't a clue. Nor did I care.

I had developed faith. Lucky thing.

It was just what I needed to overcome the sight of Franklin's flabby, naked, seventy-plus-year-old ass, which greeted my face.

I had arrived in Passy, a neat village at the top of a hill half a mile outside of Paris, on the morning of March 15, 1781—two months and six days after setting sail from Boston. I don't know what I was expecting from Franklin, officially monikered the "Sole Plenipotentiary to the Court of Versailles, Ambassador of the Thirteen United Colonies to France," but I most certainly wasn't expecting the reputedly austere, venerable, world-renowned scientist and inventor (who had invented everything from the odometer to the Franklin stove, as well as the concept of fire departments, fire insurance, and daylight saving time) to moon me with such gusto.

Maybe it was simply that he despised me. Yes, that had to be it.

I had rung at the mammoth mahogany doors of the Hotel de Valentinois, Franklin's residence lent him by a French entrepreneur. Surrounded by a chain of pavilions, multilevel flowering gardens, terraces filled with spraying fountains, and an orangerie that stretched for miles, it was a palace fit for a king. There was a note tacked to the door:

I'M IN THE TUB. ENTREZ, S'IL VOUS PLAIT.

Hmm. Not quite the welcome for which I'd hoped. *Vive la France.* I let myself in.

There was one servant in sight. An uptight little man directed me to Franklin's boudoir, advising me to *scratch* and not knock at the door, as this, in France, was how it was done with royalty. (Franklin? *Royalty?*)

I knocked.

"Entrez, si vous insistez!"

And there he was, as God made him. Ugh.

I entered cautiously. "Mr. Franklin?" I asked meekly, and presented myself. "John Lawrence, sir, at your service."

"My morning bath—I hope I don't offend," he said, ass stuck far out, bending to touch his toes, "but I've found exercise to be quite

critical to my health and posture. Being the busy *sole* plenipotentiary that I am, my days so chock-full, I am afraid I haven't the luxury of altering my routine, of taking time away for youngsters fresh
from America wishing to seek my favor, a letter of recommenda-
tion, or perhaps . . . is it a position you crave, young man?"

"I have a letter from General Washington, announcing the mission with which I have been entrusted, most kind sir."

He brought himself around to face me. The view was not much
better.

"I know who you are and what you intend. I am as popular here
as pastry, just as well regarded and well loved. I had news of you
within a day of your arrival in L'Orient, and as I'm sure you've calculated, Passy is normally six days' travel from that dreary port.
What this means, of course, is that couriers, of their own volition,
rode day and night to alert me to your presence because they cared
not to have me surprised by the likes of you."

"I see," I mumbled, shifting nervously from side to side.

"Of course, there isn't anyone you *didn't* tell of your arrival! For
starters, while your eagerness to accomplish your mission can be
understood, being green, avid, and foolish as you clearly are, I dare
say that sharing your objective with the harbor boatswains and various milkmaids you met en route regarding your intended correction of my professional failings is beyond excuse. And your testy
tête-à-tête with the Marquis de Castries—most embarrassing."

As to the incident with Castries, the Minister of Marine from
whom I was to seek a French fleet, Franklin was right to find fault
with me.

On my way to Passy I was hailed by a stalled carriage just ahead
of mine. When the velvet-waistcoated gentleman passenger (who
explained that his horses quite suddenly and inexplicably had been
seized with cramps) turned out to be none other than the Marquis
de Castries, I, losing all regard for his unhappy situation, dove in.

A perfectly thunderous cavalcade of attacks against his government came out of my mouth, accusing France of everything from

betraying America with empty promises to placing icebergs "suspiciously" in the way of my frigate *Alliance* as it crossed the Atlantic. Yes, indeed, I got rather carried away. . . .

Of course, a scuffle ensued. The marquis eventually challenged me to a duel, which, thank God, I had the momentary sense to dismiss as "beneath me to accept," thereby adding insult to injury. The whole ridiculous joust ended on my insistence that he send a huge and powerful French fleet to America this instant or I'd take up my sword against France! The marquis dared me to do just that, lying that he'd been planning to commission a fleet to America, but now, based on this "filthy encounter," he would order the fleet to avoid the United States' shores altogether and head for the West Indies instead!

Not an auspicious start.

"Chalk it up to seasickness? Or homesickness, perhaps?" I asked meekly, begging Franklin's indulgence.

Franklin replied, "Perhaps. Well, I think I've got the perfect cure for *that* . . . and my own biliousness as well."

He farted proudly.

"You have forty-eight hours, my young friend, to rest yourself—here, if you like—after which I'm shipping you back to Boston. As cargo, if I must."

At which point I brandished the letter Washington had written expressly for Franklin and none other. It read:

Honorable Sir,

The present infinitely critical posture of our affairs made it essential . . . to send from hence a person who had been eye-witness to their progress and who was capable of placing before the Court of France in a more full and striking point of light than was proper or even practicable by any written communications.

*What I have said to him, I beg leave to repeat to you, that
to me nothing appears more evident than that the [termination]
of our opposition will very shortly arrive if our allies cannot afford us . . . aid, particularly in money and in a naval superi-
ority which are now solicited.*

Yours very truly,
G. Washington

Franklin folded the letter and said not a word.

Checkmate.

"So I'm afraid we're stuck with each other until my mission is
done," I ventured.

Franklin adopted a more conciliatory tone. "Truthfully, what
actions do you imagine yourself taking here in France that I haven't
attempted already?"

He called to an attendant for his waistcoat.

"Does our esteemed General truly believe you have a skill that
surpasses mine? And if so, on what basis has he made this judgment?"

"I'm—not certain, of course, sir."

"Speak, my man!" Franklin roared. "Speak to me of what everyone back in America thinks of Benjamin Franklin!"

Wheeling about on his bunioned toe toward me:

"Speak to me of my rumored love of the ladies; of the fabulous
feasts I host at government expense, of the high living; the endless
promenades and concerts and soirees where I spend my mornings,
afternoons, and evenings in attendance, of my girlfriend Helvetius
who wipes her ass with her dress, and of my would-be fiancée,
Madame Brillon, who kisses her dog on the lips!

"Speak to me of my lack of interest in The Cause, my hundreds
of servants, and my wine cellar filled with one thousand one hundred and forty bottles of wine. Of my self-infatuation, my hedo-
nism, my atheism, my overstated charm!

"Speak to me of all that and I will say it is all part of the job, you silly infant! As you shall shortly see!"

"I'm not here to question your reputation, sir. I'm simply here to do a job—"

"Then do it! But do it without my aid. You are on your own."

And with that, he ended the audience, exiting the boudoir, slamming the door behind him. I wondered if he'd realized he was missing a stocking and had forgotten to put on underclothes.

"A part of the job . . . you shall shortly see . . ." he'd said. No, I wouldn't and couldn't see. For whatever Franklin was doing, it wasn't working. The great man who had harnessed electricity had himself been harnessed by the French as a cosseted plaything.

Later that night, while Franklin was out at a "function" to which I was pointedly not invited, I don't know what came over me, but I was compelled to sneak into the ambassadorial wine cellar and count the number of wine bottles that Franklin had stored.

There were exactly one thousand one hundred and forty.

And the next day, when the aforementioned Madame Brillon stopped by Franklin's office for "morning tea," which meant spending the day in his private sitting room riding his lap like a horsie, I knew exactly who I was dealing with. I didn't also need to witness the pleasure Franklin took in Brillon French-kissing her Great Dane to see that for all practical purposes, Franklin's diplomatic mission was long since done.

I never met the Lady Helvetius, thank goodness. When I heard she was arriving, I left the Hotel de Valentinois bound for Versailles immediately, for I had no desire whatsoever to watch a fine lady put her skirt to a dubiously hygienic purpose for which it had never been designed.

CHAPTER 33

Palace of Light

Queen Marie-Antoinette stunk like a skunk.

I smelled her coming as I stood on a mezzanine a full story above the courtyard through which she was passing.

I had just exited the office of Vergennes, minister of foreign affairs, to whom, as an official emissary of General Washington's, I was making a vigorous plea for cash, dangling the threat of British military power which would inevitably be mobilized against France if America were trounced.

"The British will not be forgiving, Minister. I can tell you that. And without the American conflict diverting Britain's military resources, France will find herself having to defend against England's wrath on her own, confronted by what will prove to be the most spectacular display of British naval and military power the world has yet to see."

Vergennes shifted in his seat.

"France has declared herself, sir," I continued. "And having done that, it seems to me that she has no choice but to put her money where her mouth was when, over three years ago, our alleged alliance was forged. England will seek revenge if she can. You have it in your power, esteemed Minister, by assuring victory with your aid, to make it impossible for England to succeed in such retaliation."

He belched. I could see now why Franklin and he supposedly got along.

Vergennes wasn't as impolite as Franklin, simply more interested in whatever it was he was eating, which nothing I said could stop him from picking at (even as he complained that it tasted suspiciously of rat). In fact, until he offered me *"un petit goût"* of the stew to help him figure out the species of meat involved—which was, at the moment, clearly of more concern to him than the possible decimation of all France—I wasn't entirely convinced he knew I'd entered the room.

Nor did he salute me when I left minutes later, disheartened and fatigued. But for my smelling Marie-Antoinette in the courtyard below, my entire French assignment might well have ended then and there, in eye-opening defeat, over a bowl of it-looked-like-rat-not-raven-to-me soup.

What can I say about Versailles, the center of administration of all France, one of the most richly ornamented chateaux ever built? There was so much silver, gold, gilded bronze, and crystal that even on this cloudy morning I had to squint to find my way down the marble staircase to the courtyard where I was hoping to get a look at the queen.

On a sunny day, apparently whole legions of courtiers could get lost if they didn't shield themselves from the sun with wide-brimmed hats. But since those were out of fashion these days, everyone was walking around Versailles blind as a bat.

Standing there in the Hall of Mirrors (a profusion of floor-to-ceiling pier glasses and Bohemian crystal chandeliers lit by seventeen arched windows offering a view outside of stunning labyrinthine gardens and magnificent expanses of water, all re-flected in the mirrors inside), it seemed clear to me why King Louis and his Queen Marie-Antoinette had such famous trouble conceiving children. They probably couldn't find each other in all that glare.

Various drawing rooms constellating the palace, each more grotesquely ornamented—a solid gold fire screen, really!—than the next, were filled with the most imaginative array of (I guess they were human) fops and fopettes spending their days waiting and waiting and waiting for the nearsighted king to notice them. Poor thing: Evidently his royal vision was so bad that Louis could only recognize people by their sound.

Oh, the noises coming out of that desperate crowd. Entire fu-tures hanging on the right bon mot, the perfectly timed compli-ment, the occasional eye contact (good luck!) or hint of a smile. The packed bosoms or dicks (who knew for sure what the king preferred?), each hoped beyond hope to catch the king's eye. A life of living hell, if my one day as a courtier was any indication.

Now to the subject of how I even came to be in this Hall of Mirrors. The goal was to be invited to dinner, or perhaps the opera or a play, by the king, and in so doing to enter the inner sanctum of power, the possibility of great riches, and untold fame.

My access to the palace was due, to a degree, to Marie-Antoinette's good favor. I say "to a degree" because had I known that to be a courtier all anyone really need do was rent a hat and walking stick from one of the dozens of street vendors providing cheap versions of aristocratic paraphernalia just outside the palace gates and then, looking smart, walk right in, I could have made things easier on myself. Still, I was in, with a slight edge on the rest of the fops-in-attendance, due to the queen's good graces following a curious accident, presaging an "opening."

As I was smelling her approach from above outside Ver-gennes's lair earlier that day, Marie-Antoinette, in a brocaded pannier skirt that was stiffer and wider than a horse-drawn carriage, came wobbling around a corner into view. The edge of her skirt hoop struck a column of marble and the impact knocked her off her feet, tossing her to the ground. Her hair, all three and a half feet tall of it, arced across the courtyard, shedding its ornaments in flight.

I do not jest. There was an entire miniature village affixed to that wig: a tiny hamlet, a porcelain bridge spanning a wooden river, a chapel with windows of painted glass, dozens of pretty green trees, all bounded by a pebble stone wall fronted with a sign—LE XANADU—and topped with ostrich feathers.

At least that's how I imagined the various bits and bobs fitting together when I, after watching the queen laid low, ran downstairs to help. While she remained sprawled across the courtyard floor and her retinue of horrified servants and ladies of the court were wrangling with her hoop to help her up, I collected the scattered pieces of the rustic diorama previously gracing her pate.

Once a lady was down in one of those dresses, apparently she was down for the count. It took six ladies-in-waiting several minutes to rock the royal beauty, wigless, back to a standing position.

And it took about the same amount of time for me to resolve in my mind the mystery of her malodorousness. It was her scalp. Or rather, the wet glue spread all over it evidently used to affix the fabulous "Xanadu" concoction to her head. "Pomade," they called it—a goo so foul it made me gag and, I later learned, so toxic that it dissolved flesh and over time leached into the brain and caused madness. Added to the stench of the pomade was, upon closer inspection, the horrific sight of diverse insect life scuttling about inside the coils of hair on her wig: a dense accumulation of lice, roaches, and ants. I guess the palm-sized pitchfork wielded by most wig wearers to pick out debris didn't exactly fulfill its intended function.

Unable to induce myself to touch the wretched assembly of powdered plaits, stinking to high heaven and crawling with vermin, I gave up.

"Ugh!" I groaned, loudly enough for the queen and her fair ladies to hear. A hush—deafening, dangerous—fell across the courtyard.

Would the insulted queen have my head on a platter?

Dead silence. And with it, ah yes, the opening . . .

The queen actually smiled at me: wee and unenthusiastic, but still, a smile.

"*C'est ridicule, n'est-ce pas, comment la reine pue? Vous-avez beaucoup de courage, monsieur—j'aime bien faire voitre connaissance. Comment appelez-vous?*" ("Ridiculous, is it not, how much a queen is made to stink? You have much courage, sir. I'd like to know you. What is your name?")

And she extended her hand to me.

I introduced myself, "Monsieur John Lawrence," explaining that I was "fresh in" from America and a friend of General Washington's.

It was as if I'd said I was from Mars, for all the recognition that the names "America" and "Washington" seemed to evoke. But wouldn't it be the way of this Revolution that the most ignorant woman on earth would be my—and America's—saving grace? Once again, expectations would be defied. For the Revolution didn't care that Marie-Antoinette would never come within fifty feet of a book if she could help it and was so stupid she had trouble remembering the number of "Louis" kings preceding her own husband ("*Il est le seizième, n'est-ce pas?*"—"He's the sixteenth, is he not?").

What the Revolution cared about was our connection: the simple, plain satisfaction she took in my daring to bemoan her grotesqueness; the overwhelming, palpable relief she took in being treated as any woman who was gliding about smelling like carrion and cheese. And wouldn't you know she was the very thing the Revolution needed, providing access—lo and behold!— to her husband, King Louis (number sixteen).

If I promised not to desist in my candor (fortunately for me, "honesty" was currently in vogue at dinner parties), Marie-Antoinette "nominated" me to sup with the king later in the evening. She asked nothing of my purpose in Versailles, and when I offered to explain, she waved me away. She wanted only to see me dressed more plainly, in the color "*caca dauphin*," a new shade of brown created to commemorate her recently born son's first bowel movement, evidently a symbol of his vitality. This, she claimed, was a color the king liked, not for the respect it connoted, but because, for some reason, he could see brown.

She counseled me to loll about in the "Gentlemen's Drawing Room" in the palace's west wing, around about nine; to stand close by the third door to the right, by which, begging my confidence, she assured me that the king would enter. She said she could manage the introduction to the king. After that, for the invitation to dinner, I was on my own.

So that's how I came to stand, restlessly and without refreshment, among the glare-stricken lookie-loos and royal hopefuls bowing, curtsying, and scraping their way through one of the thirteen opulent drawing rooms of Versailles; how I came to spend an entire day with those who, laying their bet on a particular drawing room and door through which it was rumored the king might on this day pass, would while away the waiting hours playing faro, dancing the minuet, gossiping rapaciously, performing party tricks, and feeling each other up and down. (Window seats and corners that were particularly well lit or flattering to complexions, chairs that were "slimming," were laid claim to up to twenty-four hours ahead of the king's rumored passage!)

Of course, I had no idea, should I even get my introduction to the king, what on earth I'd say or do. I simply decided, sheer impulsiveness having gotten me this far, that I'd take my position by the third door to the right and just do my job—whatever it took. The entire world, it seemed, was convening in this drawing room and at that third door. And everyone else was in brown too.

It was nine o'clock when the king showed up, the fluffy Marie

in some shepherdess getup (replete with staff), hanging apatheti-
cally on his arm. He was so short and so astonishingly fat, I instantly realized I was wrong about the Hall of Mirrors being the
reason Louis and Marie-Antoinette took forever to produce this
evidently unconstipated dauphin. Oh, others had claimed he was
impotent; that her vagina was crooked; that he had an organ that
could enter easily enough, but once in, hurt like hell pulling
out—or even that he preferred small boys. They had it all wrong.
Louis XVI was just obese and exhausted, and probably by the time
he found his instrument among the folds of flesh while attempting to perform his conjugal duties, his moment of passion had
passed.

He didn't walk, he waddled. And yes, no question, he was
feeling, not seeing, his way through the crowd. They kissed him,
they licked his boots. They complimented him on his shoe size,
his bag-wig, his eye color, even his gut ("Bulbous, no? Like
mounds of tulips in spring!").

Never mind that he had the shakes, the sweats, and a ball of
phlegm circling somewhere deep in his throat. *Il était splendide!*

The pushing and shoving was so severe I thought I didn't
stand a chance. But the queen, as promised, cleared the crowd
with her crosier. She whispered to the king, *"C'est lui, mon roi, qui
ma sauve aujourd'hui—le petit Americain qui connais Washington."*

The king summoned me to him. "Tell me something that will
please me!" he demanded. There was a collective gasp in the
room. Would I pass the test?

So this was it. Rescuing Deborah; saving Washington; protecting the army from dissension, mutiny, murderous executions;
the future of America—all of it, this instant, in my hands. "Your
country calls," quoth the story. And that invocation was good
enough for me.

A rush of images came to my mind: my father's trembling
hand ripping my beloved Apollo's head off; Ezekiel swinging in
the breeze; soldiers too emaciated to fight; Deborah hurling her-

self atop her dead daughter's body; Washington counting on the likes of Deborah and me to win him this war . . . a cavalcade of memories in no particular order or patterned line, eliciting at once great sorrow and gratefulness and fear. Conflicting emotions mysteriously producing in me the confidence, easy and plain, to speak my mind. To share with the king of France my entire story, the ordeal of the Revolution not as written or later conveyed by History, but as it was lived, by me, from its beginnings in the swamp to its pivotal turning point in the halls of Versailles. Down to and including my return to America one month hence in a ship laden with millions of francs in gold coin.

I knew as I spoke the story that it would become true. And it did. The words I found were these:

"Oh, my liege, if only you could see . . . in the sad look in your queen's eyes . . . in her little shepherdess costume . . . in her all-too-famous royal parades out to hilltops at dawn to watch the rising sun . . .

". . . In her love of spinning wheels and frolicking in the meadow, playing at being 'free' . . .

". . . In your own wild overeating, as much as three hams, four chickens, and two whole cakes at a time . . .

". . . In your passing the time playing blacksmith, bent over an anvil . . .

". . . In hiding out in the woods all by yourself, drinking yourself into oblivion . . .

". . . In your well-documented desire to touch as many of your subjects as possible, especially those not in brown whom you cannot see . . .

". . . In your decision to fling open the doors to Versailles to the public . . ."

If only the king could see that America had no monopoly on the urge for freedom. That really the thirst for liberty was no different than his own urge to be done with "*caca dauphin*," to depart from the stale crust of tradition and start anew on a different path,

one of which we were all deathly afraid but recognized, deep
within, was necessary, inevitable, and right.

"My time in the Revolution, Your Excellency, has taught me
to look past what I see. And here at Versailles, I see gaudy beauty,
to a point. But mostly I see pain, I see blindness, and also I see—
in both you and your queen—an urge, wild and fiery and busting
through your flesh, to break free."

The king blinked.

"America isn't a country so much as a state of mind, good sir.
A quest for a new order, based simply on recognition for who, not
what, one is. To America, you're not His Lordship, not King
George's nemesis, not Louis XVI, you're a fat man who can barely
see and happens to have been born into good fortune. And your
wife is lovely enough, but really she's a homely woman who'd be
happier spinning flax in a cottage. And would be prettier and less
stinky without the wig . . .

"America, Your Majesty, is nothing more than who you are
deep inside: that still point you feel compelled to hide, yet wanting out, now or never, before life passes you by. . . .

"By helping America, you help not only France and the
colonies, you help yourself, Louis, and your wife, Marie-Antoinette.
You help the world and you help me."

At which point I descended to my knees and with head bowed
was preparing to kiss the king's feet when he stopped me.

"*Non, non,*" was all he said, pulling his foot from my hand,
then wheeling about and retreating through the door from
whence he had come, asking that only his wife, and no entourage,
follow him.

That night I imagine they dined alone.

I never spoke to Louis or Marie again. I didn't need to. The
letter promising twelve million francs and a fleet of navy ships
that was delivered to the Hotel de Valentinois the next morning
said it all.

Within a week, I was heading home.

CHAPTER 34

Washington Dies

earing John's story on my deathbed was like being gently lifted from nightmare back to dream. From specious immortality to true life. That's not to say the story didn't hurt; the pain it caused me was the most excruciating of my long and lonely life.

The loved ones and doctors surrounding my bed saw only that I writhed in agony, shaking, trembling, coughing blood and sputum, swatting at the air (actually the memory of Hancock and Adams, who weren't even there). "I am just going," I intoned. Naturally they took these near-to-final words to mean that I was approaching death.

Not yet. Where I was "going" was to Yorktown, Virginia, to revisit with John Lawrence the final siege. For there was still much work to do before I could die.

As I said at the start of my account of these final moments at Mount Vernon, I knew full well that if I didn't find George fast, I'd be embalmed for perpetuity. But what I didn't tell you—above and beyond my terrible fear of being buried alive, which I'd had all my life—was why I so desperately yearned for surety of death. Because like the difference between a butterfly that your mind remembers pinned to a board in an insect collection and that your heart remembers fluttering about in the sun, I wanted, in death, to live in people's hearts rather than endure merely in History books.

For a man who knows himself is one who is loved. And a man who is loved is eventually understood. As John Lawrence was my opening, I, the father of my country, at the dawn of a new millennium, want to be America's opening, bringing her to herself as I was brought to George. The opening, in my case, being the one extended to me by my long-lost subordinate officer.

So, like John waking to his war wound in Valley Forge after he'd whipped Alice and realized Deborah was alive, I too was finally waking to my own mortal injury. (I'd never once been shot in war; God was saving me for a particular, more long-lasting agony he had devised.) And I hoped, as with John's renewed love for Deborah, mine would be renewed for George, abandoned outside a tent on the battlefield at Yorktown. So, to the final siege . . .

It was at this point when Louis acceded to John's demand, delivering several tons of gold, that I interrupted John's telling of the story of the Revolution to ask a question (although in my bedroom at Mount Vernon, all they heard was a low groan):

"You called him *Louis?*" I chuckled.

"Yes," John replied. "Just as Deborah called you George."

"Not to my face—you said so yourself, in the story!"

"I did indeed. I stand corrected," John replied.

"Do let me take it from here," I demanded. "Let me speak of the last few weeks of the war." I cleared my throat (the doctors in my room thought I was choking one last time).

"I will speak it as you do, as a tale. Since I can see now that is the only way to hold in view the miracle of how we won the war. For your story has enabled me to see, in this inscrutable pain that has been pressing against me all through my tenure as a hallowed man, the blurred memory that was sitting like a weight inside my soul." I composed myself.

"The Battle of Yorktown, by George Washington, the man."

I stopped before I began. "Come to think of it, John, *you* don't know this story either, for after Yorktown we never again spoke."

"Quite right, but we'll get to that!"

I started anew.

"September 1781. I was waiting for you, John. I was frightened you wouldn't come through."

An honest beginning. I settled into my portion of the tale. . . .

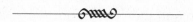

If your efforts had not met with success, John, my secret plan of cornering the British somewhere in the South, preferably Virginia, and squeezing Cornwallis from the north and south, would of necessity have been dashed in favor of the only other alternative: wholesale surrender.

It is true, as you said in your story, that for all practical purposes I sat out the war from Valley Forge on. History loves to ignore the importance of the strategic necessity of keeping an eye on Clinton *and* keeping him in New York. By focusing as it does on the terrible deprivations of my winter at Morristown (soldiers eating their own shoes and all that), and by playing up my preoccupation with plans to one day attack Manhattan (a misguided notion at worst, perhaps: History at least allows me that).

The truth is, History has no business defending my time outside New York. In fact, especially insofar as its perspective goes, confined as it is to events of record or note, I should be roundly denounced, banished from the pantheon of great military commanders, if not tarred and feathered. Even to a man none too bright, such as I was, the idea of attacking New York was anathema. Clinton had seventeen thousand splendidly fed, supplied, dug-in men to my mere eight thousand and eight hundred. And Manhattan was surrounded by water on three sides!

My purpose was twofold. Taking a page from the chapter of Bunker Hill, I *wanted* to look like a fool to keep Clinton off his toes. Thank goodness he was stupider than I thought—when it came time to make him believe I'd be attacking Manhattan, he took the bait!

A *full year* before Yorktown I wrote in my journal that I had no intention of ever attacking New York. Why does History consistently ignore this? Because then History is left with even less justification for my hiatus from war than she has already! Far better the "great George Washington" be somewhat misguided in his intentions than be an out-and-out slacker.

Not that I discouraged reports I wanted to attack Manhattan, even if it had me looking the fool. In fact, I did everything I could to make certain such rumors would be spread—even within the ranks of my own side.

In May 1781 I traveled to Rhode Island, where Rochambeau and his few French troops were installed, asking him for his help in the eventual raid. He consented reluctantly and privately mocked me, as well he should have.

In June I wrote Lafayette, informing him of my plans to invade New York. He too thought I was mad, doubly so, since I foolishly committed this folly to paper and most letters I wrote were inevitably intercepted. What the devil was I doing relaying such sensitive information in plain language, neglecting to encode it?

Pity Lafayette didn't pick up on the other letters also enclosed: one to Martha, filled with domestic detail, and another to my dentist, ordering new springs for my teeth. Quaint touches which I was hoping would work to dissuade Lafayette from believing in the letters' authenticity (the Washington he knew would *never* mingle war correspondence with shopping lists!), but leaving Clinton thinking that such correspondence with intimates was proof-positive that I intended to attack New York.

It worked. Clinton went into a tizzy!

Even as I was waiting for you, John, wondering how on earth you were faring (and privately fearing the worst), I was commissioning thousands upon thousands of men to prepare to launch an all-out assault on New York. Everyone was duped, even my own officers and troops, who up to the very last minute were convinced I was out of my mind.

So I say to History, stop protecting me! For you know not what you say! And you do disservice to yourself, to your countrymen, to me!

Actually, not everyone was easily tricked, certainly not the countless schoolteachers and housewives and booksellers I'd sent into New York to further leak the news. Nor were the engineers fooled whom I'd retained to build big ovens across the Hudson, on the Jersey side, to make it appear as though I were setting up camp. Or the bakers I hired to fill the air with the scent of fresh-baked bread ostensibly to be fed to the gathering American troops.

Somehow *they* all knew. No one said anything, of course. It was just a look in the baker's daughter's eye, the engineer's smirk, the spring in the bookseller's step, the crowds that awaited us when eventually, albeit quite suddenly, I took that right turn to New Jersey, back across the Delaware, to Pennsylvania and on down, hoping, praying, that a French fleet would be meeting up with us soon.

To the Chesapeake I was bound. It was on faith alone I was operating to keep Clinton away and leave Cornwallis whittled and withered in Virginia, ready to be vanquished. All I had to do was break the rules, create an environment hospitable to planting—till some fertile territory in which the Revolution could grow.

I sent a twenty-six-year-old American boy (you, John) to France, a twenty-three-year-old French boy (Lafayette) to Virginia, and a middle-aged, defrocked Quaker (Greene) to North Carolina, then rolled the dice!

With Cornwallis's annihilation of the American army at Camden in August 1780 (thanks to General Gates taking to the North

Carolina hills!), the South had been placed securely in British hands. I passed over scores of men who were better qualified militarily to appoint pacifist Quaker Nathanael Greene, an ironmaster with a debilitating limp, to rescue the region.

At the time, Greene's experience was scant, which was good, for this allowed him other qualities I sensed I could trust: his scatological humor was always good for morale, along with his rollicking imitation of Tristram Shandy. Add to this his independent-minded belief that the quashing of injustice was more important than blind obeisance to the chief Quaker tenet never to take up arms (a transgression for which he was read out of the Meeting of Friends).

On hand for him in North Carolina were eight hundred men (as compared to Cornwallis's thousands) on starvation rations (three days' provisions). They were demoralized, naked but for codpieces made from moss, addicted to plunder, and anarchic. He took the job with my promise to leave him alone. Every tactic, every maneuver, every line of march or order of battle would spring exclusively from his own brain, I assured him.

Additionally, I made available to Greene one sharpshooter named Daniel Morgan. Now here was a man who knew the land. (In truth, with Arnold he was in great part responsible for Gates's famous Saratoga victory which Congress loved rubbing my face in so much—but that's another story.) Morgan was a boyhood friend from my native Virginia and absolutely nuts. Crazy enough to plan (next to Bunker Hill) the most successful battle of the war, based entirely on his acceptance of a soldier's irrepressible instinct to run like hell when cornered—especially when forced to come within fifty yards of fast-approaching bare British steel.

So, let them run then. All the better for Morgan; for he could turn retreat to account. He chose a plain dotted with widely spaced trees that would give his superior opponent Tarleton and his horsemen easy maneuverability, while at the same time allow them to completely corner his own men by backing them up against a river offering no escape. This was for two reasons: to make his men fight like hell and to invite Tarleton into a trap.

Certain that his dashing enemy would charge ahead, thinking he'd caught the Rebels unawares (for who on earth would freely choose the valley of Cowpens to mount a defensive stand?), Morgan placed the men most likely to run in the front line. He ordered them to receive the first onslaught of the British attack, to defend themselves with just three volleys, and then to *run*.

They did exactly as they were told. And as a result, the Battle of Cowpens became legend.

Morgan guessed correctly that the running soldiers would give Tarleton the impression of a panicked retreat and that Tarleton, being bloodthirsty, would pursue fast and furiously—pushing Morgan and his men deeper into the plain where, from behind a little sandy hill, four hundred handpicked, camouflaged Continentals would come out from hiding and fall upon Tarleton's dragoons with more savagery than the war would ever again see.

Even more ingenious, these Continentals were directed to run too, themselves taking cover as yet another hidden cache of American cavalrymen burst upon the enemy's right flank and rear like a swirling tornado. While at the same time, the re-formed militia swung to the left and the Continentals took dead center anew, firing straight on.

The British didn't know what hit them. "It was like a whirlwind, the shock was so sudden and violent we could not stand it," wrote one soldier.

Tarleton fled moments later, having lost nine-tenths of his men: six hundred soldiers. Also two fieldpieces, thirty-five baggage wagons, and eight hundred stands of arms fell into American hands.

For our part: sixty wounded and twelve killed.

For all practical purposes, the British light infantry had been destroyed.

When British General Cornwallis (whom Clinton had sent to

shore up the South back in 1779) heard the news, he tried to avenge Cowpens by going after Morgan himself, only to be coaxed by both Greene and Morgan into a not-so-little chase through all of North Carolina and up into Virginia—as far away from the Cornwallis power base in Hillsboro, North Carolina, as they could lead him.

Throughout the chase, Nathanael Greene, like Morgan, made a brazen and precedent-breaking military choice not to concern himself with winning or losing, instead just to keep Cornwallis zigzagging through the countryside in drenching rains and mud. Greene knew he hadn't the manpower to outfight Cornwallis, but there was advantage in that too. Lighter by several thousand pounds, he could move fast enough to force Cornwallis to lighten his load in order to keep up, to consign his army's baggage and possessions to the torch, to hack his wagons to bits, to jettison his food supply, salt, and medical stores, and to drop his sick and wounded by the side of the road. To deplete Cornwallis's resources sufficiently to put their forces on par.

Two hundred and twenty-seven desertions later, with no heavy equipment left and devastated troops, Cornwallis would finally meet Greene in a humiliating stalemate at Guilford Court House, North Carolina, in March 1781. Although Greene was disappointed in not being able to declare victory, for all practical purposes triumph was his. Immediately thereafter, Cornwallis made a blue streak out of the Carolinas (he was a lot lighter now) and retreated to Virginia—bringing him one step closer to his undoing.

And what kept Nathanael Greene going, you ask, given the criticality of his situation? With no provisions but what could be plucked, shot, and stewed on sight? With no ready supply of ammunition? With no boots or clothing for his few hundred men?

The answer is simple: Mrs. Steele, a tavern keeper. Quite literally out of the darkness she came, inviting Nathanael inside one chilly night. "I am alone, tired, hungry, and penniless," he confessed. "I cannot pay."

He ate at her board gratis. And after he was done, Mrs. Steele brought him two bags filled with cold hard cash. "You need them more than I do," she said, placing them in his hands. And so, with Mrs. Steele's bags, the war chest of the Grand Army of the Southern Department of the Continental Army came to be.

After Cornwallis fled the Carolinas for Virginia, it was Lafayette's turn. The relay race to the finish was on.

I had parted with Lafayette reluctantly, as the French marquis had been of great assistance since 1777 and was like a son to me: I was very attached. But with Benedict Arnold (yes, that old traitor was back, as a *British* general) sacking Richmond, Virginia, and Cornwallis holding the line, I felt I had little choice but to send someone I trusted, which these days meant someone I loved. I didn't care that Lafayette's assignment brought criticism from my detractors. He had zeal and was driven by ideals.

And—ah, I might as well be out with it. The truth is I picked Lafayette because I wanted him in the thick of victory somewhere in the South (preferably the Chesapeake) to celebrate with me when we won.

And what about Lafayette? How did he dog Cornwallis six more months, outnumbered as he was, two and sometimes three to one? With the help of a black slave, that's how, who posed as a servant to Cornwallis and kept Lafayette informed of the earl's movements by the week, the day, the hour.

So with all these pieces in place, I still maintained my ruse of attacking Clinton in New York and praying that I would meet up with you, John. I heard news of the imminent arrival of Admiral de Grasse and his French fleet and thought: Good work, John!

But how did de Grasse and his French fleet know to come to the Chesapeake? Even you, John, didn't know where they would end up after leaving France, and so could not have told him. Ah, now there, John, is the greatest mystery of all! No one *has ever* figured that one out! But only because no one wants to believe the claims of one spymaster and cavalry man, Allen McLane, who after the war claimed to have sailed to de Grasse's ship in the West Indies well in advance, and convinced the French naval commander—*somehow*—to sail to the Chesapeake.

"Apocryphal," they say. "Impossible! Mr. McLane could never have taken such a mission. How could he possibly have had access to de Grasse, unless Washington had sent him. . . . And why on earth would Washington send an old, reckless cavalryman on such an assignment?" Besides, at the time this encounter allegedly took place, in July 1781, I was supposedly preparing to invade New York.

Well, there were a lot of things I knew that I couldn't or shouldn't have. Maybe it's because I knew the right people—at the right time.

Yorktown, you see, wasn't a battle, more like a fait accompli waiting to happen.

Indian summer. Bright, hot mid-October sun. I prayed for clouds to lessen the visibility of the workmen who would be digging the trench opposite Cornwallis's main defense in Yorktown, where the American and French cannon would be installed and readied for battle.

When the clouds didn't come, the sappers and miners began digging anyway. As they did, on October 5, 1781, the weather turned to rain.

In the mire spreading across the plain, I walked out on the line, cloaked to disguise my rank, ignoring those exhorting me to pull back to safety.

October 6. I returned to the line with a pickax and struck a few blows.

October 9. The rain lifted. Brilliant sunshine. American soldiers ran up our new red, white, and blue flag.

I came forward and fired the first cannon shot myself.

In twenty-four hours, Yorktown and its harbor took thirty-six hundred volleys.

By October 11, Cornwallis had already lost seventy men. Our

guns were moved closer to town, where Cornwallis was ensconced in a bunker, living underground.

October 14. We decide to attack two advance British redoubts near the river.

"Rush on, boys," Rochambeau (with whom I was sharing command) ordered his soldiers, all of whom had marched to Yorktown with me from New York. "I have great need of you tonight," he added.

And so, with muskets unloaded so as to remove all possibility of noise, the combined French and American brigades crawled their way through the abatis to storm both outposts, in total silence.

Then there were only the sounds of clashing steel. Like bells.

Americans poured over the walls from every direction into the darkness. Among them, I caught a fleeting glimpse . . . of both you, John, and Deborah.

True to the nature of the Revolution, the most critical battle of the American War for Independence—indeed, one of the most important battles the world has ever seen—was over in five minutes. The British flung down their muskets and begged for quarter, and with that, the war was done.

Oh, Cornwallis attempted an escape, crossing the river at his rear, a maneuver that, since I was powerless to stop it, was causing me grave concern.

No worries. A miracle ensued, one which I'd have never believed had I not witnessed it with my own eyes. Nature, again, intervened.

Driving rains and near-hurricane winds hailed without advance warning from the northeast, scattering and toppling Cornwallis's rescue boats, carrying them straight back to our shores.

October 17. A young British drummer boy wearing a red coat and carrying a drum climbed up on a rock and beat the signal for a parley. An officer appeared behind him, waving a white flag.

That night, a rare meteor shower streaked across a deep black sky leaching iridescent stars. And that night, I, George Washington, cried. I said "God bless you" to the stars and I wept neither from joy nor relief, but from appreciation for all the wonders I had been privileged to behold.

October 18. The sun returned. The surrender ceremony was set for two o'clock in the afternoon, along Yorktown Road. Cornwallis, feigning illness, didn't show. Instead, he sent a deputy to surrender his sword to the Americans.

I declined to take the sword myself, assigning it to a deputy instead. History has always assumed this was my way of parrying Cornwallis's slight (which clearly Cornwallis meant it to be), the intent behind this construed to mean that I, the lofty commander-in-chief of the Continental army, would not allow Cornwallis to surrender to me via an aide.

That wasn't it at all. I turned the sword over because I felt I had to. It didn't belong to me, but to the spirit of the men and women who had stood by me. Fought with me. Died next to me. I had come too far, however slowly, in my apprehension of this intelligence to touch that saber. And I think that somehow Cornwallis knew that too. He had been beaten not by me but by the Americans—by the Revolution.

The British soldiers, shaken, were ordered to lay down their arms and march back. Most were drunk, weeping and crying out loud. Some hugged and kissed their guns, bidding them farewell. Then they were ordered to walk the gauntlet of French and American lines, away, away. . . .

A bright and shining scarlet line, away, away. . . .

Through it all, the British band played a melancholy tune to these words:

> If ponies rode men and if grass ate cows
> And cats should be chased into holes by the mouse
> If summer were spring and the other way 'round,
> Then all the world would be upside down.

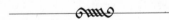

The tune is an old British nursery rhyme: "The World Turned Upside Down." And indeed it was, on that hillside.

Yes, I can see him now. . . .

It's George. . . .

George: before the parties celebrating victory . . . before the parades through the streets . . . before Congress quite consciously adjusted its attitude toward me to create a hero where "there hadn't been one" because "America needed that" (better the credit go to Washington, as lame as he was, than France!).

Before the marble busts . . . the laurels . . . the portraits . . . the pushing, shoving crowds I began to fear . . . the cups, saucers, hatpins, pipes, and kitchen utensils bearing my likeness and name . . .

Before the presidency . . . the endless ceremony . . . the levees . . . before the deathbed phobias of being buried alive . . .

Before all that was a man, humbled by Revolution, incapable of taking that sword. A man whose transition from dreams of glory to the struggle for justice began in Cambridge when, chin in hand, he laid eyes upon that exotic creature kissing her black friend. It was something new. Like the man I would have to become—open, in between, truthful, American.

So come back, my friend, myself; leave the field and come home.

And in my bedchamber at the end of a century, the room fixed in silent grief, amid the fields and creatures I had loved, I, George, held up my hand and uttered two words, signaling I was ready to go:

" 'Tis well."

CHAPTER 35

John Arrives

As for me, John Lawrence, I landed in Boston in August 1781, and instead of immediately joining the march to Yorktown along with Rochambeau and Washington and some fifteen thousand troops, I hastened to Long Island, to the *Jersey* prison ship, resolved to rescue Deborah, whose location I'd learned via the Revolution underground shortly after my release from prison earlier that year.

As with my experience in France, it didn't matter to me that I didn't know how I would rescue her.

I, like George, had come too far for that.

I decided to let the fact that it was impossible for me to imagine life without Deborah guide me on my way, resolving only to stay on that shore and wait until rescue presented itself—forever, if need be. As near to Deborah as possible was where I belonged.

I arrived at the Connecticut coast to find, however, that the ship was gone.

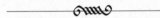

"Sunk to the bottom of the sea," I was told by a village fish-wife. "Set on fire by a prisoner. Most everyone lost . . . but me."

I turned, and my life was redeemed.

"Deborah."

"John."

She gave me her hand: "I knew you'd come." She smiled.

She had burned that floating hell to the waterline. By holding a fragment of glass up to a tiny slice of sun squeezing through a crack in the hull, she'd managed to ignite a bit of seaweed and bring the ship down.

It had taken months. But she knew she could wait, forever if need be.

And so, exchanging no words and holding hands, we ran, like once we had to the ferry. Only this time we were bound for Yorktown.

We caught up with Washington's troops on the seventeenth, the day the redoubts were occupied and felled.

It was in the darkness of the redoubt that I felt her fingers crawling up my chest, into my mouth, holding it slightly open for her lips, which, after sixteen years, she finally found again.

That night, Washington feted Cornwallis, while from outside, his soldiers listened and watched. And I could feel the presence of George, already locked outside.

How could this be that George and the people were shut out? I asked Deborah all night long.

The next morning there was a note inside the tent we had shared, after becoming lovers at last. It was from Deborah, and it read:

There's work to be done. I'm off. I love you, John. Be near. We shall meet again, as sure as Ezekiel swings upon the scaffold. As sure as his dust blows pell-mell in the wind.

And we did indeed meet again.
Upon my grave.

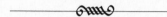

Shortly after Yorktown, I left military service for politics, with the idea of raising a black battalion, a standing army of former slaves to be summoned as the first line of defense against marauders, against attack. Since my father, Henry, was in Paris, along with John Adams and Benjamin Franklin, negotiating the treaty with England (*plus ca change, plus c'est la même chose*), I took it upon myself to offer up the slaves he'd purchased since he'd been made president of Congress.

My career in politics, needless to say, was short-lived. Freeing black men was clearly not what the Founding Fathers had in mind.

So what did *I* have in mind? I asked myself.

For there was quite simply no way to live what I knew. No way to speak it, to do it, to let it be known. Helpless as I had been with the Green Dragon back in Boston in '65, I turned to my imagination, imagining a day, maybe even two hundred years past my time, when things would be different. When the Revolution just might finally have taken hold. And once I did that, there was simply no place for me to live but there, in that far country in my mind.

Washington would go on to be crowned President. Soldiers would head home penniless and farmers in Massachusetts would plot a revolt against taxes and indebtedness, taking up arms against then-Governor Bowdoin in Shays's Rebellion of 1786 in the very same way they had once fought the power of Hutchinson. And I would come home to myself—in my swamp.

That was where I took my life.

I spurred my white horse and rode, without warning or ado, straight into British gunfire outside Charleston, a city King

George still held and would surrender only after the treaty was signed in 1783. The last sound I heard as I fell from my horse was the clattering of Apollo's necklace, my personal bell, announcing my liberation into the life of the imagination.

And, of course, there she was. Kneeling among the bulrushes, holding my hand, as my blood seeped away into the cool green mud. The dragon stood behind her, finally at peace.

One year later, she came to my grave. She was wearing the uniform of a soldier, again disguised as a man.

The war was over.

The Revolution wasn't.

Kneeling at the stone for which my father had paid, she told me she had loved kissing me in the redoubt that day and that she would always love me as both a woman and a man. Fine with me.

Deborah spent the rest of her life dressed as a man, speaking publicly and without humility of her trials, contributions, and travails in the Great War. Few believed her. George Washington never spoke of her.

She didn't care.

She knew the truth.

She died smiling.

She only visited my grave that once. She planted a single daffodil and she said, "Me know you."

Such is the way of America.

May she always smile Deborah's smile.

*No Country on Earth ever had it more in its power to attain . . .
blessings. . . . Much to be regretted indeed would it be, were we
to . . . depart from the road which Providence has pointed us to, so
plainly. . . . The great Governor of the Universe has led us too long and
too far . . . to forsake us in the midst of it. . . . We may now and then
get bewildered; but I hope and trust that there is good sense and virtue
enough left to recover the right path.*

—George Washington to Benjamin Lincoln,
June 29, 1788

AUTHOR'S NOTE

JOHN LAWRENCE is loosely based on one Lieutenant Colonel John Laurens, who, in 1777, at age twenty-seven and with no military training whatsoever, began his tenure as one of Washington's chief aides-de-camp. Captured in the siege of Charleston and later released, he was dispatched by Washington to France to solicit help from French King Louis XVI. He managed the task somehow, returning to America in August 1781 with a ship weighed down with gold coin and a nice little snuffbox as a personal gift from Louis himself. He fought at Yorktown and was handpicked by Washington to negotiate the terms of surrender with Cornwallis's aides. Shortly after the surrender, his attempts to form a black battalion of freed slaves brought such ignominy upon his head that he was forced to abandon all political ambitions, taking charge instead of a tiny military fort in the swamps outside Charleston, where on August 27, 1782, he rode directly into the British line of fire for reasons that were inexplicable at the time and was killed.

DEBORAH SIMPSON is a composite of several characters who actually lived, primarily Deborah Sampson, who, as "Robert Shurtleffe," enlisted and fought in the Continental army as a man. Her story is melded with those of several other spies, from John Honeyman (who paved the way for American victory at Trenton) to Lydia Darragh (who conveyed intelligence to Washington at Whitemarsh, Pennsylvania, from enemy-occupied Philadelphia) to John Champe (who was sent to kidnap traitor Benedict Arnold after his defection), and many more ordinary people with whom Washington regularly conferred.

ALICE, an entirely fictional character, was inspired by voluminous accounts of children who contributed to the war effort from Lexington on, often disguising themselves as young men eight to ten years older than their actual tender age in order to fight.

ACKNOWLEDGMENTS

So many people to thank, and so to begin: Marguerite Topping, whose painstaking research, unflagging commitment, precise eye, and keen judgment lofted me during my many darkest hours; Marci Poole, for her insistence, so early on, that this was a book needing to be written; Paula McDonald, for listening and keeping the redundancy of my torments to herself; Rick Wolff, for his generosity of spirit, smarts, and unbelievable knack for being in my way when he ought and making his protection of my creative space a professional priority; and Owen Laster, for his prodigious talent, and for lending his support. And finally, to Therese, Beatrice, Crackers, and the goddess of quiet.